THE KILLER EVERYONE KNEW

and Other Captain Leopold Stories

D1453010

THE KILLER EVERYONE KNEW

and Other Captain Leopold Stories

By Edward D. Hoch

Introduction by Roland Lacourbe

Crippen & Landru Publishers
Cincinnati, Ohio
2023

Cover Design by Gail Cross

ISBN (limited clothbound edition): 978-1-936363-76-6
ISBN (trade softcover edition): 978-1-936363-77-3

FIRST EDITION

*Printed in the United States of America
on recycled acid-free paper*

Jeffrey A. Marks, Publisher
Douglas G. Greene, Senior Editor

Crippen & Landru Publishers
P. O. Box 532057
Cincinnati, OH 45247
USA

Email: Orders@crippenlandru.com
Web: www.crippenlandru.com

CONTENTS

PREFACE

THE BEST OF

CAPTAIN LEOPOLD

*«You never go anywhere, Captain, that you don't bump into a murder —
a Christmas Party, class reunion, vacation, even a family funeral.»*
(—"No Crime for Captain Leopold").

*«In the best Leopold tales, Hoch fuses the detective gamesmanship stuff
of the Ellery Queen tradition with elements derived from Simenon and
Graham Greene, burying unexpected nuances of character and emotion
and meaning beneath the surface of his deceptively simple style.»*
—Francis M. Nevins

Among the impressive gallery of recurring characters from the fertile imagination of Edward Hoch are: the curious Simon Ark, who has dedicated his long life (he claims to be two thousand years old !) to fighting the Forces of Evil; the audacious English spy Jeffery Rand, a lost soldier from the Cold War; the singular Nick Velvet, who only steals objects that are unusual, too large, or without any obvious value; the adventurer Ben Snow, following the trails of the Far West in its heyday; and the bucolic Sam Hawthorne, a simple country doctor persistently faced with seemingly impossible situations. But none of these resembles the common mortal more than Captain Leopold. And, after Simon Ark, he is the devoted readers' second favorite of that marvelous storyteller, Edward Hoch.

7

Far from being an exceptional individual, Leopold is just a police-man of the most conventional kind—even though most of his inves-tigations are not. In contrast to Simon Ark, Edward Hoch wanted to create an ordinary character, typical of his time, and subject to the same daily trials and tribulations as the rest of his contemporaries. He is a competent official, respectful of the rules, who runs the Violent Crimes Section of the force in Monroe, a prosperous town in Connecticut, not unlike Rochester, New York, where Edward Hoch lived all his life. The reader does not learn Leopold's first name until the seventieth installment of his saga. Asked by the seductive law-yer Molly Calendar, Leopold himself makes a vague allusion to it, loath to reveal it openly:

"There is that French detective with the same first name. People used to kid me when I was younger," he concedes one day without being more specific (*Suddenly in September*). Devotees of detective fiction quickly worked out that the allusion was to Maigret, the cel-ebrated creation of Georges Simenon. An unexpected patronymic reluctantly confirmed several times later: "Call me Jules. It's my name, even though I never liked it" (*Leopold in the Vineyard*).

Assisted by the faithful Fletcher, who will later be promoted from sergeant to inspector, he is a fair, honest, and scrupulous man, liked by his men and disheartened by the existence of corrupt policemen (*Christmas Is for Cops*), but also continually tormented because he feels responsible for the death of one of his subordinates who was not, admittedly, beyond reproach (*Captain Leopold's Secret*). Leopold is only thirty-four years old when his first wife leaves him for the deceptive siren call of Hollywood. She will later be murdered in one of the most brilliant variations on the theme of the locked room (*The Leopold Locked Room*). Afterwards, following a brief affair that also ends very badly (*The Rusty Rose*), Captain Leopold decides to remain a bachelor. His determination is soon tested by the arrival of the charming Connie Trent on his team. She has a sociology degree and was an undercover narcotics agent, and assists him in a case involving drugs (*Captain Leopold Gets Angry*), but Leopold believes himself to be too old to rebuild a life with a younger woman. Although she willingly accompanies him to a soirée (*Captain Leopold Drops a Bomb*), his feelings towards her are those of a father. He does succumb later, however, by marrying Molly Calendar, a seductive lawyer thirty years his junior (*Finding Joe Finch*), but not before hesitating for some time about the fact that they would eventually find themselves in conflict, given that they belonged to organizations with radically different goals... But the benevolent Molly resigns as a defense lawyer to become a business lawyer, thus avoiding conflict with her husband's activities.

Faithful to his post, Captain Leopold moves around rarely. On one occasion, he is away in order to attend the funeral of an old uncle (*Captain Leopold Goes Home*). On another, he goes to the aid of Connie Trent, in trouble in Atlantic City, the gambling spot of the East Coast (*Captain Leopold's Gamble*). On yet another, he doesn't hesitate to help a colleague in the course of a visit to Manhattan (*Leopold in New York*). Not to mention his participation in a fishing trip to Nova Scotia in the company of Lieutenant Fletcher (*Captain Leopold Goes Fishing*), nor his incognito infiltration of a spa in order to unmask a dangerous drug trafficker (*Captain Leopold Incognito*).

His career is scattered with routine investigations experienced by police all over the world: unmasking a homicidal maniac planting incendiary bombs in public places (*The Demon at Noon*); hotly pursuing an elusive thief who steals—but does not kill—only on rainy days (*The Rainy-Day Bandit*); confronting the possible start of an epidemic of unknown origin (*Captain Leopold Looks for the Cause*); and unraveling a hostage situation with a very unlikely outcome (*Captain Leopold and the Three Hostages*). He notches up some notable exploits over the years, turning up in a circus where a young boy has been found hanged (*Circus*); at the dog races (*Captain Leopold Goes to the Dogs*); in an amusement park where a woman claiming to be a witch has cast a spell (*The House by the Ferris*); in another where a young girl has mysteriously vanished from a big wheel (*The Vanishing of Velma*); and in a night club where a magician kills a member of the audience apparently by accident in the course of his act (*Bag of Tricks*).

At sixty-five years old and after six years of marriage, Captain Leopold retires, following the successful conclusion of a difficult case (*The Summer of Our Discontent*), and it is his faithful deputy, Lieutenant Fletcher, who takes over. From his pleasant apartment on Bradford Bay in Monroe, he offers his services to the community through diverse activities, such as teaching classes at the Police

Academy (*Leopold's Class*), where one of his students is Lisa Fletcher, the daughter of his lieutenant and his wife Carol. He also helps out his wife Molly — who, after her husband's retirement, resumed her career as a defense lawyer — by carrying out a number of investigations as a private detective (*Leopold's Guns, Loaves and Fishing*). And, even though he is officially retired, he continues to assist his old friend Fletcher with numerous cases.

At the turn of the century, Edward Hoch declared that he expected to end the exploits of Captain Leopold at the hundredth case. His character having retired in the ninetieth story (*The Summer of Our Discontent*), he didn't see the need to continue the saga any longer. As luck would have it, he got his second wind and exceeded his earlier announcement, bringing the grand total to one hundred and eight.

So Captain Leopold's cases became Edward Hoch's most prolific series, and the verve and imagination with which his creator varies the ingredients always capture the reader's attention, all the more because the weirdness of many of the situations is in sharp contrast to the seeming banality of the cases themselves.

One can only admire the ease with which he inserts the theme of the eternal triangle (husband, wife, and lover) into a staggeringly clever criminal intrigue (*The Phantom Lover*). He brings a new inspiration to the time-worn themes of the serial killer (*Death in the Harbor*, *Captain Leopold and the Arrow Murders*). Not to mention the victim shot to death during a fire in a room surrounded by firemen (*Puzzle in a Smoke-Filled Room*), or the extraordinary case of the rich widow who claims to have witnessed a crime committed against a man... already dead for the last sixty years (*The Crime in Heaven*). Elsewhere, he builds an elaborate structure using the basics of ballistic science (*The Clever Mr. Carton*), and confronts his hero, a fierce opponent of the death penalty, with the terrible dilemma of a repeat offender who kills again once his sentence is served. And one of the most puzzling cases of his hero's career involves the robbery of a fortune in precious stones from a diamond merchant's window, no trace of which can be found on the person of the thief, captured only a few seconds later (*A Melee of Diamonds*).

His subordinates know that they can count on him if they encounter difficulties in the course of their work. Thus he moves mountains to find an explanation as to why one of his officers would fire two bullets into the heart of a man... already stabbed to death (*End of the Day*), comes to the aid of Lieutenant Fletcher's son Mike when he is accused of accidentally killing a neighbor with a .22 Long Rifle (*Captain Leopold Plays a Hunch*), or investigates the death of an Assistant District Attorney on his birthday, killed at his residence by a home-made bomb (*Captain Leopold Drops a Bomb*). Danger is everywhere, and even reaches the inside of a police station when a young man in custody is killed by an explosive (*A Little More Rope*), or when a murder is committed in an interrogation room (*Captain Leopold Beats the Machine*). On other occasions, Leopold manages to solve an incomprehensible murder inside a prison cell (*Suddenly in September*) who", faces death threats from the wife of someone he sent to prison and was killed by one of his cellmates (*The Murder of Captain Leopold*), and goes to the rescue of his faithful friend Fletcher and his daughter when their lives are threatened (*Leopold's Aim*). So it is that he acquires such a reputation for invincibility that some of the other police services suspect him of fabricating evidence (*Captain Leopold on the Spot*).

During his long and successful career, Captain Leopold is occasionally asked to solve some truly bizarre cases, such as the baffling impossible crime problems (*Captain Leopold and the Ghost-Killer, Captain Leopold and the Impossible Murder*), not to mention two other very curious disappearances (*Leopold and the Broken Bride, The Murder in Room 1010*). As for the intrigue in *The Oblong Room*, it is only a classic police investigation on the surface. It focuses less on *who* killed the victim than *why*. And the motive, once discovered, will be one of the strangest in detective fiction*... On other occasions, he is asked to shine the light on an affair which bears more than one similarity to the story of Dorian Gray (*The Nameless Crime*), meets a master criminal who describes the convoluted crime he arranges for others to commit (*The Most Dangerous Man Alive*), unmasks a mysterious bandit dressed as a clown (*The Killer and the Clown*), and discovers who is the double Leopold committing crimes in his name, in

---

* *The Oblong Room* and *The Leopold Locked Room* are the most frequently republished Hoch stories (at least ten times each).

the manner of the evil *döppelganger* of German folklore (*The Second Captain Leopold*).

The selection offered in this collection includes some of Captain Leopold's best cases. Three of them have already been mentioned above (*The Crime in Heaven, Puzzle in a Smoke-Filled Room, The Phantom Lover*). And he also will have to prove the innocence of a woman found near a murdered man, in a hotel locked room (*The Murder in Room 1010*); or take another look at a case of homicide perpetrated four years earlier, when the suspected criminal, questioned under hypnosis, convinced the psychiatrist that he is innocent (*The Killer Everyone Knew*). Two important periods of his romantic life are mentioned, when he flirts with Molly Calendar (*Captain Leopold Beats the Machine*), who will become his second wife (*Finding Joe Finch*), before he reluctantly retires after an active career (*The Summer of Our Discontent*). Which does not prevent him coming to the assistance of his faithful subordinate Fletcher (*Leopold at Rest*), and even taking his place when the new captain is finds himself in hospital as the result of an assassination attempt and is unable to perform his duties as the new police chief (*Leopold Lends a Hand*). Last, in his spare time, at a journalist's request and after new evidence being found, he re-examines an old murder case of being at a time when the man condemned for the crime is on the verge of being executed (*The Mystery That Wouldn't Stay Solved*).

***

My wife Danièle and I had the great pleasure of meeting Edward Hoch and his charming wife Patricia, and we treasure the memory of a delightful and affable man, full of warmth and with a great sense of humor. Surprised and apparently flattered that two aficionados from the Old World could be interested in his work, he was more than willing to answer our feverish questions. The result of that meeting, in September 1995, was the publication of the interview in *"Polar"* (dedicated to detective fiction and edited by François Guérif), followed by the first French collection of his short stories featuring Dr. Sam Hawthorne, subsequently published in their entirety by Crippen & Landru in four volumes, from 1996 to 2018. We selected fifteen stories, written between 1980 and 1992, that would remind French readers of the exceptional literary longevity of an author known in the nineteen-sixties and seventies with nearly two hundred short stories published in the French editions of *Alfred Hitchcock's Mystery Magazine* and *Ellery Queen's Mystery Magazine*. Then, we became regular correspondents, with Ed asking for technical or geographical information for stories he was planning to locate in Paris or somewhere in France. That was particularly true of *Paris Masque* (January 2005), the last-but-one adventure of Jeffery Rand, which he had decided would take place in the restaurant Le Jules Verne, situated on the second floor of the Eiffel Tower. He would occasionally send us first drafts of stories to ask our advice. It was through this correspondence that we realized the meticulous care this scrupulous craftsman took when writing his stories. A refinement which can be seen on every page of the little jewels of detective fiction that are the cases of Captain Leopold, precisely because the author forced himself to remain anchored in the most rigorous reality. And, in so doing—even if some stories do involve strange situations—chronicling the evolution of criminal investigation techniques during the last few decades of the XXth century.

Roland Lacourbe
(Paris, September 2021)
Translated by John Pugmire

Biography:

Film historian and fascinated with detective fiction, Roland Lacourbe is the French expert of locked room mysteries, and John Dickson Carr of whom he published for the first time ever, the translation of the complete collection of radio plays. He introduced in France the works of Joseph Commings, Hake Talbot and helped rediscover Edward D. Hoch.

THE WOMAN WITHOUT A PAST

Judy Thomas was celebrating her twenty-eighth birthday, though in a way she'd been born only ten months earlier. She didn't like to think about that tonight, though—not when she was dancing with Carl and thoroughly enjoying herself.

Judy had met Carl Forrester less than a month after she moved to the city and took the job at the license bureau. He'd come in one day for a hunting license, and they'd started chatting. One thing had led to another and she'd gone out to dinner with him a few days later. Before she quite knew what was happening Carl Forrester had moved into her apartment with her.

She hadn't exactly been swept off her feet. It was more likely, she rationalized, that her loneliness in a strange city led her to accept the first offer of friendship and love that came along. When, after a few months, he suggested they pool their incomes and buy a small house together, it seemed like a good idea to her.

Carl was a salesman for a line of office furniture, and his income with commissions was far more than hers. But she was able to suggest a small mail-order business they could get into together, and it proved moderately successful. By the time they moved into a ten-year-old ranch home just inside the city limits, Judy felt that she was holding up her end of the deal. The house was in a quiet neighborhood of mainly retired couples, with few of the children and animals one might have found in a suburban subdivision. Judy fell in love with the house and the neighborhood, though for their own reasons they avoided most of the neighbors.

"What are you thinking about?" he asked as they returned to the table from the dance floor. The restaurant they'd come to for her birthday dinner was about a mile from home. It was a quiet place with good food.

'Thinking about? Us, I suppose."

"You're thinking we should get married."

"No," she insisted. "Nothing like that."

"I almost bought you a ring for a birthday gift."

"I'm not ready for marriage yet, Carl. There's so much about me you don't know."

"I'm four years older than you. I might have a few secrets too."

He asked for the check and they left the restaurant. The summer night was clear and moonlit, and they drove home with the car windows open. Judy felt the warm breeze on her face and decided this was just about the happiest she'd been. All this, she marveled, in only ten months. It was certainly better than Florida had ever been.

Carl turned the car into the driveway of their little ranch home. Though it was barely ten o'clock, many of the other houses on the block were already dark. The older people retired early.

"This is the nicest birthday I've had," Judy said.

Carl unlocked the front door. "It's not over yet."

He stepped into the darkened living room and Judy heard two sharp sounds a little louder than coughs. Carl Forrester stiffened and toppled backward.

Judy screamed once, frozen in terror, and then she saw the man step from the shadows. He stood looking at her, holding a long-barreled target pistol in his right hand.

She turned to run and made it out the front door just as the bullets caught her.

Judy Thomas was still sprawled in the doorway when Captain Leopold reached the scene. The man, Carl Forrester, was inside the house. "Both of them were killed instantly." Sergeant Connie Trent informed him. "Small-caliber bullets. It could be a professional hit?"

"Let's keep that out of the newspapers. They do enough speculating on their own. What do you know about the victims?"

"Judy Thomas was a clerk at the license bureau downtown. The neighbors tell me Carl Forrester is a salesman of some sort, but they don't know where. Both of them lived here. They bought the house together about six months ago."

"People don't bother getting married any more."

"Some of them don't," Connie agreed.

"The neighbors hear anything?"

"The man across the street phoned the police. He's right over here."

An elderly man who walked with a slight limp came forward. "I'm Genner," he said simply. "I live across the street."

"What did you see, Mr. Genner?"

"First I heard it. Heard her scream just after they came home. I looked out the window and I saw her go down in the front door. She was trying to run out."

"Did you hear shots?"

"Guess I did, but they weren't very loud. Didn't realize till later that's what they were."

"Did you see the killer?"

"There was a man over here—I saw that much. He came out of the house after she fell down and ran into the bushes."

"Old or young?"

"I couldn't see his face, but he moved pretty fast. I'd say he wasn't too old."

"Black or white?"

"I told you I couldn't see his face. He was all in shadows."

"Did he run to a car?"

"I didn't see where he ran. He just went into the bushes."

"Have there been any recent robberies in this neighborhood, Mr. Genner?"

"Not lately. Not this year. We're peaceful here."

"Did you know Mr. Forrester and Miss Thomas well?"

"Hardly at all. They kept pretty much to themselves."

"No visitors, parties?"

"Not that I ever noticed."

"That's all for now," Leopold decided. "We'll be talking to you again."

He left Genner on the sidewalk and followed Connie into the house. The bodies had been photographed and removed, and only a few curious neighbors still watched from across the street. "No sign of robbery," Connie told him. "A window at the back of the house was forced, but apparently the killer just sat and waited for them to return. Nothing seems disturbed."

"Sat and waited?"

"This chair by the window—you can see the cushion is depressed as if someone was sitting on it. And there's cigarette ash on the table. He took the butt with him but left the ashes."

Leopold sighed. "If only there really were a monograph on the distinction between the ashes of various tobaccos."

"Shall we start questioning the other neighbors?"

Leopold was prowling around the room, opening doors, inspecting closets. In one he knelt to open a large cardboard box. When he straightened up he answered Connie's question. "It's almost midnight now. Wait until morning to start on the neighbors. And ask Fletcher to check on the victims' backgrounds. I especially want to know where Forrester worked as a salesman."

"Why's that?" Connie asked.

"There are forty-eight cans of ether in the closet."

It was almost noon the following day before Lieutenant Fletcher came into Leopold's office. He looked unhappy as he settled into his favorite chair.

"You're not going to like this, Captain."

"What is it—the double murder on Magnolia Street?"

Fletcher nodded. "Judy Thomas has worked at the license bureau for ten months, ever since she moved to the city. Before that her life is a blank."

"What do you mean?"

"Just that—she has no past! Her employment records show she was born in Baltimore twenty-eight years ago, but there's no record of it down there. Her social security number was newly issued when she came here ten months ago. She listed no living relatives. And the Maryland company that gave her a reference doesn't seem to exist."

"Interesting," Leopold admitted. "What about her fingerprints?"

"Nothing on record here. We've sent them to Washington."

"How about the man—Forrester? Where does he work?"

"He sells office furniture for a Midwest manufacturer. His territory covers all of New England."

"You know we found a case of ether in the closet."

"Yeah."

"Unless they're using it for furniture polish these days. that seems a bit odd."

"I know some addicts who try mixing it with cocaine for an extra high," Fletcher said. "But they usually burn themselves up."

"Have Connie check on it. I want to know if any local addicts have been using ether. She still has some contacts from her undercover days."

"What about Judy Thomas?"

"Talk to her co-workers. She must have mentioned something about her past."

"I'll get right on it, Captain."

It was late afternoon when Connie Trent returned with her report. She was tired and footsore from calling on neighbors. "They didn't know a thing. It seems Genner was the only one who even spoke to the dead couple. I feel as if I've wasted the entire day."

"No, you haven't, Connie. Somebody had to do it. Did Fletcher ask what you knew about ether, other than its medical use?"

She nodded. "Using it as a drug is nothing new. Ether has been around since the thirteenth century, and its narcotic use by doctors and students dates from the late eighteenth century. It was regarded then as an effective substitute for alcohol, producing intoxication without a hangover. In fact, a little more than a teaspoon of ether is enough to make a person drunk."

"What would forty-eight cans do?"

"I can't imagine. Of course you know it's rarely used as an anesthetic any more because it's so inflammable. It has had brief spurts of popularity as an intoxicating drug, generally in countries where alcoholic beverages were in short supply—America during Prohibition, and Germany during World War Two. Mixing ether with cocaine can be very dangerous as well as expensive, but it's still done in some circles. In fact, some head shops actually sell kits for it."

Before Leopold could respond, Fletcher hurried in. "Sorry to interrupt, but I thought you'd want to know about the fingerprint report from Washington, Captain."

"What did they say?"

"No record. They've nothing on her."

"Another dead end." Leopold scowled across the desk.

"She must have a past somewhere," Connie argued. "She didn't emerge full-grown from an egg ten months ago."

"You think her past caught up with her?"

"I don't know," Connie admitted. "Maybe there was something in the man's past."

"One other thing," Fletcher continued. "I found the restaurant where they had dinner. Forrester had the credit-card receipt in his pocket. Their waitress said they were celebrating the woman's birthday."

By the following morning Connie had traced the case of ether to a firm that manufactured it as an industrial solvent. Carl Forrester had purchased it there earlier in the week, supposedly for use by his furniture company. Leopold decided it was time to call on the company's regional sales manager, who would have been Forrester's immediate superior.

Greg Porson was a younger man than he'd expected, still in his early thirties, and his office in a suburban shopping complex was obviously not designed to receive frequent visitors. Porson removed a stack of catalogues from a chair and motioned Leopold to have a seat.

"When I heard the news I couldn't believe it! Carl was one of my best salesmen. Was it a robbery?"

"There are no signs of robbery, but we're investigating every possibility," Leopold said. "Did you know the young woman, Judy Thomas?"

Greg Porson shook his head. "I knew Carl was living with someone, but I never met her."

"Do you know how he met her?"

"No."

"Did he ever say anything about her past?"

"Not that I remember. He was on the road a great deal and we didn't have an opportunity for any personal chats."

"Just what did Carl Forrester do for you?"

"Sold office furniture. Called on businesses all through New England. Mainly in large cities, of course. Our firm manufactures quality wood products—desks, chairs, credenzas. We also handle a line of metal filing cabinets, though we don't manufacture those ourselves."

"Do you have any use for ether, possibly as a solvent?"

"Ether? Certainly not in the selling end, and I doubt if it's used in the manufacturing process."

"Carl Forrester had a case of ether in the closet of his home."

"Strange."

"We thought so. Tell me, have any of your other salesmen had troubles like this—assault, or break-ins at their homes?"

"No. I only have two other people under me, and one of them lives in Boston. But I haven't heard of any trouble."

"Thank you for your time," Leopold said, rising to leave. "I may have more questions later."

"Any time," Porson said, walking to the door.

Leopold drove back to his office. If there was to be a break in the case, he hadn't yet seen any sign of it.

After lunch Fletcher reported more of the same. They'd been unable to trace Judy Thomas's whereabouts prior to her arrival in the city ten months ago. "What about this company that gave her a reference? Was the letter forged?"

"I've been checking on them," Fletcher said. "Mid-States Exporting. Their letter said she worked in the office for two years and did satisfactory clerical work. The company actually existed last year, but it seems to have gone out of business. The Baltimore police don't know anything about it, and anyway there's no trace of Judy Thomas having lived at the address she gave."

"But why would she fake a reference to get a job at the county license bureau? It certainly doesn't pay much."

"She handled various licenses and gun permits," Fletcher pointed out. "And even passport applications."

"Well, keep checking on it. And contact some of your underworld connections about the possibility of a robbery. I suppose there's still a possibility that the killer was a thief who was interrupted in his work and killed them both as he fled from the house."

"I don't like it, Captain. We know he sat and smoked a cigarette. And if he panicked at their unexpected return, why didn't he flee the way he'd come, through the open rear window? No, I don't think it was robbery. The killer was waiting for them."

The conversation was interrupted by Connie Trent. "Captain, there's a man outside to see you. Max Swann from the New York office of the Justice Department."

"What does he want?"

"He says it's about the Thomas-Forrester murders."

Leopold grunted. "Show him in. We'll finish this later, Fletcher."

Max Swann was a darkly handsome man in his mid-thirties with raised black eyebrows that gave him a slightly startled appearance. He shook hands with Leopold and came right to the point. "Washington forwarded your routine request for a fingerprint check on a woman known as Judy Thomas."

"That's right. She was murdered a couple of nights ago, along with a man named Carl Forrester."

Max Swann nodded. "I checked the newspaper accounts. Any leads?"

"None."

"Those small-caliber pistols are popular with hit men."

"Why did Washington forward our fingerprint request to you. Mr. Swann?"

The dark-haired man shifted uncomfortably. "You understand I'm revealing this only because she's been murdered."

"I understand," replied Leopold, who didn't understand a thing.

"I'm assigned to the Justice Department's witness relocation program. As you must know, in recent years it's become one of our most potent weapons against organized crime."

Suddenly it was all clear. "That's why she had no past! Judy Thomas was a government witness and you gave her a new identity!"

"That's correct," Swann admitted. "Her real name was Sylvia Blount and she testified for the government in a big Florida narcotics smuggling case. Her ex-boyfriend, a fellow named Earl Perez, got twenty years in prison, but he had lots of friends who swore they'd kill her. As is government policy in such cases, we resettled her and gave her a new identity. I handled her case personally."

"Tell me about her. What sort of woman was she?"

Max Swann shrugged. "Good-looking, a great personality—but she had the unfortunate gift of attracting the wrong sort of man. She was always hooking up with losers."

"Did you know Carl Forrester?"

"Not personally. I came up here to see Sylvia—Judy—a few months ago and she told me she was living with someone. But she liked her job and seemed to be happy."

"What about the phony references you furnished her?"

"You mean the Maryland company? That was a firm we set up a few years ago in a sting operation. It came in handy when we needed fake references."

"Did she tell you what Forrester did for a living?"

"Sold office furniture, I think."

Leopold toyed with his pencil. "Do you think this fellow Perez's friends found her and killed her?"

"I don't see how, unless she got in touch with someone from her past. And why should she do that?"

"Why, indeed?" Leopold wondered. "Unless she'd gotten involved with drugs once more and needed someone's help."

"She swore to me she'd never do that again. I think she'd learned her lesson."

"She's certainly learned it now."

"When Washington identified those fingerprints they notified me and suggested I see if there's any way we can help the investigation."

"Indeed there is. We'll want a full list of Perez's friends and relatives—anyone who might have wanted her dead."

"I've brought you everything I have," Swann said, reaching into his pocket. "Here are names and addresses, as far as we know them."

There were a half-dozen names on the list, with addresses mainly in south Florida. Tying the killings to one of these people was going to be next to impossible, unless they got lucky with an informer. "Can I call on you for help if I need it?" Leopold asked.

"Certainly. Here's my card. The office always knows where to reach me."

As Max Swann was leaving Leopold thought of one more question. "What sort of narcotics was Earl Perez smuggling?"

"A little of everything. Mainly cocaine."

Connie came in with some coffee from the machine in the hall, and Leopold told her about Max Swann's visit. "So she's not a woman without a past anymore."

"No. Now all we have to figure out is which one of them was really the intended victim. Was the killer after Forrester or the girl?"

"Isn't she the logical one?"

"You're forgetting those cans of ether. Forrester bought them, so he may have been the target."

Connie Trent opened a manila envelope and shook it onto Leopold's desk. "This is what he had on him when he died. Here's something from his wallet that I missed before."

"What is it?"

"A receipt for a post-office box in the name of New-Art Apparatus Company."

"Check it out. Get a court order to open it up."

"Tomorrow?"

"Right now."

There were four letters in the post-office box, all addressed to New-Art Apparatus. Three seemed to be in answer to magazine ads, enclosing checks for fifteen dollars for unspecified "kits." The fourth was from a local "head shop" dealing in drug paraphernalia, ordering a dozen of the "kits." Leopold decided a visit was in order.

He, reached the Stay A-Head Shoppe just before six, and the short, bearded young man behind the counter looked him over for a moment before saying. "We're just closin', mister."

Leopold flipped open his wallet. "You can stay open for me."

"What is this—a bust?"

"Not if you answer some questions. What's your name?"

"Rudy Vega. I just work here."

"You do the ordering?"

"No," he answered too quickly. "Well, sometimes. Look, this stuff isn't against the law. Not yet, anyway. Not in this state."

Leopold handed over the letter. "That's your name on this order form, isn't it?"

"Yeah, I guess so."

"What sort of kits are these?"

"Just some glass piping. Nothing much. Couple of bottles come with it."

"Bottles of what?"

"A little ether," he answered quietly.

"For mixing with cocaine?"

"We don't know what people do with it," Vega insisted.

"But Carl Forrester sold these kits to you?"

"Carl who? Naw, never heard of him. It was all done through mail order."

They went back to the house on Magnolia Street. This time Leopold and Fletcher had a better idea of what they were looking for, and they found it in a dark corner of the basement. Odd-shaped glass pipes and small bottles already bearing labels that read *Caution: Highly Inflammable!*

"They were making the kits here," Fletcher decided. "And selling them by mail to head shops."

Leopold agreed. "And they were probably both in on it."

"So who killed them?"

"Someone from the present, or someone from the woman's past." Leopold picked up one of the empty bottles. "These were filled with small amounts of ether, but the buyer had to furnish his own cocaine for the mixture. There's nothing illegal in what they were doing."

"Think someone killed them to take over the business?"

"I doubt it, Fletcher. The thing just isn't that big. A few fifteen-dollar orders. Even if they made a ten-dollar profit on the kits it's still small change these days. Who'd commit two murders over a mail-order business that small?"

"They might have had contacts with cocaine dealers."

"It's possible."

"What's next, Captain?"

Leopold thought about it. "We have one advantage over the killer, if it is someone from the woman's past. He doesn't know we know about that past. In fact, the newspapers are just beginning to tune in to the fact that she doesn't have a past. If we could lure him back here for some reason, he'd probably feel safe in coming."

"How do we manage that?"

"Let's go call on that neighbor, Genner, across the street."

Mr. Genner listened quietly as Leopold spoke, nodding from time to time. Finally he said. "You want to set me up as a decoy for the killer."

"I wouldn't put it quite that crudely, Mr. Genner. Chances are he won't risk trying to get at you. But it's the only hope we have. Naturally you'll be well guarded. In fact, with your permission Sergeant Fletcher will stay right in the house with you at night."

"All right," he decided. "Go ahead. We have to do something to keep the neighborhood safe."

The following afternoon's paper carried a picture of Genner, together with a statement by Leopold that he was the only eyewitness to the killings. Genner said he felt certain he could identify the killer once the police apprehended him.

They waited a week and nothing happened.

The killings of Judy Thomas and Carl Forrester gradually faded from the press, replaced by newer violence. After a few nights at the Genner home, Fletcher turned the duty over to someone else, and after a week's time they prepared to abandon it altogether.

As Leopold pointed out, it had been a long shot at best. He'd phoned Max Swann twice during the week at his New York office, but the Justice Department had nothing new on the case. Swann had agreed to hold off any announcement of the dead woman's identity until they had tried Leopold's scheme, but as the week ended without results, both men were ready to give it up.

"Why don't you wait through the weekend?" Swann suggested. "If nothing happens by Monday I'll issue a statement announcing that the dead woman was in our witness-relocation program. There's always a chance that might uncover something new."

"Fair enough," Leopold agreed. "I'll phone you on Monday."

But on Sunday afternoon it was Max Swann who phoned Leopold at home. "We just got a tip that Earl Perez's brother Frank passed through New York on his way up to your city. This may be the break you've been waiting for."

"Do you have pictures of him?"

"Better than that. I can come up myself. I'll spot him for you."

Leopold phoned Fletcher and Connie and arranged to have the Magnolia Street block covered with plainclothes police. It would be difficult on a Sunday, when deliverymen and telephone crews didn't usually work, but he knew Fletcher would handle it. Next he called Mr. Genner and warned him to be on guard.

He picked up Max Swann at the railroad station in late afternoon. The dark-haired Justice Department man was nervous as he got in the car. "I hope you've covered everything, Captain. If Frank Perez is your killer, he's a dangerous man."

"Don't worry," Leopold said.

They drove to a spot about two blocks from the Magnolia Street address. It was dinnertime on a summer Sunday, and there was the odor of burning charcoal in the air. A bit of smoke drifted up from behind one house, and farther down the street a few boys were playing catch. A teenaged girl rode her bicycle along the sidewalk.

"He may not make his move until dark," Swann said.

"Probably not. We might have a long wait." He switched on the car's two-way radio. Then he asked Swann, "Did you bring a picture of Perez?"

The Justice Department man opened his briefcase and took out a blown-up candid shot of two men together on a street. "The one on the right is Earl. His brother Frank is on the left."

"Tough-looking customers."

"They certainly are. She must have been crazy to get tangled up with them." Swann took a revolver from the briefcase and slipped it into a holster on his belt.

As darkness fell over the neighborhood, an carful of Sunday visitors pulled away from one house with a few beeps of the horn. Leopold started the motor and followed them down Magnolia Street. "Oddly enough, two cars are less noticeable than one," he explained. They drove by the Genner house but all seemed quiet. There were lights on in the living room.

Leopold picked up the microphone, explaining, "I've got a direct connection to Fletcher in the house. Fletcher, can you hear me?"

"Sure, Captain."

"All quiet there?"

"You bet. Looks like another false alarm."

"We'll see."

Leopold circled the block and pulled into the driveway of a house that backed up to Genner's on the next street. "We've had people here all day," he explained. "We'd be too suspicious on the street after dark."

Connie Trent opened the door to admit them. "Looks like a long night, Captain."

"Afraid so. How many people do we have?"

"Eight. Two at each end of the street. Fletcher in the house, and the three of us here."

"Backups?"

"I can send a couple of joggers down the street for a one-shot. More than that would be suspicious."

Outside the streetlights were going on. "Send them," Leopold decided.

Suddenly Connie's radio crackled into life. It was Fletcher calling them. "A guy coming up the front walk with a delivery of flowers, Captain."

"On a Sunday night? That's him!"

Leopold hit the back door first, with Max Swann close behind. They jumped a low hedge and ran across Genner's backyard. Leopold already had his revolver out as they rounded the corner of the house.

The man with the flowers was just ringing the doorbell. Leopold recognized him from the photograph. It was Frank Perez. When he saw them he dropped the basket of flowers, exposing the long-barreled target pistol in his hand.

Leopold's hand was still coming up with his own gun when Max Swann reached around him and shot Frank Perez once in the left temple.

Lights were coming on and a few people were looking out their front doors, attracted by the shot and the sudden arrival of police cars from both directions on the street. Fletcher stepped over the fallen flower basket to examine the body of Frank Perez. "Nice shooting, Captain," he said.

"Swann beat me to it," Leopold admitted. "My reflexes must be slowing down."

"I was ready for him," Swann said. "I figured he'd have a gun out, to shoot Genner when he opened the door."

Fletcher peered at the fallen target pistol. "And with luck this'll be the same weapon he used across the street."

From somewhere off in the distance they could hear an ambulance siren. Old Mr. Genner came to the front door and stared down at the body. "I guess you fellas knew what you were doing after all," he said, and went back inside.

When the photographers finished their work Fletcher took the pistol and headed downtown for a ballistics check. Meanwhile, Leopold was going through the dead man's pockets while Connie examined the car he'd come in. "It's rented," she reported. "Nothing of his in it. He was ready to ditch it if necessary."

Leopold took a folded piece of paper from the dead man's wallet and held it to the light. On it was written, *Genner 143 Magnolia,* with the underlined notation, *Before Monday!*

He carefully refolded the paper and put it in his pocket. Then he walked out to the street and stood for a time gazing at the empty house where Judy Thomas and Carl Forrester had died. The flashing red lights of the ambulance bathed it in an unnatural glow, and it seemed that the house itself was bleeding. He sighed and walked back to where Max Swann stood with Connie.

"Let's go for a stroll around the block," he suggested to the Justice Department man. "We'll be back in a few minutes, Connie."

"How will this be handled?" Swann asked as they walked. "Do shootings like this automatically go before the grand jury?"

"Oh, yes—you'll have to testify."

"Damned nuisance. It'll mean another trip up from New York."

"Perhaps we can arrange for you to stay here," Leopold suggested.

"What?"

"I've been something of a fool, Swann. I caused that man's death, and though he's no great loss to the community it bothers me."

They rounded the first corner and started down the side street. "That day in my office, you mentioned that Thomas and Forrester were killed with a small-caliber pistol. We purposely kept that fact out of the papers. The only one who could have told you that was the killer himself."

"Now look here—"

"Carl and Judy used only a post-office box number for their kit business. Swann, only you could have given out her new name *and her address.*"

The man beside him said nothing and Leopold slipped a hand into his pocket, taking out the piece of paper he'd found in Perez's wallet. "See what this says? Genner's name and address, and the notation, *Before Monday!* Genner's only connection with Monday was in the conversation you and I had on the phone the other day, when you suggested I wait till Monday before pulling off the guards at Genner's home. Of course that's not what you told Perez. He probably thought Genner was going to be shown some photographs of him on Monday, and he walked into the trap you laid for him."

"He was going to shoot you!" Swann insisted.

"Maybe, maybe not. You killed him before we found out what he was going to do. With Judy and Carl dead you couldn't take a chance on Perez telling someone you'd tipped him off to her location. So you lured him up here to his death."

"Is that what you're going to tell the grand jury?"

"Yes," Leopold replied. "Now suppose you tell me why you did it."

They rounded the second corner, passing under a streetlight. There was no excitement here, a block from Magnolia. Most houses were dark, except for the blue flicker of television sets. After a time Max Swann said, "I guess I loved her. That was my big mistake, thinking someone like Sylvia—like Judy—could ever be faithful to a man. She betrayed Earl Perez on the witness stand, and she betrayed me in Carl Forrester's bed. I came up here to see her and found out she was living with him. Even worse than that, I watched through a basement window and discovered they were packaging ether kits!

"This was the girl I had loved, the girl I'd started on a whole new life! Can you understand that?"

"I think I can," Leopold said quietly.

"God, I even left my wife for her."

They rounded the third corner and Leopold said, "What did you do about it?"

"Brooded. After I saw her up here, saw what she'd become, I thought about it for weeks. Finally I decided she didn't deserve the new life I'd arranged for her. So I put her back in the old life. I phoned Earl Perez's brother and told him where she was."

"Did you know he'd kill them both?"

"I didn't care. Forrester was just unlucky. But later I figured if Perez wouldn't let that witness live he wouldn't let the neighbor live either. I needed Perez dead, so I'd be safe myself."

They walked along in silence for a time, and then they were back on Magnolia Street. The ambulance was gone, and some of the police cars. Connie Trent was standing on the sidewalk waiting for them.

"Weren't you afraid I might kill you?" Max Swann asked Leopold.

"Of course not," Leopold answered. "We're on the same side of the law, aren't we?"

"Where have you two been?" Connie asked.

"We just took a walk around the block. Mr. Swann here has a statement to make, Connie. I think you'll want to read him his rights and then get it all down on paper."

CAPTAIN LEOPOLD BEATS THE MACHINE

This is truly the age of the machine, Captain Leopold reflected as he scooped the crisp new ten- and twenty-dollar bills from the metal drawer of the automatic teller. Seven o'clock in the evening and he was able to do his banking! Then he went next door to his office on the second floor of Police Headquarters and was confronted with the recalcitrant coffee machine.

"Damn it, Fletcher," he grumbled, "they can make machines that translate foreign languages and do our banking and draw maps and even predict the weather. Why in hell can't they make a machine that gives us a decent cup of coffee without robbing us blind?"

"Want me to run down to the corner coffee shop, Captain?" Lieutenant Fletcher volunteered.

Leopold gave the machine a final kick and miraculously it came to life. A cup dropped perfectly into its proper position and steaming coffee began to flow. "I guess that's all it needed," he said, removing the cup and sampling the coffee. "Didn't improve the taste much though."

He carried the coffee back to his office while Fletcher followed along. Both of them were working the four-to-midnight shift, a busy one during the summer months when warm weather seemed to breed more street crime and random violence. "It's been a quiet night so far," Fletcher observed, slipping into his favorite chair opposite Leopold's desk.

"Let's hope it stays that way."

"I got a postcard from Connie today. She's enjoying Hawaii."

Leopold grunted. "Someday *I'm* going to take a vacation and see all the places everyone else sees."

"You love this job too much to be away from it for—"

Fletcher was interrupted by the sudden arrival of Jason Maxwell, an assistant district attorney they rarely saw outside the Hall of Justice. "I'm sorry to interrupt, Captain Leopold, but I need a favor."

Maxwell was a young man in his early thirties, with slick black hair that looked as if he waxed it. Leopold and Fletcher knew him mainly as one of the plea-bargainers from the D.A.'s office who made their job that much harder. "What sort of favor?" Leopold asked.

"We've got something big going down. I'd like to borrow your interrogation room for about an hour."

"What's wrong with the D.A.'s office?"

Maxwell put on a pained expression. "Rusto has decided to talk. I need a private place to take his statement."

Fletcher gave a low whistle. Tommy Rusto was a small-time hood who'd been picked up following the car bombing of Vice-Mayor Mark Prior three months earlier. The D.A.'s office was convinced Rusto had planted the bomb, and they had enough circumstantial evidence to get an indictment. But what they really wanted was the name of the person who'd hired Rusto. He'd refused to make a statement until now, but apparently the scheduled start of his trial the following week had given him second thoughts.

"He's going to name names?" Leopold asked.

"Seems like it." Maxwell smoothed down his already slick hair. "Look, you understand how it is. There are too many people at my office who've got a line to City Hall. Even here there's a risk, but not as big."

"Go ahead," Leopold decided. "It's been a quiet night so far. We're not using the room."

"Thanks. May I use your phone?"

Leopold nodded toward the desk and Maxwell dialed a number at the county jail across the street. "I'm in Captain Leopold's office at headquarters. We can use the interrogation room here. Bring him over. —Of course, with his lawyer! This thing has got to be airtight!"

When Maxwell hung up Leopold said, "If the press gets a sniff of this, you'll have reporters all over the place."

"I'm hoping they don't. I've already been on the phone to the Justice Department and we can get Rusto into their witness relocation program. Once I get the statement from him he'll be spirited away and kept under wraps until we need him for the Grand Jury. I don't think he'd be safe here, even in a cell."

"Will Justice keep him for you?"

Jason Maxwell nodded. "At the military prison on Marshall Island. No one will get to him there."

"Who's his lawyer?"

"Molly Calendar," Maxwell answered, making a face. "I'll tell you, there is one hard lady! I've been up against her in court twice and lost both times. Every time I think she's being nice to me she suckers me into some sort of trap."

"I know what you mean," Leopold agreed.

"Do me another favor, Captain? Sit in on this session with Rusto. I need all the help I can get."

"Why not videotape it? Then you won't have to worry about having witnesses present."

But the Assistant D.A. shook his head. "Calendar won't go for it. She says having her client on videotape that could be played on television would be like signing his death warrant. He wouldn't be safe no matter what new identity they gave him."

Fletcher got to his feet. "Are you going to need me, Captain? I should check on the arrest reports."

"Just one thing, Fletcher—ask Ainsworth or someone to clean up the interrogation room, empty the ashtrays and dump the coffee cups."

Within minutes there was a bustle of new arrivals at the squad-room door. Leopold and Maxwell looked out to see a handcuffed prisoner being led in, closely followed by Molly Calendar. Leopold had never met Tommy Rusto before but he looked much as he had in the newspaper photos—somber and mousy, with eyes so deep-set they almost disappeared into his head. Two of the jail guards accompanied him, one on either side, and a male stenographer followed behind. Leopold steered them through the squad room to the large interrogation room down the hall past his office. The guards were dismissed and Leopold signaled to Detective Ainsworth. "Did you straighten things up in there?"

"Sure, Captain." Ainsworth was a slow-moving veteran Leopold had inherited from the robbery detail. He took over custody of the prisoner from the jail guards, dropped the handcuff keys into his pocket, and led Rusto to the interrogation room.

"I'll want you to guard the door," Leopold told him.

Inside the interrogation room, Molly Calendar was glancing around. "Is this the best you can do, Captain?"

"We find it quite adequate," Leopold murmured. His contacts with Molly Calendar had been few, but there wasn't a man downtown who didn't recognize her long-legged stride from a block away and perhaps dream about what it might be like to spend a night with her. Now, facing her at close range, Leopold found it difficult to summon up any sort of erotic thought. She was a cool professional, stage-directing the entire proceeding to her client's best advantage.

"Look at the woman," Maxwell muttered under his breath. "You'd think she was introducing the next governor of the state rather than a man about to confess to murder."

Jason Maxwell grunted and seated himself across the table from Rusto. "Is your client ready to make his statement, Miss Calendar?"

"Certainly, Prosecutor."

"We plan to tape-record it and transcribe it stenographically at the same time. Is that satisfactory?"

"We objected only to videotape, for the reasons previously stated."

Maxwell nodded. "You've met Mr. Springfield, the stenographer. And I think you know Captain Leopold."

She eyed him disinterestedly. "We've met."

"Very well. Let's get on with it."

Tommy Rusto whispered something in Molly Calendar's ear. "One more thing, Prosecutor—" she said.

"I'd appreciate it if you used my name during the session."

"Very well, Mr. Maxwell. One more thing. Since we're in a well guarded room at Police Headquarters, could my client's handcuffs be removed?"

Leopold stepped to the door and opened it. "Ainsworth, do you have the key to the prisoner's cuffs?"

"They're right here, Captain."

"Come in and remove them, and then stay close."

Once the handcuffs were off, Tommy Rusto rubbed his wrists and seemed to relax a little. Jason Maxwell cleared his throat and signaled Springfield to begin transcribing. "Please tell us your name."

"Tommy Rusto. Can I have a cup of coffee?"

"What?"

"My client would like a cup of coffee," Molly Calendar said. "Is that a problem, Mr. Maxwell?"

The Assistant D.A. appealed to Leopold. "Do you have any coffee?"

"I'll get it," Leopold sighed. "Sometimes the machine doesn't work too well." He stood. "How about the rest of you? Would anyone else like coffee? It's not the best in the world."

No one reacted with interest.

Ainsworth was standing by the door as Leopold emerged. "Do you have some change for the coffee machine?"

"Not a cent, Captain. I'm flat broke except for a couple of bus tokens. Got to sneak next door to the automatic teller for a withdrawal."

Leopold went over to Fletcher's office and broke a dollar bill. "How's it going, Captain?" Fletcher asked.

"We haven't even started yet," Leopold said flatly.

He dropped a quarter into the slot and then remembered to call into the interrogation room, "Cream and sugar?"

"Black," Rusto replied.

Leopold pushed the proper button and watched the cup fill to the brim. At least the thing seemed to be working now without the necessity of a kick.

He carried the paper cup of coffee in, put it at Rusto's elbow, then resumed his seat next to Maxwell. "Is that everything?" the Assistant D.A. asked. Rusto nodded. "Good. Let's take it from the top. Name?"

"Tommy Rusto."

"Occupation?"

"Self-employed."

"Do you wish to make a statement about your activities on the evening of April fifth of this year?"

Rusto moistened his lips. Before he could speak, Molly Calendar interrupted. "I want the record to show that my client is making this statement as part of an agreement that the charges against him will be lowered to a single count of conspiracy to commit murder, and that in return for his testimony at the trial he will be released from prison and relocated with a new identity."

Jason Maxwell waved aside her words. "Let's hear what he has to say first. At this point I'm not even certain there will be a trial."

"Oh, there'll be one," she said. "Go on, Tommy."

Rusto reached out and raised the coffee cup to his lips. "The evening of April fifth. That was the night I placed the bomb under Mark

Prior's car. I stood across the street and set it off by remote control when I saw him getting into the car."

"And who paid you to do that?"

"This coffee tastes—"

Those were the last clear words Tommy Rusto ever uttered. The paper cup still full of coffee went flying from his hand as he toppled off the chair.

Leopold moved first, thinking he was having some kind of fit. But within seconds the convulsions ceased, and the truth became horribly obvious to them all.

"He's dead!" Leopold announced.

The poison was a form of potassium cyanide—the so-called suicide pill much favored in spy novels. Except for the standard drug-overdose cases routinely encountered in any metropolitan police department, Leopold had little experience with poison. His first reaction, after the medical examiner had confirmed the cause of death, was to label it a suicide.

"It couldn't be anything else," he argued. "I got the coffee from the machine and gave it to him myself. No one touched it except Rusto."

"My client did not commit suicide," Molly Calendar insisted, hitting the table with her open palm to emphasize the point. "Why should he, when he was about to strike a deal leading to his eventual freedom?"

"He got cold feet at the last minute," Jason Maxwell suggested. "He knew if he made that statement he'd be hunted by paid hit men until the day he died. So he took the easy way out."

"Rubbish!" Molly Calendar exploded. "I know my client. He had faults, but he was no coward. He knew exactly what he was doing in making that statement and he was willing to live with it."

Leopold had a thought and summoned Ainsworth in. "What's the name on that coffee machine?" he asked him.

Ainsworth went to look. "Nevins Vending Corporation," he reported.

"Phone them and get someone over here to open the machine. The poison could have come from inside."

"It's after ten," Ainsworth reminded him.

"Call them at home if you have to. I want somebody down here."

Ainsworth's phone call brought prompt action. Within a half hour the vending company had dispatched a service man named Barker to open the coffee machine and examine it. Leopold and Fletcher peered over his shoulder as he worked. "It looks O.K. to me," he said. "Nothing clogging the tubes, and the sugar is just sugar."

"The poisoned coffee was black. No cream or sugar," Leopold said.

"Then there's no way it could have been poisoned," Barker said. He closed up the machine again, then tried a coin to show that it was operating perfectly. "I can't understand why you have trouble with this machine, Captain. It's one of our best models."

Leopold grunted.

"Need me any more?"

"No. Thanks for coming in."

When Barker had gone, Fletcher said, "I guess we're back to the suicide theory."

Leopold shook his head dubiously. "I think Molly Calendar's right. A man like Rusto wouldn't kill himself. Besides, he seemed genuinely surprised when he tasted that coffee."

"Could someone have flipped a poison capsule into his cup from across the table?"

"With all of us watching? Springfield was taking shorthand, Maxwell and I had our eyes on Rusto all the time, and Molly was probably watching him, too. We'd certainly have noticed if something dropped into the cup."

"Could anyone have put poison in it while you were carrying it?"

"Impossible. No one was outside but Ainsworth and he was never close enough."

"Then we're back to the machine."

"Yeah. Look, Fletcher—suppose Tommy Rusto wasn't the intended victim. Suppose it was just chance that he got the poison. Suppose an employee of the vending company had it in for cops and decided to poison one of us—any one, it wouldn't matter who. The poison could have been put in one of that stack of cups inside the machine. The cup could drop down with the poison inside it and we wouldn't notice because it's immediately filled with coffee."

Fletcher snapped his fingers. "That guy Barker! Maybe he's got a record."

"Check him out, Fletcher. I don't really believe that's how it happened, but check him out anyway."

Leopold was supposed to go home at midnight, but at quarter to twelve he was still in his office with Jason Maxwell and Molly Calendar. Neither had shown any inclination to depart, possibly because word of Rusto's death had already brought a raft of newspaper and television reporters to the building. They were under siege, and no one was eager to fend off the barrage of questions awaiting their departure.

"They were going to build a tunnel from here to the jail once," Leopold mused. "Imagine escaping *to* a jail."

"It would come in handy as an escape route tonight," Maxwell agreed. He turned to face Molly Calendar. "You must know what Rusto intended to say in his statement, Molly. As his lawyer, you had to advise him on whether to make it."

"Of course I know."

"Then the killing of Rusto didn't really silence him." She shook her head. "No. But you must know that what he told me was privileged information."

"But your client's dead!"

"And it's hearsay evidence besides," she said evenly. "No court would admit it."

Leopold leaned forward. "He actually told you the name of the person who hired him to bomb Prior's car?"

"Yes."

"If Rusto was murdered, it's more than likely that person is the killer."

"I realize that. But just try to prove it."

"The name would be a good starting point."

Jason Maxwell tugged at his necktie. "Damn it, Molly, you've got to give us the name."

"You have to realize it was a machine intrigue from the beginning. Vice-Mayor Prior was killed because he offended the political machine in this county. Specifically, he was about to reveal certain financial ties between Nick LaGooda and—" she paused just a second "—District Attorney Hope."

"My God," Maxwell whispered.

"He may be your god, but he's certainly not mine. Hope has been the link between the political machine and organized crime for a long time. Don't act all that surprised. This isn't the first time charges have been made against him."

"Something was said during the last campaign, but I thought that was just politics. Are you trying to tell me Tommy Rusto was going to accuse Andrew Hope of—"

"Not Hope, no. He was going to finger Nick LaGooda. But the motive for the crime would surely have come out."

"So you're saying that either LaGooda or the District Attorney had a motive for keeping Rusto from talking," Leopold said.

"That's correct." Molly glanced uneasily at Maxwell. "You see why I was reluctant to go into this?"

Not too reluctant, though, Leopold decided. The part about Hope's involvement wasn't really necessary but she'd chosen to reveal it in Jason Maxwell's presence anyway. "All right," he said. "I'm going out to have a talk with Nick LaGooda. Maybe that will lure some of the press away so you two can make your escape."

He stopped at Fletcher's office but it was empty. "Do you know where the Lieutenant is?" he asked Ainsworth.

"You asked him to check on the vending-machine people, Captain."

"That's right, I did." Leopold glanced at his watch. It was five minutes before the end of the shift at midnight. "I guess it'll have to be you then, Ainsworth. I'm sorry, but I'm going out to call on Nick LaGooda and I'd feel better having someone with me."

"Sure, Captain," Ainsworth said. "You gonna bring him in?"

"Not unless he gives me trouble."

Both of them were feeling hungry and they stopped on the way for a quick hamburger. Ainsworth paid for his with a shabby five-dollar bill and waited for change. Outside, he shifted behind the wheel of the unmarked car. "You think LaGooda is behind Rusto's death? You think he got one of the vending-machine people to gimmick the coffee machine?"

"I'd like to think so," Leopold said, "because nothing else seems possible. But neither does LaGooda gimmicking the machine, if you think about it."

Nick LaGooda lived in a large house in an old but wealthy section of the city. The man who answered the door showed no sign of letting them inside. "Mr. LaGooda has retired for the night. It's twelve-thirty."

"Police business," Leopold said. "Get him down here."

"I can't—"

"Either he talks to us here or we take him to headquarters. The choice is his."

The man mumbled something and disappeared. When he returned, he opened the door wide and ushered them into the ornate living room. Leopold barely had time to take in the spotlit paintings and oriental rugs when Nick LaGooda appeared in a royal blue dressing gown. He was tall and almost priestly in appearance, his wavy white hair carefully in place.

"What can I do for you, Captain, at this hour of the night?"

"A friend of yours was killed a few hours ago. Tommy Rusto."

LaGooda nodded. "I heard the bulletin on the eleven o'clock news. But I hardly knew Tommy. I wouldn't call him a friend."

"Before he died, he implicated you in the killing of Vice-Mayor Prior."

Nick LaGooda snorted. "Too bad he didn't live long enough to make the accusation in a courtroom."

"May I ask where you were this evening?"

"Right here at home. With witnesses."

"Did you speak to anyone on the phone?"

"I speak to people on the phone all the time. I have a great many business interests."

"Do any of them involve Andrew Hope?"

"The D.A.? I steer clear of him."

Leopold felt himself at a frustrating dead end. "Have you had any contact at all with Tommy Rusto since his arrest?"

"I told you, I barely knew him. I haven't had any contact with him in years. I used to see him around the old neighborhood, that's all."

"How would you describe him?"

LaGooda shrugged. "A small-time loser."

"Why so?"

"If he wasn't a loser he'd still be alive. Right?"

On the way back to headquarters Ainsworth asked, "You gonna question anyone else?"

Leopold thought about the District Attorney but dismissed the thought. Not at one in the morning. "No. Drop me off and you can go home."

He found Fletcher back in his office and asked, "Find out anything?"

Fletcher shook his head. "Barker seems clean. A shoplifting arrest when he was eighteen, but the charge was dismissed. Nothing in the last ten years. He's the one who services our machine, so he's the only one who could have tampered with it."

"Ainsworth and I went out to call on Nick LaGooda."

"Yeah? Did he break down and confess?"

"What do you think?"

"I think I want a cup of coffee. How about you?"

"Did the lab boys finish with the machine?"

"Yes, but what could they do? Everyone in the squad room has their prints on it, and we still don't know that the poison was in the machine."

"Where else could it have been?" Leopold asked, following Fletcher out to the machine.

"I was thinking maybe we should listen to the tape and review the stenographic notes Springfield made. We might find something." He dropped a quarter in the slot and pushed the button for coffee with cream and sugar. Nothing happened. "Damn!" Fletcher whacked the machine with the heel of his hand. Still nothing happened.

Leopold squatted down to inspect the tube through which the coffee filled the cups. It seemed clear of any obstruction. "I can't see what the trouble is."

"The cup didn't even drop down. The coin must be stuck somewhere."

Leopold agreed. He gave the machine a kick, as he had earlier in the day, and suddenly the cup appeared and the coffee began to flow into it.

"I wouldn't mind all this trouble if the coffee was worth drinking," Fletcher grumbled. He dropped another quarter for Leopold and this time there was no trouble.

"Cyanide?" Leopold asked, placing the cup to his lips.

"I don't think I'd taste the difference."

But the coffee tasted the same as usual and after the first hesitant sips both of them drank freely from the cups. "You know something?" Leopold mused. "Suppose the poison was never in the coffee in the first place."

"How do you mean? They found traces in the overturned cup, didn't they?"

"Those could have been added by the killer during the confusion when Rusto was stricken. Suppose the killer had some other way of administering the cyanide. Suppose he used Rusto's dying remark about the coffee to his advantage and dropped a little poison in the cup while we worked over Rusto."

"But how did he administer the poison, Captain? That would be as impossible as getting it into the coffee without being seen."

"I suppose so," Leopold admitted. "Let's go home. Maybe things will be clearer after a night's sleep."

But in the morning as he prepared breakfast at his apartment, Leopold was surprised by the newspaper headlines: RUSTO POISONED AT POLICE HEADQUARTERS. ATTORNEY CHARGES LAXITY CAUSED CLIENT'S DEATH.

He read the account with mounting anger, aware now that Molly Calendar hadn't made good her escape from the press the previous night. They'd gotten a statement from her to the effect that ineptitude and negligence on the part of the police and the D.A.'s office had led to the death of Tommy Rusto as he was about to provide important new evidence concerning the bombing death of Mark Prior.

Leopold let the toast burn while he phoned Molly Calendar's office. It was just after nine o'clock but she was at her desk. "I was tired," she admitted. "Perhaps I was too hard on the police. But it's not every day I have a client poisoned before my eyes in a room with a detective captain and an assistant district attorney."

"I think we should have a talk," Leopold suggested. "At your office?"

"Fine. I'll be here."

Leopold arrived an hour later and was ushered into the library conference room used by members of Molly Calendar's law firm. It was a prestigious one, the city's second largest, and though she was only a junior partner Molly was highly regarded around town. Leopold sat across the polished conference table from her. "We have to work together if we're going to solve this thing," he told her.

"I agree, Captain. I'm not fighting you. But he was my client, after all."

"After I leave here I'm going to listen to the tape Springfield made. I might notice something we missed before."

"A good idea," she agreed.

"Do you have any ideas that might help me?"

She sighed and stared down at the table. "This is off the record but I feel I should say it. What form was the poison in?"

"Cyanide salts, most likely. There were traces in the bottom of the cup. The killer would probably have carried them in a small vial. Death was almost instantaneous, from paralysis of the heart, brain, and respiratory system."

"Does the average person, or even the average killer, carry a vial of cyanide salts around in his pocket?"

"I doubt it," Leopold said.

"Then the killer had to know in advance he'd have an opportunity to use it. I didn't know we'd be using your interrogation room with a coffee machine just outside the door. Tommy Rusto didn't know it. Springfield didn't know it. Only Jason Maxwell knew it because he was the one who asked to use it—right?"

"Right. But our room wasn't essential to the killer's plan. Wherever Rusto made his statement, he could have asked for a beverage—at least a glass of water. It doesn't have to be Maxwell, and even if it is we're still faced with the problem of how he got the poison into the coffee."

"I suppose so," she admitted reluctantly.

"I have to go now, but I really want your help. Call me if anything else occurs to you."

Leopold went next to the Hall of Justice, where he found the stenographer, Springfield, waiting for him. A quiet little man who rarely said much, Springfield had been around the courts and the D.A.'s office for years. After all that time, Leopold was surprised how little he knew about him.

"Here's the tape," he said, slipping it into the player. "I turned it off right after Rusto had his seizure. And these are my own notes that I transcribed this morning."

They listened to the tape, Leopold glancing occasionally at Springfield's notes, which listed those present and identified who was speaking. Leopold heard himself leave the room to get the coffee and then return with it. Nothing of importance had been said in his absence, but he was surprised that he seemed to be gone so long. Then he remembered that he'd had to get change from Fletcher. He'd—

"Hello, Leopold."

He turned to see Jason Maxwell enter the room. The tape had just reached the point of Rusto's seizure. Maxwell stood frozen, listening, until it lapsed into silence and Springfield shut it off. "Find anything?" he asked Leopold.

"Not on the tape, but it got me thinking about something."

"I've been thinking, too. That's why I came down here when I heard you were with Springfield. Can we talk?"

They left the stenographer's office and strode along the wide marble corridors outside the line of courtrooms. The benches were crowded with families and witnesses talking in anxious groups. It was a side of the legal process Leopold rarely witnessed. Even when he had to testify, it rarely involved the long waiting periods most people faced—the machinery of justice, grinding as slowly and uncertainly at times as the coffee machine at headquarters.

"Have you come up with an idea?" Leopold asked Maxwell.

"One. Molly Calendar. Tommy Rusto didn't have the money to pay a firm like hers. Someone else was paying her to take on the defense, probably LaGooda himself. And maybe he paid her for something else, too."

"To kill him, you mean? That's ridiculous." Leopold found himself feeling surprisingly defensive toward Molly. "She could have influenced Rusto not to make a statement in the first place. She didn't have to kill him to keep him quiet. He'd surely have listened to her advice. As for the money, if LaGooda was paying the bills he'd do it through Rusto, not directly."

"Maybe," the Assistant D.A. answered uncertainly.

"You know," Leopold said, "the same argument could be made about you. If Andrew Hope is involved, you're involved. Maybe you were doing him a favor to advance your own career."

"What a preposterous idea!" Maxwell exclaimed, loudly enough to turn a few heads on the benches.

"Nevertheless I may find myself in a position where I have to question the D.A."

"I can answer any questions you have for him. He didn't even see Tommy Rusto yesterday."

"Did he know the statement would be made at headquarters rather than in your office?"

"Why—yes. As a matter of fact, he's the one who suggested I call you and ask to borrow the interrogation room."

Fletcher and Ainsworth came on duty at four o'clock to find Leopold replaying the tape of Tommy Rusto's final moments. "I think I'm onto something here," he told them. "I want you both to listen to this."

They settled down in Leopold's office. "The papers are sure making a big thing of it," Ainsworth said. "Blaming us, as usual."

"I'm beginning to lean toward the suicide theory myself," Fletcher said. "Nothing else makes sense."

Leopold took three quarters from his pocket. "Let me get us some coffee before I start the tape." He stepped into the hall and started toward the machine. "Will you help me carry it, Ainsworth?"

"Sure, Captain."

Leopold handed the first cup to Ainsworth and carried the next two in for himself and Fletcher. Then he rewound the tape to the beginning and started to play it. Fletcher and Leopold each took a sip of their coffee and Ainsworth lifted his to his lips.

At the first taste he made a face and choked. "What the hell!" The paper cup fell from his fingers and he seemed to clutch at his stomach. Leopold started to move, but Ainsworth was faster. His hand came away from his stomach gripping the police revolver from his belt holster.

Fletcher hurled himself at Ainsworth and the force of the blow tipped Ainsworth's chair over backward. As he hit the floor, Ainsworth fired one wild shot that went out the door. Then Fletcher had the gun and it was over.

"No evidence," Leopold said, shaking his head. "No real evidence, but we nailed him."

"It was a good thing you phoned me at home about your suspicions or I never would have been ready for him. He moved fast."

Leopold had already phoned Maxwell with the news, and while he and Fletcher waited for Ainsworth to be booked he said, "Once I knew that Hope had suggested Rusto's statement be taken here, I asked myself why. Assuming he or LaGooda had a paid killer able to reach Rusto, why could he strike best at Police Headquarters? The most likely answer was that he worked here, that he was a police officer or a detective. I imagine Hope called LaGooda and LaGooda called Ainsworth, and the trap was set. LaGooda furnished Ainsworth with the cyanide crystals to use as best he could."

"But how did you know it was Ainsworth? And how did he poison the coffee? He never went near it. He was standing outside the door the whole time."

"When I stepped out in the hall to get Rusto's coffee, I asked Ainsworth for change. He said he had no money at all, that he'd have to make a withdrawal from the automatic teller next door. But when we drove out to LaGooda's house later he paid for his hamburger with a used five-dollar bill. But those machines only give crisp new money. Old money would jam the mechanism. Ainsworth lied about being out of change."

"Why would he do that?"

"Well, what did it cause me to do? I had to walk across the squad room to your office and ask you for change. For the space of nearly a minute I was away from the coffee machine and my back was to it. Ainsworth had overheard the conversation in the interrogation room and knew I was after coffee for Rusto—and just for Rusto. He used those crucial seconds to poison the machine."

"But how?" Fletcher demanded, staring distastefully at his own cup of coffee.

"There's a little tube that delivers the coffee to the paper cup. I was looking at it earlier. Ainsworth simply stuffed the end of that tube with cyanide crystals, wetting it first with his finger so they'd stick. They only had to stay in place for a minute, until I dropped in my quarter and the hot coffee swept them into Rusto's cup, removing all traces of the poison from the machine. Of course, he was taking a chance. If someone else, including myself, decided to get coffee and took the first cup, we'd have died instead of Rusto. But murderers have to take risks."

"And what did you do this afternoon?"

"I used salt crystals the same way, and gave Ainsworth the first cup out of the machine. When he tasted the salt in his coffee, he knew I'd guessed his method. I didn't know how he'd react, but when he went for his gun I was glad you were prepared."

Jason Maxwell appeared at the doorway, out of breath. "Ainsworth wants to make a statement. I think we're back in business!"

"No coffee for *anybody* this time," Leopold warned, starting out of his chair.

Fletcher had preceded him out of the room and he called back, "Captain!"

"What is it?"

"The coffee machine is leaking! Ainsworth shot a hole in it when his gun went off!"

FINDING JOE FINCH

It was shortly after Captain Leopold and Molly Calendar announced their plans to marry that Lieutenant Fletcher and his wife had them over for dinner. Leopold and Fletcher had been a team for more than twenty years, and he was pleased that Fletcher approved of his decision.

"It's about time you married again, Captain. None of us is getting any younger, and you were divorced before I ever knew you."

"I've been single too long," Leopold agreed. They were chatting over the dinner table while Molly helped Fletcher's wife Carol in the kitchen.

"Have you set the date yet?"

"It'll be sometime in the next few months—certainly by summer. Molly has some court cases she needs to get scheduled, before we know when we can get away for a couple of weeks."

"Is she going to continue with her law practice?"

Leopold nodded. "That's the plan, although she'd like to join one of the big firms and get out of the public defender's office."

"Talking about us?" Carol asked as she came from the kitchen with coffee. Molly followed with a tray of dessert. Leopold was pleased to see them getting along together. He'd always liked Carol.

"Of course," Fletcher told her with a smile. "What else do men talk about?"

Molly served the strawberries with whipped cream and settled into the chair opposite Leopold. "See what a good wife I'm going to make?"

Carol Fletcher sat, too. Since their children were grown and gone from home, she'd become more assertive, more independent. "Now if only they'd learn to be good husbands," she said, only half in jest.

"There she goes again," Fletcher sighed. "Pretty soon she'll be telling us we should quit the force and take an honest job in a factory."

"Well, I'd have a lot more peace of mind if you worked with Joe over at Greenways."

"Your brother Joe?" Leopold asked her. "How's he doing?"

Carol shrugged. "We don't see much of him. My point is that at least Stella doesn't have to lie awake nights, wondering if he'll get home alive."

The conversation quickly switched to other topics, and as near as Leopold could remember later that was the only reference to Joe Finch all evening.

But two events the following Tuesday reminded Leopold of the conversation, though at first they seemed unrelated. Shortly before noon, the payroll office at the Greenways plant was held up and robbed by a lone gunman wearing a ski mask. A plant security-guard who chased after him was shot and killed. And while Fletcher was at the scene investigating the crime, his sister-in-law, Stella Finch, called headquarters looking for him. Leopold took the call and identified himself. He'd met Joe Finch and his wife only once, some years earlier, at a Fourth of July cookout in Fletcher's backyard.

"What can I do for you, Stella?"

"Joe didn't come home for lunch, and I was wondering if he'd stopped by there to see Fletcher's."

"I haven't seen him, Stella, but he's on a case right now at the Greenways plant. Maybe they ran into each other out there."

"Maybe," she said, sounding dubious.

"Does Joe come home every day for lunch?" Leopold asked.

"A couple of times a week. He said he'd be home today."

"If Fletcher ran into him, I'll have him give you a call, Stella. Okay?"

"Fine," she said. "Thank you, Captain."

He hung up and got back to work helping Connie Trent with a week-old murder case she was handling. An arrest had been made and it was a matter of preparing the evidence for the District Attorney's office. They were both still working on it when Fletcher returned at midafternoon.

"What's the story?" Leopold asked.

Fletcher gave a frustrated sigh. "An inside job, for sure—but they've got over five hundred employees. No one but an employee could have gotten past the guards at the gates. He slipped a ski mask over his face, pulled a gun, and got away with more than fifty thousand dollars."

"Don't they pay by check?"

"Yeah, but they have a check-cashing service for employees and always keep a large amount of cash on hand. Nothing like this ever happened before."

"What about the man who was killed?"

"A forty-six-year-old security guard named Marvin Wise. The cashier pressed a silent alarm and Wise came running just in time to see the bandit running away. He went after him and got two bullets in the chest."

"No sign of the killer?"

Fletcher shook his head. "We searched the immediate area for clues, thinking he might have dropped the ski mask or even the money, but there was nothing. It's a big place."

"What was he wearing?"

"Jeans and a zipper jacket—like half the guys in the place. It happened just before noon when the employees were going out to lunch. Chances are our man was long gone before we even arrived."

"All right. Type up your report and we'll go over it later." As Fletcher headed for his office Leopold added, "Oh, did you see your brother-in-law out there?"

"Joe? No. Why?"

"His wife called here looking for him. He was due home for lunch."

Fletcher grunted. "Why'd she think he'd be here? I haven't seen him in a month."

Leopold and Connie went back to work, leaving the question unanswered.

Sergeant Turner from the Missing Persons Division phoned Leopold at Molly's apartment that evening. "Sorry to bother you, Captain. When you weren't at home, I thought I'd try you there."

"That's all right, Turner. What is it?"

"Got a report of a missing person, Joseph Finch. Brother-in-law of Lieutenant Fletcher. I couldn't reach Fletcher and I thought you should know about it. Mrs. Finch says he didn't come home from work and his foreman says he never came back after lunch. I know you guys had a robbery and murder at Greenways today—"

"Yeah," Leopold said. "Thanks for letting me know, Turner. I'll try to get back to you in the morning."

He sat staring at the telephone. "What's the trouble?" Molly asked, coming in from the kitchen.

"I don't know." He told her about the call.

"You think the two are related?"

Before he could answer, the phone rang again and Molly took it. She handed him the receiver with a smile. "Captain, this is Fletcher."

"Yes, Fletcher. Sergeant Turner just called me."

"About Joe?"

"Yes. Has he turned up?"

"I'm afraid not. We're over at Stella's now. She's a wreck."

"I'll come over," Leopold said. He hung up and went for his coat.

"You're going out?" Molly asked.

He nodded. "They're over at Stella Finch's house. She's upset. Joe still hasn't come home."

"Do you want me to come along?"

He shook his head. "Get some rest. I'll call you in the morning."

"She was right about being married to a cop."

"Carol. Yes, she was right." They kissed and she saw him out the door.

When he reached the house on the suburban street just north of the city, lights were on in nearly every room. Carol greeted him at the door and led him into the living room where Stella Finch was waiting for word of her missing husband. A framed recent photograph of him, with a bushy black beard she said she disliked, sat prominently on the table next to her.

"I'm sorry about all of this, Mrs. Finch," Leopold said.

"Call me Stella," she said. "We met once."

"I remember." What he remembered was a funny, gossipy little woman whose company he'd enjoyed on a summer afternoon. She bore little resemblance to the older, sober Stella Finch he saw now.

"We've checked all the hospitals," Fletcher told Leopold. "Nothing."

Leopold sat down opposite Stella Finch. "I hope you'll forgive me," he said, "but I have to ask you some rather personal questions. How have things been between you and Joe? Had you noticed any changes in him recently?"

"What sort of changes?"

"Less affection, perhaps."

"I—I don't know."

"Were you having any money problems?"

"We've always had those. They don't pay much at Greenways."

"Stella, a man was killed there this morning and fifty thousand dollars was stolen. Is there any possibility that Joe could have been involved in that?"

It was Carol who answered from across the room. "You're talking about my brother! Are you calling him a thief? And a murderer?"

"I'm not calling him anything, Carol. I'm just trying to help find him."

"Missing Persons isn't your department. He doesn't even live in the city limits. You want him because you think he's implicated in that robbery."

Leopold sighed. "Be reasonable, Carol. The robbery and murder took place at Greenways just before the lunch hour. Joe was last seen on his way to lunch. There could be a connection. Maybe Joe happened upon the killer in the parking lot and got taken as a hostage." He turned back to Stella Finch. "Is there any chance Joe could purposely be involved in something like this?" he asked.

"No. No, I'm sure he couldn't be."

"But you tried to phone Fletcher when Joe didn't come home for lunch, even though they hadn't seen each other in a month. Why did you think he might have gone to headquarters?"

"He said something last night about wanting to see Fletcher. I didn't know what for, and I only half remembered him saying it. But when he didn't turn up I thought that was where he might be."

"Did Joe ski?"

"No."

"Did he own a ski mask?"

"No."

"Had he said anything recently about needing money?"

"I told you, we've had money problems from the day we were married. Our son Ned got to college on a scholarship or he wouldn't be there at all. I've worked off and on to help out, and I'm looking for another job now." She was close to tears.

"Captain," Fletcher said quietly.

Later, as they were leaving, Leopold told Fletcher, "I got a bit carried away with my questioning. I probably shouldn't have pressed her so hard right now."

"You were horrible!" Carol said and got in the car.

"They're family," Fletcher tried to explain.

"The security guard, Marvin Wise, had a family too."

"I know." Fletcher looked sympathetic, then made a decision. "Look, if it starts to seem that Joe was involved, you'll have to put someone else on the case."

"We can talk about that later. Tomorrow morning, we'd better take a run out to Greenways."

The plant occupied some two hundred acres at the edge of the city, much of it warehousing and shipping departments for the score of plastic products manufactured at Greenways—goods as diverse as high-impact auto parts and foam wrestling mats were made there, with workers often being shifted to assorted production jobs to meet fluctuations in demand.

When Leopold and Fletcher arrived at mid-morning, they were met at the front gate by the head foreman, a tall, competent-looking man named Bernie McGrath. "Did you catch him?" he asked immediately.

"No luck yet," Fletcher said. "This is Captain Leopold. We'd like to look around your plant."

"Sure thing."

Leopold shook hands with McGrath and said, "I understand the production workers have individual lockers."

"That's right. We like them to wear white cotton coats on some of the jobs. They keep them in the lockers along with their personal belongings."

Leopold took a folded paper from his pocket. "We have a search warrant here for the locker of Joseph Finch."

McGrath didn't even look at it. "They all supply their own locks. You'll have to break it open."

"We brought a spare key from his home," Fletcher explained. "The warrant was just to save time in case you gave us an argument."

"Look, fellas, you'll get no argument from me. You think Finch pulled the job?"

"What do you think?" Leopold wanted to know. "Are you a friend of his?"

"I know him. He's just one of the guys to me. Always seemed like a nice fella."

"No trouble?"

"None at all."

"How about with the women employees? Does he like the ladies?" Leopold sensed Fletcher's displeasure at his question.

"Oh, sure. Nobody special, though, if that's what you mean."

"Who does he work with?"

"Well, we shift people around. This month Joe's been running a machine that extrudes plastic beading for automobile upholstery. Come on, I'll show you."

The plant was surprisingly clean and airy, with wide aisles between the banks of machines and the individual work areas. As they paused at an untended machine, a blond young woman across the aisle asked, "You running tours now, Bernie?"

"Sure, Gert, why not?" The foreman smiled at her, then turned his attention to the machine, showing them an overhead hopper filled with tiny blue plastic pellets. "We can mix these pellets to match any color at all and then extrude the beading like Gert there is doing on her machine."

"Was this where Joe Finch was working yesterday?"

McGrath nodded. "Come on, I'll show you his locker."

He led them down a narrow hallway to a large locker room filled with several rows of dull-green-metal boxes. Finch's was number 335. Leopold opened it with the duplicate key Stella had given him. A white-cotton coat was hanging in there along with an old red sweater. The only other thing in the locker was a blue ski mask.

Leopold lifted it out gingerly. Without a word, Fletcher produced a plastic evidence bag and Leopold dropped it inside.

That evening over dinner Leopold told Molly about the latest developments. "The lab is checking the ski mask for hairs. There's still no sign of Joe. We've had to issue a warrant for his arrest."

"Is Fletcher taking it hard?"

"Of course. He had to go home and break the news to Carol."

"It just seems so unlikely that a brother of hers could—"

"I didn't know him well," Leopold interrupted. "Even Fletcher hadn't seen him in a month. People change, and sometimes they can hide that change from those closest to them. We know he had financial problems. Maybe they just got to be too much for him to handle."

The meal was not the pleasant affair he'd hoped for. The cloud of Joe Finch seemed to hang over the table. Molly said she'd had a tiring day in court, and after dessert Leopold paid the bill and drove her home. By nine o'clock he was back at his own apartment.

As he was unlocking the door, a nearby voice called his name. He turned to see Carol Fletcher step out of the shadows. "Carol! What's the trouble?"

"You know what the trouble is. The real question is how we're dealing with it. I've just had a terrible row with my husband. I was out driving around to cool off and I thought maybe you could help."

"I'll do whatever I can," Leopold assured her. "Come on in."

She entered the apartment and sat down without removing her coat. "He says my brother may have killed that guard."

"Fletcher has a job to do, Carol. Just as I have."

"And his job comes before his family, right?" she asked bitterly.

"That murdered guard had a family, too," Leopold reminded her. "But that's not the point. Fletcher's not trying to railroad your brother. He's only trying to get at the truth."

"Do you have to love your work this much?" she asked, trying to fight back the tears. "Does it go with the badge?"

"We don't love it, Carol. If Joe did cause someone's death, would you want him to get away with it?"

"Yes, I think I would. He's still my brother."

Leopold took a deep breath. "Carol, I have to ask you this. Are you or Stella helping him? Do you know where he's hiding?"

"I won't answer that! You have no right to ask it!"

"I have every right, Carol, as a police officer and as a friend."

She stood up, her anger overtaking the tears. "I thought I could come to you for some sort of help, but you're all the same, aren't you?"

"Fletcher and I are the same," Leopold told her. As she rushed out of the apartment he called after her, "Go home to him, Carol."

He went to the bedroom where the telephone was, intending to do the sensible thing, phone Fletcher and then phone Connie to put a tail on Carol in case she did know where Joe Finch was hiding. Instead, he merely sat on the bed feeling very tired. He'd argued with Carol Fletcher and now she was an enemy. The conflict between duty and family was too much to overcome, as Fletcher was finding out. Maybe it was impossible for a good policeman to be a good husband, too. Maybe his dream of marrying Molly Calendar had been doomed from the beginning.

On Thursday morning, Leopold went out to the Greenways plant alone. Fletcher had asked to be transferred from the case that morning, and Leopold had respected his request. He assigned Connie Trent in Fletcher's place, and asked him to brief her on it. But right now he was alone because there were people he wanted to interview. First on his list was the robbery victim.

Kevin Bryer was a young man with a neat mustache and a businesslike manner. He worked in the Greenways payroll office and he'd been alone there Tuesday morning when the robber entered. "Do I have to tell it all again?" he asked plaintively when Leopold introduced himself.

"I'm afraid so. One more time."

"All right. What do you want to know?"

"How long have you worked at Greenways, Kevin?"

"Two years next month."

"Ever have any robberies before?"

"No. Nothing. I was thinking the job was a bit dull, in fact—just cashing checks and things like that."

"Tell me everything that happened Tuesday morning."

"Well, there's not much to tell. I was alone a little before noon when suddenly the door opened and this guy with a ski mask over his head is standing there, pointing a gun at me."

"What sort of gun?"

"A short-barreled revolver. A .38, I think—like the detectives use on TV."

Leopold brought out his Smith & Wesson. "Like this?"

"Yeah."

"What did he say?"

"Nothing at all. He just motioned with the gun and I knew what he wanted."

"Maybe he was afraid you'd recognize his voice. How was he built?"

Kevin Bryer shrugged. "About your height, but thinner."

"White or Black?"

"White. I could see the skin on his neck and around the eyes."

"What about his hands?"

"He was wearing gloves."

"What else did he have on?"

"Baggy jeans and a leather jacket with a sweatshirt under it. None of the clothes seemed to fit too well."

"What about his feet?"

"I didn't notice."

"So you gave him the money?"

"Sure thing—he was waving that pistol at me. I tried some small bills first but he pointed the gun and made it clear he wanted bigger ones."

"All without speaking?"

"Yeah. So I shoved over some stacks of hundreds, and that was when I managed to trip the silent alarm that brings the security guards. He shoved the money into a bag he was carrying and backed out the door about a second before Marvin Wise came running up. I saw Wise take off after him, and then I heard two shots."

"Did Wise fire?"

"I guess not. They said the bandit shot him twice."

"Which way was he running? Toward the gate?"

"No, back into the plant."

"So you figure it was an employee."

"It had to be," Bryer replied. "They're pretty strict at the gate. No one gets in without an appointment, and then they have to be escorted by a security guard. Otherwise it would be too easy to steal things."

"Why the tight security? Your plastic products don't seem that valuable."

"Oh, some of them are. But mainly it's because we do lots of sub-contract work for the auto industry. If we didn't have tight security, they wouldn't let us work on parts of their new models."

"I see. Tell me, do you know Joe Finch?"

"Yeah, I know him a little, like everyone who comes in here for their pay. I heard he's disappeared."

"Any chance he could have been the one who held you up?"

"I've been thinking about that, and I'm not sure. I suppose he's about the right build, but I just don't know."

Next Leopold went in search of Bernie McGrath, the foreman, and found him checking a sheet of production figures. "Oh—hello there," McGrath said. "It's Captain Leopold, isn't it? What can I do for you?"

"Two things. The first is a question about your security guards. I've been walking around here pretty freely without seeing any, except at the gate when I arrived. How many are there?"

"Well, we have one at each of the four gates, and then there are another four on duty inside the plant. When we're running extra shifts, we have to hire extra gate guards, of course, but the security service provides them. Right now there are just the eight."

"Next question: Could I talk to the men who were working with Joe Finch on Tuesday morning?"

"Sure." McGrath consulted a stack of pink time-sheets. "Come this way."

Soon they were back among the extruding machines, and Leopold noticed that another man was now operating Finch's machine. "Tommy," McGrath asked, "were you working with Joe on Tuesday?"

The slim young man turned and looked at them. "No, I was filling the hoppers. I saw him, but we didn't get to talk."

"Who was on this machine across the aisle?"

"Gert Provest."

"Where is she now?"

"She's out in the warehouse, getting a load of pellets."

McGrath nodded. "We'll see her there."

They went back out through the locker room to a large connecting building where wheeled hampers full of colored plastic pellets stood in line. Leopold paused to scoop up a handful of the pellets. "There must be a million of them in each hamper," he marveled.

"Possibly—but it's only enough for one hour's production when the machines are running at full speed. The pellets are mixed to achieve exactly the right color match, then heated to their melting point and extruded as vinyl beading. The operator checks the color periodically and keeps the hopper full of pellets."

Leopold remembered Gert Provest from the previous day. She was a plain, thin girl in her twenties who wore her bleached hair in a tight bun at the back of her head. A few pimples on her cheek were covered with salve. She stopped pushing one of the empty hampers long enough to answer Leopold's question. "Tuesday? Sure, I was working the machine across from Joe."

"Did you go to lunch when he did?"

"I didn't take a lunch break. We were short-handed, and when I shut down my machine I worked out here for an hour, loading pellets into these hampers while the guys went to eat." She positioned one beneath a narrow chute and pulled a lever, releasing a steady stream of yellow pellets from some unseen source.

"Pushing these hampers when they're full must be hard work," Leopold said.

She turned to face him, their eyes at the same level. "I figure I get a man's pay, so I do a man's work."

"Did you see Joe at all during the lunch hour?"

Gert Provest shook her head. "Not after he left his machine."

"How did he seem that morning? Nervous, tense?"

"He was the same as always."

"Was he especially friendly toward you or any of the other young women? Did he ever invite anyone out for a drink after work?"

"No." She smiled slightly. "He was married, wasn't he?"

"Yes, he was married," Leopold agreed. "Thanks for your help, Miss Provest."

As they returned to the manufacturing building, Bernie McGrath asked, "What about Joe's car? It hasn't been found, has it?"

"No," Leopold agreed. He hadn't given any thought to the car. "Where did Joe park it?"

"Everyone's assigned a space in the lot across the road." McGrath walked to a desk at one end of the first row of extruding machines and flipped through the pages on a clipboard. "Joe Finch has space number C-44."

"Thanks for your help," Leopold said, "I'll try not to bother you again."

"No bother at all."

Leopold crossed the street and walked up and down the rows of parked cars until he found the space marked C-44. It was empty. The car was gone, along with Joe Finch.

Back at headquarters, Fletcher listened glumly to Leopold's account of his visit to Greenways. "I could have told you the car was gone," he said. "That's the first thing I checked when Joe turned up missing. It's in the wanted bulletin we sent out on him. What's so important about the car?"

"I don't know, Fletcher. Maybe I'm clutching at straws." Leopold glanced around the squadroom. "Did you brief Connie on the case?"

"Yeah. She's gone out to talk to the dead man's widow. She thinks maybe Wise recognized the bandit and that's why he was killed."

Leopold shook his head. "It was a spur-of-the-moment killing, to avoid capture. But I might take a drive out to visit Stella Finch."

"Stella? What for, Captain?"

"I want to ask her about Joe's car."

When he reached the Finch house a half hour later, it seemed at first to be empty. Then he saw that Stella's car was in the garage and he rang the bell. After a time she answered it, and he suspected he'd awakened her. "Have you found him?" she asked.

"No, Stella, I'm sorry. There's no new word. But I have a couple of questions I'd like to ask you if it's all right."

"Come in," she said reluctantly, stepping aside so he could enter. The curtains were drawn and the living room was in semi-darkness. "What was it you wanted to know?"

He turned to face her without sitting down. She made no move to open the draperies. "It's about Joe's car. Did he have it at work Tuesday?"

"Of course. He always drove it to work."

"Stella, I've been thinking about the car. And about the ski mask."

"What about them?"

"Why would Joe bother wearing the mask if he was going to reveal his identity anyway by fleeing in his car immediately after the robbery?"

"I have no answer to that question because I'm not ready to admit that Joe did all this."

"Neither am I. But if Joe didn't use his car to leave the scene with the stolen money, he used it for some other purpose. He didn't drive downtown to see Fletcher. Is it possible he came home for lunch after all?"

"Certainly not. I'd have seen him if he did. I wouldn't have called you if he'd come home."

"You might have," Leopold said, "if something happened here at the house—if you wanted it to seem as if he was still at work."

Her face was a frozen mask. "Are you accusing me of something, Captain?"

No, he realized, he wasn't. He had no evidence to accuse her of anything. And yet, if Joe Finch hadn't robbed the company and hadn't driven home, where had he gone in his car? "I'm accusing you only of being less than frank, Stella. You must know why Joe might have been going to see Fletcher."

She turned away, and he realized that for all her stony exterior she was close to tears. After a moment she replied, "Joe wanted a gun permit. He thought his brother-in-law could help him. I didn't have any reason to think he went down to headquarters on Tuesday, but when he didn't come home that was the only possibility that came to mind. So I called you."

"A gun permit? Why didn't you tell us earlier?"

"Because a gun was used in the robbery and killing. I was afraid it would look suspicious. But he hadn't even bought it yet. He was just looking at one to have around the house."

Leopold sighed. "Was he going to buy it from someone at work?"

"No, from a gun shop. Joe would never do anything illegal."

"All right," Leopold said. "Thanks for telling me, Stella."

Leopold had arranged to meet Molly for a late lunch at one o'clock. She had to be back in court by two, and he could tell from her face that it wasn't going well. "I'm getting a complex about judges," she said, filling him in quickly on her frustrating morning. In return he told her about Carol Fletcher's visit the previous night and his call on Stella Finch. "I shouldn't be bothering you with my troubles," Molly decided. "You've got enough of your own."

"I was especially bothered by Carol," he admitted. "It got me thinking that maybe cops shouldn't marry. Maybe it's best to stay celibate, like priests."

"Oh, rubbish! You're too sensible to believe that!"

"I'm wondering about us, Molly. I see this thing tearing Carol and Fletcher apart and I wonder what something similar would do to us."

"I suppose it would make us miserable. But it wouldn't make us stop loving one another."

He went back to headquarters feeling better. Connie was waiting for him with a report on her interview with Marvin Wise's widow.

"I didn't think you'd find much there," he said.

"You were right. Until Finch turns up, I think we've hit a dead end with this case. Here's the lab report on that ski-mask you found in his locker."

"Thanks, Connie. Anything in it?"

"No hair, but they found a greasy spot of some sort."

Leopold let his eyes scan down the report until he found the phrase "a common over-the-counter medicinal ointment."

He said to Connie, "Get Fletcher. We're going out to Greenways."

"I thought he was off the case."

"He's back on it."

Leopold sought out a hectic Bernie McGrath. "Which color of those vinyl pellets are you running least of right now?"

The foreman looked blank, then replied, "Tan, I suppose. We haven't used any number-five tan in weeks."

Leopold thanked him and hurried away. He entered the big warehouse and walked down the rows of pellet-filled hampers until he found three tan loads tucked away in a corner. As soon as he got close, his nose picked up the trace of a familiar, unpleasant odor. He started scooping tan pellets out of one of the hampers, tossing them onto the adjoining loads. In a few minutes he uncovered an arm, and then the rest of the body. Joe Finch had been found at last.

"I was afraid you'd find him," a voice behind him said. He turned and saw Gert Provest pointing a revolver at him.

"I've come to arrest you, Gert," he said.

She fired twice as he dropped to the floor, and then Fletcher and Connie moved in from either side, grabbing and subduing her before she could fire again. "It's all right, Captain!" Fletcher called out.

Leopold watched Connie put handcuffs on her, then said grimly, "You'd better come with me, Fletcher. You stay here, Connie—read her her rights."

Fletcher walked over to the hamper. He stared at the body of his brother-in-law and managed to say, "I knew he wasn't a killer. I knew something bad must have happened to him."

"Something bad, yes. Gert Provest stole the money and killed the security guard. She ran in here, or into the adjoining locker room, to remove her ski mask and the baggy clothes she'd worn over her blouse and jeans. Joe was unlucky enough to see her, so she killed him, too. She was probably wild with panic after shooting the guard. Maybe he had his key out to open his locker. Anyway, she got the keys and put his body in an empty hamper, then rolled it over to a chute and filled it with vinyl pellets. I figured if she was trying to hide the body she'd choose a color that wasn't used much." He turned to the handcuffed woman. "He'd have been found sooner or later. What were you going to do with him?"

"The weekend. I could have gotten him out over the weekend."

"How'd you know where to look, Captain?" Connie asked.

"Once I suspected she'd done it, this was the only likely place the body could be. I knew she'd spent the lunch hour here in the warehouse, loading hampers while the guys were at lunch. She'd told me that much. I figured it was easy for her to go out the door and run around to the payroll office in her ski mask. After she came back and shot Joe, muffling the sound or hoping it wouldn't be noticed among the regular factory noises, she hid him under the pellets and then put the ski mask in his locker to implicate him. She had his car keys, along with the others, so she drove his car out of the lot and hid it. Want to tell us where, Gert?"

"Down the river bank," she mumbled without looking up.

Leopold went on. "I'd pretty much ruled out Joe as the killer from the beginning. Bryer, the man who was robbed, glimpsed the skin of the killer's neck beneath the ski mask. Joe had a bushy beard, and even if he'd tucked it into the mask I was pretty sure some neck hairs would have shown. And there'd almost certainly have been stray hairs inside the mask when the lab examined it. But there weren't any, because Gert wears her hair in a tight bun. What we did find were traces of the greasy salve she uses on her face."

"But the description indicated the killer was a man," Connie protested.

"A thin man, as she is thin, wearing baggy clothes to conceal her shape. The killer never spoke during the robbery. Bryer said he, or she, was about my height, which she is."

Fletcher looked grim. "Can you two take care of things here? I have to tell Carol and Stella."

"Go ahead," Leopold said. "Tell them how sorry I am."

When Fletcher left, Connie said, "It hasn't been easy for him."

"No, and this now is the hardest part of all."

Three weeks later, Leopold and Molly were married at a small wedding in a church near the courthouse. Fletcher was Leopold's best man. Carol Fletcher cried after the ceremony, but Leopold knew they were tears of happiness.

THE MURDER IN ROOM 1010

Captain Leopold had barely known Max Hafner during the younger man's years on the Police Force. Hafner had been assigned to Narcotics and Vice, in the days when those specialties rarely overlapped the homicides and violent crimes that were Leopold's concern. All this had changed in the present decade, but Max Hafner was gone from the Force, earning a comfortable living running a security firm that doubled as a private-detective agency.

"Sure, I know Max," Sergeant Connie Trent said, responding to Leopold's question on a chilly November morning. "I used to work with him on Narcotics. That was a long time ago, though. He's been off the Force nearly ten years."

"He called me at home last night," Leopold said. "Wants to have lunch with me today, like we were old friends."

"Maybe he's going to offer you a job."

Leopold chuckled. "The thought crossed my mind." His wife, Molly, had suggested the same thing after the phone call. Of course, Leopold would never leave the Force, and who would want him at his age? Still, he sometimes envied men like Hafner, who'd had the vision to strike off on their own while they were still young.

"Hold out for fifty thousand," Connie advised, only half in jest. "Max Hafner can afford it."

The lunch itself proved to be a pleasant affair at an expensive French restaurant across the street from City Hall. Leopold had eaten there only a few times in the past, always when someone else was picking up the check. Seated across the table from Max Hafner, he tried to remember what this portly, middle-aged business man had looked like in a police uniform but the image wouldn't come. During lunch, they spoke casually of some mutual friends on the Force.

"Is Connie Trent still with you?" Hafner asked. "She was a great little girl."

"She still is. She's a sergeant now, and one of our best."

"Fletcher, too? I think he made lieutenant just before I resigned." Leopold nodded. "Still there."

"You know, I hired a few of the boys when they left the department. I like to think of Hafner Security as a second Police Force at times."

Leopold finished his dessert. "I have to be getting back soon. If there was anything special you wanted to bring up—"

"Of course—I keep forgetting your time's not your own when you work for the city. I'll get to the point. You're aware that we handle a little private-detective work along with the security that constitutes the bulk of our business?"

"Yes," Leopold admitted cautiously. Here it comes, he thought. A job offer.

"Right now we have some need for a good battery-operated tape recorder small enough to fit into a woman's purse. A voice-activated one would be best. Could you recommend a good brand?"

"What?"

"A tape recorder, I asked—"

"I heard you. The question just took me by surprise. Was that all you wanted to ask me?"

"That's all I can think of at the moment."

Leopold mentioned a brand name the department used, and after Max Hafner paid the check they parted with a handshake.

When he returned to the office, Connie was waiting for him. "Well? Did you take the job?" she asked with a grin.

"He didn't offer me one. He wanted to know a good brand of tape recorder. He spent nearly fifty dollars on lunch to ask me about tape recorders. And then he didn't seem all that interested in what I told him."

"Do you think he had some other reason for inviting you?"

"It beats me," Leopold admitted. "Maybe once he saw me again, he decided I was too old for the job he had in mind."

Molly called later in the afternoon, curious about his luncheon. He told her the same thing he'd told Connie. "It was strange. I could have understood it better if he'd been a close friend on the Force, but we hardly knew each other. I think he changed his mind about what he originally wanted to say to me."

"You sound almost disappointed. Would you have accepted a job if he offered one?"

"Of course not," Leopold said. "But I wouldn't have minded the pleasure of turning him down."

Two days later, Leopold had virtually forgotten about the luncheon. It was midafternoon of a busy day when the call came in from the St. George, one of the city's largest hotels. Connie took it and hurried into Leopold's office. "There's a dead man in one of the rooms at the St. George, Captain. Looks like a homicide."

"Is Fletcher in?"

Connie shook her head. "Still out on that bank robbery."

"I'd better go with you, then. Old Duncan Kincaid will fire off a letter to the newspaper if I don't cover this."

The St. George occupied an entire block facing Veterans Park in the center of the city. At one time it had been part of a nationwide hotel chain, but a few years back Kincaid, a local developer, had bought it with the help of an investment syndicate. Though Leopold was no great admirer of Kincaid, he had to admit the hotel had been kept up in style. The dark wood paneling gave the lobby a warm, rich look and the ebony statue of St. George slaying the traditional dragon made a nice centerpiece.

An ambulance and a squad car were already at the hotel when Leopold and Connie arrived. The first officer on the scene led them to the elevator and then to the tenth floor. "The front desk had reports of a woman screaming," the officer explained. "A security man went up to Room 1010 and tried to open the door. The chain lock was on, so he had to cut it. Inside, he found the screaming woman, barely conscious, next to the body of a murdered man."

They found another officer in the hotel room with ambulance attendants who were attempting to calm a pretty, dark-haired woman.

"See if you can talk to her, Connie," Leopold directed, turning his attention to the body on the king-sized bed around the corner from the door. The man was fully clothed and the spread was still in place, its pale-pink design saturated with a wide circle of blood. The dead man, who seemed about the same age as the woman, had been stabbed several times in the chest and stomach. The bloody knife lay on the carpeted floor near the woman's chair.

Connie finally managed to calm the woman and she was strapped to a stretcher for the trip to the hospital. "She doesn't seem to be wounded," Connie told Leopold as the stretcher was wheeled out. "Just hysterical and maybe a little high on something. I couldn't be sure."

"Did she kill him?"

"She claims not. Says she doesn't know how it happened. She dozed off and woke up to find him like that."

"Dozed off in the middle of the afternoon?"

A large Black man in a three-piece suit entered the room. He was still carrying a pair of long-handled heavy-duty cutters. "Are you the security man?" Leopold asked, introducing himself.

"Right, Sam Mason's the name."

"Tell me what happened."

"We had a report of a woman screaming in this room. I could still hear her when I got up here. When she wouldn't open up, I used the pass-key on the door. I saw the chain was on, so I had to get these cutters."

"The dead man was on the bed like he is now?"

"Just like that. I didn't touch him. I tried to calm her down and then I told the manager to phone the police."

"What did she say?"

"She kept insisting she didn't kill him. Hell, if she didn't do it, she locked the door after the killer left."

Connie reached behind one of the chairs. "Here's her purse, Captain."

Leopold opened it. "I don't suppose there's anything—" He stopped in mid-sentence. The purse contained a small, voice-activated tape recorder. It was the same model he'd recommended to Max Hafner.

A few hours later, Hafner sat across the desk from Leopold at Headquarters. "The old place hasn't changed much," he remarked. "I'm glad to see you finally got rid of that coin-operated coffee machine, though. It never worked right."

It was too late in the day for small talk and Leopold came right to the point. "Max, do you know a woman named Anita Buckman?"

"Anita—It does sound familiar."

"Think hard, it's important," Leopold said grimly.

"Well, yeah—I have a client by that name."

"You'd better tell me about her."

"What's this all about?"

"Murder, Max. Your client was found alone with a dead man in a locked hotel room this afternoon."

"Has the victim been identified?"

"A man named Ken Armstrong. He used to teach at one of the local high schools until he was accused of molesting a female student. Since then his life's been all downhill. He was arrested last year for living off the earnings of a prostitute, but the charge was dismissed."

Max Hafner moistened his lips with his tongue. "I'd better tell you about it."

Leopold nodded encouragingly.

"Her husband was being blackmailed and she came to me for help. He'd had a fling with a prostitute and somebody took pictures. They got some money from her husband but then they came after her—told her her husband could lose his job at one of our town's more staid banking institutions. She wasn't about to pay more blackmail, but she didn't want the publicity of calling in the police, either, so she came to me. I figured our best bet was to have her record the payoff meeting and then force the blackmailers to lay off under threat of arrest. That's why I asked you about tape recorders the other day."

"This Armstrong was the blackmailer?"

"I assume so. A man contacted the husband and then phoned Anita Buckman."

"What's the husband's name?"

"Rudolph Buckman. Rudy Buckman. He's a vice-president in the trust department at Community Trust Company. Conservative, like I said."

"Everything seems conservative in this case, including the staid old St. George Hotel. Is that where Mrs. Buckman and the black-mailer agreed to meet?"

Hafner nodded. They agreed to meet in the lobby. Somehow he must have lured her up to a room."

"Room 1010." Leopold decided it was time to get a bit tougher with Hafner. "Look here, Max, do you expect me to believe you took me to lunch the other day just to find out what model of tape recorder I'd recommend? You've probably been using them for years. Chances are you know more about them than I do."

Hafner looked uncomfortable, running a hand across his broad stomach. "I'll be frank. My first intention was to tell you about this case and to ask a favor. I wanted someone in that hotel lobby backing up Mrs. Buckman in case the blackmailer turned violent. I'm too well known around town to do it myself and you can see I'm not in the best shape for any rough stuff."

Leopold shrugged, shifting to a friendlier tone of voice. "So tell me what changed your mind at lunch."

"I suppose I realized I couldn't expect you to furnish a plain-clothes officer as a backup without filing a formal complaint, and that was what Anita Buckman wanted to avoid. While we were eating, I happened to see Sam Mason pass the window and I remembered he was head of security at the St. George. I decided to use him instead, and avoid bringing my own people in on the investigation. Then I simply made up that question about the tape recorder."

"At least you followed my advice," Leopold told him, taking the miniature recorder from his desk drawer. "Care to listen to this?"

"Of course. It should tell us what happened in that room. I'm sure Mrs. Buckman acted in self-defense."

"She denies all knowledge of the killing—says she blacked out for a few minutes and woke to find him stabbed to death on the bed." Leopold pressed the Play button and leaned back to listen to the tape for the third time.

It started with some lobby sounds, half-heard voices loud enough to activate the recorder. Then a woman's voice, quite close, asked, "You're the one who phoned me?"

A man's voice responded. "That's right. Did you bring the money?"

"In my purse. Where are the pictures of my husband?"

"Upstairs. I had to make sure you came alone."

"I'm alone."

"Come up with me. It'll only take a minute."

"All right."

There were more random noises and the chime of an elevator bell, then: "Here we are."

"You don't have to lock the door."

"We don't want anyone interrupting us, do we? Let's see the money."

"What about the pictures?"

"Right here."

"God, you're an animal!"

"It's your husband, lady."

"Who's this woman?"

"I guess you could call her a mutual friend of your husband's and mine. Her name's Rhoda?"

"And you took these pictures?"

"I admit it.—Rudy's bank wouldn't like these, would they?"

"You scum!"

"Relax. I've got a bottle of rye here. How about a drink?"

"No."

"I'll pour you a weak one, anyway, in case."

"Is this how you make your living?"

"I do lots of things. I used to teach high school."

"I'll bet."

"No, really. Here, take a swallow and then you can give me the money."

"This tastes terrible! What's in it?"

"Let's have the money."

"No! —I feel strange! The room's starting to spin!"

"That's your imagination."

"What did—?"

A jumble of sounds, and then Armstrong's voice came on again. "What in hell are you doing?" A gasp, then the rest of the tape was filled with Anita's screams until it ran out and Leopold switched off the recorder.

Max Hafner stared at him. "You say the room was locked from the inside?"

"Yes. And the chain lock was on."

"From the tape, it sounds like she killed him. But she might have been drugged at the time. Did you check the bottle of whiskey?"

"It's being analyzed now."

Hafner shook his head sadly, "Why would she kill him when she had the evidence against him on this tape? He wasn't a threat to her or her husband any longer."

"You said you decided to use Sam Mason to keep an eye on her. Have you talked to him?"

"No. I hadn't heard a thing about this when you called me in here."

"Weren't you curious?"

"I have a busy office, Captain, and a small staff."

"All right, Max. I'll call you if I need anything else."

"Do you think Anita Buckman killed him, Captain?"

"I try to keep an open mind at this stage of the investigation."

"Is there any other possibility?"

"At least one," Leopold told him.

At the hospital, Leopold encountered Rudy Buckman for the first time. He was a pale, blond-haired man in his thirties who looked as if he'd spent too much time inside his bank.

"Is it really necessary to have a policewoman on guard outside my wife's room?" he asked after Leopold introduced himself.

"I'm afraid it is, Mr. Buckman. "Your wife is a suspect in a murder case. The only suspect we have at the moment."

"Are you here to question her?"

"I'd like to speak with her if she's able."

"She's calmed down quite a bit. The doctor wants to keep her overnight."

Leopold followed him into his wife's room, nodding to the officer on duty at the door. Anita Buckman was in bed but wide awake. "I'm feeling all right now," she told them. "Why can't I go home?"

"The doctor will release you in the morning," Buckman assured her. "He just wants to be sure you're all right."

Leopold cleared his throat. "I wonder if you're feeling up to making a statement, Mrs. Buckman. I must advise you that you have the right to remain silent or have a lawyer present. Any statement you do make may be used against you."

"I didn't kill him!"

"That's what I'm here to determine."

"Do you want a lawyer, Anita?" her husband asked.

"No! I have nothing to hide."

"Suppose you tell me what happened," Leopold suggested.

"That detective, Hafner—"

"Max Hafner."

"Yes. I went to him about the blackmail."

"I wish you'd told me," Rudy Buckman said. "If I'd known Armstrong was shaking you down, too—"

"You didn't come to me, Rudy. I couldn't go to you." She took a sip of water from the paper cup by her bedside. "Hafner said I could turn the tables on the blackmailer by getting a tape recording of the transaction. It seemed like a sensible solution and I agreed to it. The blackmailer—you said his name was Armstrong?"

"Ken Armstrong," Leopold verified.

"He told me the pictures were in his hotel room and we went up to get them. I saw them, Rudy. They were awful. You and that woman—"

"What happened then?" Leopold asked, trying to keep her on track.

"He insisted I have a drink of whiskey. I only had a swallow, but it made me dizzy. I don't remember what happened, except that all of a sudden he was on the bed, bleeding. I think I started to scream then."

"Did Armstrong let anyone else into the room?"

"No. And I remember him locking the door when we entered."

"Could someone have been hiding in the closet or the bathroom?" Rudy asked. "Or under the bed?"

"I—suppose so."

"But they couldn't have gotten out," Leopold was quick to point out. "Sam Mason, the hotel security man, had to cut the chain to enter the room."

"I—"

"Don't say anything more, Anita. I'll get you a lawyer in the morning." Buckman turned to Leopold. "I think that's enough for now, Captain."

"All right. We'll continue this tomorrow at my office."

Leopold left the hospital room and walked to the elevators. Visiting hours were coming to an end, but he had one more stop to make elsewhere.

Sam Mason was off duty by the time Leopold reached the St. George Hotel. "You just missed him," the desk clerk said. "I'll tell you, though, sometimes on rough days he stops for a nightcap at the Fountainhead down the block."

"Was this a rough day?"

The clerk rolled his eyes. "You'd better believe it."

Leopold was on his way out of the hotel when he was stopped by Duncan Kincaid, the gray-haired developer who owned the place. "Captain Leopold!"

"Mr. Kincaid! I didn't know you involved yourself in the day-to-day operations here."

"I came down because of the killing. It's not good for the business to have a murder in one of the guest rooms. Has the woman confessed yet?"

"She claims she didn't do it."

"But Sam Mason tells me the room was locked from the inside. He had to cut through the chain."

"She right."

"If she was alone with him she must have stabbed him."

"We're working on it, Mr. Kincaid. We hope to have a break in the case soon."

Leopold found Sam Mason nursing a bourbon at the Fountainhead bar and sat down beside him. The man squinted at him in the dim light. "Leopold, isn't it?"

"That's right. I wanted to ask you a couple of questions about this afternoon. About the murder in Room 1010."

"I told you everything I know."

"What about the dead man, Ken Armstrong? Ever notice him hanging around the lobby?"

"Not before today."

"Do you happen to know a friend of his named Rhoda? A prostitute?"

"Rhoda? There's a fancy call girl by that name. Rhoda Quigley. If I see her in the lobby I escort her out. I haven't seen her lately, though."

"Where does she live?"

"Beats me. You probably got a file on her at Headquarters."

"Do you know Max Hafner?"

"Private dick, isn't he?"

"That's right, that and security. He says he slipped you a few bills to keep an eye on Anita Buckman when she met Armstrong this afternoon."

"Hell, man, I can't do outside work! Mr. Kincaid would have my ass for it."

"I'm not asking about the rules. I'm asking if Hafner had you watch her."

"Well, yeah, I guess he mentioned it."

"Didn't do a very good job, did you?"

"I followed them up to the room, but there was nothing more I could do after they went inside. I went downstairs to call Hafner, and then I got the report of the screaming."

"Was Hafner at his office?"

"No. He was out."

"Then what did you do?"

Mason swallowed the rest of his bourbon and said, "When I heard about the screaming I went back up there. The chambermaid gave me the pass-key and I unlocked the door, then I had to go get the cutters and cut the chain. When we went in, Mrs. Buckman was still screaming and this Armstrong guy was dead on the bed."

"The chambermaid was with you? She saw you cut the chain?"

"She sure did."

Leopold tried not to show his disappointment. He had had the idea that Sam Mason might have cut the chain after stabbing Armstrong. But with the chambermaid as a witness that possibility faded away.

Back at his office, Leopold phoned home to tell Molly he'd be late, then he settled down to review the relevant objects that had been found in the room—the knife, the bottle of whiskey, a camera, Anita Buckman's purse, and the tape recorder. In addition to the recorder, the purse had contained an envelope full of cut-up newspaper, apparently a half hearted attempt to fool the blackmailer at payoff time, if it came to that. Once she had the transaction on tape, Anita would have had to get out of that room fast. As it turned out, she hadn't been fast enough.

Leopold turned his attention to the 35-mm camera. It had been found on the closet shelf and apparently belonged to Armstrong. There was a full roll of film in it, with no shots exposed. "What do you make of this?" he asked Connie when she came in with the lab report.

"My guess is that he was going to try for some photos of Mrs. Buckman, too. The whiskey was loaded with knockout drops. More than that one swallow and she'd still be sleeping. You've got to say Armstrong had nerve, Captain. He gets Buckman's wife up there to pay blackmail for her husband and knocks her out with the idea of taking off her clothes and getting some shots of her for future blackmail."

"That's speculation."

"What else makes sense. Why else would he try drugging her?"

Leopold thought about it "Maybe you're right."

"She must have had the knife in her purse and she used it when she felt herself going under."

"Then why deny it? No jury would convict her for stabbing him under those circumstances."

"I don't know," Connie admitted. "Maybe she's afraid."

"Let's see those photos of the crime scene," Leopold said. He shuffled through them, passing quickly over those of the body and concentrating on the others. There was one of the door, showing the chain cut neatly in half with five links hanging from either side. The broken pieces of the split link had fallen to the carpet.

"Here's something else to check on, Connie Armstrong's partner in the shakedown may have been a call girl named Rhoda Quigley. See if there's an arrest record on her and pick her up for questioning."

It was when he thought about Rhoda Quigley that he suddenly realized how stupid he'd been.

Molly was waiting for him when he reached home a little before nine. "I'll heat something up for you," she suggested.

He kissed her lightly on the lips. "Just make me a sandwich. I may have to go out again."

"What now?"

"I'm waiting for a call from Connie. It's that murder at the St. George."

"I thought they found the woman in the room."

He gave her a tired smile. "That would be too easy." He took off his coat and then went back to examine the lock on their front door. "Nine," he said more to himself than to Molly.

"What's that?"

"Nothing. Just bringing my work home from the office." The ringing of the telephone interrupted them. "I'll get it," Leopold said. "It's probably Connie."

"Not already. You haven't eaten yet."

"Captain," Connie said, "I've got Rhoda Quigley here at Headquarters. She wasn't hard to find."

"I'll be right down, Connie."

Molly handed him a ham sandwich on his way out the door.

Rhoda Quigley was a well-dressed young woman with brown hair and a winning smile. She didn't look like a call girl, and Leopold couldn't imagine her working the streets as a prostitute. She might have been selling real estate or working in an insurance office. "Am I under arrest?" she asked him with a sly smile.

"That depends on you. Do you know a man named Ken Armstrong?"

"I knew him. The TV news says he was killed this afternoon."

"That's correct. What about a man named Rudy Buckman?"

The smile began to fade. "Just what is it you want to know?"

"The penalty for blackmail in this state—"

"I wasn't involved in any blackmail. What Ken did with those pictures was his own affair."

"But you knew he was taking them."

"Yes," she admitted softly.

"You've done this with other clients?"

"I figured it wasn't harming anyone. Ken just liked to look at pictures. Some people get their kicks that way."

"What did he do—hide in the closet?"

She hesitated. "Can I smoke in here?"

"Go ahead."

She lit a cigarette and inhaled deeply. "No, he didn't hide in the closet He was afraid the guy would hang up his coat or something. I'd keep the John busy while Ken sneaked in. It wasn't difficult. You couldn't see the door from the bed."

"Wasn't it locked?"

"He'd tricked it up somehow. We always used the same room."

"Which one was that?"

"Room 1010 at the St. George Hotel."

"I see." Leopold studied her. "I'd suggest you get a lawyer in here before we take your formal statement."

He went out to find Connie. "I want you to find a judge to issue a search warrant," he told her.

"Tonight?"

"Right now."

"It's a holiday, you know. Some of the judges might have taken a long weekend."

"Holiday? Oh, Veterans Day—I forgot about that. Try Judge Newman. He'll be in town."

"All right. Give me the name and address for the warrant."

Leopold wrote it out for her. He paused momentarily over the address, but finally printed it out decisively.

"You see, Connie," he explained an hour later as they drove to their destination, "it should have been obvious to us from the beginning that Anita Buckman didn't kill Armstrong. Someone else *had* to be in that hotel room."

"How can you be so sure?"

"Because something very important was missing from that room. Armstrong brought Anita Buckman up there to show her the photographs of her husband with Rhoda. We know from the tape recording that he did show her the photos. But what happened to them? They weren't among the things we found in the room. The only possibility is that someone entered the room and removed them."

"It might have been Sam Mason, after he cut the chain."

"Why? To deliver them to Hafner? That wouldn't make sense. The pictures were proof that Anita was being blackmailed, and she was Hafner's client. Besides, the chambermaid was with Mason when he broke in. No, the pictures were removed by the killer, and that means it wasn't Anita."

"Who, then? And how did they get into the room?"

He turned the car into the street they were seeking. "Someone to whom the pictures were all-important. Not another blackmailer, and certainly not Rhoda Quigley. She'd done this sort of thing before. Armstrong must have had numerous prints of her in the arms of clients. As for the *how* of it, my own observations were confirmed by my interview with Rhoda Quigley. Obtaining a passkey for the room was never a problem. The killer might have had one from a prior visit, or tricked the chambermaid into borrowing hers just long enough to make an impression of it in putty. The problem was the chain lock.

"I noticed in the police photograph that Mason had cut the middle link, leaving five links on each side. That meant the chain had eleven links in all. Of course these vary by manufacturer, but I did notice that my chain lock at home has only nine links. It seemed the chain on the door of Room 1010 was a bit longer than normal. Then Rhoda told me Armstrong always used that same room for his photo sessions. He'd gimmicked the door so he could sneak into the room with his camera while Rhoda and the potential blackmail victim were making love. He'd simply substituted a different chain, one long enough so he could reach his hand in to unlatch it—and to relatch it later. To anyone locking the door from the inside it would have seemed normal."

Connie nodded. "We had a hotel thief last year who used that method. He'd enter an empty room during the day with a passkey, substitute a slightly longer chain, and then return at night when the occupants of the room were sleeping and there were wallets lying around."

Leopold stopped the car in front of the address he had written down an hour earlier. "The killer had to know about this system, or at least be able to figure it out from his own experience. And he had to be intimately concerned with those photographs. Rudy Buckman is the only one who fills the bill."

Buckman opened the door when they rang. "It's a bit late for a call, isn't it, Captain? I was about to go to bed."

"We have a search warrant here, Mr. Buckman."

"For what?" he asked, immediately on the defensive.

"The pictures you removed from the hotel room today after you killed Armstrong."

"That's crazy!" Buckman stepped aside as they entered the house and Connie moved on to the living room.

"You knew there was a way past that lock," Leopold said. "When you heard him drug your wife, you burst in and stabbed him. Then you must have decided you wouldn't mind if she went to prison for the murder. You took the pictures—a big mistake—and relocked the door. You didn't take them to work because the bank was closed for the holiday. I doubt if you'd have risked throwing them into a trash can. You brought them back here, didn't you?"

"Captain," Connie called, "there are a few ashes in the fireplace—and the unburnt corner of a photograph."

"Call the lab boys. They'll get an image off those larger pieces of ash." He turned back to Rudy Buckman and read him his rights as he took out a pair of handcuffs.

A week later, Max Hafner invited Leopold to lunch again. "I understand Buckman confessed."

"That's right. It's all over but the trial. He'll try to plead some sort of justification, I suppose, but the jury isn't likely to forget that he was willing to frame his wife."

Hafner toyed with his glass. "You know, Captain. I'm going to make you an offer I should have made long ago. Would you be interested in retiring from the Force and coming to work for me? I could certainly use someone with your brains and knowledge."

Captain Leopold smiled, feeling good. "Thanks, Max, I appreciate that. But I'm not ready to retire yet. And today the lunch is on me."

"**Y**ou don't seem to understand," Captain Leopold was telling the stout middle-aged woman across the desk from him. "Mrs. Roberts, this is the Violent Crimes Squad. What you want is the Swindle and Embezzlement Squad."

"What's more violent than murder?"

"We need a corpse," Leopold explained. "According to your story, the murder victim was a man who's already been dead for fifty-five years."

"But he was still murdered," Mrs. Roberts insisted. "I heard it with my own ears."

Leopold pressed a button on his intercom. "Connie, are you free? Could you come in here for a few minutes?"

When Sergeant Connie Trent entered his glass-walled cubicle, Leopold introduced her. "Connie, Thelma Roberts has a special problem that warrants some investigation. She feels it belongs with our squad. I'm not convinced of that, but maybe you could look into it and decide. Mrs. Roberts, could you repeat your story for Connie exactly as you told it to me?"

"Certainly." She smiled at Connie as if recognizing someone who would be sympathetic to her argument. "My grandfather was Hugh Paxton—are you familiar with the name?"

"I'm afraid—"

"No, of course not, you're much too young. Well, he was an important man in this city—a banker and alderman everyone admired. Paxton Park is named after him. I was only six when he killed himself during the Depression, but I still remember him coming to see me a few times when I was little. He had a booming voice and a big walrus moustache. When my husband died of cancer recently and I had no one to turn to, I remembered my Gramps. I went to him for help."

Leopold saw Connie's mouth drop open and he hurried to explain. "Mrs. Roberts consulted a medium, Connie. A woman on West Side Avenue who goes by the name of Madame Vane."

Connie made a note on her pad. "And Madame Vane put you in contact with your grandfather?"

"That's right, on my second visit. She held a small séance and his voice came to me clear as a bell."

"Did the others hear it, too?"

"Yes, everyone did. First there was a spirit guide by the name of Grey Elk. They're often Indians, you know."

"I didn't know," Connie admitted.

"Grey Elk said he would go and find Gramps. We had to wait a long time, and even Madame Vane was beginning to lose hope but then we heard his voice, just like I remembered it. 'Hello, Thelma,' he said. It was like I was six years old again. I felt so good."

"Did you ask him about your problems?"

"Not that time. He said he couldn't talk long. But he told me to come back the following week. All week I could hardly sleep in anticipation. My friend told me he wouldn't come, but he did. The Indian guide brought him again, just like the first time. I told him about my husband dying and we talked a long time about my life and how hard it's been. I told him about the money I had and asked his advice on investments."

Connie made some more notes. "How long ago was this?"

"Three weeks ago Tuesday."

"It was the same voice as the first time?"

"Of course—it was the voice of my grandfather."

"Was that the last time he spoke to you?"

"No, I went back the following week for a third séance. He came again, and that's when it happened."

"What happened?"

"The Indian guide, Grey Elk, murdered him."

"You can't be serious," Connie said.

"I heard it with my own ears! Don't tell me I can't be serious! I expected more respect from the police department!"

"I'm sorry," Connie said, trying to avoid Leopold's steady gaze. "Please continue. Tell me exactly what happened."

"Gramps was speaking to me, as he'd done twice before. We were talking about the small inheritance my husband had left me. Then the Indian started shouting at him. I don't know what it was about, but I distinctly heard someone say, 'Put down that gun!' Then there was the sound of a gunshot. After that there were no more voices."

"What did you do?"

"I was frantic, of course, I wanted to call the police but Madame Vane assured me they have no jurisdiction in the afterlife."

"She's quite correct," Leopold interjected.

"I insisted on returning the following Tuesday evening. She agreed and we held another séance with the same controls. Nothing happened at all."

"No voices?"

"Nothing. I returned again last night with the same result. Madame Vane refused to take my money and told me the sessions are now at an end. She seems frightened by what happened. So this morning I came to you."

Hearing her story for a second time, Leopold had no doubt of the woman's sincerity. She really believed what she had heard. "Sergeant Trent will call on Madame Vane and take a statement from her, Mrs. Roberts. You can be assured that we'll look into this."

The woman managed a weak smile. "Thank you. I hope I did the right thing in coming to you like this."

"That's what we're here for," Connie told her. "I'll be in touch with you."

But when Thelma Roberts had gone, leaving her alone with Leopold, Connie said, "Is this some sort of a joke, Captain? You can't be serious!"

"The woman is serious, Connie, and that's what matters. I tried to steer her to the bunko squad but she wouldn't hear of it. She honestly believes that her grandfather who's been dead for fifty-five years has been murdered in the afterlife by an Indian named Grey Elk. It looks to me as if this Madame Vane is working some sort of scam. A friendly visit from you could nip the thing in the bud."

"If you say so," Connie agreed reluctantly. "But don't expect me to come up with any bodies from the beyond."

Connie had started by checking with the bunko squad—Swindle and Embezzlement—to see if they had an arrest record for Madame Vane. She turned up only one instance, two years earlier, when the woman, whose real name was Madeline Vane, had been arrested for grand larceny. The charges were later dismissed for lack of evidence.

Madame Vane's home on West Side Avenue was a big brown house that probably dated from the early years of the century. The other houses like it on the street had long ago been split into apartments for the young singles who'd found the area convenient to their downtown offices. This one was still together, with Madame Vane's living quarters on the second floor and the first floor given over to her business. There was no sign to indicate what the business was—only a small brass plate above the bell bearing the single word *VANE*.

Connie pressed the bell and waited.

A man in his forties who might have been a servant answered almost at once. "Good afternoon, Miss."

"I'd like to see Madame Vane."

"Do you have an appointment?"

Connie showed her badge and identification. "Police. I just want to ask some questions."

He pursed his lips and retreated a few steps, as if to remain out of her reach. "I will see if Madame is available. Please wait here."

Connie stood in the hallway as he disappeared through a large oak door. The dark wood of the staircase had been polished to a dull glow and a small Chinese lamp on a table gave off the only light that penetrated the place. She glanced around for windows, but in this area there were none.

"Step this way, please," the man said from the doorway. "Madame can give you ten minutes."

Connie followed him into a sitting room decorated in fine Victorian style. It was too bleak for her taste, but she could appreciate the quality of the décor. She sat on a straight-backed chair and after a moment Madame Vane made an impressive entrance. She was a tall, slender woman dressed in a shimmering black gown that almost reached the floor. Her black hair was pulled back severely into a bun and her pale face was set off by a beauty mark high on the right cheekbone.

"You wished to see me?" she asked. "Have the neighbors been complaining about my business again?"

"No, this is another matter." Connie showed her identification. "I'm Sergeant Connie Trent of the Violent Crimes Squad."

"Violent—"

"A woman named Thelma Roberts has been to see us." Connie ran quickly through the major points of Mrs. Roberts' story. "Is that what happened?"

"I do conduct séances here," the woman admitted. "I don't believe there's any law against it."

"If Mrs. Roberts is telling the truth, this whole thing seems like the first step in a scheme to defraud her somehow."

Madame Vane's pale face remained impassive. "I have not asked her for money other than my usual charge for sessions. In fact, I told her yesterday that I would no longer take her money. I want nothing more to do with the woman. She is too disruptive."

"In what way?"

"*I* have no control over what happens in my sessions. I simply summon the spirits. Some nights nothing happens. On other nights we are more fortunate. Either way, I am not responsible."

"I see. You contend that these séances are authentic, that you have no control over what the spirits say."

"How could I control that?"

"There are numerous tricks used by mediums, as you must know."

"By charlatans, not by me."

Connie could see she was getting nowhere. "Is Mrs. Roberts' account substantially accurate?"

"I couldn't say. I was in a trance the entire time."

"Have you used this spirit guide, Grey Elk, before?"

"Yes, many times."

"And since?"

"As Mrs. Roberts told you, no spirits were contacted these past two weeks."

"What do *you* think it means, Madame Vane?"

"I have no idea."

"Do you think Grey Elk killed the spirit of Thelma Roberts' grandfather?"

"No, certainly not. How can there be murder in the afterlife? Occasionally, messages from the beyond are scrambled in the ether, just as radio signals are. The message may have been garbled by a transmission from Earth."

"Are others present at your séances?"

"We need at least four to conduct a proper session. We sit around a table and hold hands—but I'm sure you must be aware of the traditions."

"You sit in the dark?"

"Yes."

"Were there four of you on these nights in question?"

"Yes. Mrs. Roberts, myself, Colonel Armbruster who lives next door, and Oliver. You met him when you arrived."

"Your servant?"

She smiled slightly. "No, Oliver is my husband."

"Could I speak with him?"

"Certainly. I'll go find him." She rose and went out the door.

Connie stood up and walked to the window, lifting aside the heavy draperies to look out at the street. There was little activity, and her unmarked police car sat undisturbed at the curb. She let the drape fall back in place and turned her attention to a nearby bookcase. There were a few recent novels in book-club editions and a much-thumbed volume on the history of spiritualism. A few old phonograph records in their original sleeves were on the bottom shelf and Connie bent to examine them, wondering what was keeping Madame Vane.

One of the record jackets proclaimed *Our City's Centennial—1830-1930: Its Leaders Speak.* Beneath it was a Bing Crosby record that was almost as old. Connie straightened up just as the door opened and Madame Vane returned with her husband. "I'm sorry it took me so long to find him," she explained. "I didn't realize he was outside doing yard work."

Oliver stepped forward, still maintaining the attitude of a servant. "You had some questions for me, Miss?"

"You're Madame Vane's husband?"

"That's correct."

"What is your full name?"

"Oliver Peebles."

"You took part in the séances with Mrs. Roberts."

"That's correct."

"And you heard the seeming act of violence between the spirits of Grey Elk and Hugh Paxton?"

"It was all very garbled. I believe Mrs. Roberts may have heard more than the rest of us. I heard a noise that could have been a gunshot, but I doubt if it was."

"Have you ever heard anything like it before during a séance?"

"No," he said. "But conditions weren't good that night. There was something in the air. Bad vibrations."

Connie turned her attention to Madame Vane. "And you were in a trance during the entire time."

"That's correct."

"What about the fourth member of the séance—your neighbor, Colonel Armbruster? Could I speak with him?"

"You can if you want," Madame Vane replied. "He has an apartment next door, in the green house. He's retired and is usually at home."

"Thank you," Connie said. "I may be back later."

Oliver Peebles saw her to the door. "My wife is a bit edgy over this business," he said. "I hope it will be cleared up soon."

Connie walked next door to the green house and rang the bell for Colonel Armbruster. When no one answered, she rang a second time.

A tall grey-haired man came around from the rear yard carrying some garden tools. "You come about the apartment for rent? It's a real bargain. My tenant just moved to L.A. to be a TV star."

"No, I'm from the police," Connie explained, showing her ID. "I'm looking for Colonel Armbruster but he doesn't answer his bell."

"Saw him at the window not ten minutes ago. I'm Charles Day, the landlord. Come on, I'll take you up to his room."

It was at the top of the stairs on the second floor. Day knocked loudly on the oak door but no one answered, "I know he didn't go out." He produced a ring of keys from his pocket. "We'll just take a look."

The first thing Connie saw through the opening door was a vase of flowers broken on the floor in a puddle of water. Beyond it, the early-afternoon sun revealed the body of a man. The landlord gasped as she hurried to him. "Is this Colonel Armbruster?"

"Yes! Is he—?"

"It looks like he was hit with that brass bookend. Yes, he's dead."

By the time Leopold arrived, the medical examiner and the police technicians had finished their work. "We're ready to remove the body," Connie told him. "I was just waiting until you had a look at it."

"I was over the other side of town when Fletcher reached me. What's it look like?"

"Blow to the head. He died almost instantly."

"How long ago?"

"Maybe ninety minutes. I found the body nearly an hour ago."

"Any witnesses?"

"The landlord, a man named Charles Day, knew he was up here, Armbruster was retired. Day was working in the yard. He didn't see anyone go in, but there's also a back door and a front door."

"How did you happen to find the body?"

"Colonel Armbruster was one of the people at Madame Vane's séances." She went on to tell him the rest of it as Leopold studied the body from various angles and then ordered it removed.

"Let's go next door and talk to Madame Vane," he said.

She was waiting at the front door as if she'd been expecting them. Leopold recognized her at once from Connie's description. "Good afternoon, Madame Vane. I'm Captain Leopold from the Violent Crimes Squad. I don't know if you've heard about your neighbor—"

"Mr. Day told me when I saw the police cars and phoned him. It's a terrible thing. This was once such a safe neighborhood."

"Sergeant Trent tells me Colonel Armbruster took part in your séances."

"That's right. Whenever I needed someone, Colonel Armbruster could always be depended upon."

She had stepped away from the door, allowing them to enter, and Leopold let Connie lead the way. When they were seated in the parlor Connie had described to him, Leopold asked, "What determined whether you needed someone, Madame Vane?"

"Well, we always need at least four for a séance. Five or six is acceptable, but there must be four."

"Why is that? Is it a mystic number of some sort?"

She seemed embarrassed by the question. "Actually, it's the number I need to link hands around the table."

Leopold rose and walked over to a round table at one end of the room, covered with a fringed green cloth. "This table?"

"Yes."

"Do you mind if I examine it?" Before she could respond, he removed the cloth and ran his hand over the wood. "An old table."

"It belonged to my mother," Madame Vane told him.

He dropped to one knee and peered under it. "They made them sturdy in those days."

Madame Vane stood up. "Is there anything else, Captain?"

"Yes, I'd like to speak with your husband. You see, the murder of John Armbruster adds a touch of reality to this entire investigation. Armbruster is certainly dead, and if he's dead perhaps Hugh Paxton is, too."

"Well, of course he's dead! I couldn't have communicated with him in the afterlife if he was still among us!"

"Is your husband available?" Leopold asked.

This time, instead of going to fetch him, Madame Vane simply called his name from the doorway. "Oliver! Come here!"

He appeared almost at once. "Can I help?" he asked quietly, squinting at Leopold and Connie.

"You took part in the séance with Colonel Armbruster the night Grey Elk shot Paxton?"

"Yes, I was present when it happened—whatever it was. I'm not prepared to describe it as a shooting. As I told the sergeant earlier, it was all very garbled. Mrs. Roberts believed she heard a gunshot, but then we all hear what we want to hear, don't we?"

"You're saying she wanted her grandfather's spirit killed? I understood she loved the man."

"That was in her childhood. Maybe now he was telling her things she didn't want to hear, things only she could understand."

"Show me where Armbruster was seated at the séances."

"Right here, between Madame Vane and Mrs. Roberts. I was across the table from him."

"So you were seated between the two women as well."

"That's the ordinary seating arrangement when there are two men and two women," Madame Vane pointed out.

"Did Colonel Armbruster have any enemies?"

"Not that we know of," Oliver answered. "He was retired from the Air Force and lived here on his pension. Everyone liked him."

"Somebody didn't," Leopold observed. "If either of you remember anything else of importance, please call the office."

Back at headquarters, Connie brought in a couple of coffees and seated herself across the desk from Leopold. He glanced up at her from the duty roster. "Is Fletcher still on that gang stabbing at the high school?"

"Right. He's trying to get a confession out of the suspect but it's a tough one."

"How about you? Can you stay on this with me?"

"Sure."

"Any ideas?"

Connie sipped her coffee. "About which case—Paxton or Armbruster?"

"Paxton doesn't really concern us, does it?"

"Only if it was the beginning of an attempted fraud that ended with Colonel Armbruster's murder."

Leopold grinned. "You've got a theory, Connie, let's hear it."

"All right, how's this?" She hunched forward, arms on his desk. "Thelma Roberts calls on Madame Vane and tells her about Grandfather Paxton and the rest of the family—she wants to contact her grandfather for financial advice. It's a perfect opportunity for Madame Vane, who got in trouble once before with an attempted fraud. She and Oliver arrange a séance to contact Granddad in the spirit world. After a few sessions, something happens."

"Exactly! But what? Logically, Paxton's voice should have told Mrs. Roberts to invest her money in some project linked to Madame Vane or her husband. Instead, there's a shot and Grey Elk seems to have killed Paxton."

"Think about that, Captain. Why a shot? Wouldn't an Indian more likely use a dagger or an arrow—some sort of silent weapon?"

"Connie, are you trying to find logic in this? Grey Elk's probably no more an Indian than I am. In fact, his voice and Paxton's voice could be coming from the same person."

"Yes, there's the voice. Thelma Roberts swears it was the voice of her grandfather."

"A voice she hasn't heard since she was six years old."

"Still, she described it as booming. How would they even know that much?"

"She probably told them the same thing."

Connie shook her head. "No. The voice had to be almost right or it would have spoiled everything. It had to awaken memories of her childhood in Thelma Roberts."

"Are you telling me you think Paxton is still alive somewhere, over a hundred years old?"

"No—but there may be another possibility."

Connie walked over to the public library's main building a few blocks away. The Local History Division was on the second floor and an attractive young woman looked up from behind a microfilm reader as Connie entered. "Pardon me. Is the City Historian in?"

"I'm afraid you've missed him. We'll be closing for the day soon. Perhaps I can help you."

"I'm interested in the city's centennial celebration back in nineteen thirty."

"Oh, yes. Of course we had a sesquicentennial in nineteen eighty—"

"No, it's the earlier one I'm interested in. There was a phonograph record, I believe. Something about the voices of our leaders."

"*Our City's Centennial—Its Leaders Speak.*"

"That's the one!"

"I believe we have a copy in the file. Just a moment, please."

The young woman returned with the record, its sleeve showing the same faded illustration Connie had seen in Madame Vane's parlor. This was a long shot, she knew, but Mrs. Roberts had mentioned that her grandfather was an alderman.

"May I listen to this?" she asked.

"There's a record player in the audio-visual department down the hall, but we're not supposed to lend these items."

Connie showed her ID. "This may figure in a murder investigation."

"Oh! In that case—"

Connie found the record player, set the turntable at the old 78 rpm speed, and listened. The recording was scratchy, but she made out the voice of the then city's mayor, followed by other officials. There was some band music and then more speeches. Halfway through the first side, Hugh Paxton was introduced. She listened as he read a few sentences about the city's history in his booming voice and that was it. She listened to both sides, but he did not return. But it was enough. His voice was on the record and the record was in Madame Vane's parlor.

She returned the record to the Local History Division and went back to headquarters. Leopold listened to her report with growing interest. "That's fine work, Connie," he said. "All we needed is something to link Madame Vane with that voice. I think we can show now that the messages from the beyond were faked by someone imitating Hugh Paxton."

"One of those two men? Oliver Peebles or Colonel Armbruster?"

"Or a third person as yet undiscovered." Leopold hesitated, playing with his pencil, tapping the eraser against the desktop. "Only one thing bothers me. Why would Madame Vane leave that centennial record so openly in the bookcase?"

"It meant nothing to *me*. It's a wonder I even noticed it."

"She was gone from the room long enough for you to wander around and find it."

"She was looking for her husband. Maybe he was next door killing Colonel Armbruster."

"And maybe they were both waiting outside the door until they were sure you'd found the record."

Connie felt herself growing flushed. "That's not likely, Captain. They had no way of knowing I'd be coming there today."

"Thelma Roberts was in that room just last night, remember. Would they leave the record out where she might see it? She must have heard it as a child. Perhaps she still possesses a copy. That might be why she was so certain of hearing her grandfather's voice."

"Thelma Roberts was in a dimly lit room, totally dark during the séances themselves. And I told you it was on the bottom shelf, mixed in with several other old records."

Leopold's face relaxed into a smile. "I was only playing the devil's advocate for a moment, Connie. I think you did a fine job. Confronted with this evidence, there's a good chance Madame Vane and her husband will talk—about the attempted swindle, if not about the murders."

"Murders? You think there *were* two?"

Captain Leopold nodded. "It's a possibility."

When Leopold returned to Madame Vane's home the following morning, Connie was with him. Oliver Peebles admitted them, saying, "Madame rarely sees visitors this early."

"I think she'll see us. Mrs. Roberts will be joining us here shortly. We want your wife to conduct another séance."

"I don't think—"

"What is it, Oliver?" Madame Vane appeared at the top of the stairs. She wore a long red robe and no makeup.

"Sorry to bother you this early," Leopold said with an easy smile. "We've arranged to meet Mrs. Roberts here. We'd like to duplicate the events of that séance two weeks ago—the last time she heard her grandfather's voice."

"I'm afraid that will be impossible. I hold séances only at night."

She'd come down the stairs to join them, standing at her husband's side. Somehow she no longer seemed to dominate him—they were simply two middle-aged people trying to make an easy dollar.

"I think you can manage," Leopold told her. "Do you mind if we have a look in the parlor?"

"At what? You saw yesterday there was nothing under the table."

But Leopold was already in the parlor, at the bookcase Connie had described, and picking up the pile of phonograph records. The centennial recording was still among them. "Do you want to explain this, Madame Vane? There's a recording of Hugh Paxton's voice here."

"Of course there is. Mrs. Roberts gave me that—so I could hear him speaking before I held the first séance. How else do you think I'd come upon a copy?"

"She gave it to you?" Leopold was dumbfounded. Thelma Paxton had never mentioned such a thing. But maybe they hadn't asked her the right questions.

"That'll be Mrs. Roberts now," Connie said as the doorbell rang.

Oliver went to admit her and Thelma Roberts entered the parlor somewhat breathlessly. "I came as soon as I could," she told Leopold.

"I've suggested to Madame Vane that we hold a final séance," he said. "I think it will go a long way toward clearing the air if she can contact Grey Elk one more time. Meanwhile, though, I want to ask you about this record. Did you ever see it before?"

Thelma Roberts nodded. "I brought it with me the first time, so Madame Vane could hear his voice."

"Are you satisfied now?" Oliver asked Leopold.

"I will be as soon as we hold our séance. Mrs. Roberts will take part as she did before."

"The aura isn't right for it," Madame Vane protested weakly. "Besides, we need another man to take Colonel Armbruster's place."

"I'll sit in," Leopold told her.

"I—"

"Let's get started," he said.

She sighed and turned to her husband. "Oliver, would you make the necessary preparations?"

"Certainly." He left the room and Leopold heard him ascending the stairway.

"What preparations are those?" Leopold asked Madame Vane.

"I wear a special robe daring the sessions, and these draperies must be closed to insure utter darkness."

Oliver returned with the robe and helped his wife into it. Leopold had half expected it to be covered with stars and crescent moons, but it was a plain purple garment. If there were any hidden pockets, he couldn't detect them. The middle-aged man went about the routine of closing the drapes with great care, while his wife instructed them on the seating arrangements. "Everybody will be exactly as they were, except that Captain Leopold takes the place of the Colonel. Now please tell me exactly what you want, Captain."

"Try to make contact with Grey Elk. Ask him if Colonel Armbruster has crossed over yet. Then ask him about Paxton."

Oliver Peebles adjusted the last of the drapes. "What about this woman?" he asked, reaching for the light switch. "She can't be in the room if she's not part of the circle."

"I'll wait outside," Connie volunteered. She went out, closing the door behind her.

Oliver took his position between Madame Vane and Mrs. Roberts, across the table from Leopold. They all linked hands as Oliver turned out the lamp and plunged them into darkness. All was silence for a moment and then Madame Vane spoke, "I'm directing a message across the ages to the outer darkness. I'm seeking to speak with the spirit guide known as Grey Elk—"

Leopold felt the moist palms of the two women against his own. He tried to adjust his eyes to the darkness, to see whether Madame Vane's other hand was still joined with that of her husband, but he could make out only dim shapes.

"Come to me, Grey Elk. Be my guide once more."

Silence.

Then her voice droned on in a sort of lament. "Grey Elk, Grey Elk, I appeal to you. We need you now. Grey Elk—"

More silence.

"Grey Elk—"

"Who calls?"

The voice was soft, but it seemed to fill the room, coming from all sides at once. Leopold felt the women's hands tighten in his grasp.

"Grey Elk, it is Madame Vane. Your voice is clear. Do you hear me?"

"I hear you."

"Grey Elk, we seek our old companion Colonel Armbruster. Has he passed over yet?"

"It is too soon."

"And what of Hugh Paxton, departed these many years? May we speak to him today? His loving granddaughter is here, awaiting further word from him."

There was a clatter of some sort and Grey Elk's voice distinctly said, *"What the hell!"*

Suddenly a new voice echoed through the room. *"Police! You're under arrest for the murders of Colonel John Armbruster and the man known as Hugh Paxton!"*

It was Connie's voice. Leopold smiled and broke the circle of hands. "Turn on the lamp," he ordered Oliver Peebles. "It's over."

Madame Vane blinked in the sudden glare of light. "What happened? It's dangerous to break a trance this suddenly."

"Who was that voice?" Thelma asked.

"It's Sergeant Trent, upstairs," Leopold explained. "If Grey Elk committed a murder in the afterlife, that's where she went to arrest him."

"Grey Elk is upstairs? I don't understand this."

Connie came in then with her prisoner, handcuffed and submissive. It was Charles Day from the house next door.

"Were you surprised it was Day?" Leopold asked Connie back at headquarters when Charles Day had been booked and fingerprinted.

"Not really. When I went to interview Armbruster, Day told me he'd seen him at his window ten minutes earlier. But the medical examiner said he'd been dead a good half hour before I found the body. Day was trying to alibi himself, to set the time of death for after he was already downstairs and outside in the garden; if we dig in that garden, I think we'll find another body — the man Day killed two weeks ago at Madame Vane's house."

"Any idea who that would be?"

"I could take a guess. Charles Day told me he had an empty apartment because a tenant moved to Los Angeles to be a TV star. That meant the man was an actor, and maybe it was an actor who imitated Paxton's voice over their other-worldly intercom system. Maybe the story of the Los Angeles move was just Day's cover story for the actor's sudden disappearance."

It was still speculative grounds for an arrest, and Leopold couldn't relax until late that afternoon when Madame Vane decided to talk. Encouraged by a promise that she wouldn't be prosecuted as an accessory if she agreed to testify, she started dictating a statement to a police stenographer.

"I still believe the first killing was an accident," she told them, "but if Mr. Day killed the Colonel there was no excuse for it. The Colonel was a regular at our séances, and when we needed a voice for the Indian guide I asked the Colonel to ask his landlord. I paid him a hundred dollars for fifteen to twenty minutes' work and Mr.

Day was happy to get it. After Mrs. Roberts brought in that record-ing of her grandfather, I had the idea of trying to imitate his voice, too. Day told me he had an unemployed actor as a tenant who might be happy to earn some money. I paid them each a hundred dollars a session."

"How much was Mrs. Roberts paying you?" Leopold asked.

"Five hundred for each session where there were results."

"What happened at the last one?"

"This actor—his name was Freddie Mason—had a few too many drinks and decided to liven up the session. Charles Day swears he took out a gun and was going to fire it into the air, he struggled with him, and the gun went off. Whatever happened, Mr. Mason was dead in our upstairs room and Mrs. Roberts thought it was her grandfather she had heard being killed. Oliver helped Mr. Day carry out the body, but I didn't dare have another session. When Mrs. Roberts came back for more, I simply failed to produce results. We couldn't substitute another actor's voice at that point. This morning you were so insistent we decided to risk it, with Grey Elk telling some story that would satisfy her. Oliver phoned him to come over when he went upstairs for my robe."

"The voices had to come from somewhere," Connie said. "Upstairs seemed a likely place, so I checked there first."

"What about Colonel Armbruster?" Leopold asked.

"After Mrs. Roberts was there the last time, he said he wouldn't be a party to the deception any longer. He knew Mr. Mason was dead, of course, and he threatened to go to the police. I suppose that's when Mr. Day killed him."

Later Lieutenant Fletcher looked in on Connie and Leopold. "What have you two been up to today?"

"I collared a killer," Connie announced with some pride. "And I had to go to heaven to do it."

THE KILLER EVERYONE KNEW

It should have been one of the least mysterious cases of Captain Leopold's career. Nearly everyone in the Harborview Café that night four years ago had known Ralph Simmons, and they'd all identified him as the young man who'd taken Laurie Mae Nelson out to her car in the parking lot and strangled her. He was arrested the following afternoon, hiding beneath the porch at his sister's home. A grand jury had indicted him, and he was tried and convicted within six months, still protesting his innocence. That should have been the end of it, but it wasn't. A criminal psychologist, Dr. Arthur Frees, came to know Ralph Simmons following his sentence of twenty years to life in State Prison. He came to Leopold one bright day in early June with his opinion that Ralph Simmons was innocent.

It was a relatively busy day for the Violent Crimes Squad, following the first really warm night of the year, and Leopold was immediately sorry that he'd agreed several days earlier to the meeting with Frees.

The psychologist was a short, bearded man with a ready smile and a twinkle to his eyes. "It's a pleasure to meet you, Captain," he said, giving Leopold a warm handshake. "I've followed your career in the press for some time."

"I didn't think anyone did that except my wife," Leopold smiled. "What can I do for you today, Dr. Frees? You said it was about a convicted killer named Ralph Simmons."

"That's correct. I've been working with inmates at the State Prison for the past year, especially with convicted murderers. With their permission, I've been regressing them through hypnosis to the actual moment of their crimes, recording their words as they describe the murders. I've gotten some fascinating, really breakthrough material."

"It's too bad hypnosis and polygraphs aren't admitted in a court of law," Leopold commented drily.

"It's true that they're not, but polygraph results still carry a great deal of weight, in certain circumstances. My hope is that someday authentic sessions of hypnosis will be even more useful."

Leopold was anxious to get to the point. "You regressed Ralph Simmons while he was under hypnosis?"

"I did. In his mind he returned to the night four years ago when Laurie Mae Nelson was strangled."

"And?"

"Captain, the man is innocent. He was nowhere near the scene of the crime that night. The story he told is true."

Leopold shook his head. "With all due respect to your professional skill, Doctor, Ralph Simmons was positively identified by four witnesses in a court of law. He was in a bar where he was well known, he picked up a girl and took her out to her car, as he'd been known to do with young women before. This one resisted a bit too strongly and he strangled her. The case was really quite routine."

"Except that you got the wrong man. A jury convicted the wrong man. A judge sentenced the wrong man."

Leopold had pulled the file on the Simmons case in anticipation of Frees' visit. He opened it now to refresh his memory. "Four witnesses testified at the trial. All were positive in their identification."

"But none of them actually carried on a conversation with Simmons. They said hello when this man came in and that was all. It could have been someone who looked a great deal like him."

"I know. That was the defense argument. I'll admit such mistakes are made occasionally. The criminal justice system isn't perfect. But no one has ever produced this so-called double. If such a man exists, what happened to him?"

"I understand there was a water festival taking place at the time, with tall ships and various special events. A great many tourists and other strangers were in the area."

Leopold closed the file. He studied the bearded man across the desk, looking for the familiar signs of a do-gooder more interested in promoting some favorite cause than in actually freeing an innocent man. Certainly an article in a prestigious medical journal about a convicted murderer freed through the use of regression by hypnotism would give a boost to Frees' career. But there was something more here. The psychologist seemed sincere and open in his belief in the man's innocence.

"Exactly what did Simmons say under hypnosis?" Leopold asked him.

"I brought the tape and a transcript with me."

"I don't have time to listen now, but if you'd be willing to leave them—"

"Certainly," Frees said. "I have copies. Here's my office number at the University. I spend a good deal of time at the prison, but this is the best way to reach me. My secretary will take messages."

Leopold saw him to the door, not convinced he'd be giving the material on his desk any more than cursory attention.

He played the tape at home a couple of nights later. His wife, Molly, now in corporate law after an earlier career as a public defender, listened with interest as a voice identified as that of Ralph Simmons narrated in trancelike tones the routine events of the summer night four years ago. He hadn't been anywhere near the Harborview Cafe that night, he said, but in the morning he heard the police were searching for him. He went to his sister Ruth's house and hid under her front porch.

When the tape ended, Leopold asked, "What do you think, Molly? Is he on the level?"

"I wouldn't believe him for a minute on the basis of that tape alone. There's a reason why testimony under hypnosis isn't admitted in a court of law. It's too easy to fake. We have no way of knowing if Simmons was really hypnotized or not."

She was right, of course. No matter how dedicated and convincing Dr. Frees was, his tape and transcript carried no weight whatsoever. No judge would consider it grounds for a new trial, and no district attorney would give a moment's thought to reopening the case.

Still, the next day when Leopold reached Dr. Frees on the telephone, he said, "It's interesting, though certainly inconclusive. I'll take another look at the evidence."

"May I tell Ralph that?" Frees asked, making no effort to disguise his pleasure.

"I wouldn't get his hopes up. I only said I'd review the evidence. If it convinced a jury, it's probably still strong enough to convince me."

"If you're willing to pursue it, Captain, might I offer a suggestion? You asked what happened to the real killer if he was a double for Simmons. Remember the water festival with the tall ships? I was just reading in the paper that there's another festival down at the harbor next week and some of those same ships are returning. What if the real killer was a crewman on one of those ships?"

"That's pretty much of a long shot, Doctor. I'll keep it in mind, though."

"Thank you, Captain."

Leopold knew about the water festival on Long Island Sound. It always attracted crowds and there was usually a great deal of drinking. Laurie Mae Nelson hadn't been the only victim to die during one of the festivals. Just last year a young kid home from college had been knifed to death in a fight with another youth. Leopold had assigned Lieutenant Fletcher to ride herd on the crowds this year, working with the uniformed forces to move in at the first sign of trouble. It might not be a bad idea if he spent some time down there, too.

The harbor area was already crowded on Tuesday evening, the first night of the festival, though it was nothing compared to what Leopold knew the weekend would bring. He parked his car about a block from the Harborview Cafe and strolled casually among the groups of young people. Some carried beers, drinking as they walked, but they were generally well behaved. Off in the distance, at pier-side, he could see the masts of three tall sailing ships outlined against the evening sky. He decided to walk down there before checking out the cafe.

All the ships were open for public tours, with a box or can near the gangplank to accept donations. Leopold quickly established that only one of them had actually visited the harbor four years ago. The crew member at the gangplank wore a pirate's costume, with a bandanna covering his hair and a black patch over his right eye. "Step right aboard," he urged Leopold. "Only thirty more minutes tonight to tour the good ship *Bountiful*. It's free and it's fascinating."

Leopold went aboard and wandered around, inspecting the deck area and the cramped crew quarters below. There were perhaps a half dozen crew members, all young and muscular. They seemed anxious to end the tours and mingle with the festival crowd on shore. One older man wearing a peaked cap had an attitude of being in charge. "Are you the captain of the *Bountiful?*" Leopold asked him.

"That's me, Cap'n Bright. What can I do for you?"

"I seem to remember the *Bountiful* was in port four years ago."

"That's right. We've been sailing all up and down the east coast since then. We wintered in Puerto Rico this year."

"Got the same crew along this time?"

"Hell, no. These young guys like to move around. They're with me a year or two at most, then they get a regular job or meet a girl or something. Barry over there, the pirate at the gangplank, has been with me five years. He'd have been along last time, but no one else."

Leopold carried a photograph of the convicted man, but because of the bandanna and eye patch, it was impossible to tell if Barry bore any resemblance to him. Leopold chatted with Captain Bright for a few more minutes and then departed.

There was little more to be learned at the Harborview Cafe. It had passed to new owners in the intervening years and the place had been completely remodeled. There was an attractive young woman behind the bar, mixing drinks while she carried on a running conversation with a couple of college kids. Leopold took a stool and waited until she'd finished. "Does Max Rhineman still work here?" he asked her.

She shook her head. "Max died of a heart attack last year, before I came to work here. I never knew him."

"Sorry to hear that."

"What'll you have?" she asked, wiping off the polished wood in front of him. Her long black hair glistened.

"Draft beer. What's your name?"

"Sally. I'll bet you're a cop."

"Does Ruth Simmons still live around here?" he asked with a grin.

"Say, you know all the old names, don't you? She's the one whose brother got sent away for killing the girl out in back of here." She drew a tall draft beer, wiped off the excess foam, and set it in front of Leopold. "Yeah, Ruth's still at the same place. She comes in after work sometimes. Her husband dumped her years ago and she's still pretty lonely, I think."

"I can imagine," Leopold murmured. He hung around a while longer, sipping his beer, then left without finishing it.

It was Thursday afternoon before Leopold had an opportunity to visit the harbor area again. The evenings there had been remarkably calm thus far. That morning, he had told Fletcher about Arthur Frees and his work at the State Prison. Fletcher was not impressed.

"You're actually spending time on this, Captain? He's got nothing that's admissible in court. Ralph Simmons was guilty as sin. Four or five witnesses swore to it."

"Four. I've been refreshing my memory on the case. The bartender, a married couple, and a young woman all swore it was Simmons who took the girl outside."

"Sure, everyone knew him. Who else could it have been? He had no real alibi, just claimed he was wandering around at the carnival."

"That's what he said under hypnosis, too."

"Captain—"

"I know, I know. I just told Dr. Frees I'd look into it and that's all I'm doing. I'll drive down there this afternoon and talk to Simmons' sister."

As he'd been told, Ruth Simmons still lived in the same house, down a side street that led to a marina about a half mile up the river from the main harbor area. There were the usual bait shops and boating-supply places at the end of the street, and the Simmons house reflected the gradual deterioration of the entire neighborhood. It was a two-story frame dwelling with faded yellow paint that was beginning to peel.

Ruth Simmons was sitting on the front porch drinking a beer when Leopold got out of his car. She eyed him curiously, remembering him no better than he remembered her from four years earlier. "I'm Captain Leopold," he told her, climbing the steps to the porch. "I believe we met during the police investigation of the Nelson case."

She sat up straight in her chair, as if preparing to fend off an attack. "You're the one who pulled Ralph out from under the porch?"

"No, that was one of the arresting officers. Mind if I sit down?"

"Go ahead." She was around thirty, dressed in blue shorts and one of the Water Festival T-shirts being sold all over the area. Her yellow hair was faded like the paint, in need of touching up at the very least. She wore it clipped very short.

"Have you been to see your brother lately?"

"I was up to the prison last month. I try to get there every month, but it's a fair drive from here. The round trip plus the visit takes half the day."

He told her about the psychologist's experiments. "It doesn't mean a thing, of course. It won't win a new trial. But judges have been known to give some weight to lie-detector tests, if only off the record, provided there's other new evidence as well."

"Why this renewed interest in my brother's case?"

"Dr. Frees makes a very good impression. He strikes me as a man who knows what he's talking about. That doesn't mean he can't be fooled, however. Your brother might be fooling him."

"It's funny Ralph didn't mention any of this when I visited him."

"He may have had his reasons."

She drank more beer. "Want one?" she asked him, holding up the bottle.

"Thanks, but I'm on duty. What can you tell me about the night Laurie Mae Nelson was killed?"

"Nothing I didn't tell in court. I've been living here alone ever since my husband took off five years ago. Sometimes Ralph used to spend the night here, especially if he'd had too many beers and didn't trust himself to drive back downtown to his apartment. He'd been here a lot that week because of the festival and all."

"Did he have a girl at the time?"

"Not really. He knew a few who hung out at the bars."

"Did he ever bring any of them back here?"

"No," she snapped, then amended: "Well, maybe once or twice."

"Did he ever bring Laurie Mae Nelson here?"

"No. I never even knew the girl—she wasn't from around here."

Ruth Simmons was correct in that. The dead girl had been from a town in the next county. She'd driven over because of the festival. None of the witnesses from the cafe remembered having seen her there before. "Did Ralph come here the night of the murder?"

"I found him sleeping here on the porch the next morning. The door was locked and he didn't want to wake me. He sometimes did that when he came by late. Then we heard on the radio that the police were looking for him in connection with the killing. When he saw a police car heading down this way, he went and hid under the porch."

"Where were you the night Laurie Mae was strangled?"

"Same place I am most nights, same place I'll be tonight. I work the five-to-midnight shift at Golftown." Golftown was a miniature-golf-and-driving range across from the public beach area on the Sound.

"So you didn't see your brother at any time during the evening?"

"No, but if he says he was just walking around I believe him. Those witnesses just described somebody who looked like him, wearing jeans and a T-shirt like all the guys wear in the summer."

"They all knew Ralph," Leopold pointed out.

"And they'd all had a few beers. They didn't really talk to him. They could have been mistaken."

Leopold got to his feet. "Thanks for your time. Miss Simmons."

"I still go by my married name. Ruth Cutler."

"Pardon me—Mrs. Cutler." He paused on the top step. "Are Ellie and George Wainwright still living down here?"

She shook her head. "They were both killed last year in a crash on the expressway."

Leopold grunted. "How about Lucy Aarons?"

"Oh, sure, she's around. Works at the custard stand down by the public pier."

"Thanks."

It was almost evening and he walked down to watch the crowds on the carnival rides. Kids and young people, mostly. Screaming girls, boys pretending to be brave. The lights were beginning to come on, though darkness was still some time away.

"Captain Leopold!" a voice called out.

Leopold turned and saw coming toward him Dr. Frees wearing a plaid sport shirt and smoking a pipe, looking for all the world like a college professor on his summer vacation. "I hoped I might find you here," Frees explained. "And I wanted to check out the scene myself. —Did you know that three of the four witnesses against Ralph Simmons have died since the trial?"

"I just found that out," Leopold admitted.

"Doesn't that seem strange to you?"

"Two were killed in an auto accident. I'm checking on Max Rhineman, the bartender. He was in his late sixties and it seems to have been a heart attack. Probably the deaths are just coincidence. What would anyone gain by killing them so long after the trial?"

"What if they'd been paid to lie about Ralph?"

"All four of them?"

"Stranger things have happened, Captain."

"Well, Lucy Aarons is still alive. I'm on my way to talk with her now."

"May I come along?"

"I suppose so."

They walked past the merry-go-round and the bandstand where a rock group was setting up its amplifying equipment for the entertainment to follow the fireworks at ten o'clock. Leopold recognized Captain Bright strolling through the crowd with his pirate crewman.

"See the fellow dressed as a pirate?" Leopold asked the psychologist.

"Yes."

"Does he look anything like Ralph Simmons?"

"It's difficult to tell with the eye patch, but I'd say no."

The custard stand by the public pier was a busy place as darkness descended. The pier itself was the best viewing area for the fireworks, to be launched from an offshore barge, and a long line had formed to buy custards before the start of the action. Leopold avoided the line and leaned over the counter to speak to a young woman with an empty cone in her hand.

"Pardon me, you're Lucy Aarons, aren't you?"

"That's me." She filled the cone from a shiny chrome custard dispenser.

"Captain Leopold from the Violent Crimes Squad. I'd like a word with you. It's about your testimony in the Simmons case."

"See that line? I can't talk now. Catch me between ten and ten-thirty. All the concessions close down during the fireworks."

"All right," he agreed. It was only an hour's wait.

He and Frees walked out to the end of the crowded pier. "This is a dangerous place at night," the psychologist remarked, "even with the lights on. They should have a railing along here."

"Write a letter to the public-safety commissioner," Leopold suggested.

"'Will that get action?"

"No. Nothing will get action until someone falls off and drowns." He paused. "I have to tell you, Doctor—the odds are strongly against reopening the Simmons case."

"I'm trying to change those odds."

They started back toward the custard stand when Leopold saw the pirate from the *Bountiful* without his eye patch. "There!" he told Frees. "Do you see any resemblance now?"

"The pirate? I didn't notice his face. I'll go after him. I'll catch up with you later."

He disappeared into the crowd and Leopold continued on. He saw a patrol car parked at the edge of the crowd and walked over to find Fletcher speaking with the officer inside. "Pretty calm so far, Captain," Fletcher said. "We busted up a fight in a parking lot, but there's been nothing like the trouble in previous years. There are some undercover narcs working the crowd—that's probably putting a damper on the drug action."

Leopold was satisfied. "I have to speak to someone at ten, then I'll be heading home."

The first skyrocket shot up from the barge as he reached the custard stand. It was already closed and he caught a glimpse of Lucy Aarons walking onto the pier with another young woman. Although her long hair was pinned up off her neck, Leopold recognized her as Sally, the bartender from the Harborview Cafe. He hurried after them.

There was a multiple burst of fireworks overhead, plumes of color lighting the night sky. Leopold glanced up for an instant, and when he looked back the two young women were lost in the crowd ahead. The pier was filled with people now, moving in both directions. He hurried on, edging past the spectators as best he could. A brilliant series of multicolored mushroom shapes seemed to march across the sky, accompanied by crackling bursts of sound. The watching crowd gasped at the beauty of the display, and for a moment all movement on the long pier seemed to cease.

Then a woman screamed and there was a splash.

A wave of panic swept across the pier. Someone else screamed and two young men immediately dove into the water after the fallen spectator. While the fireworks streaked across the night sky, Leopold pushed his way back along the pier for help. Finally he saw Fletcher hurrying toward him, attracted by the screams.

"Someone's in the water," Leopold called to him. "Get an ambulance and the scuba squad!"

"They're standing by, Captain."

By the time he returned to the other end of the pier, the young men had located the victim and were attempting to lift her from the water. Once she was on the pier, they started administering artificial respiration in relays. Leopold identified himself and bent to get a better look at the girl.

It was Lucy Aarons, and it was clear to him that she was beyond revival.

It was a long night for Leopold, but he was back in his office by ten A.M. Fletcher came in with two cups of coffee and settled into his favorite chair across the desk. "You look as if you could have used a few more hours' sleep, Captain."

"Couldn't we all? What did you find out?"

"Well, you were right. The Aarons woman drowning last night means that all four of the eyewitnesses against Ralph Simmons have died since his trial. But it's got to be a coincidence. The bartender, Max Rhineman, was a heavy drinker and a smoker and he had a heart attack one night. It happens all the time. The young married couple—well, that was a sad story. Their little sports car was hit head-on by a truck that had wandered onto the wrong side of the road. The driver admitted he'd smoked a couple of marijuana cigarettes and he's in prison now for a few years."

"Lucy Aarons could have been pushed from that pier," Leopold suggested.

"Sure, but there were plenty of people around, Captain. The odds were against her drowning before they pulled her out."

"Is the autopsy in?"

"Not yet." Fletcher finished his coffee. "I've got that bartender, Sally Olcott, outside. You want to see her now?"

"Send her in."

The attractive barmaid entered and took a seat. "I can't add anything to last night's statement," she told him. "Lucy and I got separated in the crowd."

"I just have a few questions, Miss Olcott. You weren't working at the Harborview four years ago when Laurie Mae Nelson was killed?"

She shook her head. "I was living in California at the time. They didn't hire me until Max Rhineman had his heart attack."

"How did you happen to know Lucy Aarons?"

"She was a regular at the Harborview, and we struck up a friendship. We were both unmarried, about the same age—"

"Did she ever mention the Nelson killing?"

"Oh, sure. I'd gone to school with Ralph Simmons—I even visited him a few times in prison. No one else ever went except his sister. and I know he was grateful for the friendship. Naturally Lucy and I talked about the case."

"Did she have any doubts that he was the killer?"

"None. She said it was Ralph in the bar, and that he picked up Laurie Mae and they went out to the parking lot. There was no doubt about it—everyone knew it was him."

"What about last night? Did you go to the custard stand to meet her?"

Sally nodded. "I was off, and she closed up during the fireworks, so I went down to meet her. We strolled out on the pier for a better view, but there was such a crowd we got separated. Then I heard a scream and a splash."

"Wasn't she afraid to go out there? It's not a very safe place without a railing, especially at night."

"Oh, Lucy was a good swimmer. In fact, I can't understand—"

"She was a good swimmer?" He knew good swimmers drowned sometimes, but it was unusual.

"Sure. Sometimes when we were both off, we'd go swimming in the Sound together. Both of us were sort of between boy friends and we didn't like to swim alone."

"You've been very helpful," Leopold said. "We may call on you again."

She turned at the door and gave him a grin. "I knew you were a cop."

Leopold chuckled and phoned the medical examiner.

There was very little water in Lucy Aarons' lungs. She hadn't drowned. She'd died from a thin, almost unnoticed chest wound that had penetrated the heart. The medical examiner speculated that it might have been made by a long hatpin or something similar.

Arthur Frees arrived at Leopold's office just before noon. "With all the excitement last night I never got back to you. I followed that pirate back to one of the tall ships. He looks a *little* like Simmons, but no one could honestly mistake one for the other. His name is Barry Kinski, by the way. He's the captain's nephew."

But Leopold was barely listening. His mind was on Lucy Aarons and how she'd died. "You heard who fell off the pier last night?"

Frees nodded. "Lucy Aarons. What do you make of it?"

"I don't know. Vengeance for her testimony, perhaps. But if that's the case, why wait nearly four years?"

"You mean you think someone killed her?" The psychologist seemed surprised. "I thought it was an accident."

"No accident. She was murdered." Leopold came to a quick decision. "I'd like to visit Ralph Simmons at the State Prison."

"When?"

"Tomorrow. Can you help arrange it?"

"Absolutely."

Late in the day, Leopold drove down to the harbor area once more. There was always the possibility that the Aarons killing was unconnected to the Simmons case, but he'd never been a great believer in coincidences like that. He parked his car in the bathhouse lot and walked across the street to Golftown. It was just after five o'clock and Simmons' sister, Ruth, was working behind the counter, passing out buckets of balls for the driving range and well-worn putters for the miniature-golf course.

"You heard about last night?" Leopold asked.

"I heard," she said with a nod. "I can't say I'm shedding any tears. She's one of them that testified against Ralph."

"And now they're all dead."

"Yes." She filled another bucket of scuffed golf balls. "It's as if someone was taking revenge for their testimony against my brother."

"You'd be the most likely one for that," he pointed out.

"I wouldn't have waited four years to kill her. Besides, I was working here last night—I couldn't have killed her. You need to look for someone who had a reason to wait four years."

"Who could that be?"

She shrugged. "Maybe someone who's been away for four years."

Leopold started to leave, then turned to ask, "How did you know Lucy Aarons had been murdered?"

"It's in the afternoon paper," she answered blandly.

Later, before he headed home, Leopold spoke to Lieutenant Fletcher. "There are more fireworks tonight, aren't there?"

"That's right, Captain. Ten o'clock."

"I want you to stroll over to Golftown during the fireworks and see if they close down like the other concessions."

"What's up?"

"Just an idea I have."

Leopold arrived at the State Prison by late morning the following day and found Dr. Frees waiting for him by the main gate. "I have a regular session with Simmons today," he explained, "and I received permission to have you sit in on it."

"Fine. That's just what I wanted."

The meeting took place in a prison office that Frees used for his work. When Ralph Simmons was brought in by a guard, he seemed pleased at Leopold's presence. He was a handsome young man with black wavy hair and a deep voice. His handshake was firm, and Leopold was reminded that those hands might have strangled the life from Laurie Mae Nelson. Simmons remembered him better than he remembered Simmons. "Pleased to see you again, Captain. Does this mean I've been granted a new trial?"

"No," Leopold said carefully. "I just wanted to speak with you and Dr. Frees."

Frees himself seemed embarrassed. "Talk of a new trial is still premature, Ralph. I'm doing everything I can, but there are legal problems."

"You hypnotized me. You took me back to the night of the murder. You know I didn't do it."

Leopold decided to take a firm hand. "Ralph, did Dr. Frees tell you that would be enough to get you a new trial?"

"Sure!"

"I said it could be a factor in winning a new trial," the psychologist corrected him. "I never promised—"

The blood had drained from Simmons' face. "Then what are you here for?" he asked Leopold.

"Lucy Aarons was murdered Thursday night down at the harbor. You remember Lucy, don't you?"

"She testified against me at the trial."

"Do you still hold a grudge against her?"

"Not really, but she was too drunk that night to know who was there and who wasn't."

"How does your sister feel about it?"

"Ruth? She never gave a damn about me. I could rot in here for all she cares."

Dr. Frees offered to try hypnotic regression again, to convince Leopold of Ralph's innocence, but Leopold had heard enough. "I have to be heading back to the city. I still have an unsolved murder case on my hands."

"Let me walk out to the gate with you."

"If you like."

As they walked to Leopold's car, Frees said, "I know you're upset with me, and perhaps I did go too far in holding out the hope for a new trial, but it was the only way I could get him to agree to the sessions with me. At first he didn't want to be hypnotized at all."

"I'll bet he didn't. He was afraid you could really do it."

"Look here," Frees said, "if you're suggesting he wasn't really hypnotized—" He caught himself and changed his tone. "My own theory is that someone else was the killer."

"Who?"

"Well, maybe it *was* that ship crewman who dressed as a pirate—Kinski. He's back here after four years and maybe the Aarons woman showed signs of recognizing him and doubting her testimony."

Leopold shook his head. "Your man is guilty, Dr. Frees. You might as well face the fact. There was a certain authority in his voice when he told me just now that Lucy Aarons was too drunk that night to know who was at the bar. If he wasn't there himself and didn't see her all night, how could he speak with such assurance?"

"Well," the psychologist answered uncertainly, "someone might have told him."

Leopold shook his head. "It won't wash, Doctor. The man's guilty. When he realized he wasn't susceptible to hypnotism, he pretended he was, anyway. He faked that whole regression for your benefit."

"If that's true, then what about Lucy Aarons? Who killed her, and why?"

It was some seconds before Leopold answered. "In a manner of speaking, Doctor, I believe you were partly responsible for her death."

That afternoon Leopold drove to Ruth Cutler's house down by the marina. She wasn't on the porch and the house was locked. On a hunch, he decided to try the Harborview Cafe. There he found her sitting at the bar with a drink in front of her, chatting with Sally, who was on duty.

"Just who I'm looking for," Leopold said, taking the stool next to her. "I drove up to the State Prison to see your brother this morning."

"What for? Do you think he slipped out of prison long enough to kill Lucy Aarons, too?"

"No, that matter is close to being cleared up."

"Would you like a drink?" Sally asked.

"Just a Coke."

"Cleared up?" Ruth repeated. "Does that mean you know who killed Lucy Aarons?"

Leopold nodded. "More important, I know why she was killed. It wasn't because she testified at your brother's first trial. It was to keep her from testifying at his second trial."

"What second trial?"

"Dr. Frees, the criminal psychologist working with Ralph, did a highly unethical thing. In order to gain your brother's cooperation in an experiment in hypnotic regression, he led Ralph to believe there was a good chance of uncovering evidence for a new trial. That wasn't true. The courts would never admit statements made by the accused under hypnosis—they can be too easily faked. But Ralph believed a new trial was imminent, and that led to the killing of Lucy Aarons."

"I don't understand what you're getting at," Ruth said.

"There was no material evidence against your brother at the first trial, only the eyewitness testimony of four people. Coincidentally, one died of a heart attack and two died in an auto accident, so that Lucy was the only witness left alive. If a judge ordered a new trial, the entire case would rest on Lucy's testimony. If she died, too, the district attorney wouldn't even be able to retry the case. Ralph would walk out of prison a free man. So what did Ralph do? He persuaded someone to kill Lucy Aarons."

Ruth took a deep breath. "You think I killed her. But I told you I was working at Golftown when it happened."

"The concessions close during the fireworks. It occurred to me that you could have walked over to the pier and killed Lucy in that crowd without ever being noticed."

"I didn't—"

He held up his hand in a calming gesture. "I know. Fletcher checked out Golftown last night. You don't close during the fireworks."

"Then how could I have killed her?"

"You didn't." Leopold reached across the bar and took a firm hold of Sally's wrist. "Miss Olcott, I'm taking you downtown for further questioning, after which you may be charged with the murder of Lucy Aarons. You have the right to remain silent. You have the right to an attorney—"

"You look tired," Molly said when Leopold returned home late that evening. "And you must be starving."

"It's been a long day, but thank heaven I wrapped up the Aarons killing. Just fix me a sandwich. That's all I need."

"Who did it?" she asked, going into the kitchen.

"Sally Olcott, a barmaid at the Harborview Cafe. She's made a full statement in the presence of her attorney. It seems she went to school with Ralph Simmons and started visiting him in prison. She fell in love with the guy and he talked her into killing Lucy Aarons, to remove the last living witness against him. Dr. Frees had convinced him the courts would probably order a new trial and he decided that without any witnesses the case would be forfeited in his favor."

"I thought you were suspicious of the sister," Molly said, bringing him a turkey sandwich and a beer.

"Ruth Cutler, yes. She seemed likely, except that she really didn't like her brother that much. When Fletcher confirmed her alibi, I got to rethinking the entire case. The killing occurred after I started asking questions in the harbor area. Someone was convinced I was acting on the possibility of a new trial, so they had to kill Lucy quickly. But in my conversation with Ruth before the murder I made a point of the fact that the hypnosis testimony would never be admitted in court. She knew there would be no new trial.

"The only other person who'd had contact with Simmons in prison was Sally Olcott, who told me herself that she and Ruth were his only visitors. I didn't discuss the new trial with Sally, so she assumed there would be one. It turns out she'd gained Lucy's friendship, and gone swimming with her several times in the hope of staging an accident. But Lucy was too good a swimmer, so she used a hatpin Thursday night on the pier, hoping the autopsy would miss the wound.

"When I narrowed the suspects down to Simmons' two visitors in prison, that weapon was a clue for me. The safest place to carry one comfortably and unnoticed is in the hair. Ruth's hair is cut short like a man's, while Sally has long hair, which she wore pinned up that night."

"In a way Simmons was responsible for the murder."

Leopold sighed. "In a very big way. Of course Sally really was, but Dr. Frees started it all by misleading Simmons about a new trial and I compounded it by asking questions that spurred Sally into action. If Ralph Simmons was the killer everyone knew, Lucy Aarons was the victim everyone killed."

CAPTAIN LEOPOLD'S BIRTHDAY

"I know how you hate surprises," Leopold's wife Molly told him one morning in August. "Fletcher and Connie want to have a surprise party for your birthday next week."

Leopold stared down at his bowl of cereal. "Do they have to? I'm not at an age to be reminded of birthdays." He was thinking of the Police Department's mandatory retirement policy, looming closer each year and now only twelve short months away.

"Just a small gathering—Fletcher and his wife, and Connie and her new boy friend. Only the six of us. They want to do something for you."

"Talk to me about it later," he said, rising from the table.

"You haven't finished your breakfast!"

"I'm late already. There are some important cases in the works."

Molly sighed. "Not even coffee?"

"I'll have it at Headquarters. They've been brewing it better lately."

"Well, I have to be in court myself at ten. A very dull negligence case."

"Good luck," he called over his shoulder as he went out the door. She didn't ask him if he'd be home for dinner. She'd given up on that long ago. There actually were no important cases for Captain Leopold that day. There hadn't been in over a week. It seemed as if all the violent criminals in the city had taken the month of August off this year, reversing the long-standing trend. Leopold viewed it as akin to a summer drought, an abnormality that would soon pass. "These things average out," he told Connie that morning when she brought his coffee. Still, he didn't like the leisure it afforded him. At his age, and with his temperament, leisure wasn't something he looked forward to.

Sergeant Connie Trent, for her part, enjoyed a week without over-time. She'd been dating an engineer at the city's pollution-control bureau, and their relationship had reached the stage where they were having dinner together every evening she didn't have to work.

She was reviewing the few interesting cases on the morning report while Leopold drank his coffee. "Did you hear that Marty Doyle died last night?" she asked him.

"Marty! What happened?"

"Heart attack, I guess. It was quite sudden."

Marty Doyle had been a lieutenant on the Arson Squad for almost as long as Leopold had headed Violent Crimes. He'd taken an early retirement last year at fifty-five. He hadn't lived long to enjoy it, Leopold thought. "I'll have to attend the wake," he said. He had lunched with Marty once or twice since his retirement, but they weren't close socially. He remembered that Molly had taken a dislike to Doyle's wife when she had too much to drink at his retirement party. What was her name? Greta? Yes, he thought that was it. They had just one child—a daughter Leopold thought had moved out of town earlier this year.

Molly was surprised when he arrived home by five o'clock. Her own case had been settled out of court while the jury was being selected, and she'd decided to give herself a few hours off. It was a slow month in the courts, too, with many judges away on vacation.

"How did *your* day go?" she asked Leopold.

"Quieter than I expected." He tossed the afternoon newspaper on the table. "Marty Doyle died yesterday. Heart attack. I should go to the wake tonight." She nodded and said, "I'll go with you. Greta will need comforting." He was always amazed at how Molly remembered the names of people after meeting them only once. "I thought you disliked her because of her drinking."

"Well, it was her husband's retirement. She deserved to live it up."

They arrived at the funeral parlor around seven-thirty and made their way through the gathering crowd. Some of the mourners were familiar faces from Headquarters, others were family members and neighbors. Molly spotted Greta Doyle in a simple black dress near the coffin and led the way to her.

"Thank you for coming," the widow said, trying to smile. She was a handsome woman of around fifty, who'd built up too much weight around the hips with the coming of middle age. Leopold could imagine the lovely girl she'd been when she and Marty had first fallen in love, and the glowing mother she must have become when their daughter was born.

"I'm very sorry," he murmured. "I knew Marty for most of my working life. He was a fine man."

"What happened?" Molly asked.

"He was watching television and complained of a pain in his arm and chest. Then he collapsed. The ambulance came with the paramedics, but it was too late. An hour after it happened, I was on the phone to June, having to tell her he was dead."

"Your daughter?" Leopold glanced around the room. "Is she here?"

"She's sitting over there." Greta indicated a pretty girl Leopold remembered now from the retirement party. She was wearing a blue dress and he noticed she was pregnant.

The Doyles' next-door neighbors approached Greta and she introduced them as the Kingsleys. He was a tall, good-looking man who towered over his wife. Leopold and Molly said a silent prayer at the casket and moved over to where June Doyle sat alone. "You probably don't remember me," he said. "I'm Captain Leopold from Headquarters. I knew your father a long time."

She started to her feet and Leopold urged her to stay seated. "Thank you," she said. "It's getting near my time. The doctor says another two weeks."

"It's too bad you had to come home under these circumstances," Leopold said. "Where are you living now?"

She hesitated. "Philadelphia."

"I'd lost touch with your father after he retired. I didn't even know you were married."

She blushed and looked down at her hands. "I'm not."

"Oh." It was Leopold's turn to be embarrassed. "I'm sorry, that was—"

"It's all right. You're not the first."

Molly stepped in quickly. "Will you be going back to Philadelphia after the funeral, June?"

"I'll stay for the weekend and go back on Monday."

"We'll be at the service tomorrow," Molly told her, although she and Leopold hadn't yet discussed it.

Leopold spoke with Lieutenant Fletcher and his wife, Carol, who'd just come in, then said a few final words to Greta before he and Molly headed for the door.

When they were safely in the car, he said, "I really put my foot in it with June."

"The poor girl. She may not be married by choice, but it can't be an easy time for her—and losing her father so suddenly can only make it worse. That's why I thought we should go to the funeral. You don't have to work on Saturday, do you?"

"No," he admitted reluctantly. "Not this week."

Molly turned to face him. "What's been the matter with you lately? Is it just the pre-birthday blues or is there some other reason?"

"I don't know, Molly. It doesn't help to see a friend who's younger than you in his coffin."

"It started before today. You know it did."

She was right, of course. Molly knew him perfectly after only five years of marriage. Maybe it was pre-birthday blues and he should try to snap out of it.

They drove in silence for a time and then she asked quietly, "What should I tell Fletcher and Connie about the party?"

"Sure," he said. "It's okay."

Leopold and Molly attended the funeral the following morning and then stood under the August sun with the other mourners around the simple gravesite. Molly accepted an invitation from June Doyle to return to their house. There, the neighbors had set out enough food to provision a small army. Leopold had never been to the Doyle home before and he was surprised that the neat but modest house— on a street with other neat but modest houses—was equipped with ail the latest gadgets. There was a VCR on a shelf beneath the television set, a cordless telephone in the kitchen, and a small personal computer in the den. "Marty was teaching me to use it," Greta explained, leading them through to the family room where the food had been spread out on folding tables. "He'd used one at work, of course, but I just couldn't get the hang of it."

"It's good to see you again, Greta," said Leopold. "And June."

"Yes," she answered, her mouth drawn into a tight, grim line. "I'll soon be a grandmother."

As Brenda Kingsley, the next-door neighbor, helped to serve the guests, her husband, Roy, carried in a large tray of meat and cheese from the kitchen. He was a jovial, outgoing man of around fifty— Leopold thought he remembered hearing once that he was a car salesman, Leopold had just started chatting with him when Greta Doyle reappeared by his side.

"Captain, I wanted to ask you what should be done about Marty's gun collection. It's not very large and I wonder if it has any value at all."

"I'd be happy to look at it," he told her.

She led the way upstairs to their pleasantly cool bedroom and took several cloth-wrapped bundles from the closet. Arranging them on the bed, she carefully unwrapped each one. It was a collection of weapons such as many detectives and police officers acquire over the course of a career—his service revolver, a .38 Smith & Wesson he'd purchased, a German Luger that was probably a war souvenir ("His uncle gave him that," Greta confirmed), a small Beretta automatic, a Colt .45 with a worn Army holster, a belt holster he'd no doubt used on duty, and a target pistol with, more surprisingly, a silencer that fit over the end of the barrel.

"I suppose I shouldn't be telling you this," she said. "He took that from a suspected arsonist once, about ten years ago. Then the man knocked him down and escaped. He thought he'd look like a fool if his superiors knew he'd actually disarmed a suspect and then let him escape, so he just kept the weapon and said nothing."

Leopold noticed she was close to tears and realized the strain she had been under, "I don't know a cop anywhere who doesn't regret some fool thing he's done," he tried to console her. "This collection has no special value, but it would probably bring several hundred dollars from a gun dealer. If you decide to sell the others, I could turn this one in and say it was found on the street somewhere."

"Thank you," she said. "I'll keep that in mind." As she started putting the guns away, he said, "Let me know if there's anything you need, Greta."

Back downstairs, June Doyle was talking with a young man in his twenties. She introduced him to Leopold. "Captain, this is Pete Brody. I attended Community College with him."

"How are you, Pete?"

"Fine, sir."

Leopold tried to calculate how old June must be, and guessed her age at around twenty-five. When Brenda Kingsley called over and asked Brody for help in carrying out some empty bottles, he was left alone with June. "How long have you been in Philadelphia?" he asked her.

"Since March. After I found out I was pregnant, I decided it might be best if Mom and Dad didn't know. I had a college friend with an apartment in Philadelphia and I moved in with her. I was waiting on tables until last month."

"You mean your parents didn't know you were pregnant?"

She shook her head. "How's that for bad timing? Two weeks before I'm due, Dad drops dead and I have to come back for the funeral. Now everyone in town knows."

"Did you think about getting married?"

She glanced away. "It wouldn't have worked out."

"Does the child's father know you're pregnant?"

"I've never told him."

Pete Brody came back to continue his conversation with June and Leopold drifted away. The crowd was thinning as friends and neighbors said their good-byes. Leopold glanced at his watch and saw that it was just before noon. He asked Greta if he could use her phone to check in with Fletcher, who was pulling Saturday duty at Headquarters. It was fairly quiet in the living room and he called from there. "How are things, Fletcher?"

"Nothing exciting, Captain. Where are you?"

"Molly and I are back at the Doyle house, but we'll be leaving soon."

"It sounds pretty quiet there."

"People are beginning to leave."

"The only thing we've had all morning is a call on the 911 emergency number reporting a knifing on the west side. I'm waiting for a report—it sounded like family trouble."

"All right. If you need me, I should be at home the rest of the afternoon."

Fletcher didn't need him, and the weekend proved to be a quiet one. Molly cooked some of his favorite dishes for Sunday dinner, in preparation for his birthday, and Leopold began to feel better. It was only a date on the calendar, after all.

It was after dark, shortly before nine o'clock on Sunday night, when the telephone rang. Leopold answered it and heard a vaguely familiar voice. "Captain Leopold?"

"Yes?"

"This is June Doyle. I wanted to talk to you. I'm calling from my mother's house. Wait—" There was a pause, and when she came back on she whispered, "Look, could you call me back here in a couple of minutes? I think I hear someone on the porch—"

"All right," he agreed. "I'll call you right back."

After she hung up, he realized he didn't know the Doyles' phone number. He had to find it in the book and dial it. She answered at once. "It's all right, Captain. I didn't see anyone out there. I was worried it might be a prowler. Mom is out and I'm here alone."

"Where'd your mother go?"

"There's a meeting to plan a neighborhood picnic for Labor Day and Mrs. Kingsley convinced her it would do her good to get out." She coughed and covered the phone for an instant. "I hope I'm not getting a cold with the baby on the way."

"What was it you wanted to talk to me about, June?"

"Well, has my mother said anything to you about my situation— my pregnancy?"

"Not a word. Why would she?"

"I just thought—" a clock faintly chimed the hour at her end "— that she might have said something. She's barely spoken to me since I arrived home."

"I was never that close to your parents, June. I just worked with your father. But I know he loved you."

"That's one of the reasons I had to go away. I thought it would kill him if he knew."

"I can assure you your mother hasn't mentioned it outside of say-ing she'd soon be a grandmother."

"I see. I'm sorry I've taken up your time like this, Captain, but I want to make peace with Mom before I leave tomorrow afternoon and I needed some reassurance."

"Happy to do what I can. Good night, June."

"Good night— Oh! There's a police car out on the street with a flashing red light. Maybe there was a prowler, after all!"

"I'll check with Headquarters. If there's any trouble, I'll tell them to look in on you."

"Thank you. Captain Leopold."

After he'd hung up, Molly asked from the living room, "Who was that?"

"June Doyle. A case of nerves, I think. She says there's a police car on her street. I'd better call downtown."

Neither Connie nor Fletcher was on duty, but he spoke with the dispatcher. She reported a 911 call from a telephone at 145 Mapledale Drive. "I'm at home," Leopold told her. "Ring me if it's anything serious."

He hung up and went to join Molly. "It was a 911 call from the house next door. I don't know what that means. June thought she heard a prowler earlier."

The call came five minutes later from the duty sergeant. "Captain? You wanted to be notified about the 911 call from 145 Mapledale?"

"That's right. What was it?"

"We've got a middle-aged white male dead of a gunshot wound at his home. No formal identification yet, but it appears to be a man named Roy Kingsley."

"I'm on my way," Leopold said.

By the time he arrived, there were four squad cars and the technical-unit van parked in the street. Connie Trent had been on call and she was already there, dressed in a blouse and slacks and looking as if she'd spent the day at the beach. "What is it, Connie?" he asked.

"A man named Roy Kingsley. We just got positive identification from his wife. He was shot once in the head. He was lying just inside the front doorway. They had a 911 call, and when the officer responded he found the front door ajar."

Leopold had been introduced only briefly to Kingsley and had never really spoken with him, but it was still a shock to see him dead. "Marty Doyle lived right next door," he told Connie. "I met Kingsley at the funeral home on Friday and then again yesterday."

The body was inside the door as Connie had said. The telephone receiver was on the floor by one hand, at the end of an extra-long cord that led to a wall phone mounted around the corner in the living room just beyond the entrance hall. "He'd been dead only minutes when the officer arrived," Connie said. "The 911 call was clocked in at 9:00:25."

Leopold bent to examine the body. "Shot once in the forehead. There are some powder burns on the face, so the gun was fairly close." He straightened up. "There was an earlier report of a prowler."

She nodded. "I've got a car out checking the neighborhood."

"Send another. You don't need four parked out in the street like this. Where's Mrs. Kingsley?"

"In the family room, straight back to the rear of the house. Come on."

The place was larger and just enough fancier than the Doyles' home, Leopold decided, to prove that selling cars was more profitable than being a cop. In the wood-paneled family room Brenda Kingsley was quietly sobbing. Greta and June Doyle were trying to comfort her.

"I went outside when I saw the police cars," June told Leopold.

"June thinks it was a prowler," Greta said.

"We're searching the neighborhood," he assured them. "Mrs. Kingsley, I'm terribly sorry about this."

Her expression was one of rage as much as sorrow. "Where can we be safe if not in our own homes? What's this city coming to!"

There was no way to answer her, so he said instead, "I understand that you women were at a neighborhood meeting tonight."

"At the last minute I decided I couldn't go," Greta said. "Brenda and I got to the house and I just didn't want to face so many people. I left her there and walked around for a while, and then I went back home. I got there just after the second police car arrived and June came running out of the house to see what the trouble was."

Leopold motioned to Connie. "I'd like to speak with Mrs. Kingsley alone for a few moments—could you take statements from Mrs. Doyle and her daughter?"

Connie took the Doyle women to the kitchen, and when they were alone Brenda Kingsley said, "Just yesterday I was wondering how

Greta was going to be able to live without Marty. Now Roy is gone, too."

"Did he have any enemies, Mrs. Kingsley? Do you know of anyone who might have wanted to kill him? Anyone he worked with, say?"

She shook her head. "Everybody liked Roy."

"Might there have been some trouble over a car he sold? A dissatisfied customer, perhaps?" She shuddered. "People don't kill over things like that."

"You'd be surprised."

"Well, there was nothing I knew about." Her eyes filled and she reached for another tissue. "My God, I never dreamed anything like this could happen to me."

"Tell me this, Mrs. Kingsley—were your husband and Marty Doyle involved in anything together? Any sort of business deal, possibly with a third person?"

"No, nothing like that. They were neighbors, that's all. The four of us were friendly, but there were never any business dealings between the men."

Connie came back into the room. "I'm sorry to interrupt, Captain. We've picked up a young man a couple of blocks away. He was spotted cutting through a back yard."

Leopold got to his feet. "We'll talk again, Mrs. Kingsley. I *am* terribly sorry about what's happened."

"Thank you," she managed.

He followed Connie out to the street. "He's in the car. He says he knows these people, so I didn't want to bring him into the house."

"Knows them?" Leopold followed her to the squad car and bent to look into the back seat. The young man was June Doyle's college friend, Pete Brody.

Leopold opened the back door and climbed in beside him. "Hello there, Pete. We met yesterday."

"Yeah. Hello, Captain."

"I didn't realize you lived around here."

"I don't, really. I was just out for a drive and then I decided to take a stroll, it was such a nice night."

"Any weapon on him?" Leopold asked the patrolman in the driver's seat.

"Nothing, Captain."

"What *is* this? What's going on here?" Brody demanded.

"A man was killed—Roy Kingsley, June's neighbor."

"Killed! You mean, murdered?"

"That's it."

"Was it a robbery?"

"We don't know. Why do you ask? June thought she heard a prowler earlier, shortly before the killing."

"Hey, you can't think I was involved! I was nowhere near this house."

"The officer picked you up just a few blocks away. That's not very far."

Brody was silent for a time, staring out at the Kingsley house. Finally, he said, "June suggested yesterday that I might come by and see her before she went back. It sounded like a good idea. I've always liked June."

"Where's your car?"

"I parked it over on Adams Street, three blocks away."

"You came to visit her and parked three blocks away?"

"Yes."

"Did you see her?"

"When I got here, there were all these police cars so I changed my mind."

Leopold counted silently to thirty, then asked, "Why was it, Pete, that you came to visit her and parked your car three blocks away?"

The young man blurted it out. "I didn't want folks to see my car. They might think I was the baby's father."

"Are you?"

"No! June and I are just friends. I only dated her a few times."

Leopold opened the door and slid out of the back seat. Connie was waiting on the sidewalk. "Take down his statement, Connie, and then drive him over to his car. Ask him nice and politely if you can search it for a possible weapon."

"Right, Captain."

The police photographer came out of the house with his camera. "We're all finished, Captain. Can they take the body?"

Leopold nodded. "Tell them to go ahead."

On Monday morning he was in the office early. When Connie came in with their coffee, he said, "You got a nice tan yesterday."

She sat down and crossed her legs. "We went to Brian's cottage on the Sound. It's his folks' cottage, really, but they're in England."

"Do you like him, Connie?"

"He's a nice guy." Her face crinkled into a grin. "Two years younger than I am. I'm robbing the cradle."

"How did you make out searching Pete Brody's car?"

"No problems. No weapon."

"What about the other neighbors?"

"Nobody saw or heard a thing. No one was looking out at the street. They were mostly watching television or busy in the kitchen if they were home at all."

Leopold handed Connie an address. "This is where that neighborhood meeting was held last night. Greta Doyle admits she changed her mind when she and Brenda Kingsley arrived and she didn't go in. I want you to find out what time Brenda arrived and how long she stayed."

A few minutes after Connie left, Fletcher arrived. "You wanted the 911 tape from last night, Captain."

"Just the part around nine o'clock."

"Here's what you want, from Kingsley's phone. There's no voice, but the connection was made at 9:00:25."

Leopold listened to the silence. There might have been a soft thud, but he couldn't be sure. "They traced the number?"

"They didn't have to. It was right up there on the screen in front of the dispatcher. When she couldn't rouse anyone, she sent a car at 9:02:10. It was only a half mile away on regular patrol."

Leopold nodded. "I was still on the phone with June Doyle when he arrived. Speaking of that, I have one or two questions for her, too, before she goes back to Philadelphia. Questions about Pete Brody."

"I've got the Medical Examiner's preliminary report if you want it."

"Let me have the high spots."

"Kingsley died almost instantly from a single bullet to the brain. It was a small caliber, probably a .22, but the slug was pretty well flattened by the impact. Fired from much farther away, it might not have been fatal. Death occurred about nine P.M., which is consistent with the other evidence. The bullet traveled upward, but of course Kingsley was a tall man."

Leopold sighed. "I'd better go out and see June Doyle's mother again, too."

He found Greta just pulling out of the garage. "Do you have a minute?" he called to her, getting out of his car.

"I'm in a hurry, Captain—June's gone into labor. Pete Brody just took her to the hospital in his car. That's where I'm going."

"I'll follow along," Leopold said. "One thing first, though—could I take another look at Marty's gun collection?"

"What for?"

"Roy Kingsley was shot, and you have guns in your house. I have to check all the angles."

"I can assure you he wasn't shot with one of Marty's weapons!" Her eyes had gone cold with anger, but she turned off the ignition and led the way back to the house.

Upstairs, she unwrapped the guns as she'd done the previous day Nothing seemed to have changed. Leopold picked up the target pistol and sniffed the barrel. It might have been cleaned and oiled recently, but he couldn't be certain—he hadn't examined it that closely the first time. And the bullet had been too mashed for identification purposes.

"Marty cleaned them often," she said, as if reading his mind. "He was fooling with them just last week."

"All right," Leopold said, returning the weapon to its oily wrap ping. "I don't want to delay you any longer."

As they went out to their cars, he said, "Why him? Why did Brody take June to the hospital?"

"He stopped by to see her. That's when the pains started."

"What was their relationship when June was living at home?"

"You'd have to ask her that. I know they dated."

Leopold followed Greta to the hospital and when he went inside, she was already speaking with the nurse at the desk.

"The doctor's with her now," Greta told Leopold, "but he thinks it'll be a while. Pete has gone on home."

"I think I will, too, Greta," he said. "Please call me when you have any news. I'd like to know that June and the baby are all right."

Greta telephoned him at Headquarters on Tuesday morning. "The baby didn't arrive until after one this morning and I figured you'd be asleep. It's a healthy boy. Both of them are doing well."

"Thanks for calling, Greta. I'll try to get over to the hospital and see her later today."

He told Connie about the baby. "Greta has a grandchild less than a week after Marty died," she said. "And he never even knew about it."

Leopold nodded. "Is there anything new in the Kingsley killing?"

"One item that'll interest you. I spoke to the woman who had the meeting at her house Sunday night. Greta didn't show up, as we already knew, but neither did Brenda Kingsley."

"What?"

"She has no alibi for the time of the killing, Captain."

"That *is* interesting. Did you ask her about it?"

"Yes—she told me that when Greta left her on the sidewalk, she didn't feel much like going to the meeting, either. After thinking about it, she got back in her car and drove down to the Sound."

"While Greta was walking around the neighborhood. That would be something of a coincidence, wouldn't it?"

"Do you think one of them is lying?"

"I told Greta I'd stop by the hospital to see June," Leopold said. "Maybe I'll see what she has to say about it."

At the hospital, Leopold told June, "I hear he's a beauty." June smiled.

"Today's my birthday, too," Leopold told her. "He and I were born on the same day—just a few years apart."

"I'm glad he has someone like you to share a birthday with."

"Is your mother around?"

"She's getting some tea down in the lounge."

Leopold spoke briefly to Greta on his way out. "June seems to be coming along fine."

"Did you see the baby?"

"No. Another time. I'm on my way to Mrs. Kingsley's house."

"Do you have any suspects?"

"No." He added, as casually as he could, "Would you say she and her husband were on good terms?"

"They always seemed to be. Surely you don't suspect Brenda! If nothing else, she was at that meeting."

"As it turns out, she wasn't. When you didn't go in, she decided not to, either. But we don't really suspect anyone yet."

He could see she wanted to ask more, but instead she said, "I hope June can make something of her life now. It's going to be difficult for her without a husband."

"Perhaps it will work itself out."

"She never *would* share her troubles with us—with Marty and me. She always thought she could fool her father. I think she took a certain pleasure in it."

"You have no idea who the baby's father is?"

"Pete Brody seems the most likely, but I just don't know."

Leopold's thoughts were running in another direction, and when he called on Brenda Kingsley that afternoon he came to the point quickly. "You say you were just driving around at the time your husband was killed."

"That's right," she said, moving nervously about the kitchen. "Look, Captain—I have to be at the funeral parlor. I'm not having calling hours, but I need to make arrangements for the service tomorrow."

"I understand. I'll try not to keep you. I was just wondering about your husband. I'm sorry to put it so bluntly, but was he faithful to you?"

She sat down hard on a kitchen chair, her eyes full of fury. "How dare you ask me a question like that?"

"It's my job, Mrs. Kingsley. Unpleasant at times, but my job. You see, prowlers just don't walk up to somebody's front door and start shooting. Three things happened here in the last several days. First, Marty Doyle died of a heart attack. Second, his death forced his daughter June to return from Philadelphia and reveal her pregnancy. Third, your husband was murdered. Since event number one caused number two, isn't it just possible that number two caused number three?"

"What are you saying, Captain? That June's return somehow caused Roy's death?"

"Was there a relationship between them, Mrs. Kingsley?"

"Roy was fifty-one years old. June is twenty-four."

"I'm still asking the question." Leopold turned to stare out the window. There was the same age difference of twenty-seven years between Molly and him. "You might have shot Roy if you found out about it. Or Greta Doyle might have shot him for doing that to her daughter. I suppose even Pete Brody might have done it if he really loves June."

"I can't help you, Captain. Please leave me now."

The clock in the front hallway was chiming two as he left the house.

June opened her eyes to find Leopold seated next to her hospital bed. "I must have been dozing. I didn't hear you come in."

"That's all right. You need your rest. I've only been here a few minutes."

She smiled sweetly. "If you keep coming to visit me like this, nurses are going to think you're the father."

"I almost wish I were, June. It might be simpler that way."

"What do you mean?" She'd come fully awake now.

"Roy Kingsley was the father, wasn't he?"

She stared at him.

"It's the only thing that makes sense—that gives you a motive for killing him."

"That's crazy! I'm the only person who *couldn't* have killed him! I was talking on the phone with you when he was shot, remember?"

Leopold smiled sadly, "You may become a footnote in the criminology books, June, as the first person who ever committed a murder while talking on a cordless telephone to establish an alibi."

Her eyes closed for an instant, then opened again. "What are you talking about?"

"Your first mistake was with the telephone. You had to call 911 because you knew they'd record the time of the call and set the time of death. That was important if you were going to use your conversation with me as an alibi. You phoned me, then asked me to call you back so I'd be sure you were really at your home phone. Of course you were talking on the cordless phone I saw at your house on Saturday. You were probably out the door by the time I called back, well across the front yard to the Kingsley house. The range of cordless telephones varies, but usually they can be used more than a hundred feet away from the main unit before there's too much static. Certainly your house and the Kingsleys' were close enough."

"What mistake are you saying there was with the telephone?" she asked without meeting his eyes.

"Not the cordless phone—the one you used to call 911. When Roy Kingsley opened the door, you shot him in the forehead at close range, using the .22 target pistol and silencer from your father's collection. You were talking to me all the time, of course, and you coughed and covered the mouthpiece for a moment to muffle the silencer even further and cut out any shout that Roy might make. Then you stepped inside the hallway, cradling the cordless phone against your shoulder, and dialed 911 on their wall phone. When the connection was made, you dropped the receiver by Kingsley's body and left the house, returning to your mother's as you completed the conversation with me. The trouble is, while the telephone receiver reached to Roy's dead hand, the unit with the dialing mechanism was still attached to the wall some feet away, Kingsley couldn't have stood in the doorway and dialed 911 as he was shot because he was too far away to reach the dial."

"Couldn't he have dialed first and then walked to the door without speaking?"

"Then the sound of the shot—at least the muffled cough of the silencer—would have been on the tape. The only sound on the tape was the thud of the receiver hitting the rug when you dropped it. But there's more, June. I heard a clock chime the hour as you talked, just after your cough and obviously before you dialed 911. There's no clock near the phone in your house—which I used on Saturday to phone Headquarters. The chiming clock is in the Kingsley hallway. I saw and heard it as I was leaving there this afternoon." He reached out to touch her hand. "Why did you kill him, June?"

But she only shook her head and said nothing.

"I suppose when you had to come back and reveal your pregnancy, you decided to confront him. He rejected you, so you got your father's gun and you shot him. Your mother told me how you liked to fool your father. Fooling me with the telephone trick would have been more of the same to you. I was a policeman like your father had been, a figure of strict discipline who had to be outwitted and fooled. If I hadn't been home on Sunday night, you probably would have called someone else your father worked with."

She was crying silently. "Roy said the baby wasn't his. He called me a whore—after all I did for him!"

Leopold stood up. "I'm sorry, June—I am. Sorry for you and sorry for your baby."

"What will you do now?"

"I've already done it. There's a guard stationed outside the door. I'm going to read you your rights, and from now on anything you say may be used against you. If you wish to have a lawyer present—"

Driving home, Leopold was miserable. It was as if not only Marty Doyle had died, but his daughter as well. If Marty had lived just a week longer, June's pregnancy might never have been revealed and her confrontation with Roy Kingsley might have been avoided.

He was still thinking about it when he walked into the house and heard the shouts of *"Surprise!"* He'd forgotten it was his birthday. He'd forgotten about the party.

He looked around at the smiling faces—Molly and Fletcher, Fletcher's wife Carol, Connie and her friend Brian—and then he smiled, too.

THE RETIRED MAGICIAN

W hen Rex Furcula gave his farewell performance at the Majestic Theater in Montreal, it happened that Captain Leopold and his wife Molly were in the audience. They'd been married just a year at the time and had driven up to Montreal for their first anniversary. Though neither of them was a great fan of magic, they found Furcula's final performance fascinating.

A few months later, Molly showed Leopold the evening paper. "Remember Rex Furcula? He's moving here. The paper says he's bought the Stafford place on the Sound for his retirement home."

"I heard that place was on the market for close to a million." Stafford was a senior partner in the city's largest law firm. He'd died at seventy-six after a brief illness and the family had put the property on the market. The brick house itself wasn't large, but there was a small carriage house and the six acres of land bordered on Long Island Sound, with its own boathouse and dock.

It was a one-day story for the papers, and Leopold heard nothing more of Rex Furcula for two years. His retirement was complete, and if he took part in the city's night life it was as a private citizen, unrecognized by others. Then came a warm morning in late July when Sergeant Fletcher brought the word to Leopold.

"There's been a killing reported at the Furcula place on the Sound. Should I handle it or—?"

"I'll come along," Leopold told him. "Who was killed?"

"A woman. No further identification yet. A patrol car's at the house now."

"Let's go."

Leopold's city had a public beach at the end of Ocean Avenue and private homes along Beach Street, which ran east and west from Ocean Avenue. Rex Furcula's home was located about a mile east of the public area, hidden from the street by a dense stand of fir trees. Leopold recognized the retired magician at once: there was no mistaking the tall slender man with the black goatee and piercing dark eyes. On the posters for his show, he'd seemed the quintessential stage magician but here in retirement he was still the same impeccable wizard come to meet his audience.

"I'm Captain Leopold. What's happened here?"

"I'm afraid my sister has been killed," Furcula said.

Leopold left Fletcher to get the pertinent information and proceeded to the carriage house. Patrolman Miller, who he knew slightly, was standing by the door. He stepped aside to let Leopold enter. "Woman named Theresa Cottswood, Captain. She lived here with her brother and his wife. It looks like she might have surprised a burglar."

Walking into the brick carriage house, Leopold had the sudden feeling that he was backstage at a theater. The walls were lined with garishly painted trick cabinets, mirrors, and draperies. There were magicians' tables and top hats, a wonderment of wands, and even a black cauldron left over from some witches' sabbath. Some of the things he remembered from the performance he'd seen in Montreal, others were strange to him. But he tore his gaze away to focus on the grey-haired woman on the floor. Her head was bloodied from the force of repeated blows, and a blood-stained length of pipe lay nearby. Her skin was cold to Leopold's touch. She'd been dead for some time.

Before long, the police technical unit arrived and Leopold left the scene to them. He returned to Fletcher and Rex Furcula. "You say the dead woman is your sister, Mr. Furcula?"

The black-bearded man nodded. "Poor Theresa—what a way to die—at only fifty-two!"

"She was younger than you?"

"That's right. I'm sixty-one."

"When did you find the body?"

"Around ten o'clock, just before I phoned. She didn't appear at breakfast and when I checked her room the bed was empty. I looked everywhere in the house for her and finally came out here. I noticed that a small pane of glass on the door had been broken and I came in to investigate. That's when I found her."

"You say her bed was empty. Had it been slept in?"

"I believe so. It was rumpled."

"And yet she's not wearing nightclothes, even though the medical examiner says the body temperature indicates she may have died around six this morning. Was anything missing in there?"

"I didn't really have a chance to look. I'm a retired performer, Captain—a stage magician—and the carriage house contains all my stage equipment."

"Has your sister lived here with you since your retirement?"

"No, only for the past year or so. Her husband died of a heart attack, and with this large house I felt we should take her in."

Leopold glanced up toward the house. "Is your wife—?"

"She's away. I don't expect her back until next week."

"So the two of you were alone here."

"Yes."

"Don't you need servants for a place this size?"

"A woman comes in to clean and cook dinner, and we have a service to take care of the grounds."

Patrolman Miller appeared and interrupted them. "Excuse me, Captain. I was just checking around for possible clues and I discovered the door to the boathouse has been forced open. Do you keep a boat in there, sir?"

Furcula's mouth dropped open. "Of course. My powerboat."

"It's not there now."

They hurried down to the boathouse at the water's edge. Furcula's boat was indeed missing, the winch turned to lower it into the water. "Give a description of the boat to Fletcher," Leopold told Furcula. "If we can find it, we may have our killer."

Later that afternoon, a police helicopter searching the coastline of Long Island Sound spotted the missing craft run up on some rocks about five miles away. The thief apparently had been knocked unconscious in the crash and flung into the shallow water, where he drowned. He was later identified from fingerprints as twenty-seven-year-old José Martinez, a New Yorker with a criminal record that included arrests for burglary and possession of drugs. What he was doing on the north shore of Long Island Sound was never explained, but it seemed clear that he had killed Theresa Cottswood when she surprised him in the carriage house. A week later, the case was closed.

Out of necessity, Captain Leopold had held several meetings and conversations with Rex Furcula during the course of the investigation. He found that he liked the man, and when Furcula's wife returned home for the funeral he liked her, too. Stella Furcula was much younger than her husband, a thin blond woman in her early thirties. It developed that she'd been the magician's assistant during his last few years before he retired.

"Rex used to saw me in half every night," she said. "Twice on matinee days."

"How long have you been married?" Leopold asked her.

"Nearly three years. We were married during his final tour."

"It must be dull for you now."

"Oh, no, I enjoy it. But I wish we got to see more people. Are you married, Captain?"

"Yes."

"Would you and your wife come out to dinner some night?"

It was the sort of vague invitation Leopold occasionally received during the course of an investigation and he thought no more about it, but about two months later Molly greeted him one evening: "Remember Rex Furcula? His wife phoned today to invite us to dinner next week. What do you think?"

"Interesting. What did you tell her?"

"I said I'd have to check your schedule and call her back tomorrow."

"Would you like to go?"

"Why not? We don't see that many new people these days. It might be fun."

Molly wore a short, glittery dress and Leopold put on the suit he usually wore to political dinners. They drove out to the Furcula house the following Thursday evening, arriving a few minutes after seven. Stella Furcula answered the door herself, and if she was surprised that Molly was no older than herself she gave no sign. The two women chatted amicably as Furcula took the Leopolds on a tour of the house.

"I know you saw most of this during the investigation," he told Leopold, "but I thought your wife might be interested."

"I'm sure she is."

It was still light out when they crossed the yard and entered the carriage house. "Rex is really proud of this collection," Stella told them. "He shows it at every opportunity. It's too bad that terrible thing had to happen here."

They paused at a large poster showing the showman in satanic garb, with the title "The Wizard of Magic" circling his head like a halo. Then Rex pointed out his collection of trick cabinets and mirrors and drapes.

"What are all these wands for?" Molly asked.

Furcula smiled. "Each has a different purpose, my dear. This is a coin wand." As he spoke, a half dollar magically appeared at the end opposite to where he held it. "Or perhaps you'd prefer the auto-gravity wand that remains on a table even though three-quarters of its length is beyond the table's edge. And here's a cigar wand, similar to the coin wand." He smiled, his slender fingers caressing each wand. "The swallowing wand." He smiled at Stella and she obediently opened her mouth. The wand seemed to descend into it for two-thirds of its length.

"Is that the sort of thing you used to do on stage?" Molly asked her.

Stella nodded cheerfully. "When I wasn't walking through brick walls or being sawed in half."

"And," her husband resumed the tour, "the vanishing wand."

It seemed to do exactly that, before their eyes.

At dinner, the conversation was brisk and Molly managed to learn a few professional secrets. "We saw the final performance in Montreal," she told Stella over the soup course, served by a plump Irish cook named Nellie. "You mentioned walking through the wall and being sawed in half. How in heaven's name did you manage those? They looked impossible to me."

Stella glanced at her husband. He gave a slight nod and she said, "I suppose I can tell you. Those tricks are pretty widely known. Both require a really thin girl—which I think explains my original appeal to Rex."

Furcula smiled. "There was more to it than that."

"In the wall trick, a trap door opens in the stage under the rug or sheet the wall rests upon. It lets the fabric sag a bit, and with the screens shielding me from the audience I managed to wiggle beneath the wall and come up on the other side. Then the trap door closes and the floor seems solid again when the screens are removed.

"Sawing the lady in half, there are two of us, of course. The other girl, doubled up in one half of the box, sticks her feet through the holes as I climb in. I double up and occupy only the other half, with my head and hands showing. That way the box can be separated after sawing."

"Amazing," Molly said. "Did you know all this, Jules?"

Leopold laughed. "More or less, but it's nice to have it confirmed by a professional."

Dinner was delicious, and after another hour of pleasant conversation Leopold and Molly headed for home.

"That was nice," she said as they drove through the night. "We should invite them back one evening. I like Stella, and he's pleasant enough."

Early the following week, while Leopold was poring over the weekend reports, Fletcher interrupted him. "Sorry to bother you, Captain, but I've got someone on the phone from Masterplan Insurance. They're getting ready to pay off a life policy on Theresa Cottswood, and because of the violent nature of her death they want to be certain we're satisfied the case is closed."

"It's closed," Leopold confirmed. Then, as an afterthought, he asked, "Who's the beneficiary—her brother?"

"That's right. They took out identical life-insurance policies on each other about a year ago."

"How much?"

"A million each."

Leopold whistled quietly. "The magician's going to have a nice retirement, if he hasn't already."

It was a month before Molly suggested having the Furculas for dinner, and Leopold agreed. The evening proved equally as pleasant, although Molly's generous cocktails before dinner gave Stella a bit of a glow. "I miss performing," she said at one point. "It's different with Rex. He doesn't need the money and he was ready to retire, but I'm still young."

If Furcula was unhappy with the remark, he didn't show it. "It's difficult for a younger wife. Do you find it so, Molly?"

"Well," Molly said, "we're both still working, and after Jules retires I plan to continue my legal career."

"Stella has outside interests," Furcula told them. "She still attends a magicians' convention every year."

"*Do* you?" Molly said. "That must be fascinating."

Stella nodded. "That's where I was the week Theresa was killed. Sometimes I think I'd like to put together a little nightclub act, using some of Rex's old equipment."

"But it's difficult for a woman," Furcula explained. "For one thing, Stella's fingers aren't the right shape for the sort of close-up magic you do in nightclubs." He reached over to take her hand. "Notice her fingers. They're short and a bit pudgy—not the long, slender kind a close-up artist needs."

"Oh," she told him, pulling her hand away, "with the right equipment I could be as good as you any day."

The increasingly serious banter was beginning to disturb Leopold and he changed the subject. "Why are magicians often portrayed as devils? That poster of yours—"

"It's only one of many I used. The conjurer's problem has always been to convince journalists that his act is of special interest to the reading public. From early in this century, famous magicians have portrayed themselves as in league with dark forces. It's all promotion, like this little goatee I wear."

Stella laughed. "It's grey, you know. He only blackens it with a wash-out dye when he's going out or making a public appearance."

"You're giving away my secrets," Rex told her.

Molly retreated to the kitchen to check on dinner and Leopold hoped it would be coming soon.

At the end of the evening, when the Furculas departed, Leopold said, "I'm always uneasy when people argue, even in a light manner."

"The drinks hit Stella a little hard."

"You shouldn't make them so strong."

In bed that night, as he was falling asleep, Leopold suddenly came awake, sitting upright. "What is it?" Molly asked.

"His beard!"

"What about it?"

"If he only dyes it black when he performs or is going to see people, why was it black the morning his sister was killed? Why did he dye it black unless he knew that he'd be seen by outsiders?"

"Oh, go to sleep, darling," Molly complained, rolling over in the bed.

But Leopold didn't sleep for a long time.

The following Monday morning Leopold called Sergeant Connie Trent into his office and asked to see the files on the Theresa Cottswood case. "I thought that was closed," she said.

"It is, but I want to look them over. After José Martinez died in the boat accident, I left it pretty much in Fletcher's hands. I was thinking over the weekend how little I knew about the victim."

The files weren't thick, since the official investigation had been a short one. Leopold started reading the report on Theresa Furcula Cottswood and her brother. Both had been born of middle-class parents in Cleveland, Ohio. Theresa had married a tailor with his own small shop, but he'd died the year before he turned fifty. She'd lived alone until her brother retired from the stage, then he'd bought the house on the Sound and she'd moved in with him and his new wife. That must have been about the time they'd taken out the joint life-insurance policies. There were no other living relatives, and Leopold supposed the policy had been meant as a measure of security for Theresa if Rex died first and left his house and other possessions to Stella.

That was about all. Police questioning of the neighbors had turned up very little—Furcula and his family kept pretty much to themselves and the adjoining houses were not close. The retired magician wasn't a wealthy man and the estate was heavily mortgaged, though he'd kept up his payments.

Leopold closed the file with a sigh. It told him very little. The file on José Martinez told him even less. He'd been a street punk from New York, with the usual sort of juvenile record before he'd graduated to drugs and burglary. Nothing bigger, though: fancy motorboats didn't figure into his lifestyle.

Leopold sighed. He put away the files and turned to other business.

Leopold and Molly hadn't really expected to receive another invitation from the Furculas, and certainly not as soon as the following week. But Stella phoned one evening to invite them over for a small cocktail party they were giving. An old colleague, a mindreader named Argos, was performing at a local dinner theater, and they wanted to fête him while he was in town. The party would be on Monday, because that was the only night he didn't perform.

"It should be entertaining," Molly said.

He wasn't so sure, but they went nonetheless. They arrived at six o'clock to find half a dozen cars in the driveway. Inside, a catering service was helping the cook, Nellie, pass trays of food and drinks among the dozen or so other guests. Leopold recognized some local theater people and art enthusiasts and learned it was the first invitation to the Furculas' for most of them.

He and Molly were drinking white wine when Stella spotted them and hurried over. "You were wonderful to come. Rex and I know so few local people, even after two years, but we wanted to put on this little affair for Argos."

The mindreader was probably still in his forties and seemed pleasant. Stella knew him well enough to challenge him, and when she asked him to guess Leopold's occupation he struck out badly, coming up with a bank vice-president. After Stella and Molly enjoyed a good laugh, Leopold's police connection was revealed.

"They met during the investigation of Theresa's murder," Stella explained.

Argos turned serious. "I was terribly sorry to hear about that. I wish I could have gotten here for the services."

"I was out of town myself when it happened," Stella told him. "At the magic convention. I made it back in time for the funeral. Rex took it very hard."

Leopold's memory of his first meeting with Furcula didn't include any tears or emotion. He remembered thinking that the man had seemed quite calm until the discovery of the stolen boat.

There was a small framed photograph of Rex and his sister on the piano, their faces overexposed as they squinted into the sun. "That would have been about ten years ago," Argos guessed, squinting back at the picture, "just after I first met them."

"Did Theresa travel with him?"

"No, her husband was still alive. But she often came to see him if he was appearing in her part of the country. I appeared with Rex in something called *A Night of Magic,* in Cleveland, and she came back-stage. She was a lively woman, very likable."

"Yes, she was," Stella agreed. "I loved her like my own sister."

Leopold left them with Molly and moved off toward Nellie. Taking an hors d'oeuvre from the tray, he said, "Nellie, do you have a minute?"

Nellie peered at him. "Oh, it's Mr. Leopold, isn't it? Captain Leopold?"

"That's right, Nellie. I just wanted to ask you something about the night Mrs. Cottswood was killed. Were you here that night?"

"No, sir—I didn't start until the following week. That would be Susan Ander you'd be wanting. She left the Furculas' employ about that time."

"I didn't know that. Why did she leave?"

"I couldn't say, sir. She was already gone when I arrived. She moved to Baltimore."

"Do you know her address?"

"Yes, and her phone number, too. It's on file in the kitchen."

"Could you get it for me?"

She hesitated only an instant. "Certainly, Captain."

Leopold drifted back to the others. Nellie didn't reappear immediately, but before they left she came up to him with a folded piece of paper. "Here's that information you wanted, sir."

"Thank you, Nellie."

"What was that about?" Molly wondered.

"I'll tell you later."

But Stella Furcula had also noticed the exchange. "I hope Nellie wasn't slipping you the recipe for my onion soup." She smiled.

Leopold laughed. "Nothing so devious. I was asking her about Rex's sister and she told me you had another cook at that time."

"Yes—Susan. She was devoted to Rex's sister. Sometimes they went to the movies together, and occasionally Theresa gave her one of her dresses. Rex was very surprised when she left."

"Was it because of the killing?"

"I suppose it might have had something to do with it. She didn't even stay for the funeral."

"Odd, if they were so friendly."

"Rex thought she seemed frightened when she gave her notice, but by that time the police had found the wrecked boat and that man's body; she knew there was no killer still at large."

"Would you have any objection if I contacted Susan?"

"Certainly not. Give her our best wishes if you do."

When Stella moved away to mingle with the other guests, Leopold watched to see if she headed toward Rex with a report on this kitchen intrigue, but she didn't go near him, and the next time Leopold noticed her she was deep in conversation with Argos, the guest of honor.

On the way home, he filled Molly in on what he'd been up to. She shook her head and reprimanded him. "They're going to think you're still investigating them. I thought the case was closed months ago."

"It was. It still is. I just wonder what frightened the cook away."

"You asked Stella for permission to speak to her? What if she'd said no?"

"I'd have done it anyway."

It took Leopold three phone calls over the next two days before he was able to reach Susan Ander. She was a mature, pleasant-sounding woman. "You say you're a police captain? Whatever are you phoning me for?"

"I'm a detective captain, actually," Leopold told her. "I was called into the investigation of the murder of Theresa Cottswood. We never realized there was a live-in cook on the premises at the time."

"There wasn't. I just came in to cook and clean, like the one they have now. I wasn't there when it happened."

"You were friendly with the deceased?"

"We were good friends."

"Might I ask why you left the Furculas' employ so suddenly?"

"Theresa's murder was a terrible shock to me. I'd had an offer of a job down here and decided to take it. I told Mr. Furcula, phoned the landlord at my apartment, and just left. I didn't even stay for the funeral service. I wanted to remember her alive."

"Where are you working now, Miss Ander?"

"At a restaurant here in Baltimore. A seafood place by the harbor."

"I have to ask you a very frank question. Did you have any reason to suspect that Theresa Cottswood's death might have been caused by her brother?"

"By Mr. Furcula? Certainly not! They were very close."

"What can you tell me about the boat that was stolen by José Martinez?"

"It was Mr. Furcula's boat, but he didn't use it often. He took it out on weekends sometimes, in good weather."

"What time did you usually arrive at the house?"

"Around eight o'clock. The family liked to have breakfast before nine."

"Thank you for your help, Miss Ander. I may want to contact you again if I have more questions."

Leopold returned to the file once more and picked out the statement of a fisherman who'd been first to arrive at the scene of the boat accident. "I'd seen him pass me earlier," it read. "I thought there was a man and a woman in the boat, but I may have been wrong. When I found the boat up on the rocks, there was only the man. The accident had thrown him into shallow water and he'd drowned."

He buzzed for Connie. "Do you have the autopsy report on Theresa Cottswood?"

"Nope. Everything's there." She rummaged around in the file and came up with it. "Right in front of your nose, Captain."

He sighed. "I guess my eyes are failing me. Is there any evidence she tried to fight off her attacker?"

Connie skimmed the relevant paragraph. "Fingernails normal, unbroken. No fresh wounds on the hands. Just a cut that had scabbed over and a week-old burn."

"She didn't try to fight him off. Does that mean she knew him?"

"He might have hit her from behind."

"Blows on the temple like this would suggest she was partly turned toward him."

"Captain, are you trying to say that her brother killed her?"

"No, I'm—" What *was* he trying to do? "Connie, I want you to find out where that magic convention was held—the one Stella Furcula attended. Try to get a complete list of attendees. They usually keep such things for next year's mailing list."

That evening at home, Leopold was in a bad mood. When Molly asked him why, he admitted, "I've grown to like the Furculas. But I may have to reopen the case."

"Because of something you learned while we were their guests?"

"In a way. I still have a duty to perform and I can't let that interfere."

"You think he killed his sister for the insurance money?"

"There's another possibility I'm checking on, but I like it even less."

"It could have been just what it seemed, Jules."

"In a magic act, nothing is ever quite what it seems," he reminded her.

By midmorning of the following day, Connie had the information he'd requested. "The magic convention was held in Omaha this year. The organizers faxed me a list of the delegates."

Leopold accepted the several pages she offered, saw that the list was alphabetical, and scanned down the first page. "There's no Argos," she told him. "I already looked."

"Sometimes I think you can read my mind."

"You mentioned meeting him at Furcula's house, and he's been performing in town. It seemed likely."

"Argos is probably just a stage name. He may have been registered under his real name, which we don't know." He turned the page and found Stella Furcula's name.

"Of course, this list is no proof the people actually attended," Connie pointed out. "It just means they paid the registration fee."

Leopold grunted. "Omaha." He closed his eyes and leaned back in his chair. A few minutes later he sat up, almost surprised to see the look of concern on Connie's face.

"Are you all right?" she asked.

"I'm fine. Get us a couple of plane tickets for this afternoon."

"To Omaha?"

He shook his head. "Baltimore. We're going to see the Furculas' cook."

It was raining in Baltimore when their plane landed. Connie had phoned ahead and a detective from the local police department met their plane. They drove to Susan Ander's apartment on Light Street and rang the bell, but nobody answered.

"She mentioned working at a seafood restaurant down by the harbor, but there are a lot of those," Leopold said, pressing the buzzer again. When nothing happened, the Baltimore detective, whose name was Schwartz, suggested they wait in the car.

As they walked back across the street, Leopold suddenly touched Connie's arm. "There she is," he said, indicating a bare-headed woman of about fifty who was walking toward them, carrying a bag of groceries.

"How do you know?"

Leopold didn't answer. Instead, he stepped across the damp sidewalk to intercept her. "Pardon me—you're Susan Ander, aren't you?"

"Yes." She looked from one to the other, her eyes blinking behind her eyeglasses. "What is it?"

"I'm Captain Leopold—I spoke with you on the phone."

"Oh, yes, Captain."

"This is Sergeant Connie Trent and Detective Schwartz of the Baltimore police."

Schwartz took over. "We'd like you to accompany us to headquarters for questioning, ma'am."

"Are you accusing me of something?"

"Suspicion of murder."

Susan Ander gave a short, sharp laugh and turned to Leopold. "Do you think *I* killed Theresa Cottswood?"

Leopold shook his head. "No, I think you killed the real Susan Ander, Mrs. Cottswood."

The part of the case that Leopold hated most was confronting the Furculas the following morning at their home. "I don't understand you," Stella said. "What are you trying to tell us?"

"I'm afraid what I'm telling you isn't news to your husband, Stella. After all, he's the one who falsely identified the body as that of his sister."

Rex Furcula sat down, the color drained from his face. "Where is Theresa now, please?"

"Still in Baltimore. If she doesn't waive extradition, we'll file the necessary papers tomorrow."

"You can't prove murder."

"We can prove insurance fraud. She's the walking proof of it. We'll use that to extradite her and then work on the murder charges. Our best case against her is probably in the killing of José Martinez. Either one of you might have killed the cook, Susan Ander."

"Rex!" Stella screamed. "What is this? Tell him it's not true!"

He ran a tongue over his dry lips. "I never killed anyone, Captain. I knew nothing about it until it was over."

Stella appealed to Leopold. "I don't understand any of this."

"It was a plot to defraud the insurance company out of a million dollars," Leopold explained. "Theresa Cottswood hired Susan Ander as cook a full year ago, choosing someone about her size and age and coloring. She waited until a time when you were away because it was important that you didn't see the body. Then she called Susan there early that morning, took her out to the carriage house, and beat her to death with a length of pipe. Martinez was someone she—or you, Rex—hired in New York to come up and help her get away in the boat. Of course, he didn't know what was in store for him. Theresa had him run the boat onto some rocks down the coast and then knocked him out and left him to drown. She went to Baltimore and took a job under Susan Ander's name, because it was important the cook appear to be alive until after the insurance settlement. Afterward, she could move again and drop out of sight, then start a new life with her money. Is that about right, Rex?"

Furcula lowered his head, running a hand across his face. "I was afraid you'd find out. It's why I struck up this friendship with you, so I'd know if you were suspicious. Theresa always had these crazy schemes, even when she was in school. I suppose I did, too, but I became a stage magician and used them to entertain people. Killing a person meant no more to Theresa than when I sawed Stella in half. It was fantasy—I think she half expected her victims to return for a curtain call after it was over."

Stella had been sitting with an expression of growing horror on her face. "How did you know all this, Captain?"

"I didn't, not right away. I considered the possibility that Rex killed his sister, or even that you sneaked back here from the convention and killed her, possibly with the help of Argos."

"But—"

"But then all the little clues began to point the way toward the truth."

"What little clues?"

Leopold began counting them off on his fingers. "The only picture of Theresa on public display here is a decade-old snapshot of Rex and her squinting into the sun, their faces overexposed. It gives nothing, really, but a general impression. I knew Susan Ander was about the same size because your cook told me Theresa sometimes passed her dresses on to Susan. That was why the victim was fully dressed, even though the crime must have taken place around six in the morning. Susan arrived wearing one of those hand-me-down dresses, no doubt on Theresa's instructions."

"What about the boat?" Stella was crying now.

"Martinez was hired to steal it, of course—and to become the fall guy in the murder plot. A fisherman thought he saw a woman in the boat with Martinez before the accident, and that got me thinking. I thought of you, Stella, as I've said, and then I thought of Susan Ander. Her story of her sudden departure didn't make sense. She and Rex both insisted she wasn't here the morning of the murder, yet she admitted leaving the job suddenly because of the killing. But why wouldn't she have been here? She started work at eight that morning and the body wasn't found until ten.

"I began considering her as a suspect, but then a funny thing happened. Sergeant Trent was checking the autopsy report for me and she happened to mention there were no recent hand injuries, as in a struggle—there were only a scabbed-over cut and a week-old burn. These struck me as the sort of injuries one receives in the kitchen— minor cooking injuries. Was it possible that the dead woman was the departed cook, Susan Ander? Her landlord never saw her when she moved out that day. He only received a call from her, and Theresa could have imitated her voice after knowing her and socializing with her for a year. The body wasn't on view, and Theresa's few friends—including you, Stella—saw only a closed coffin at the grave. So I went to Baltimore yesterday, and when I was able to pick out the supposed Susan on the street I knew my theory was correct."

"Can you prove that to a jury?" Rex Furcula asked.

"The fraud charge will be easy enough, and she was alone in the boat with Martinez when he was killed. As for Susan Ander, I think we can bring down indictments against both you and your sister."

"I told you it was her idea," Rex protested. "She planned the whole thing. I was simply to collect the insurance money and turn it over to her. I wanted none of it."

Stella took his hand, wanting to believe him. Leopold only said, "We'll let a jury decide. Perhaps you can pull off one more trick and stay out of prison. But you might get more sympathy if you let your goatee stay grey for the trial."

PUZZLE IN A SMOKE FILLED ROOM

There hadn't been a fire in two weeks, and Randy Dwyer's days on the job were beginning to blend into one another with a boring sameness that made him anxious for his shift to end. The men of Fire Company 5 took turns doing the cooking for the group, but even that did little to break the monotony. Randy Dwyer was almost relieved on the days when they were sent out to check hydrants.

Usually in the evenings, after dinner, he'd play euchre with three of the men on his truck. Mike Rascow usually won, but it was fun anyhow, and helped break the monotony. It was Monday night, in the midst of their regular games, when the alarm finally sounded. Tony Loma went running to the tape to read the location. "House fire," he reported, "122 Baldwin—called in by a neighbor."

"Let's go!" Rascow shouted, throwing down his cards. Jack Yount was already at the wheel of the pumper, throwing the switch that activated the overhead door and the flashing red lights outside the station. Dwyer and the others grabbed their coats and helmets from the rack as they ran. Their boots and other equipment were already on the truck. Within ninety seconds of getting the alarm, they were on their way.

"At last, a little action," Rascow said. He had a black moustache which he had to keep trimmed so it wouldn't interfere with his oxygen mask.

Usually they rode inside the engine in the compartment just behind the driver, but tonight, because the weather was warm and they were feeling good, they stood on the backstep, clinging to the rails like firefighters of an earlier decade.

The whine of the siren cut through the night as Jack Yount guided the engine down the main street for about a mile before turning right into Baldwin. They saw the flames immediately, shooting from the second floor of the house—a frame dwelling built in the 1930s.

Mike Rascow was off the engine before it came to a full stop, pulling a length of hose after him. He quickly unscrewed the nozzle cap from a fire hydrant two doors down from the burning house while Dwyer attached the other end to the hydrant intake on the side of the pumper. They had done this so often it was almost automatic by now. Tony Loma was setting up an extension ladder against the side of the house.

"Anyone still inside?" Randy asked a woman in pajamas and a robe who had come running out to meet them.

"My husband!" she cried. "He went up to bed early and he may have been smoking! You've got to save him!"

Another engine, from Company 8, had just pulled up. Rascow took the hose and Dwyer led the way into the house, carrying his axe. Yount was following Loma up the outside ladder. The smoke was thickening, but not yet deadly. Dwyer ran up the inside stairs to the second floor, hearing the breaking of glass as Loma smashed through one of the windows from outside and he and Yount started playing their hose into the burning bedroom.

Dwyer could see a man in his underwear huddled in one corner of the room, trying to escape the fire's fury. Rascow doused Dwyer with water from the second hose as he rushed into the room. The blaze seemed to be centered on the mattress, but it had already spread to a dresser and a closet. As Dwyer reached out a gloved hand toward the cornered man, he heard the crack of an exploding cartridge. He had an instant to remember what they'd taught him at the fire academy about homeowners who kept a gun and extra ammo in their bedrooms.

Then there was the crack of a second shot and he felt something pierce his chest.

Firefighter Randy Dwyer was pronounced dead on arrival at the city's Brooke Medical Center, the victim of a bizarre but not-unheard-of accident in which the intense heat of the fire had detonated the powder charge in several pistol cartridges stored in the homeowner's bedroom. Firefighters were taught to retreat from a location at once if they heard the sound of shots or explosions, but there'd been no time for Randy to escape. A tumbling lead slug had torn open his chest and penetrated his heart.

Captain Leopold attended the young firefighter's funeral as part of a small police-department delegation. After the prayers at the cemetery, he met the man's widow, a slim, handsome woman who wore her black dress more like a fashion model than a wife in mourning. "I'm very pleased you're here, Captain," she said with a trace of British accent. "And his chums from the fire department, of course. For as long as I knew him, Randy wanted to fight fires."

"If there's anything any of us can do, Mrs. Dwyer," Leopold said.

As they walked back to the car. Sergeant Connie Trent, who'd accompanied Leopold, remarked, "You could probably get a lunch date with her if you play your cards right."

"Not nice, Connie," Leopold said.

The three firefighters who'd worked with Dwyer were standing on the sidewalk with a plain young woman. They'd served as pall-bearers and seemed ill at ease now that their formal role was ended. Leopold introduced himself. The one with a moustache replied, "I'm Mike Rascow. This is Tony Loma and Jack Yount. And my wife Clara."

"These freak accidents," Leopold said. "They're terrible for you all."

Driving back to Headquarters, Connie said, "I guess you never know when your number's going to come up."

"It's just as well we don't."

He hadn't been back in the office more than five minutes when Lieutenant Fletcher appeared in the doorway with a cup of coffee. "We got problems, Captain."

"Bring me a cup, too, and you can tell me about them."

Fletcher went back for a second coffee. When he returned, he settled into a visitor's chair. "You know that fireman, Randy Dwyer, who was killed Monday night?"

"I just came from his funeral. What about him?"

"Doc Bueller just sent up the autopsy report. There was no question about the cause of death so he didn't hurry it."

"Anything unusual?" Leopold asked, already knowing there must be something.

"Yes. Doc Bueller dug the bullet out of Dwyer's chest and examined it under a microscope. You know the fire was supposed to have set off a box of cartridges in the bedroom."

"Yes."

"The slug they dug out of Randy Dwyer had lands and grooves on its sides. It had been fired from a gun barrel, probably from a .38-caliber revolver."

There was a simple explanation, Leopold told himself as he drove out Baldwin Street to the burned house. The original police report had stated that the owner of the house, Aaron Pettigrew, had a license to possess the revolver and that he used it exclusively for target practice. Leopold knew a number of spoils shooters and hunters had loading equipment, purchasing gunpowder, cartridge cases, and lead slugs in quantity and making their own bullets at home. He often wondered how much money this saved them, but perhaps Aaron Pettigrew was an especially saving sort. He might even dig his used slugs out of the targets to reuse them, which would explain the lands and grooves. They'd have been from the previous time the bullet was fired, not the time it killed Randy Dwyer.

That was Leopold's theory, at least. Aaron Pettigrew took less than a minute to demolish it. "No, I never do my own loading. It's too much trouble." He was a small, deeply tanned man in his forties who moved with the gracefulness of someone who took care of his body. "To tell you the truth, I don't do much target shooting, either. I just keep the gun for protection. These days you never know."

There was still a possibility that the heat from the fire had exploded the cartridge in the gun's chamber, propelling it out the barrel. "Could you show me where the weapon was stored during the fire, Mr. Pettigrew?"

"If you don't mind rummaging around in the ruin. Come on up with me."

The first floor of the house had suffered only some water damage, and the fire itself had been confined to the upstairs master bedroom.

"You're still able to live here?" Leopold asked.

"We're staying across the street with neighbors till some of it gets fixed. I'm off from work today because I'm waiting for the insurance adjuster. Otherwise you wouldn't have caught me home."

"Where do you work?"

"At the Westside Health Club."

"The police report says the fire was caused by smoking in bed. How does that square with your health-club image?"

"I don't smoke on the job. I'm trying to give it up completely, but once in a while a cigarette relaxes me."

He led the way to the burned-out bedroom. The ruined mattress had been thrown out the window by the firemen, but the other furnishings were still intact, if a bit charred by the blaze. The walls and ceiling were scorched, too, and the draperies were all but burned away from the windows. "The gun and ammunition were in the top drawer of my dresser here. I'd taken the gun out to clean it and the box of cartridges was lying on the bed."

"You were in the room all the time?"

"Yes. The fire trapped me in the corner—I couldn't get out."

"Then you saw the fireman get shot?"

"Well, as much as you can see anything in a smoke-filled room. He was the first one through the door, just as the fire reached the box of cartridges on the bed. I heard one go off, but before I could shout a warning there was another and he fell."

"The cartridges all went off?"

He nodded. "There were only a dozen left in the box and they all went in about two minutes."

"Where was the gun during all this?"

"Well, it was in my hand. I grabbed it when the bed caught on fire."

"Could I see it?"

"I just put it back in the same place the next day," Pettigrew said, pulling open the charred dresser drawer. He handed over a .38-caliber snub-nosed revolver that still had traces of soot on it. Leopold opened the cylinder, but the weapon was unloaded.

"Were there bullets in it the night of the fire?"

"Of course not," he said, slightly indignant." Only a fool tries to clean a loaded gun."

"Could I take this along for a test firing?"

Pettigrew hesitated. "Do I have a choice?"

"Certainly. Although I can get a court order easily enough."

"Take it. Just bring it back in one piece."

"Are there any cartridges?"

The small man shook his head. "They all got burned up. I haven't had a chance to replace them."

Leopold nodded. "Could I speak to your wife, too?"

"She works during the day, selling real estate. You can catch her in the evening."

"I'll do that."

He went downstairs and out to his car. Pettigrew didn't do his own loading and the gun had been empty when the fire started. That seemed to eliminate the only two possible ways in which Randy Dwyer could have been shot with a bullet that had rifling marks on it. Still, it would be better to wait for a ballistics report on the gun.

Fletcher had the report first thing the following morning. "The bullet *was* fired from Pettigrew's gun, Captain. Now what?"

"I suppose we have to question the other witnesses. Pettigrew's wife, the three other men from Engine Company 5—" He had another thought. "Was Dwyer conscious before he died? Did he say anything?"

"I don't know, Captain. We could check with the ambulance attendant and the hospital."

"Let me talk to them. Meanwhile, you track down the men he was working with. See when we can have them all in here for a session."

"Together?"

"The first time, yes. Then we might talk to them individually."

While Fletcher went to work on that, Leopold drove out to Brooke Medical Center and talked to the people on duty in the emergency room. One nurse was on duty Monday night, and she assured him Randy Dwyer had been dead on arrival—the house physician had pronounced him dead as soon as they slid him from the ambulance.

"Could I speak with the ambulance attendant?"

She consulted her records. "That would be Vince Scarlata at Star Ambulance Service."

He thanked her and went on his way. Driving out to the Star Ambulance garage, he wondered what he actually expected to learn. There had been a case earlier in his career in which the victim had been shot to death in the back of an ambulance, but he hardly expected a repeat of that. Randy Dwyer had been shot and killed in Aaron Pettigrew's smoke-filled bedroom. All he had to establish was how it had happened.

Scarlata was due to start work at noon, so Leopold waited for him. The attendant was a well-trained physician's assistant, he informed

Leopold, and there was no mistake in his initial diagnosis. "Dwyer was dead when we arrived. I could see it right away, but we needed a doctor to make it official so we wheeled him over to Brooke Center."

"Did anyone else ride with him in the ambulance?"

Scarlata shook his head. "Just me. He never stirred or made a sound during the trip. He was dead, Captain."

Leopold went back to his car and found a message on the computer screen to call Fletcher. He got him on the radio and Fletcher told him the three firemen would be in Leopold's office before their evening shift began at four o'clock.

Leopold wanted Connie and Fletcher in on the meeting, too, and six people could never fit into his cramped office, so they ended up meeting around the big table in one of the interrogation rooms. The three firefighters arrived together and shook hands all around. Leopold decided that Mike Rascow was the most outgoing of the three. Tony Loma spoke little and studied his hands. Jack Yount, the driver, seemed like a nice guy who was puzzled at what they were doing there. "We've got to be on duty at four," he announced, speaking for the others.

"This shouldn't take long," Leopold assured them. "An odd situation has come up regarding Randy Dwyer's death. It concerns the bullet that killed him having been fired from a gun." Rascow and Yount exchanged surprised glances, while Loma continued studying his hands. "I'm sure there's some simple explanation for it, but we have to investigate, of course. We especially want to know if there's any possibility this man Pettigrew might have shot Dwyer as he burst into the room, simply out of fright or a reflex action."

"I doubt it," Yount said at once. "We were all there with him, more or less. Tony and I were coming through the window and Mike was behind him with the hose."

Mike Rascow agreed. "Pettigrew's gun was pointed at the floor. He never raised it. We all ducked for cover when those bullets started flying, but as soon as they stopped I grabbed the gun out of his hand. Randy was already on the floor then."

"Dead?"

Tony Loma raised his head. "He sure looked dead. He wasn't moving and I could see the wound in his chest. I dragged him by the feet into the upstairs hall. After the fire was out, Mike worked over him while we waited for the ambulance."

Leopold turned to Jack Yount. "Was that the way you saw it, too?"

"Yeah, as much as I *could* see. The smoke was pretty thick."

"Did Randy get along with you guys?"

"Sure. Everybody liked him."

They talked until it was time for the men to leave, and after they'd gone Leopold sat frowning at his notes. "Nothing. We've got nothing, except that Pettigrew's gun killed him. At best we can show the gun must have been loaded, and fired accidentally, but that's no crime."

"So it was an accident." Fletcher shrugged. "Accidents happen."

Leopold shook his head and went back to his office. Maybe he was straining to manufacture a murder where none existed He looked at the morgue photos again, studying the rifling marks on the fatal bullet. He glanced at pictures of the entrance wound, exit wound, and various bruises no doubt acquired on the job. None of them told him anything.

Finally he called Connie in. "I know this sounds far-fetched, but I want you to run a check on a young man named Vince Scarlata. He's an attendant with Star Ambulance Service and he was with Dwyer on the ride to the hospital. I had a case once—"

"I know, Captain." It had been before her time, but they'd talked about it. "I'll get right on it."

He went home that night and told his wife Molly about it. "What do you think, Molly?" he asked when he'd finished. "Is there anything to it or am I just chasing smoke?"

"I'll admit there's a lot of smoke—a whole room full of it."

"Any suggestions?"

"So far you've talked to Pettigrew and this Vince Scarlata and the three firemen. If you want a suggestion, go talk to the wives."

"What?"

"Talk to Pettigrew's wife. And talk to Randy Dwyer's wife."

Aaron Pettigrew's wife was named Jenny. Leopold remembered her husband saying that she sold real estate, and the following day he managed to track her down at the office where she worked. She was a small woman who moved and talked fast. "You came about the fire, I suppose," she greeted him, extending a hand that rattled with gold bracelets as he shook it.

"Yes, if I could just have a few minutes of your time."

She led him into a photo gallery where they were surrounded by black-and-white pictures of area homes for sale. "This is about as private as it gets here. You can tell me now. It's about Aaron, isn't it?"

Leopold was taken aback for an instant. "Well, he probably told you we've been running ballistics tests on his gun."

"Sometimes he gets crazy when he smokes."

It took another instant for her words to make sense to Leopold. "Of course—pot. He'd given up regular cigarettes, but he went up to the bedroom evenings to smoke pot."

"I thought you already knew. Well, then he'd get out that gun of his and load it up. That really scared me." She was pacing back and forth as she spoke.

"He said the gun was empty, that he was cleaning it."

"He cleaned it about once a year. He was smoking and imagining he was a cowboy or something. He was in another world. That's how the bed caught on fire."

"Do you think he could have shot at the first fireman through the door?"

"I don't know. He yelled down to me that the bed was on fire, so he wasn't completely zonked out."

"Did you call 911?"

"I was about to when I heard the sirens. I guess my neighbor saw the flames and called."

"So you believe the gun was loaded and your husband was high on pot when the mattress caught on fire."

"It's a pretty safe guess. That's what I live with."

"Has he ever threatened to harm you with the gun?"

"No, he goes off by himself. When he hasn't been smoking, he's a real quiet guy. With some people it's just like drinking too much, I guess."

Leopold left Jenny Pettigrew and drove across town to the small ranch home Randy Dwyer had shared with his wife Margaret. There was a yellow sports car in the driveway and a familiar figure was just leaving the house. It was Jack Yount, the engine driver who'd worked with her husband. Yount seemed surprised and perhaps a bit embarrassed to encounter Leopold. "Hello, Captain. I just brought some of Randy's things over from the firehouse."

Leopold nodded. "How's Mrs. Dwyer bearing up?"

"As well as can be expected."

"I just thought I'd stop by and ask a few questions about Randy."

"I'll see you, then." Yount slid into the front seat of the sportscar and backed out the driveway, barely missing Leopold's car parked at the curb.

As soon as he was out of sight, Margaret Dwyer opened the front door. "I thought I heard voices."

"I have just a few questions, Mrs. Dwyer."

"Please come in."

The house was modestly furnished except for a few extravagant touches like an expensive stereo system and a large sofa that looked like something out of a British country house. "I met Jack Yount outside."

"All of Randy's friends have stopped by to bring me things. They know I'm so alone without him. There are no children, you see, and my family's back in England."

"How did you and Randy meet?"

"I married an American and moved to Boston. Soon after we divorced, I met Randy up there. He swept me off my feet."

"What did your first husband do for a living?"

"He was an insurance executive."

"Marrying a fireman must have been quite a change for you. And this city's not Boston."

"No, but I like it nonetheless. I like being able to take the train down to New York when I want to, and come back the same day."

"Will you stay here now or go back to England?"

"Oh, I'll stay in America. Everyone's been so friendly to me here. Perhaps I'll move to New York."

"I have to ask you this, Mrs. Dwyer. Did your husband have any enemies, especially among the men he worked with?"

"No—they got along splendidly."

"Did you all get together socially very often?"

"The boys did occasionally, but not the wives. Of course Mike Rascow's the only one who's married right now. Tony Loma had a painful divorce."

"What about Yount?"

She smiled slightly. "He's a bachelor. Couldn't you tell from that sportscar he drives?"

"Do you know Rascow's wife?"

"Clara? Not well. She's a mousy little thing, isn't she?"

"Did you or Randy ever meet Aaron Pettigrew, the man whose mattress caught fire?"

"No."

"All right, Mrs. Dwyer. Thanks for your help. If I think of anything else, I'll give you a call."

That night he told Molly, "I followed your advice. I talked to the wives today."

She slid a frozen package into the microwave. "What did you find out?"

"Nothing."

Then maybe there's nothing more to learn."

"Oh, my mind's full of theories, all right. Pettigrew was smoking pot at the time of the fire. He liked to load his gun and play with it. He might have shot Randy Dwyer without fully realizing what he was doing."

"That's one good theory."

"About the only one, really. Building a case for murder here is more difficult than accepting the simple fact that Pettigrew's gun was loaded, it went off accidentally and killed Dwyer. I'll have to talk to him again in the morning and get him to admit he'd put a cartridge into that cylinder."

As it turned out, Leopold didn't get back to Pettigrew. He awoke in the morning with some subconscious memory surfacing in his brain, as it often did when he first woke up. He'd missed something obvious and very important.

One of the autopsy photos of Randy Dwyer had shown an exit wound!

Was he getting that old? Couldn't he spot a major discrepancy like that without having to sleep on it for two nights?

Doc Bueller, a pleasant middle-aged man who served as a part-time assistant to the Chief Medical Examiner, had performed the autopsy. He looked a bit startled when Leopold rushed into his office before nine in the morning, waving the stack of photos he'd sent up to Fletcher's office two days earlier.

"What is it, Captain?"

"These are the Randy Dwyer autopsy photos. This one shows an exit wound. If there was an exit wound, how were you able to recover the bullet?"

"Just a moment." Bueller opened a file drawer to consult his notes. "Is it possible that some other bullet got mixed up with this case?" Leopold asked him.

"No—I remember removing it myself. It had penetrated the left ventricle of the heart."

"Then how could there be an exit wound? There's only one entrance wound."

"The lead slug might have split apart on impact with a bone. It happens sometimes."

"But you recovered the slug, with its grooves along the side," Leopold reminded him.

"When a lead bullet passes through flesh and bone, it takes a beating, Captain. If it hit the bone at an angle, the head of the bullet may have broken off and continued through the deceased's back. Visually it may have appeared mashed in, but a piece might be missing."

"How would we know?"

"Ask ballistics to weigh it, if they haven't already."

"Can I use your phone?"

"Go ahead."

Ballistics had weighed the bullet, of course. That was part of the normal testing. It was all there. Leopold hung up the phone and turned back to Bueller. "Any other ideas?"

"He must have been hit twice. If there's only one entrance wound, it's because both slugs hit him in the same spot. It's not too likely, I'll admit—"

"—unless the second shot was carefully aimed at the first wound, from close up, and angled toward the heart."

"Well, yes."

"Thanks, Doc."

Leopold went back to his office. Connie Trent entered to tell him she'd found no connection between the ambulance attendant, Scarlata, and the dead man. Leopold hardly heard her.

"He fired a second shot into the wound. Connie! The bastard fired a second shot and we never caught on."

"Who?"

"The killer. Come along with me. It's time for an arrest."

His wife opened the door when they rang. She seemed surprised to see them. "Could we speak to your husband?" Leopold asked her.

"He's just getting up. I'll call him."

When he appeared a few minutes later, Leopold said, "We want to question you regarding the death of Randy Dwyer. You have the right to remain silent and the right to have a lawyer present. I must warn you that anything you say —"

Mike Rascow moistened his lips and glanced back at his wife. "Let's go somewhere and talk."

In the car, Rascow sat in back with Leopold while Connie drove. "There were four of us in that room with him, counting Pettigrew. How'd you know it was me?"

Leopold sighed. He'd handcuffed Rascow when they reached the car, though he still didn't know if it had been necessary. The man hadn't said good-bye to his wife, and Clara Rascow hadn't spoken to him. Perhaps they'd said everything to each other already. "We've established that Dwyer was killed by a second bullet fired into the original entrance wound. Pettigrew couldn't have done that from across the room, and neither could anyone else in all that smoke. Someone used Pettigrew's gun, though. Only you could have done that, Rascow, because you told us yourself that you took the gun away from Pettigrew after the cartridges stopped exploding."

"Yeah, it was me."

"Tony Loma had dragged him into the upstairs hall and thought he was already dead, but when you bent to examine the wound you saw he was still alive. You were there with the gun still in your hand, the gun you'd taken from Pettigrew. You wrapped it with a cloth or a portion of the burned mattress-stuffing to muffle the sound and hide any powder burns, and fired a second shot. With all the noise of hoses and axes, no one heard it. The ammunition had caught fire by accident, after all. You were just helping the accident along a little, making sure he was dead. Then you just ejected the cartridge from the cylinder and left the gun on the floor. If there were any unfired rounds you took those, too, because you didn't want Pettigrew to be blamed. You wanted it to look like an empty gun."

Rascow was staring out the car window. "I figured it was perfect. I never thought about the grooves on the bullet that would prove it had been fired from a gun."

"Pettigrew probably didn't even remember whether he'd loaded it or not. When he went back and picked up the gun later, it was empty. That was good enough for him."

Connie pulled into the police garage and Leopold helped Mike Rascow from the car. "I guess I don't have to ask what your motive was," he said. "Dwyer's wife, Margaret, is quite a woman."

Rascow looked surprised. "Margaret? Is that what you think? I didn't kill him for Margaret. I killed him because he was sleeping with my wife. He was sleeping with Clara."

THE SUMMER OF OUR DISCONTENT

It had been a bad summer for Captain Leopold, because he knew it would be his last before he was forced to retire from the police department. He was already a few months past the mandatory retirement age of sixty-five, and he'd spent much of August as a guest lecturer at the police academy. That was a sure sign he'd be called upstairs to the chief's office any day now to receive the news he dreaded.

"You'd better get ready to take over my desk," he told Lieutenant Fletcher on the Friday before the Labor Day weekend. "I hear today might be the day." Fletcher was the first of three names on the civil service promotion list, and no one in Violent Crimes doubted that he'd be taking over when Leopold left.

"Much as I hate to see you leave, I'll admit that *Captain Fletcher* has a nice sound to it."

The call came at two o'clock that afternoon and Leopold took the elevator to the chief's office on the top floor. Chief Ringold was only two years younger than Leopold and would be retiring soon himself. He understood the pain of it better than most, and he sympathized with what Leopold was going through. He was a beefy, balding man with a good record, tough but fair. Over the years he'd kept hands off Leopold's department and as a result their relations had remained good, if a bit formal.

"Good to see you, Captain," he said, shaking hands and motioning Leopold to a chair opposite his polished desk.

"I guess I know what this is for."

"Well, yes," Chief Ringold told him, offering a cigar which Leopold declined. "You turned sixty-five last month and there's that department retirement policy staring us in the face. I'll be there soon enough myself. We assigned you to the academy class for August to keep City Hall happy, but now we're up against the wall and I've run out of excuses."

"I understand," Leopold said, calmer than he imagined he could be under the circumstances. "I appreciate your giving me the extra month."

"Actually, I think we can give you a little more than that. You can announce your retirement effective September thirtieth if you'd like. However, I want to appoint the new head of Violent Crimes on Tuesday, right after the holiday."

"I must say that Lieutenant Fletcher is looking forward to it."

Chief Ringold glanced at his desk, moving a few papers aimlessly. "It won't be Lieutenant Fletcher."

"What?"

"I've decided to promote Lieutenant Vivian to the position."

"Vivian!" Leopold felt the blood draining from his face. "He's never worked in Violent Crimes! He's head of the Burglary Squad!"

"It was a close call, to be sure." Ringold seemed suddenly uncomfortable. "But George Vivian is second on the civil service list and he's ten years younger than Fletcher."

"My God, Fletcher's only fifty-two! You're going to force him out with something like this!"

"No, no, I don't think so."

"Was this strictly your decision, Chief, or is there politics involved?"

"There's nothing, Captain. It was my decision alone. I was of two minds from the beginning and now with Fletcher's daughter on the force—"

"Lisa? What does any of this have to do with Lisa?"

"There was that murder case while she was at the academy. You wrapped it up nicely, but she had some involvement. If at some future time she proves an embarrassment to her father, it would be best if he wasn't head of the Violent Crimes Squad."

"She'll never be an embarrassment to her father. She's one of the finest young women I know."

"You're a close friend of the family." He put his hands together as if in prayer. "Captain, I know this is difficult for you after working with the man for thirty years—"

"Damn right, it's difficult. And unfair!"

"I'd appreciate it if you could prepare Lieutenant Fletcher, so the news on Tuesday isn't too big a shock to him."

Leopold left the office and headed for the elevator, wondering what he would say to Fletcher. He needn't have worried. When he walked into the squad room, Fletcher was at his desk reading the front page of the afternoon newspaper.

"What do you think of this?" he asked, pointing out a two-column story at the bottom of the page.

Leopold could read the headline from where he stood, *Vivian in Line for Violent Crimes Post.*

Molly knew something was wrong as soon as Leopold walked in the door. "What happened?" she asked at once.

"The chief tells me I'm retiring the end of the month."

"You knew that was—"

"Fletcher's not replacing me. They're giving the job to George Vivian."

"Vivian? From the burglary squad?"

"Exactly. Worst of all, a rumor about it ran in tonight's paper. Fletcher saw it before I could break the news to him."

"You look like you could use a drink. I'll make some cocktails."

"How was your day?" he remembered to ask. She'd been due in court on a tricky inheritance case.

"I think the judge wanted a long weekend. He adjourned the case until Tuesday." Molly had given up her criminal law practice when they'd married six years earlier, but she still practiced a fair amount of civil law. She was only thirty-eight, and there were still times when she seemed more like his daughter than his wife. "But tell me about Fletcher. My God, I thought he had that promotion locked up!"

"So did everyone. The chief gave me a lot of bull about George Vivian being ten years younger, as if that meant anything. Then he dropped Lisa's name into it."

"Lisa Fletcher?"

"He said her being on the force might cause some sort of problem."

"That's ridiculous!"

They talked about it over dinner, but there was nothing Leopold could say to give vent to his feeling of dejection and frustration. Not only was he being forced into retirement, but the man he'd groomed as his successor was being passed over in favor of someone with no experience in homicide or violent crimes.

"I should phone Carol. Maybe we can have them over on Monday."

"Fletcher's working the holiday," Leopold told her.

"Well, maybe—"

Her suggestion was cut short by the ringing telephone. Leopold answered, fearing it might be some reporter asking for a statement he didn't want to make. Instead he heard a voice he barely recognized. "Captain, this is George Vivian. How are you?"

"I—fine. How are you, Lieutenant?"

"Can't complain. Chief Ringold said he spoke with you. I'm terribly sorry the word got out to the papers before Fletcher had a chance to hear it from you or the chief."

"He wasn't too happy about it," Leopold conceded.

"That's why I'm calling. Gert and I have invited the Fletchers over for a cookout on Sunday afternoon. We were wondering if you and your wife could join us."

"Wait just a moment while I check our schedule with Molly." Leopold put down the phone and walked back to the dining room.

Molly listened to the surprise invitation and decided, "If Fletcher and Carol are going, we have to go too, if only for moral support."

"I'll hate every minute of it."

"Tell him we'll come."

Leopold returned to the phone and jotted down Vivian's address along with three o'clock, their expected arrival time. "We'll see you on Sunday," he said as he hung up.

"I'd better phone Carol when we finish dinner," Molly decided.

"Good idea."

They talked for the better part of a half hour, about the invitation and about Fletcher s frustration at being passed over for the promotion. As Molly told Leopold later, "He feels like this is the end of his career. He knows he'll be retired before Vivian ever leaves Violent Crimes."

Leopold simply stared at the floor and shook his head. "I'd rather stay on myself than see Fletcher lose that job."

"You can't stay on. You're already a month past the retirement age."

He gave her a weak smile. " 'Now is the summer of our discontent.' Who said that?"

"Shakespeare's *Richard III*, and it was winter, not summer."

"I guess it doesn't matter. We'll go Sunday. I owe that much to Fletcher, and a lot more."

George Vivian's house was a neat but modest place on the north side of the city, out near some of the better suburbs. Both cars were in the garage when Leopold and Molly arrived on Sunday afternoon, and he could see smoke rising from a backyard grill. It was obvious that either George or his wife spent a great deal of time in the garden, tending to a variety of late summer flowers whose names were foreign to Leopold. He'd met Gert Vivian once or twice at Christmas parties, and she hurried forward to greet them as they walked around the back of the house.

"So good of you to come, Captain! And Mrs. Leopold—"

"I'm Molly."

"Molly! I'm Gert." She was about Molly's age, but thinner and not as attractive to Leopold's eyes. Her dark hair was worn in a neat ponytail that seemed a bit too youthful.

"I was just admiring your flowers," Molly told her. "Those are a variety of mums, aren't they?"

While the women chatted about the garden, Leopold walked over to the barbeque grill where Vivian was just putting the steaks on. "How are you, George? Thank you for inviting us."

Vivian turned and smiled. His smile had always been warm and friendly, especially when he was trying to get a confession out of a suspect. Though Leopold didn't know him well, he'd heard good things about him. "I felt terrible about that story appearing in the paper before Fletcher knew about it. Gert suggested we have you all over this afternoon and try to get off on the right foot. I understand the chief is making the official announcement Tuesday morning."

"So he tells me." There were more sounds of greeting and he saw that Fletcher and Carol had arrived.

"Can you put the rest of these steaks on for me?" Vivian asked. "I just want to say hello."

Leopold positioned the steaks over the hot charcoal and turned as Gert Vivian arrived to ask what he wanted to drink. "Just a beer," he said.

"It's terrible, George putting you to work like this! You're our guest."

"I don't mind," he assured her, and watched as she hurried into the house again.

Fletcher walked over, trying to look relaxed and cheerful. "I didn't expect to see you this weekend, Captain."

"Well, it's a nice gesture," Leopold said, dropping his voice a notch. "I suppose we can't blame Vivian for the way things are working out."

"Lisa feels terrible. She's convinced I lost the promotion because of that trouble she was involved in."

"Nonsense! She was cleared of any wrongdoing and she's patrolling downtown." Whatever else happened, he had no intention of repeating the chief's remarks about Lisa to her father. For one thing, he wasn't convinced it was the real reason for Vivian's promotion. In the police department, as in City Hall, politics had a way of asserting itself.

They sat around with beers and cocktails until the salad was ready. Gert Vivian had really outdone herself, and smiled proudly when they complimented her. "George deserves the praise. He cooks the steaks," she insisted.

"No thanks to you!" he said with a chuckle. "Can you imagine her running out to get charcoal a half hour before the guests are due?"

"I forgot! I've had so much on my mind these last few days—"

Carol Fletcher's face darkened for an instant, perhaps thinking that it could have been her. Lieutenant Vivian must have caught the expression because he immediately changed the subject. "I'm glad you both had a free day on the holiday weekend. How do you work the holiday schedule in Violent Crimes, Captain?"

"Well, Sergeant Connie Trent is working today and Fletcher works tomorrow. I'm off this holiday but I'll be working the next—" He stopped in mid-sentence, realizing he'd be retired before another holiday appeared on the calendar.

"That sounds fair to everyone," Vivian decided, walking to the grill to turn over the steaks. "I realize I'm getting into something quite different from the burglary squad. I'll be depending on you a great deal, Lieutenant."

Fletcher grunted and took a sip of his beer. Leopold held his breath, aware that any comment Fletcher made could be bad. "I'll help in any way I can," he said finally.

The steaks were delicious, and Gert Vivian did everything she could to ease the tensions of the situation, bustling back and forth between the house and yard with fresh beer and a bowl of potato salad, all the while keeping up a stream of conversation with the other wives. It was a pleasant enough gathering for the end of summer, and nothing more was said about Vivian's promotion until Leopold and Molly were ready to leave, well after dark.

"They want me to start working with you as soon as I can," Vivian said. "At least a few hours a day, to learn how your department functions. I should go out on a couple of homicides."

"Sure," Leopold agreed. "That's the way to learn." Vivian didn't know him well enough to catch the sarcasm in the words.

Leopold was silent during the drive home. Finally Molly said, "That didn't go well, did it?"

"Oh, it was pleasant enough. If he wasn't screwing Fletcher out of his promotion, I could probably even like the guy."

"That's not his fault."

"Molly, it's got to be somebody's fault, damn it! A man like Fletcher gives his entire life to the department and this is how it all ends up!"

"What does Connie think about it?"

"I told her about it Friday after I talked to Fletcher. First time I ever saw her cry. She just kept saying how unfair it was."

"It is unfair," Molly agreed. "But Vivian and his wife seem like nice people. I hope Fletcher will give it a try before he does anything drastic."

Leopold slept late on the holiday, and he was just beginning to rouse himself when Molly came into the bedroom fully dressed. "It's nearly ten," she scolded. "You should be up. Fletcher's on the phone."

"Isn't he working?"

Leopold glanced out the window, pleased to see another sunny day, and picked up the extension. "Enjoying your holiday?" Fletcher asked.

"I was until now. What's up?"

"Sergeant Patrick O'Mera. Do you know him?"

"Slightly. He's one of Vivian's people on the burglary squad, isn't he?"

"They found him early this morning in his car. He'd been shot once through the head."

"I'm on my way," Leopold told him and hung up. He wondered if anyone had notified George Vivian yet. He phoned the lieutenant's number but got an answering machine and hung up.

"You're going in on the holiday?" Molly asked.

"One of Vivian's sergeants was found shot to death. I don't know when I'll be back."

There was a gloomy intensity about the squad room when Leopold reached it. He'd seen the mood before when a cop had been killed. Nobody said much, as if they were all thinking it could have been them. Fletcher was on the phone as he entered. When he hung up, Leopold asked, "What's the story on O'Mera?"

"His car was in the parking lot of a branch bank on Maple Street, over on the north side. With the holiday weekend no one paid any attention to it until this morning when a patrol car pulled up to check it out. The officer found O'Mera slumped across the front seat, dead. The medical examiner just told me the time of death was probably mid-afternoon yesterday, but we can pin it down a little closer than that. O'Mera was off duty but on call. He phoned in around three-thirty to say he was going out but would be back shortly. Apparently he drove over to the bank parking lot to meet someone and they shot him."

Leopold shook his head sadly. "I didn't know him well but he seemed like a good cop. Any family?"

"Divorced. Two children moved to Virginia with the mother. George Vivian is trying to reach her."

"Then he knows about it. I tried to reach him."

"I phoned him right away, Captain. O'Mera was his man."

"Yes, of course. That was the right thing to do." Leopold grimaced. "O'Mera got it just about the time Vivian was taking our steaks off the fire."

"I hadn't thought of that."

"We need to know about his friends, and if he was working on any special cases."

"He was pretty friendly with Bill Carmichael. They were sergeants together on the squad. Carmichael was the one who took his call yesterday."

"I'll talk to him. Any sort of evidence in the car? How about the murder weapon?"

"Probably a .38, but not O'Mera's. His was in his belt holster and hadn't been fired." The detective squads weren't yet equipped with the new 9-millimeter semi-automatics that patrolmen carried.

"Anything in his pockets?"

Fletcher hesitated. "It probably doesn't mean anything—"

"What is it?"

He pushed a plain white business-size envelope across the desk. Leopold recognized its grey smudges as fingerprint powder. "This was in his inside jacket pocket."

Leopold lifted the flap and saw the thin sheaf of hundred-dollar bills. "How much?"

"A thousand dollars."

"Any prints?"

"None."

"What do you think?"

Fletcher shrugged. "You always think of drug money or a bribe of some sort."

"It's hardly enough to be drug money these days."

"And he didn't work Narcotics anyway."

"No," Leopold agreed. "Let me go talk to Bill Carmichael."

He'd known Sergeant Carmichael for more than a decade, and the stocky redhead was one of Leopold's few friends in the department outside the Violent Crimes Squad itself. Now, entering the burglary squad room down the hall from his own, he saw Bill deep in somber conversation with two of his men. "How are you, Bill?" he asked.

Carmichael shook hands. "Holidays are always quiet here," he said, avoiding an answer. "It's the day after, when people return home, that we get all our calls."

"I heard about Pat O'Mera."

"Yeah, isn't it a hell of a way to go?"

"What was he working on?"

"Nothing special. Nickel and dime stuff."

The other two detectives had drifted away, aware that Leopold was there in an official capacity. "Fletcher tells me his wife moved south with the kids."

"Yeah."

"Did he have anyone else? A girlfriend?"

"Sometimes he went out with Sunny Novak. She used to be one of the 911 operators for emergency calls. Know her?"

Leopold shook his head. "On my squad they usually end up with emergency room nurses, but I suppose the burglary detail doesn't make it to Emergency too often. Were they living together?"

"Not so far as I know." He walked over to the desk that O'Mera had occupied, flipped through the Rolodex and removed a card. "Here's her address and phone number if you want it."

"Thanks." Leopold was about to mention the thousand dollars but decided that that information should go to Lieutenant Vivian first. "What did your boss say? Is he coming down?"

"He phoned right after Fletcher broke the news to him. Said he'd be in before noon."

Leopold glanced at his watch. "He should be here any minute, then. What about burglars that Pat sent away? Any of them get out recently?"

"I suppose they're getting out all the time. Let me check on a few of the more likely names for you."

George Vivian came in then, nodding to the other men and walking directly up to Leopold and Carmichael. His open, friendly demeanor of the previous day had given way to an all-business attitude. "Can I speak with you alone, Captain?"

"Certainly. Let's go back to my office."

Vivian paused and told Carmichael, "I spoke with Pat's ex-wife on the phone, but she's not coming up for the funeral. Says the kids start school on Wednesday and doesn't want to disrupt things with them."

Carmichael sighed. "Pat won't miss her."

They went down the hall and into Leopold's glass-walled office. "It's a terrible thing," Vivian said, pulling up a chair. "Just yesterday

I was trying to decide whether to suggest Pat or Bill Carmichael as my replacement when I move over here."

"The chief doesn't always listen to suggestions."

Vivian shifted uneasily in his chair. "Look, I know you wanted Fletcher to take over, and he would have been a good man for the job. But it was the chief's decision and he made it. Are we going to start off with a feud?"

"Who's feuding?"

"I asked Fletcher about the case just now and he wouldn't tell me a thing. He said you were still in charge."

"Well, I suppose I am, for the rest of September."

"Pat O'Mera was one of my men. Under the circumstances I'd like to be in on this with you. All the way."

Leopold picked up the envelope and handed it across the desk. "Maybe you can start with this. It was found in his jacket pocket. There were no prints on it."

"Money?" Vivian asked, peering inside.

"A thousand dollars. I want you to be honest with me, George. Were there ever any rumors of bribes or payoffs in your department?"

"Hell no! What is this? Some sort of attempt to discredit me? Are you planning to tell Chief Ringold that the burglary squad was corrupt under my command?" His face flushed with anger.

"Nothing of the sort," Leopold answered calmly. "You wanted to be part of the investigation so I'm telling you what we have."

Vivian tossed down the envelope with the money and tried to recover his composure. "I know nothing of any payoffs or bribes involving my department. This envelope alone proves nothing. What else do you have?"

"O'Mera was on call yesterday and he phoned Carmichael to say he was going out for a while. This was around three-thirty."

"He didn't have to call in. The holiday weekend is usually slow, and he would have been wearing his beeper anyway."

"Regardless, he did call in and talk to Carmichael. Then he drove to that bank parking lot, probably no more than five minutes from his house with the slim Sunday traffic. I think it's obvious he planned to meet someone there. Either that person gave him the money or he brought it to give the person. Instead, he was shot once at close range, probably with a .38 revolver since Fletcher made no mention of ejected cartridges. If the car windows were closed, the sound of the shot wouldn't have carried far enough in that empty lot to attract attention."

"Any possibility of suicide?"

"None. His service revolver was in its holster, unfired. There was no other weapon."

George Vivian nodded. "I appreciate the information, Captain. Forgive me for my outburst earlier. This thing has really shaken me."

"It's shaken all of us. No one likes to see a good cop gunned down." Leopold stood up, signaling that he had work to do. "And I'll speak to Fletcher, tell him you're working with us on this."

"I'd appreciate it."'

Before he could call Fletcher into the office, Bill Carmichael appeared at the door. "I said I'd check on some burglars that Pat sent away. Here's one who was released about six weeks ago. He was a nasty sort. You might want to check on him."

Leopold accepted the file and glanced at it. Kevin Kane, age twenty-eight, just released after serving three and a half years of a five-year sentence for burglary and possession of an unlicensed fire-arm. "Thanks. We'll look into it." He set the file aside. "While you're here, Bill, I need to ask you about your phone conversation with O'Mera yesterday. Tell me everything he said."

"Well, it wasn't much. He called just before three-thirty, and when I answered he said, 'This is Pat. I have to go out now, but I'll be back soon.' Then he hung up. That was it."

"You're sure those were his words?"

"Pretty sure. I said, 'Hi, Packy,' because that's what I called him, but he kept right on talking like he didn't hear me."

"You're sure it was his voice?"

"Positive. I worked with the guy every day."

"Thanks, Bill. I'll let you know if anything develops with this Kevin Kane."

By Tuesday morning it was the top story in the newspaper, and Leopold, Fletcher, and Connie Trent were all working on it, with a bit more assistance from Lieutenant Vivian than any of them wanted.

"He acts like you're already gone and he's in charge!" Connie complained.

"I told him he could work with us. Pat O'Mera was his man. He told me he was getting ready to suggest either Pat or Bill Carmichael for promotion after he moves over here. Naturally he's anxious to get to the bottom of it."

"All right. What angle do you want me working on?"

Leopold shuffled through the reports on his desk. "I'm going out to talk with Sunny Novak. We still don't have a line on this paroled burglar, Kevin Kane. Check with his parole officer and try to get an address for him."

Sunny Novak had gone from being a 911 operator to serving as a hostess at the city's swank University Club. She was tall and attractive, with a winning smile and the correct personality for escorting wealthy businessmen and lawyers to their tables. Leopold waited until the lunch hour had ended before approaching her.

"Miss Novak?"

"Yes?"

He showed his ID. "Captain Leopold, Violent Crimes. We're investigating the murder of Patrick O'Mera on Sunday. You probably read about it."

"Yes."

"Is there someplace we can talk?"

The dining room was all but empty and she led him to a nearby table. "Would you like some coffee, Captain?"

"Thank you, that would be nice."

She brought over two cups and saucers and then returned with a polished silver pot. "There, now. What can I help you with?"

"I understand you were a friend of Pat O'Mera's."

"We knew each other, I met him when I worked at headquarters, answering 911 calls."

"Did you have a romantic relationship?"

She shrugged and took a sip of coffee. "Sure, for nearly a year. Nothing wrong with that. We were both divorced and he was a nice guy."

"When did you break up?"

"About six months ago."

"Mind telling me why?"

"I guess he got interested in someone else. Those things happen. It was no big deal."

"You weren't jealous or upset?"

"Oh, for about a week, I guess. I got over it." Her green eyes suddenly flashed with apprehension. "Hey, you don't think I shot him, do you? I haven't seen him in months."

Leopold tried to calm her. "We have to pursue all possible leads. There's nothing to link you to the killing at this time. For the record, though, I have to ask where you were on Sunday afternoon."

"Alone in my apartment. I was painting the kitchen." As he got up to leave she asked, "When's the funeral?"

"Tomorrow morning, ten o'clock."

"I should go to it. We had some good times together."

Wednesday morning was warm and muggy, the sort of late-summer weather that frequently seems to occur on the first day back to school. Molly got out her best black dress and accompanied Leopold to the funeral. Fletcher and Carol were there too, along with Gert and George Vivian. At the cemetery, standing by the casket before it was lowered into the grave, he spotted Sunny Novak at the edge of the crowd of mourners, not far from Sergeant Carmichael.

Chief Ringold came over to Leopold after the graveside service. "How's the investigation going? I'd like to tell the press that an arrest is near."

"I wish that were true. I have Fletcher and Sergeant Trent working on it full time, along with me. Lieutenant Vivian is assisting us too."

The chief nodded. "I postponed the official announcement of his promotion until after the funeral, out of respect to Sergeant O'Mera, but I'll be holding a news conference this afternoon at two. I'd like you to be there since he'll be taking your place in Violent Crimes."

The last thing Leopold felt like doing that afternoon was joining in the hoopla for his successor, but he could see no way out of it. "I'll be there," he promised.

As they walked together toward the cars, Leopold asked Connie about the ex-convict, Kevin Kane. "His parole officer just got back to me this morning with Kane's address. Do you want me to question him?"

Fletcher interrupted. "Captain, I've got an idea that I'd like to pursue with Connie this afternoon. It involves some of the houses bordering that big parking lot for the bank and shopping plaza."

"The uniform men already talked to the neighbors. No one noticed a thing."

Fletcher fidgeted. "I know. I just have this idea—"

"Go to it, Fletcher, I trust your judgment. Take Connie with you. I'll question Kevin Kane myself."

He decided Fletcher might just want to be out of the building when Chief Ringold made his announcement. If that was the case, he couldn't blame him. Maybe he felt like getting drunk with Connie in a bar.

At two o'clock he was in the auditorium of the city's public safety building across the street from headquarters. The place hadn't existed when Leopold became captain of the homicide squad, as it was called in those days, but for the past two decades it had been used to announce all sorts of government promotions, especially those connected with the police and fire departments. There were only a few dozen people present, plus the television news cameras, when Chief Ringold strode to the microphone to make his announcement. Leopold was on stage, seated next to Gert Vivian, while her husband was on the other side.

"A big day for you both," he whispered to her.

"George has worked hard for this."

Chief Ringold opened with a tribute to Leopold's thirty years as head of the department. "Perhaps we'll never see his like again," the chief rambled on, "but we think we have a strong replacement in Lieutenant George Vivian, whose long and distinguished service on the burglary squad is well known to the community. Today I am announcing Lieutenant Vivian's promotion to captain and his appointment as commander of the Violent Crimes Squad. This appointment will be effective September thirtieth, the date of Captain Leopold's retirement from the department."

There was polite applause from the small crowd as the chief finished his announcement. Photographers and video cameras moved in to film the event. Chief Ringold shook hands with Vivian, Gert gave him a kiss for the cameras, and finally he and Leopold were photographed together. It was one of the low points of Leopold's career. Thirty years, for this? To surrender his job to a man he didn't really respect that much?

He tried to smile through it all, but when the photographers were finished he slipped quietly off the stage and out of the auditorium.

Kevin Kane was working at a car wash across town, and on this sunny Wednesday afternoon business was good. Leopold waited until there was a lull in the line of customers and approached him. Kane was a small man who'd had a reputation as a burglar of being able to slip through the narrowest of openings. Leopold showed his badge and said he had a few questions. "Can we go outside and talk?"

"Hey, you're not on the burglary squad!"

"No, I'm Violent Crime. Homicide, in this case."

"What's this about?"

They walked outside into the afternoon sun. "Sergeant O'Mera is the one who sent you away, right?"

"Yeah. I see he got his, too."

"Last Sunday afternoon. What were you doing then?"

"I went to a movie."

"Alone?"

"Alone. Hell, you think I killed him?"

"You might have resented those years in prison."

"The only thing I ever resented about O'Mera was the way he used to inflate the burglary reports."

"What do you mean?"

"Hell, I'd make off with a little cash and some jewelry, maybe a gun if I found one. Next day I'd read that the burglar got twice as much loot, things like computers and VCRs that I'd never bother lugging around."

"Did you tell the police about this?"

"I wasn't about to tell them when they didn't know I pulled the job. When O'Mera finally grabbed me, I told him about it. He said I was lying and that's when I knew he was the one who was taking the stuff."

Leopold had heard stories about crooked cops all his life. Coming from ex-cons, they weren't too reliable. "How could he steal things at a crime scene without anybody noticing?"

"You think it never happens? I've seen cops loading up their cars with Scotch after a burglary at a bar! If there's stuff scattered around in a bedroom, chances are the homeowner calls the police before he takes an inventory. It's easy for a cop to slip something extra into his pocket. Who's to know? The insurance company pays off and nobody really loses."

"What about the big stuff you mentioned?"

"He has a friend follow him to the crime scene with a car or even a van. If the property owners aren't around, the uniformed cops aren't likely to say anything. Maybe he even cuts them in."

"And Pat O'Mera was doing this?"

"Sure! He probably even stole drugs sometimes."

"If you resented him enough you might have killed him."

Kevin Kane merely laughed. "You try proving that!"

Leopold knew it wouldn't be easy. O'Mera wasn't the sort of cop to sit in a car with an ex-con and let him draw a gun without a struggle. But maybe there was a way to verify his story.

"Keep your nose clean," he told Kane as he left.

Sunny Novak was hostessing that evening at the University Club. Business was slow on the weeknight and Leopold had no trouble getting a few minutes alone with her.

"Now what?" she asked.

"I'm looking into a report that Pat O'Mera sometimes stole things from burglary scenes, before the property owners could determine just what was taken in the original break-in."

"I wouldn't know about that."

He decided to stretch the truth a bit. "The report says that a woman sometimes showed up and took away some items that O'Mera put in her car. That wouldn't have been you, would it?"

She moistened her lips. "Do I need a lawyer?"

"Look, I'm investigating a homicide, not a burglary. I just want to know if it's true."

"And if you're wearing a wire anything I say will turn up in court."

He sighed. People watched too much television these days. "I'm not wearing a wire, but if it'll make you feel easier you don't have to say a word. I'll ask you one question and all you have to do is nod or shake your head."

"Let's hear the question."

"Do you have any knowledge that Sergeant Patrick O'Mera ever stole anything from the scene of a burglary he was investigating?"

She hesitated, trying to read something in his eyes. Then she gave the faintest of nods. "Thank you, Miss Novak," he said quietly.

Leopold went back to his office. He hoped that Fletcher and Connie would be there but they were still out. So was George Vivian. He got out the file and checked the inventory of O'Mera's pockets. Wallet, keys, change, handkerchief, plain white envelope containing a thousand dollars in cash, .38 service revolver in belt holster, beeper, ballpoint pen, notebook. Nothing unusual. No gloves. Who'd be wearing gloves on a warm September day?

Leopold went home and had a late dinner with Molly. He refused to talk about the case. "What's bothering you?" she asked at last. "Retirement?"

"Oh, I suppose I could cope with that. Most people do. It's just that things aren't working out the way they should."

"You mean Captain Vivian?"

"Do you have to call him that?" he asked harshly.

"I'm sorry."

"I didn't mean to use that tone of voice."

"I know how you feel. I only wish there was something I could do."

He managed to smile. "You do it just by being here."

Thursday morning Fletcher was waiting for him in the squad room. "I think we've got it, Captain."

"Got what?" Leopold asked, glancing at the morning report on his desk.

"Pat O'Mera's killer."

Leopold's head jerked up. "What?"

Fletcher sat down and took some photographs from his pocket. "The other day when I was out to that bank parking lot, I looked around and saw all the yards on the next street that backed up to it. With the shopping plaza it fills most of the block. There were houses across the street too. I remembered that we were at a cookout Sunday afternoon at the time of the murder, and I wondered if some of those families might have been having backyard gatherings for the Labor Day weekend. This time Connie and I didn't ask if they noticed anything in the parking lot. We asked if they'd been out in their yard that afternoon taking pictures."

Leopold reached for the photographs. "Let's see them."

"It was only one family quite a distance away, and they hadn't even picked up their photos yet. Connie did it for them."

Leopold stared down at the color pictures of small children playing, a man in a joke apron grilling hamburgers, some older people—grandparents?—on a picnic bench with the house behind them. Another photo showed a chain-link fence at the back of the yard with the empty parking lot beyond. In the last photo two cars, mere shapes in the distance, could be seen in the lot behind an attractive woman in white shorts, posed by the fence with two of the children.

"The one on the left is O'Mera's car," Fletcher explained. "The one on the right is almost certainly the killer's car. Connie is having that portion of the negative blown up as large as she can. We can't make out any people through the car windows, but I think we can get the number on that license plate."

Leopold looked up and smiled. "Damn fine detective work, Fletcher."

"Think it'll tell us who killed O'Mera?"

"I already know who killed him, but this picture is going to convince a jury I'm right."

When Connie arrived an hour later with the enlargement, Leopold inspected it briefly and then returned it to its envelope. He took it down the hall to show George Vivian, but Carmichael told him the captain had taken a vacation day. "Getting ready for his new job, I guess."

Leopold nodded. "I guess he deserves a day off. I'll catch him at home."

He drove out to the modest house on the north side of the city. It looked the same as it had on Sunday afternoon, with both cars in the garage, but this time he could see no one in the backyard. When he rang the bell, George Vivian answered almost at once.

"Leopold! It's good to see you. Come on in."

"Sorry to bother you on your day off, but it's important. We've got something on Pat's killing."

"What is it?" He led the way into the family room and they sat down. Leopold could hear Gert vacuuming upstairs.

"I have to run through my reasoning on this, George."

Vivian snorted. "Your reasoning's fine, but we need something that'll stand up in court."

"Hear me out. The thing that bothered me about this case was Pat O'Mera's phone call to the squad room on Sunday afternoon. There was no reason for him to tell Carmichael he was leaving the house, not when he was wearing his beeper. Besides that, he simply gave his message and hung up. When Carmichael tried to say something he kept on talking."

"What does that prove?"

Leopold leaned forward on his chair. "According to Carmichael, O'Mera said, 'This is Pat. I have to go out now but I'll be back soon.' He didn't let Carmichael speak, and referred to himself as Pat, a name Carmichael never called him. Don't you see, George? It was a recording, the sort of message O'Mera might have left on a friend's telephone answering machine."

"Why would he call Carmichael and play a recording?"

"He wouldn't, but his killer would, if an alibi was necessary."

Vivian frowned. "Do you think Bill Carmichael is lying about the call?"

"No. If he were lying he'd have invented a two-way conversation with O'Mera, not this strange one-sided thing. And there's more. We found that envelope in O'Mera's pocket containing a thousand dollars."

"Are you back to that? I told you there were no bribes or payoffs on my squad."

"Someone wanted to make it look like it, though. The trouble is, there were no fingerprints on the envelope or the money. None. That meant it had been wiped clean. O'Mera didn't have gloves with him, so he couldn't have put the money in his own pocket without at least leaving smudges. The killer put it there, George, to make it look like some sort of corruption scandal. So what do we have? A carefully planned murder that probably had some motive other than corruption. A murder that probably took place *before* that phone call to the squad room around three-thirty. Remember, the medical examiner simply placed the time of death at mid-afternoon. Remember too that O'Mera didn't draw his gun, and that he was probably shot with a .38, similar to his service revolver."

"You're trying to pin it on another cop, aren't you? Bill Carmichael? Is that it?"

"I already told you why it couldn't be Carmichael. He'd have told us a different story on the phone call. I questioned O'Mera's former girlfriend and a burglar he sent away. Neither had an alibi for Sunday afternoon, so paradoxically they must be innocent. If the killer phoned in with a recording of O'Mera's voice it was because he *did* have an alibi for three-thirty and after."

George Vivian gave a snort. "I had an alibi for that time. We were all here at my house."

"Exactly, George."

"What?"

"I want to run a ballistic test on your service revolver."

Vivian was on his feet. "Are you out of your mind, Leopold?"

He opened the envelope he'd been carrying and brought out the enlarged photo. "This is your car, parked in the bank lot next to O'Mera's car."

"My car, my gun? You're accusing me of killing Pat O'Mera!"

Leopold closed his eyes for just an instant. He'd been through these scenes so many times. Was this to be the last one? "I need to have the gun, George."

"It's upstairs."

"I know you didn't kill Pat. O'Mera was taking things from burglary scenes and selling them. Sometimes he used a lady friend to drive the extra loot away before anyone checked on what was stolen. He dropped his old girlfriend for a new one about six months ago. It was the girlfriend who killed him because her husband had just gotten a nice promotion and she wanted to break it off with O'Mera. He threatened to tell her husband about their affair and that she helped him skim off some extra loot from burglaries."

"Gert—?" It was barely a whisper.

"It was her idea to invite us Sunday afternoon for a cookout. She was the one who had to dash out for a bag of charcoal just before our arrival. She was the one who was in and out of the house so much, making it easy to play a tape of O'Mera's voice that he'd once left on her answering machine. She killed O'Mera with your gun when she supposedly went for the charcoal, then came back and concocted her alibi with that tape while we were all out in the yard."

Then Gert Vivian was standing in the doorway staring at them, holding the revolver loosely in one hand. Leopold saw her, and knew he had to draw his weapon. Instead he stood up and walked slowly toward her. Perhaps this was the way it was all going to end, with a bullet through his head, the way Pat O'Mera had died.

"The thousand dollars was my cut of what he'd stolen," she said quietly. "I gave it back to him after I shot him. I wanted to be clean again. For you, George. For your job." She looked down at the weapon in her hand and held it out to Leopold. "I think this is what you're looking for. I cleaned it afterward, of course, but the bullet will match."

It was Fletcher who brought him the news two days later. "Vivian has handed in his resignation. He's quitting the department."

"I'm sorry it had to happen like this," Leopold said.

"Chief Ringold offered me the job. Captain of the Violent Crimes Squad. I felt like telling him to shove it."

Leopold glanced at him. "I hope to hell you didn't!"

"I told him I'd take it. I even thanked him. God, Leopold, what's happened to me?"

"You've just inherited my job." He put his arm around Fletcher's shoulders. "And I couldn't be happier."

Tod Baxter was a very ordinary-looking man, average in height and weight, middle-aged, with graying hair and a gap-toothed smile. He might have seen his double any day of the week among the corporate lawyers lunching at the University Club or even among the homeless men who spent their nights sleeping beneath the Broad Street bridge. Baxter himself was neither a lawyer nor homeless. He worked for his older brother Sam at the lumberyard, and came home each night to the small apartment he'd rented since his divorce three years earlier.

On this particular day, one of those October Saturdays when summer seems to be struggling for a brief comeback among the golden leaves, Tod sat at his kitchen table and thought about Marcy McGregor. More specifically, he thought about Marcy McGregor's husband, Charlie. He knew now, if he hadn't known before, that Charlie McGregor would never allow a divorce, that he intended his marriage to Marcy to last until death. Thinking about that, and knowing he could not go on living without her, he rose from the chair and went to a closet in the bedroom. There was a large box on the top shelf, filled with assorted treasures from his former life. He'd packed them up and brought it from his house at the time of the divorce, and hadn't thought of it since.

Now, looking through these memories of a happier time, he ignored most of them until he came upon the Beretta automatic pistol he'd acquired once in a Las Vegas pawn shop, buying it on a whim and tucking it away in his luggage for the flight home. The slide still seemed to function well, and he still had the box of bullets he'd purchased for target shooting but never used. He loaded the weapon, jacking a cartridge into the chamber, and put the safety catch on. Then he slipped the weapon into the pocket of his jacket and went out to the car. The thing would be decided today, one way or the other.

Baxter drove across town to the McGregor home in a fashionable area. Being a Saturday, there was a good chance Charlie would be there along with Marcy, and that was why he'd brought the gun. As he pulled up and parked in front of the house, he could see both of them working together in the backyard. Charlie was cutting the grass with his power mower while Marcy trimmed a hedge.

She saw him first and hurried forward, as if to warn him away before her husband was aware of his presence. But the mower stopped immediately and Charlie McGregor fell into step behind her. "What do you want here, Baxter?" he called out. "You're not welcome here!"

"Tod—," Marcy began, but then she saw the gun. "My God, what are you—"

Her husband saw it too and paused in midstep. He started to say something, but Tod Baxter had listened to enough words already. He aimed the little Beretta and fired point-blank at McGregor's chest.

Marcy screamed as her husband clutched his chest and went down. "The damn fool shot me! Marcy, call the police—"

Tod Baxter could see he was bleeding badly. He grabbed Marcy with his free hand and shouted, "Come on! We have to get out of here now!"

"Are you mad, Tod? I'm not going anyplace with you! My God, there's blood all over—"

A neighbor had appeared from somewhere, approaching gingerly and ready to dive for cover. Marcy was on her knees by her husband, trying to stem the flow of blood from his chest wound. He was gasping, close to losing consciousness. Baxter turned and started running toward his car.

Then he heard a siren, off somewhere in the distance, growing louder.

He turned and sprinted away from the car, into a small stand of evergreens. He realized he was still holding the Beretta in his right hand and he threw it to the ground. The siren grew louder and then stopped. Another took up the cry, coming from the opposite direction. He tried to hide behind a tree, to make himself invisible.

"Over there!" someone shouted.

He crouched down, squeezing his eyes shut as he'd done so many times in his childhood. This was a game of hide-and-seek, nothing more.

Then he heard the voice, very close. "Police! Freeze or I'll shoot!"

Charlie McGregor did not die that day, or the next. In critical condition from a bullet wound near the heart, he hovered between life and death. Tod Baxter was arraigned before a judge on Monday morning and bail was set at a half-million dollars. Later, in the visiting room at the county jail, he met with his brother Sam.

"Can't we get the bail reduced? I'll go crazy locked up like this for months awaiting trial!"

Sam Baxter, a dour, balding man eight years older than his brother, shook his head in frustration. "Your lawyer says they're afraid you'll run away. You're divorced, with no real roots in the community."

"No roots! I've lived here most of my life! I've got a job with you and you're certainly a reputable citizen."

"Kid, you tried to kill someone. You tried to kill your girlfriend's husband. Maybe you even succeeded. He's hovering between life and death. If he dies within a year from that wound, it's murder."

"Look, you did a damned foolish thing. You're going to prison for it and there's nothing I or anyone else can do to save you. God, Tod, you're forty-one years old! You chase after twenty-eight-year-old married women as if it was your constitutional right!"

"Marcy's not just any woman. She's special."

Sam Baxter sighed. "How can I talk to you when you're like this?"

"Can't you get me out?" Tod pleaded.

"Where in hell would I get a half-million dollars?"

"The lumber business must be worth that much."

"I'm going to put up my business to get you out of jail?"

"Hell, Sam, I'm not going to run away. I realize I have to pay for what I did. I just need some time to get used to the idea."

Sam shook his head, but it wasn't a final no. "Look, I can't promise anything. I'll talk it over with Rose tonight. It's got to be her decision, too."

"Thanks, Sam."

Fletcher decided during his first month as head of the Violent Crimes Squad that he would never get used to being called "Captain." Every time Connie Trent or one of the other detectives uttered the word in his hearing he turned around, looking to see if Leopold had just strolled into the squad room.

"Captain," Connie was saying this time, "do you want some coffee?"

"I do, but I don't expect you to get it for me."

She laughed as she brought him a cup. "I used to do it for Leopold."

"Things are different now, Connie. We both have to realize that."

"I think we'll manage." She sat down across the desk from him and crossed her legs. After the weekend's good weather the days had turned cooler.

"You probably heard about Tod Baxter. He's out on bail."

"Bail! You mean he raised a half-million dollars?"

"His brother put up the lumber business."

Connie Trent sighed. "Do you think he'll have another try at McGregor?"

"The judge specifically ordered him to stay away from the hospital and the McGregor home. Still, we might want to put an officer at the hospital, at least for the next few nights."

"I'll take care of it," Connie assured him. "When is the grand jury getting the case?"

"Next week, I imagine. I'm going to stop at the hospital this afternoon and see if McGregor is strong enough to make a statement."

"What about the wife?"

"She's not talking yet. Claims she didn't see a thing. Her back was turned when she heard the shot, which is a damned lie according to the neighbors."

"She's keeping her options open in case hubby kicks the bucket."

"I suppose so. She doesn't want a dead husband and a jailed lover."

Connie finished her coffee and stood up. "Back to work."

"How's the firebombing case coming?"

"I'm working with the Arson Squad on it. If they come through with the evidence I should be able to make an arrest by tomorrow."

"Good!" The city was changing, with rival groups of immigrants challenging each other's turf. He supposed it had always been that way, especially in East Coast cities, but in previous generations things were more likely to be settled with fists at the neighborhood bar. Now there were firebombs and assault weapons. And innocent bystanders. At least the Mafia used to brag that they only killed their own. Now the rules had changed, or more accurately there were no rules. A sixty-year-old woman had died in the firebombing, only because she was in the wrong place at the wrong time.

Such was not the case with Charlie McGregor, however. He'd been the intended victim from the start. A few hours later, as Fletcher stood outside the intensive care unit with the doctor, he'd put his other cases out of his mind and was concentrating on this one. "You can't see him," Dr. Greenwald told him. "He's much too weak."

"I'd like to get a statement before the case goes before the grand jury, Doctor."

"Give us a day or two, Captain. Once he's out of danger, we can start building up his strength."

"Then you think he'll make it?"

"Barring infections, he's got a better than even chance. The first forty-eight hours were the crucial ones."

"But I can't see him yet?"

Dr. Greenwald gave him a firm but understanding shake of the head. "Check with me tomorrow."

As he started down the hall to the elevators, Fletcher saw Marcy McGregor walking his way. She was wearing a fancy green dress perhaps better suited to a garden party than a hospital visit, but he was never one to understand women's fashions. "Hello, there," he greeted her. "I'm Captain Fletcher of the Violent Crimes Squad. I spoke with you on Saturday."

"I remember," she replied. "Have you been here questioning Charlie?"

"The doctor wouldn't let me see him."

"I should hope not!"

"When he's able to talk, a statement about the shooting would be helpful. The case will be presented to the grand jury next week."

"I don't understand why you need it. You have the neighbors' testimony."

"It would help to have something from the victim," he said, pausing an instant before adding, "especially since your back was turned at the crucial moment."

"Do you think I put him up to it?"

"I don't know. There have been reports that you're quite friendly with Tod Baxter. You've been seen around the city together."

"He took me on a tour of his brother's lumberyard. Is that a sin or something?"

"Of course not. Still, he must have had some motive for trying to kill your husband."

"You'll have to ask him about that."

Fletcher had asked him, and gotten nowhere. Baxter mentioned a vague disagreement. He'd taken the gun to frighten McGregor and it had discharged accidentally. No one believed the story, and the district attorney felt sure he could prove in court that Baxter and Marcy McGregor had been having an adulterous affair. Baxter had fled and tried to hide after firing the shot, and that alone could be used against him.

"Thank you, Mrs. McGregor," Fletcher told her and moved on toward the elevators. It was still mid-afternoon and rather than head directly home, he decided to stop off at Leopold's place.

Leopold had retired in September, just past his sixty-fifth birthday, following some thirty years as head of the city's Homicide and Violent Crimes Squads. Following an early marriage that ended badly, he'd remarried late in life. Now he and Molly lived in a pleasant condominium on the shore of Bradford Bay in the eastern suburbs, having just moved there from their city place. Molly was twenty-seven years younger than her husband, and at the peak of her career as a civil and corporate attorney. She was still a lovely woman as she approached middle age, and Fletcher envied Leopold the joys of retirement. Still, on this day he found his old boss alone down by the water, staring out at the calm surface of the bay.

"Hello, Fletcher. It's good to see you."

"How are things going, Captain?"

Leopold smiled. "I'm not the captain anymore, Fletcher. You are."

"Hell, you'll always be Captain to me, like an ex-president is always President. How are things going? We want to have you and Molly over for dinner one of these nights."

"Give Molly a call. I'm free any time she is."

"Is she here now?"

"No, she never gets home till six or later. It's a busy season for her."

"Do you have things to pass the time?"

"I've been thinking I should get a boat, but maybe I'm too old to take up sailing."

"You should try writing your memoirs," Fletcher suggested.

"Nobody'd be interested in them, except maybe some of the killers I helped put away." He seemed to make a conscious effort to brighten up. "How about you, Fletcher? What are you working on?"

"The usual things. This McGregor shooting was big news last weekend, but it didn't call for much detective work. Baxter's out on bail now."

"How's Connie?"

"Good. She misses you. When we set up dinner maybe I'll invite her too."

"Well, I have to find something to do with myself. The mayor appointed me to a commission on public safety, but it only meets once a month."

They strolled along the shore for a time, talking about people they both knew, and then Leopold decided to go back inside. "It gets chilly out here by the water in the late afternoon."

"Take care of yourself," Fletcher said. "I'll stop by again, and we'll set up that dinner sometime late next week."

The next morning in the squad room, he told Connie Trent about his visit to Leopold. "He was friendly enough, but I could tell he was bored. He needs something to do, Connie."

She nodded in understanding. "Most people, when they retire, go traveling. Or there are children and grandchildren to help fill the time. Leopold has no children, and Molly's still working. His days are just empty."

"I think I'll phone Molly and see what she thinks about it. I've been Leopold's friend for thirty years and I want to help if I can."

"Oh, there's a message on your desk. Dr. Greenwald phoned this morning from the hospital."

"Not bad news, I hope."

"McGregor is conscious and coherent. The doctor says you can see him for five minutes."

"I'd better go right over before he changes his mind."

Marcy was at McGregor's bedside when Fletcher arrived, and he waited a moment until she left. Then he entered the cubicle in the

Intensive Care Unit. "I'm Captain Fletcher from the Violent Crimes Squad. Can you hear me, Mr. McGregor?"

The patient still had a tube up his nose and an intravenous line attached to a vein in the back of his hand. "I hear you," he said, fluttering his eyelids.

"Do you feel well enough to make a statement about the shooting?"

"Nothing much to tell. I was cutting the grass and he pulled up in his car." He paused a moment to take a breath. "I told him to get out and he pulled a gun and shot me."

"Mr. McGregor, I'm going to tape record your words. Later, when you're feeling better, we'll need a more formal statement. For purposes of this tape, will you tell me your name?"

"Charlie McGregor."

Fletcher went through the other formalities, recording the time and place of the interview. Then he asked McGregor about the shooting and recorded his response. The nurse had entered to signal that his five minutes were up.

"Two quick questions. Who shot you, Mr. McGregor? Did you recognize him?"

"Of course. It was Tod Baxter."

"Why did he shoot you?"

"He was having an affair with my wife. That was the only way he could get her away from me."

The nurse was tugging on his sleeve. Fletcher turned off the tape machine. "Thank you, Mr. McGregor. I'll be back when you're feeling stronger."

Marcy McGregor was waiting in the hall. "I hope you didn't tire him out, Captain."

"I kept it brief. He seems to be recovering well. By next week he'll be able to give us a more complete statement about exactly what happened."

"Do you really need this?" she asked, her face twisted with indecision.

"Everything will have to come out in court. If you wish to amend your statement—"

"I do!" she decided suddenly. "I saw the whole thing. I'll tell you exactly what happened."

She'd made her decision. Charlie McGregor was going to live, and she'd decided to stick with a winner.

Saturday morning's newspaper carried the story that Marcy McGregor had decided to testify against her lover. The case would go before the grand jury the following week. It did, on Tuesday, and Baxter was indicted on charges of felonious assault, illegal possession of a firearm, and attempted murder. Now that McGregor appeared to be out of danger, Baxter's lawyer argued for a reduction of bail, but the judge kept it at $500,000.

The following Monday, Connie Trent came into Fletcher's office. "I've located Tod Baxter's former wife. She's using her maiden name again—Grace Smiley. Do you want to talk with her?"

"Wouldn't do any harm. Ask her if she could come in this week."

Grace Smiley arrived on Wednesday morning. She was a woman in her late thirties who might have been fairly attractive. It was difficult to know for certain because her features were all but obscured by layers of makeup. "I travel for a cosmetics firm," she explained, seating herself gingerly on the worn wooden chair in Fletcher's office. "I was out of town at the time of the shooting, but then it didn't really concern me anyway. I'm not surprised at anything Tod would do."

"How long were you married to him?"

"Five years, nearly six. We've been divorced for the last three. He's something in my past."

"Was there another woman?"

"Not that I knew of. My job keeps me on the road a great deal of the time and Tod objected to that. He was the sort who needed a mother more than a wife. I finally just got sick of it."

"He seems to have been having an affair with this McGregor woman. Apparently that's why he shot her husband. Were there ever indications of violent behavior when you were married to him?"

"No, not really. Certainly never against me. I wouldn't have stood still for it. Sometimes he'd go into a rage about something and break a vase or a glass. Once he hurt his hand punching a wall. I think a lot of the problem was his brother."

"Sam Baxter?"

"That's right. Sam is eight years older, and when their father died he more or less raised Tod. He was father and big brother both. He succeeded with his lumber business while Tod foundered in everything he tried. They were very close, always giving each other gifts. Finally Sam had to give him a job."

"Sam put up the bail money," Fletcher told her.

"I'm not surprised. If Tod asked him, he'd do it."

"The case is pretty open and shut. I gather you knew nothing about Tod's involvement with Marcy McGregor?"

"Not a thing. I don't know the McGregors and I haven't spoken to Tod in nearly a year."

"He did contact you then?"

"Only about some minor points of the property settlement. It wasn't as if we'd had children to keep us in touch over the years."

Fletcher stood up to signify the interview's conclusion. "Thank you for coming in, Ms. Smiley. I doubt if we'll need to contact you again."

He typed up a report on the interview and stuck it in the file.

Connie Trent was on duty Friday night, and Fletcher went to the movies with his wife. When they got home they watched one of the late-night talk shows and then went to bed. He was sleeping soundly when the phone next to the bed awakened him. The clock radio showed the time to be 3:04.

"It's Connie, Captain. Sorry to bother you."

"What? That's all right, Connie. I'm used to it. What's up?"

"I thought you'd want to know. Tod Baxter just killed himself."

A suicide wasn't usually something to rouse Fletcher in the middle of the night and send him out to view the body, but this one was different. He drove to the apartment on the west side of the city. He'd given it a careful search following Baxter's arrest but had found nothing unusual. Now, as he pulled up in front of the building at 3:30 in the morning, he saw a police patrol car, an ambulance, Connie Trent's unmarked car, and an unfamiliar red Buick.

She met him at the door and led him to the upstairs apartment. "It seems fairly straightforward. He phoned his brother to say goodbye and then shot himself. He left a handwritten note too."

Sam Baxter, the obvious owner of the Buick, was standing to one side on the upstairs landing, looking dazed. He nodded to Fletcher, possibly without remembering who he was. Inside the apartment, the body was slouched in an overstuffed chair next to a small end table holding the telephone and a half-empty glass of amber-colored liquid. Baxter had put a snub-nosed revolver in his mouth and pulled the trigger. The bullet had shattered a couple of front teeth before making a mess of the back of his head. His right hand still clutched the revolver with its bloodied barrel, drooped across his stomach.

"Check everything for prints," Fletcher instructed Connie. "Especially the gun, the phone, and that glass."

"Here's the note he left," she said. "I put it in an evidence bag right away."

It was a single sheet of notepaper that had been folded once in the middle. "Where'd you find it?"

"Right next to the glass, spread flat like this."

He read through it quickly. "Sam—I know this is the worst thing I have ever done, but I can't face the thought of prison. I hope you'll find it in your heart to forgive me. Tod."

Fletcher handed the evidence bag back to Connie. "Check it for prints and have a handwriting expert look it over. Has Sam Baxter seen it?"

She nodded. "He called nine-one-one as soon as Tod phoned him. The patrol car got here just before he did and I was right behind them. Tod was considerate. He'd left the door unlocked for us."

"Did the people downstairs hear anything?"

"They go away every Friday for the weekend. Sam Baxter thinks they have a place in the country."

Fletcher went out on the landing to speak with the dead man's brother. "I understand he phoned you before it happened, Mr. Baxter?"

"I—yes. I'm sorry, it's a terrible shock."

"Just what did he say?"

"*Goodbye, Sam.* That's all he said. *Goodbye, Sam.* Then there was this loud noise just as the connection was broken. I couldn't believe my ears! I called nine-one-one and got dressed and hurried right over. I prayed all the way that it wasn't what I thought, but—"

"Are you certain it was your brother's voice? If he only said two words it might have been someone imitating him."

"What?" Fletcher's words seemed to have confused him. "Well, it certainly sounded like Tod. As soon as I heard the voice I thought it was him."

"It just seems odd that he'd have the gun in one hand and the phone in the other, but I guess it could be done. As he was hanging up the phone with his left hand, he put the gun in his mouth and fired with his right."

Fletcher's graphic words seemed to have upset Sam Baxter even further. "You'll have to excuse me, Captain. I need some air." He hurried down the stairs to the street.

Connie came over to Fletcher. "Go a little easy on the guy, Captain. He just lost his brother."

"I didn't realize—"

"I know you didn't. You were just thinking out loud."

"Yeah." He knew he wasn't as smooth as Leopold would have been. Maybe he never would be.

On Monday morning the reports were on Fletcher's desk. The dead man's fingerprints had been on the revolver and the liquor glass, the note and the telephone. Left-hand prints on the phone, right-hand on the glass and gun. Nitrate particles in the victim's hand showed that he'd fired the weapon. And a handwriting expert had verified without doubt that Tod Baxter wrote the suicide note to his brother.

The case was closed, or would be after Fletcher spoke with Marcy McGregor. She arrived at his office later that morning. "Sorry to get you down here, Mrs. McGregor. How's your husband doing?"

"Much better, thanks. The doctor says he's out of danger and they've moved him to a private room."

"I'm glad to hear that. You know about Tod Baxter's suicide, of course."

"It was in the papers."

"That's why I asked Sergeant Trent to phone you. I just have a couple of questions. Did you have any contact with Baxter between the time your husband was shot and the suicide?"

"None whatever."

"Not by phone or in person?"

"No. I had nothing to do with him after he shot Charlie. In fact, I'd broken off with him before that, which was why he came to the house that Saturday."

"Did he send you any sort of note hinting at suicide?"

"No."

"The autopsy report shows a large amount of alcohol in the body at the time of death. Was he a heavy drinker?"

"Not especially, but I suppose if someone's on the verge of killing himself it wouldn't be unusual to have a few drinks."

He couldn't argue with that. "One more question and I'll let you go. Baxter used one handgun to shoot your husband and another to take his own life. Any idea where they came from? Both were unlicensed."

She shook her head. "He never mentioned guns to me."

"You were at his apartment from time to time?" Marcy shifted nervously in the chair. "Well, yes. A couple of times."

"Did you ever see a gun?"

"Never. He never mentioned them and I never saw them."

Fletcher put down his pencil. "Thank you for coming in, Mrs. McGregor. I hope your husband continues to improve."

"You can't believe the weight that's been taken off my shoulders. I kept imagining Tod would pop out from behind a tree some night and try to kidnap me."

"I'm glad it didn't come to that."

After she departed, he sat starring at the open case file on the desk in front of him. Open and shut.

Still, he wondered about the gun. It was a loose end.

He picked up the phone and dialed the number of Grace Smiley's home. There was no answer, so he tried the other number he had for her, the office of the cosmetics firm. After a few moments' wait she came on the line.

"Ms. Smiley," he said after identifying himself, "I'm wondering about this pistol your ex-husband used to kill himself. He used an unlicensed Beretta to shoot Charlie McGregor, and now an unlicensed Smith and Wesson to kill himself. Do you have any idea where he obtained those weapons?"

"I suppose they're the ones he got in Vegas. We went out there for our first anniversary. He was roaming around downtown one afternoon and saw some guns in a pawnshop window. He bought two of them and brought them home in his luggage. He never bothered to register them, and I never saw them again."

"All right," Fletcher said. "I just wanted to clear up that point. Thanks for your trouble."

When he hung up he was satisfied for the first time. He called Connie in and handed her the file on the McGregor shooting and Baxter's suicide. "Case closed, Connie. File it away."

She took the file and flipped through it. "This one was a first for me. I never had a suicide where the victim clenched his teeth while shooting himself in the mouth. They always practically swallow the barrel before they pull the trigger."

"Yeah. All it did was blow out his two front teeth."

When Connie left he went back to the day's paperwork. She was right, of course. Suicides shoved the gun into their mouth. Otherwise they shot themselves in the temple. Still . . .

He remembered Baxter's gap-toothed grin from one of the newspaper photos. He punched Connie's number and got her on the phone. "Connie, does the McGregor file include Tod Baxter's mug shots from when he was arrested?"

"No, but I can get them easily enough."

"Do that. And bring the file back in too."

What was it? What was he looking for? He didn't really know. For an instant he wished Leopold was back.

"Here it is," Connie announced, placing the mug shots on his desk.

Of course Tod Baxter wasn't smiling in the mug shots. The gap between his front teeth didn't show. Fletcher cursed silently and took out the autopsy photos. Death certainly did change a person's appearance.

"Connie!"

"What is it?"

"Look at the ears in these pictures!"

She studied them for a moment. "They're different."

"Damn right they're different! And the shape of a person's ear certainly doesn't change after death."

"What are you saying? The fingerprints all matched."

"The fingerprints on the gun, glass, and telephone all matched those of the deceased. Did anyone check them against Baxter's prints from when he was arrested?"

"Why should we? He was in Baxter's apartment, wearing Baxter's clothes, looking like Baxter. There was no doubt of his identity."

"There's doubt now. Have them run a check right away."

She was back in fifteen minutes. "They don't match," she announced somberly.

"Get a patrol car out to Marcy McGregor's house right away, and another to the hospital. Tod Baxter is still alive."

Fletcher phoned Leopold's home that evening, just after dinner. When Molly answered, he asked if he could come over. "Sure, he'd be glad to see you," she replied. "We're just sitting on the veranda watching the sunset."

He was there in twenty minutes, carrying a briefcase with the case file, mug shots, fingerprint records, and various bits of evidence. "It's good to see you," Leopold said. "What is this, a new case?"

"The McGregor one. Open and shut, except for one thing. The man who shot himself wasn't Tod McGregor."

Leopold frowned. "An unknown twin brother?"

"I'd better start at the beginning. It's suddenly become a very interesting case, far from routine." As Fletcher spoke he laid out the various files and photos for Leopold's inspection. "See the ears?" he asked at one point.

"The ears, yes." Leopold was warming to the subject. "An early method of criminal identification, predating fingerprints."

Fletcher went on, covering everything he could remember that was connected with the case. "To answer your earlier question, the dead man's not an unknown twin brother. We think it's a homeless man known as Pete Detroit."

Leopold smiled, pleased. "You've been busy."

"I decided that Tod Baxter was a fairly ordinary-looking person. Average height and weight, no startling facial features. Someone with the right color hair and eyes might be mistaken for him, especially after death. Since no one was reported missing after the so-called suicide, I figured if the body wasn't Baxter it might be some homeless drifter, like the ones who sleep under the Broad Street

bridge every night. We took Baxter's mug shot and retouched it a little, covering the ears. The teeth didn't show, so that was no problem.
Connie sent a couple of men up to the area of the bridge to show the
picture around. Two people mentioned a man they call Pete Detroit
who hasn't been seen lately. Near as we can tell, he disappeared just
before Baxter's suicide."

"That's good work. How do you think it was done?"

"Chances are that Tod Baxter had run into this guy and noticed
the resemblance. When he decided to fake his own suicide, he
sought out Pete Detroit and brought him to his apartment. Maybe
he let him take a shower and get dressed in some of his clothes. Then
he got him drunk and killed him, making sure the bullet shattered
those front teeth so nobody would notice they lacked that distinctive
gap. Tod got him to leave fingerprints all over before he killed him.
It had to be Tod, of course, because the fake suicide note was in his
handwriting."

"Where is he now?"

Fletcher frowned and shook his head. "I don't know, Captain. It
would help a lot to have him back in custody before we announce
this thing to the press. I've got a hunch he's not far away. Somebody
might be hiding him."

"Who?"

"Well, there are three likely suspects—his brother, Sam, has always
been very close to him, as much a father as an older brother. Marcy
McGregor was having an affair with him, and her reconciliation
with her wounded husband could be just an act. Since her husband
is still in the hospital, Tod could even be hiding at her house. The
third possibility would be his ex-wife, Grace Smiley. Who knows?
Maybe they're back together again."

"Which possibility do you like?" Leopold asked.

"None of them," Fletcher admitted. "I guess that's why I came to
you."

"It perks me up, getting the brain functioning again. There are
times, Captain Fletcher, when hunches pay off. But they can never
take the place of good hard evidence."

"Then you know—?"

"I know some things, not everything. Let's just say I know the
most important thing. Come, let's go for a ride."

"Are you going out?" Molly called from the other room.

"Just for a bit. Fletcher and I are going for a ride."

They headed back into the city, with Fletcher following Leopold's directions, and before long he realized they were headed for Sam Baxter's house. When they pulled up in front, the ground floor was brightly lit. Rose Baxter came to the door, surprised to see them. "Oh! It's Captain Fletcher, isn't it?"

"We need to see your husband," Leopold said.

As if on cue, Sam Baxter appeared behind her. "What's this all about?"

Leopold pointed his finger. "There's your man, Fletcher. Arrest him!"

"As his brother's accomplice?"

"No, no! You had the wrong motive and therefore the wrong murderer. Tod probably knows nothing about this. Sam Baxter killed that homeless man."

Later, as Leopold explained it all down at the squad room, it seemed like old times. Connie Trent was there, and a couple of the others on the night shift. Everyone was feeling good.

"It was a difficult case, full of ambiguities," he began. "Coming into it late, I had to rely upon the very accurate description of events furnished by Captain Fletcher, along with the photos and documents. There were two things—clues, if you will—that set me on the right track. The suicide note and the two guns."

Fletcher pulled the note from the file on his desk. "Here it is."

"And I'm sure the dead man's fingerprints were on that too, just like on the phone and the gun. It's not too difficult to place a gun in the hand of a drunk or unconscious man, cover it with your hand, place it against his front teeth, and pull the trigger. It even leaves the proper nitrate marks on the victim's hand, as you discovered. But look again at this note. It was found flat on the table as you see it, and yet there's a fold in it. Why?"

"Maybe he folded it and then changed his mind," Connie reasoned. "He was drunk, after all."

"Ah, but you're confusing the real Tod Baxter with the dead man, whom we'll call by the unlikely name of Pete Detroit. It was Detroit who was drunk, but Detroit certainly didn't write the note. And if you'll read the note again, you'll see that it really makes no mention of suicide: *Sam—I know this is the worst thing I have ever done, but I can't face the thought of prison. I hope you will find it in your heart to forgive me. Tod.* This is brother talking to brother, remember. The worst thing. Tod has ever done is to jump bail and leave Sam Baxter responsible for a half-million dollars. He begs forgiveness, but not in person. The note was folded because he mailed it to Sam."

"You mentioned the wrong motive," Fletcher remembered.

"Of course! When you discovered the dead man wasn't Tod Baxter, you immediately suspected Tod of the killing. But it was Sam who remembered the man who looked like his brother, Sam who sought him out, lured him to Tod's apartment, got him drunk, and killed him. Sam had put up his lumber business to guarantee Tod's bail, and now Tod was gone. Sam could lose everything unless he could convince the authorities that Tod was dead. In something like a fire or a car crash there are always fingerprints and dental records to check. By doing it with a gunshot in Tod's own apartment, he hoped no one would feel the need to check those things. The gunshot took care of the missing gap in the teeth, and he figured no one would notice the difference in ears. Maybe he even cut Pete Detroit's hair a little, or shaved him."

"You mentioned the other clue being connected with the guns."

Leopold nodded. "Of course if the note was mailed or delivered to Sam Baxter at an earlier time, he must have been responsible for the killing. Once he discovered the true meaning of the note— maybe there was a travel folder or something enclosed with it—he set about trying to save his money and his business. One of the things you told me, Fletcher, was that the brothers were close and often exchanged gifts. Grace Smiley told you Tod bought two guns in Las Vegas. He used one attempting to kill Charlie McGregor, but what about the other gun? It wasn't at his apartment because you searched the place after his arrest. Surely you would have found a second gun. If he didn't keep it, what did Tod do with it? The most likely answer is that he bought it as a gift for his brother. And that was the weapon Sam used to kill the homeless man. Both the note and the gun pointed to Sam Baxter."

"What about the missing Tod?" Connie asked.

Leopold shrugged. "We may never know. He could be anywhere by now."

As it turned out, he was in Taos, New Mexico. Four days later, when he read about his brother's arrest in a newspaper and realized the full consequences of his bail-jumping, he surrendered to local police.

LEOPOLD LENDS A HAND

L eopold pulled up before the little brick guardhouse at the entrance to the Bellview Sound Estates and flashed the shiny honorary badge he'd carried since his retirement. "I'm with Captain Fletcher's squad," he told the uniformed guard.

The guard consulted a handwritten list on his clipboard, taking no chances. "Name?"

"Leopold."

"Go on," he said, waving the car through. "It's the middle building—the unfinished one."

There were three squad cars plus Fletcher's unmarked Pontiac parked in front of the building. A truck from the technical unit stood off to one side and the medical examiner's vehicle was just backing into position. One of the uniformed patrolmen stood by the elevator and Leopold headed for him.

"Hello, Captain. How's retirement treating you?"

"Can't complain, Cahill. Captain Fletcher gave me a call. What floor are they on?"

"Top one. Number ten."

He found Fletcher and his men in one of the unfinished condominiums, standing off to one side while still and video cameras recorded the murder scene. The victim, a well-dressed man with black hair and a bushy moustache, seemed out of place on the bare concrete floor of the building, surrounded by boxes and piles of tile waiting to be installed.

"What have you got, Fletcher?" Leopold asked.

"Thanks for coming. What I've got is more cases than the Violent Crime Squad can handle at the moment. Connie's working on a drug stabbing and I've got two people on vacation. I called you because I thought you might help with some of the routine questioning."

"I'm always happy to help out. Who's the dead man?"

"Vladimir Petrov, a Russian businessman who emigrated to America about five years ago. That's really all we know so far. He'd purchased the condo on this floor—the most expensive in the building, by the way—and apparently had come here today to check on progress. He was shot twice in the chest at fairly close range."

"Anyone hear the shots?"

"There are twenty men and a couple of women working on the building today. That's what we have to find out. I thought you could help Spencer and Frawley interview them."

"Glad to," Leopold said. It reminded him of his early days as a detective, before he'd been in charge of the squad, before the age barrier had forced his retirement. Fletcher's call for help wasn't exactly in keeping with departmental regulations but Leopold was more than willing to lend a hand. His wife, Molly, was in court defending a rape suspect in a difficult case and he was pretty much shifting for himself these days.

The man who'd found the body was a crew chief named Al Haskins. His men had laid tile in the condo's three bathrooms earlier in the week, working on a subcontract from the builder of the condominium. He was a tall, slender man with dark hair and glasses, dressed in a T-shirt and work pants. "Had you seen Mr. Petrov before the shooting?" Leopold asked, jotting down notes as they talked.

"Not today. But it wasn't unusual for him to stop by and see how things were coming. He and his wife were anxious to move in."

"The guards allowed him onto the grounds?"

Al Haskins smiled. "He paid a million three for this place. No way you're going to keep him out."

"That's expensive real estate." They'd walked out onto the screened-in terrace overlooking Long Island Sound. Ten stories below, a few yachts were visible on the blue water.

"Part of it's the view," Haskins explained. "The condos are pretty much the same, but the higher you go the more expensive they get."

"What did Petrov do for a living?"

"Beats me. Some sort of art dealer in Manhattan, I think. Didn't seem to work very hard at it, though. He hung around here a lot. Sometimes his wife came too."

"So he was up here today—alone?"

A shrug. "You'd have to get that from the guard at the entrance. I told you I hadn't seen him."

"Didn't you hear any shots?"

"I don't think so. Sometimes there's a little hammering and it's hard to tell what you're hearing."

"What brought you up here?"

"Like I said, my crew had tiled the bathrooms." He led the way into one of them. "The inspector for the builder was up yesterday to check out our work. See—she puts these little blue stickers wherever there's a flaw to be corrected. I came up to see how many things had to be fixed."

"And you found Petrov."

"Yeah." He patted the two-way radio hanging from his belt. "I called downstairs and told them to get the police."

"Your people do nice work," Leopold said, inspecting the tile that lined the walls and floor of a shower stall. A grouping of four larger ones had been painted with the unmistakable likeness of Cleopatra. "Fancy."

"Petrov's wife picked those out. They're twenty-five bucks each."

Leopold returned to Fletcher and the others as the medical examiner was supervising removal of the body. "Did you check to see if the victim's wife came with him today?"

Fletcher nodded. "He was alone. The gatehouse checked him in at eleven-ten, about an hour before Haskins found the body. We haven't been able to tell his wife yet. Come downstairs with me. Spencer has been going through his car and he found something."

The victim's car, not surprisingly, was a foreign make that sold for better than fifty thousand dollars. Spencer had opened the trunk with keys from the dead man's pocket and found a painted wooden panel carefully wrapped in soft cloth. It was about six by eight inches in size and seemed very old. "A religious scene," Fletcher decided. "Some saint, judging by the halo."

"It's an icon," Leopold said. "Byzantine, possibly Russian." Fletcher raised his eyebrows and Leopold added, "Molly's been helping my cultural awareness since my retirement."

"Good for you." But something clicked in his mind and he took out a business card. "This was in the dead man's pocket too. Think there's a connection?"

" 'Rachel Dean, Art Appraisals,' " Leopold read. "The address is local. Maybe we should give her a call. Better still, have your men photograph this icon and log it in. Then I'll drive over and show it to Rachel Dean myself."

"I didn't mean to get you so deeply involved in this," Fletcher said. "I just thought you could question some of the workmen. After all, with the security around this place, it's likely that one of them shot him."

Leopold remembered the blue waters of the Sound. "Unless the killer came by boat."

Rachel Dean's shop was in a mall across town from the Bellview Sound Estates. She sold art works on consignment and the shop was a small gallery hung with oils and watercolors, some by local painters. The woman herself was red-haired, dressed and made-up to appear both younger and more attractive than she really was. Close up, Leopold could see the lines of middle age beginning to show. Leopold introduced himself, keeping the icon wrapped and under his arm for the moment.

"We're investigating a homicide," he said. "Your card was found in the victim's pocket."

"Vladimir Petrov," she said at once. "My God!"

"How did you know?"

"You've got one of his icons under your arm. I wrapped it in that cloth to protect it. What happened to him?"

"He was shot and killed at the condominium he purchased in Bellview Sound Estates. The icon was in the trunk of his car and your business card was in his pocket. What do you know about it, Ms. Dean?"

"It's Mrs. Dean, although we've been separated for years. Come into my office, Mr.—?"

"Captain Leopold, retired. I'm helping the police on this."

He followed her into a back office with a locked and barred window. Several paintings were leaning against the wall opposite her desk. He sat down in the only free chair, facing her. "Mr. Petrov contacted me about two weeks ago," she began, nervously tapping a pencil as she spoke. "He was in the process of buying this quite expensive condominium and he needed to raise some cash for the down payment. He showed me this icon and I appraised it for him."

"Did he say where he got it?"

"He'd come from Russia and brought it with him. He implied he had several more, but I never saw them."

"Could they have been stolen?"

Rachel Dean shrugged. "The art scene in the former Soviet Union is very clouded at present. We are learning about paintings that we barely knew existed. Certainly there has been a great deal of theft, as there was during the Allied occupation of Germany."

Leopold loosened the wrapping. "This is the painting you examined?"

She leaned across the desk to take it from him. "It is. I believe it to be a representation of Saint John Chrysostom, though it's difficult to know for certain."

"Do you have a copy of your appraisal?"

She pulled open a file drawer next to the desk and took out a folder. "I have an extra copy you may have."

Leopold skimmed through it. *Appraisal of one Russian ikon measuring 6½" by 8½", being an encaustic painting on a wooden panel, possibly of St. John Chrysostom ...* His eyes went to the bottom of the page. ... *Estimated value—$400,000.*

He folded the copy and tucked it into his pocket. "What does encaustic mean?"

"Painted with wax colors that are then fixed with heat. It was a technique used on many of the early icons. The technique helps to date it to the sixth or seventh century, and that's what makes it so valuable. Very few icons exist that are this old."

"Were all early icons done that way?"

"No, some were mosaics—you know, with little inlaid stones, glass, or tiles—"

"Tiles?"

"Certainly. Tiles are nothing but baked clay, usually glazed or painted. The technique was known long ago."

"Have you ever come across fake icons, with the painting or mosaic work made to appear much older than it is?"

"I never have, but I've read about such things. There are some people, especially in Eastern Europe, who are quite skilled at faking antique furniture and art objects."

"Do you think this icon could be faked?"

Rachel Dean shook her head. "I'd stake my reputation on its being authentic."

"You said he had more of them?"

"So he implied. He mentioned at least four which could be offered for sale, though I suggested it might be best to wait a bit before producing the other three."

"But he took this icon with him?"

She nodded. "I don't know why. Perhaps he wanted another opinion. Can you leave it with me now?"

"I'm afraid not. It's possible evidence in a murder case. Thank you for your help, Mrs. Dean."

"I'd appreciate your keeping me advised of the icon's fate."

"I'll try to do that," he promised.

Leopold returned the icon to Fletcher's office along with Rachel Dean's appraisal. Fletcher studied it and gave a soft whistle. "Four hundred thousand—that's motive enough for murder. We'd better lock this away in the evidence vault."

"I hope it helps with your investigation." He told Fletcher what he'd learned about the possible faking of mosaic icons.

"You're thinking of those tilers working at the condo, aren't you?"

Leopold nodded. "I may be on the wrong track, but if Vladimir Petrov was trying to fake an ancient mosaic he might seek the help of a skilled tile worker."

"There's one thing wrong with your theory," Fletcher said with a smile. "The only icon we've recovered so far isn't a mosaic. It's a wax—" He glanced again at the appraisal, "—encaustic painting."

Leopold stood up. "I'll leave that to you. Good luck with it."

"One more thing, if you're interested. Mrs. Petrov is in the interview room. Do you want to speak with her?"

"Sure, if you want me to. I've gone this far. I guess I can talk with one more person."

Sally Petrov was not what he'd expected. For one thing, she was American, with a decidedly Brooklyn accent. Her tailored tan suit looked expensive, as did the wrist watch and rings she wore. "Have you found the killer?" she asked as soon as she entered the room.

"Not yet, Mrs. Petrov. We're working on it." He introduced himself and sat down opposite her. "I gather you met your husband in this country?"

She nodded. "About four years ago, after he'd emigrated here from Russia. He had an apartment in the Russian colony down near Coney Island. We were married within six months."

"He was a great deal older than you," Leopold observed.

"Well, yeah. I'm twenty-seven now and he was forty-seven, but twenty years isn't so bad. We were both interested in art. He'd collected some while he was in Russia and I'd posed a few times for a life class. That's where we met."

"I see." Leopold watched her nervously fidgeting with a gold bracelet on her wrist. "What can you tell me about the Russian icon we found in the trunk of your husband's car?"

"He brought it over with him, from Russia. There were four in all."

"What happened to the others?"

"I don't know. He told me he had six originally, part of an iconostasis—a large screen. He got them into the country past customs somehow, and he sold two soon after his arrival here. Certainly he had plenty of money when I first met him."

"I understand he was an art dealer in Manhattan."

"He didn't work much at it," Sally Petrov said, twisting her long brown hair back behind her shoulder.

"Do you know a local dealer named Rachel Dean?"

"Not personally, but he mentioned her. She did an appraisal on one of the icons for insurance purposes."

Leopold stood up. "Thanks for your time, Mrs. Petrov. I know this must be hard for you."

"Will I get the icon back?"

"You'll have to speak with Captain Fletcher about that."

Back in Fletcher's office the younger man asked, "What did you think of her?"

"She's a cool one," Leopold replied. "I think we could safely say she married him for his money."

"Maybe she killed him for it."

"Is that your current theory?"

"I've got one other," Fletcher admitted. "Connie's free of her other case and we're going to check it out tonight. One of the workers on the tile crew, a fellow named Max Rosen, has a conviction for armed robbery. Served a few years for it back in the eighties. He's been clean since then but we figure he's worth a look."

Leopold glanced at his watch, surprised to see it was after five. "I'll be heading home. Give me a call if you need me for anything."

Molly was home before him, just slipping two frozen dinners into the microwave. "I was hoping you wouldn't be late," she said. "I'm starving."

"Hard day in court?" He kissed her lightly on the cheek.

"Not easy. I think I'm losing this one. How about you? What did Fletcher want?"

"He's short-handed. I'm helping him out on a case."

"Just like the old days."

"We'll see."

He could tell Molly was done in by her long day in court, with another session looming in the morning. They went to bed earlier than usual, just after eleven o'clock.

When the door chimes awakened him some time later, Leopold immediately looked at the glowing digits on the clock radio. It was 2:05. He slipped out of bed, trying not to disturb Molly from her sleep, and took his old .38 from the bedside drawer. As he went down the stairs he could see the red light flashing from the top of a waiting car.

He opened the door and faced Lieutenant Connie Trent, her face drained of color except for the pulsating red flasher that bathed them both.

"Connie?"

"I didn't know what to do. I had to come for you. Fletcher's been shot."

Molly came with them, because Fletcher was like one of the family. She threw on a bulky sweater and jeans and was in the car with Connie and Leopold within minutes. "What happened?" she asked Connie as they headed toward the hospital.

"Fletcher wanted to check out a man named Rosen who had a criminal record. He was working on the condo where Petrov was killed. We drove to Rosen's apartment over on Snyder Street, above a bodega. There was a back entrance, and as we approached it in the dark Fletcher saw someone moving. He drew his weapon and identified us as police. There were two quick shots and he went down—" Her voice broke as she said it. "I fired once but I couldn't see anything in the dark. Whoever it was got away. I ran to Fletcher and he was bleeding heavily from chest wounds."

"Wasn't he wearing his bulletproof vest?" Leopold asked.

"We weren't expecting trouble. You know Fletcher. Like most older cops, he hates those things."

"You never set him a very good example," Molly told her husband.

Connie swung her car into the hospital emergency room's parking lot and pulled the flashing red light from the roof of the unmarked vehicle. They hurried inside. "Captain Fletcher?" Connie asked the nurse behind the desk.

"The doctor will see you in a moment."

"I want to see someone now," Connie insisted.

"In a moment."

A greying man in a white coat appeared within five minutes. "I'm Dr. Slocum," he told them. "We're preparing Captain Fletcher for surgery now. His wife is with him."

"Can we see him?" Leopold asked.

"We've already put him under. I'm afraid you'll have to wait till later."

"What are his chances?"

Slocum glanced at the two women. "Good. Very good if I can dig those bullets out of him."

"We'll want them saved as evidence," Connie said, remembering her duty.

"Of course."

"How long do you expect the surgery to last?" Leopold asked.

"There's no telling. It should take a couple of hours, minimum."

He left them, disappearing through the swinging white doors, and Leopold asked, "Where do you stand on this Max Rosen?"

"I have a pickup order out on him, and the apartment is staked out, in case he comes back. We've no evidence he shot Fletcher, though, unless we find him with the weapon. As soon as the doctor recovers the slugs, we'll compare them to the bullets that killed Petrov."

Leopold knew Molly had to be in court, and he finally persuaded her to head home for a couple of hours' sleep, promising to phone her with any news. He and Connie had been waiting about an hour, comforting Fletcher's wife, Carol, as best they could, when the police commissioner arrived.

Commissioner Johnson was a tall black man with a voice as deep and commanding as that of James Earl Jones. He'd been appointed to the position just after Leopold's retirement and his honeymoon with the media had lasted a full year now. Those waiting for him to make a misstep were still waiting.

"How is he, Lieutenant?" he asked Connie.

"They have him in surgery now, Commissioner. The doctor says his chances are good."

"I'm glad to hear that." He turned to Leopold. "I don't believe we've been formally introduced. You're retired Captain Leopold?"

"That's right, sir. I'm pleased to meet you."

"I'd like to get your views on something, Captain. Would you pardon us please, Lieutenant?"

"Of course."

Johnson led him to an unoccupied corner of the waiting room, out of Connie's earshot. "This is an awkward place for a conversation, Captain, but I guess it's the best we can do. I'm aware that the Violent Crimes Squad had staffing problems even before tonight. I approved Fletcher's reaching out to you for routine assistance on the Petrov case. Now I fear we have a more serious problem. At best, and with the full recovery we're all praying for, Captain Fletcher is likely to be out of action for two or three months. I can't let the department drift for that long. I need an acting head of Violent Crimes and I need him now. Would you consider coming out of retirement on a strictly limited basis?"

"Connie Trent could do the job," Leopold argued.

"A year from now, maybe. I'd like her to have a little more experience as a lieutenant first. There's no one else, and I know she works well with you."

Leopold took a deep breath. "For this case only?"

"I hope so. We'll know better once Fletcher is out of the woods."

"I can help you out for that long," Leopold agreed, wondering what Molly would say about it.

"Thank you, Captain. I'm eternally grateful. As of this minute, you are acting head of the Violent Crimes division, with your old rank and pay scale." They shook hands and the commissioner said, "I should tell Lieutenant Trent."

Feeling a bit embarrassed, Leopold followed the commissioner back to where Connie was sitting. He was relieved to see her smile at the news. "That's the best thing I've heard all night. I'll call the squad room on my car radio and tell them the good news."

She went out to the car while Leopold and the commissioner spoke of technical matters involving the appointment. In a moment she was back, speaking quickly to Leopold. "Max Rosen walked into headquarters twenty minutes ago. He heard about the shooting at his apartment, and knew we'd want to see him. Spencer is talking with him now."

Leopold was on his feet. "You stay here till Fletcher is out of surgery, Connie. I'll talk to Mr. Rosen."

He didn't remember having seen Max Rosen among the few workers he'd spoken to at Vladimir Petrov's condominium. He was a middle-aged man of average height, with a short, neatly trimmed beard. "My neighbor said you were looking for me," he told Leopold in the interrogation room. "I came in as soon as I heard. I bar-tend a few hours at night."

Leopold told Spencer to take a break and settled down opposite the bearded man. "Our record shows a conviction for armed robbery, Max. What about that?"

"I served my time. That's in the past. I've been living a new life for five years now."

"Do you own a gun?"

"I can't, as a convicted felon."

"But do you?"

"No, sir."

"Did you know Vladimir Petrov?"

"Not really. Al Haskins was showing him our work one day and he told me it was a nice job. That's all the conversation I ever had with the man."

"He was killed with two shots from a nine-millimeter weapon, probably a pistol like police carry now." He placed an unloaded Glock on the table between them. "Ever seen a gun like that?"

"Yeah, I see them on these TV cop shows all the time." He brushed back his sandy hair nervously. "Look, do you think I'd have come forward if I had anything to hide?"

"Maybe. Did Petrov ever mention any Russian icons to you?"

"I told you we barely spoke. I hardly knew the man."

Detective Spencer opened the door and said, "Captain, could I see you for a moment?"

Leopold went outside. "What's up?"

"Rosen gave us permission to search his apartment. Frawly just got back from looking it over. Want to see what he found?"

Spencer and Frawly were both new since Leopold's days with the department, but he'd known them both as patrolmen. Frawly was the younger and more excitable of the two. Right now he had reason to be excited. "Look at this, Captain! I found it hidden away at the back of a closet!"

Leopold watched while the detective unwrapped the soft cloth from around the wooden panel, knowing what it would be. "Another icon," he said, studying the painted angel with all the scrutiny of an art professor. "The technique seems similar to the first one."

"I guess that clinches it, Captain."

"I wish it did, Frawly. The man who shot Fletcher may have planted it to incriminate Rosen for Petrov's murder and been caught in the act when Connie and Fletcher arrived."

Max Rosen, of course, denied all knowledge of the icon, insisting it had been planted in his apartment. "Why would I agree to a search if I knew you'd find that?" he argued.

"Because you had no choice," Leopold countered. "You knew we'd get a court order anyway."

The questioning went on past dawn, and Leopold took a break to phone Molly before she left for court. He told her what he knew about Fletcher, and then what the commissioner had asked him to do.

"Is it what you want?" Molly asked softly.

"What I want is to have Fletcher back here. What I want is to find out who shot him."

"Let's talk about it later," she said.

Connie phoned from the hospital just before nine. "It was a long operation but he's going to make it, Captain. Both bullets are out and ballistics is already running tests. They're nine-millimeter, the same type that killed Petrov. I'm on my way in."

"Go home and sleep for a while, Connie."

"I'm on my way in."

After Connie arrived, Leopold wrapped the icon in its soft cloth covering, identical to the cloth around the one in Petrov's trunk, and drove over to Rachel Dean's shop. He wanted confirmation that this one was the real thing too, and not some forgery. He couldn't imagine a killer sacrificing a valuable artwork simply to frame someone else for the crime, but stranger things had happened.

The first thing he noticed when he pulled up in front of the shop was that the front door was standing slightly ajar. He stepped inside, calling out, "Mrs. Dean? Rachel Dean? It's Leopold."

There was no answer. He walked to the back office, tried the door, and found it locked. He could see light coming from under the door, but no one answered. Then he remembered the barred back window and went outside. He walked around to the rear of the row of shops and counted down until he found the window in question. Looking through the dirty glass, he saw Rachel Dean slumped over her desk. Breaking the window would have done no good with the bars still in place. He hurried around to the front of the shop and put in a call for help. When a patrol car arrived, two burly police officers helped him break down the locked door.

Rachel Dean was dead. She'd been shot in the chest, like the others. He looked around the office, at a blood-soaked handkerchief with which she'd tried to stanch the flow from the wound, at the pencil with which she'd tried to print a dying message: *ICON.*

Just that one word. She hadn't gotten any further.

Just before noon, Leopold faced Connie and Spencer and Frawly in the squad room. He was working at one of the vacant desks, somehow reluctant to reclaim his old glass-enclosed office that now belonged to Fletcher. "We now have two murders and one close call. Happily, the news from the hospital is good. Fletcher is conscious after his surgery and the doctor says it looks good. What else do we have, Connie?"

"The bullets they removed from Fletcher came from the same gun that killed Vladimir Petrov, which is no great surprise. The one that killed Rachel Dean was a nine-millimeter too. We're after one killer, and those icons are the motives for the crimes."

"Any theories?"

She thought for a moment before responding. "From what we know, including what his wife, Sally, told you earlier, Petrov smuggled a half-dozen valuable Russian icons into this country five years ago. He sold two soon after his arrival, and when he decided to purchase the condominium at Bellview Sound Estates, he needed to sell some of the remaining four. Rachel Dean valued one at four hundred thousand dollars, but apparently didn't see the other three. I have two theories about what happened next. Petrov might have decided to keep a good thing going by faking some mosaic icons, approaching one of the condo's tilers for help." She smiled. "I got that idea from you, Captain. The other possibility is that someone simply killed him to steal the icons, and then shot Fletcher when he was caught leaving one of them at the Rosen apartment."

"Or else Rosen did it himself and is trying to appear innocent by coming in," Spencer suggested.

Leopold frowned. "How's the timing on that? Could he have killed Rachel Dean before he showed up here?"

Connie had the answer. "He walked in shortly before four A.M. The medical examiner estimates that Rachel Dean died around three, but keep in mind she was shot sometime earlier. She lived long enough to write that single word of her message. The killer shot Fletcher around twelve thirty-five. We got him to the hospital, and then I came over to get you, Captain. While I was doing that, the killer had plenty of time to go to Rachel's gallery and shoot her. Then, if it was Rosen, he showed up here before four."

"How do you explain the locked room?" Spencer asked. "She had to be alone when she was shot."

But Connie shook her head. "It sure wasn't suicide—no weapon and no powder burns. She let the killer in, probably arranged to meet him in the first place. What else would she be doing there in the middle of the night? She let him in, he shot her from across the room, and then he got out."

"Leaving the door locked behind him?"

That didn't stop Connie. "He may have been hiding someplace when the captain found the body—in a closet or under the desk."

But Leopold shook his head. "There's no closet in the room. The desk is out because, you'll remember, I had two officers help me break in the door. A hidden killer might have sneaked out past me, but not past three of us."

"So what do we do with Max Rosen?" Frawly asked.

"Turn him loose. We've been holding him for eight hours and we have no evidence to charge him."

But Connie objected. "The doctor thinks we might be able to speak with Fletcher for a few minutes this afternoon. We can hold Rosen till then, at least, in case Fletcher saw who shot him."

"All right," Leopold agreed. "Meanwhile, I want to speak with Al Haskins again. If Petrov approached any of the crew about doing some private tile work, he might know about it."

Leopold drove back out to the Bellview Sound Estates and waited at the gate while the guard recorded his name. "You know there's vacant land just east of here," he told the man. "Anyone could take a boat or even wade over and avoid the gatehouse."

The guard eyed him suspiciously. "Once the tenants move in, we'll have a beach patrol. No one will get by us."

"I hope not."

He found Al Haskins issuing instructions to a couple of his men after the lunch break. Haskins was not too pleased to see him. "What's this about you holding one of my men? Is he under arrest?"

"Max Rosen? We're just questioning him. He'll probably be released later this afternoon."

"I hope so. I need a full crew to finish up this job." He sent the others on their way and started back into the nearest doorway.

"Wait a minute," Leopold said. "I'd like to ask you a few more questions."

"I told you everything I know about Petrov's killing."

Leopold walked up to him so they wouldn't be overheard by the other workers. "Did he ever ask you or your crew about doing some personal jobs for him? Mosaic work?"

"Not me. I don't know about the others."

"Might he have asked Max Rosen?"

"Why do you keep harping on Max? I know he was in prison, but he served his time. He's trying to make a fresh start."

"We're just trying to find Petrov's killer. There was a second murder during the night, in case you haven't heard."

There was a sudden sharpness in his eyes, visible even behind the glasses. "Did that detective die? I heard about it on the radio."

"No, this was an art dealer named Rachel Dean."

He nodded slowly. "I think she was up here with Petrov once. They were discussing the right paintings for his condo."

"Was that the only time you saw her?"

"I guess so. He usually came alone, or with his wife."

"Did Sally Petrov ever come here without him?"

"No. She seemed content to let him handle things. The only thing I remember her picking out were those Cleopatra tiles for the shower."

They were standing near one of the interior doors, and Leopold realized the locking mechanism was the same as the door to Rachel Dean's office—a round knob with a locking button in the middle. "Tell me something, Al. Do you know a way someone could gimmick this lock, walk out the door, and leave it locked from the inside?"

He shook his head. "You have to turn the knob to get out of the room, and turning the knob unlocks it. See?" He demonstrated for Leopold. "If you push the button while the door's open, it pops out when you shut it."

Leopold was convinced. "Thanks for your help."

He went back to his car and radioed in to Connie. "What time are you going to the hospital?"

"Right now, Captain. The doctor says we can see Fletcher for five minutes after three o'clock."

"I'll meet you there."

"I've got something for you. I know how that locked room trick was worked." She sounded pleased with herself.

"You do?"

"I'll tell you at the hospital."

Fletcher was awake, swathed in plastic tubes that ran to his arms and disappeared beneath the bedclothes. Another tube delivered oxygen to help him breathe. Leopold wondered if one of the bullets had nicked a lung. "How are you feeling, Fletcher?"

"Real dopey. Not much pain, though. Carol was in just before you two."

Leopold nodded. They'd spoken to his wife on the way in. She was his strength, and always had been. "Did you see who shot you?" Leopold asked.

"No. Just a dark figure at the door. I thought it was Rosen." He turned his head slightly. "Connie, what's happening with the squad?"

"Don't you worry. The commissioner got Captain Leopold to lend us a hand till you're back on your feet."

Fletcher nodded just a speck. "You'll do it, Captain. You'll get the one who shot me."

"We'll get him, Connie and the rest of the squad. Rest easy now." He could see the nurse looming in the doorway.

Outside, down the hallway in the waiting room, Leopold said a few comforting words to Carol Fletcher. "He'll be out in no time, and back on the job."

She gave a weak smile. "Our son is flying in from California. He'll be here tonight."

"I'll be back then."

"Will you have the one who shot him?"

"Yes," Leopold promised.

Back in the car with Connie, he said, "Tell me about the locked room."

"It was so obvious we didn't see it. The killer shot her but she didn't die immediately. He left, and she held the handkerchief over her wound, struggling to the door to lock it in case he returned. Then she got back to her desk, tried to write a message, and died."

He took her hand and held it, smiling like a father to his daughter. "Connie, you'll make a great detective someday, but not yet. If it happened that way, why didn't she pick up the phone on her desk and call for help?"

"But—but there's no other explanation!"

"There is one. Rachel Dean told us herself, with her dying message—*ICON*. Think about it."

"I've *been* thinking about it! I don't see—"

"Give me your weapon, Connie."

"What?"

"The Glock you carry in your holster. Give it to me."

"What for?"

"It has to be tested by ballistics. You killed Rachel Dean, Connie, with your wild shot last night. It was Rachel who murdered Vladimir Petrov for those icons, Rachel who shot Fletcher when he caught her planting one in Rosen's apartment, Rachel who drove back to her office, dying, and started to write a confession. *ICON—I confess that I killed Vladimir Petrov.*"

By the time ballistics had confirmed Leopold's explanation that evening, he'd gone over it all with Connie. "I'll tell Fletcher tomorrow, but I want you to hear it from me first. You see, in a case full of icons we all leaped to the wrong conclusion. But it suddenly occurred to me that Rachel Dean couldn't have been writing *icon*, because she didn't spell it that way. On the copy of the appraisal she gave me, she used the alternate spelling, *ikon*. She was trying to write a longer word or sentence. I immediately thought of *I confess* and started looking for confirmation. Was there any? Yes, in the soft cloth used to wrap the icons. Rachel claimed she'd only seen the one recovered from Petrov's trunk, and that she'd wrapped it in that cloth herself to protect it. But when we found the second icon, hidden in Rosen's closet, it was wrapped in the identical soft cloth.

"It had obviously been in Rachel's possession and she'd lied about not seeing it."

"She was willing to sacrifice that valuable icon?"

"She still had two others, worth a fortune overseas, and I'm sure she left the least valuable one. Petrov must have mentioned once that an ex-con was working on the tiling crew and she decided he'd be the perfect fall guy for the murder. She crossed over from the adjoining property yesterday without being seen, met Petrov, and shot him. If anyone had seen her, she would simply have postponed the crime. She had the other three icons in her possession for appraisal, and must have known Petrov hadn't told his wife where they were."

"When I shot her—"

"She'd just planted the angel icon in Rosen's closet. Leaving the apartment after midnight, she suddenly saw you and Fletcher. She shot him, but your return shot in the dark hit her in the chest. She escaped back to her car, holding a handkerchief to the wound. It must not have seemed too bad at first. She drove to the gallery to patch herself up, then sat in her locked office for two hours feeling her life drain away from the internal bleeding. She couldn't call for help without revealing herself as Fletcher's assailant. Finally, in her last moment of life, she picked up her pencil and started to write a confession."

It had been a long day. Connie looked at him and said, "It's good to have you back, Captain, even for a little while."

THE MYSTERY THAT WOULDN'T STAY SOLVED

T he winter after Leopold's second retirement as captain of the Violent Crimes Squad had been long and cold, with more snow than usual on the north shore of Long Island Sound. While his wife, Molly, went off to work every morning he stayed behind, puttering around the house and trying to get his notes in order for a book he knew he'd never write.

Perhaps that was why he'd welcomed the phone call from a deep-voiced man named Zach Brewster, who introduced himself as a writer of true-crime books. "I understand you're retired now."

"That's right, Mr. Brewster," Leopold said. "What can I do for you?"

"I have a contract to write a book on the Clemmins case. I thought I might interview you about it."

The Clemmins case. Leopold's memory raced back nine years. "I haven't thought about that one in a long time, though of course it's back in the news right now."

"It certainly is! Look, I'm calling from in town. I've already been to police headquarters and Captain Fletcher gave me your name. He said it was your case. I'd like to talk to you about it this afternoon, if that's convenient."

"Sure, come ahead. I don't know how much I can tell you. That was a terrible case. Now that the execution is less than a week away the press is onto it again."

"Suppose I come right after lunch, around two o'clock."

"That'll be good, Mr. Brewster. I'll look forward to seeing you."

When Brewster arrived, on schedule, Leopold faced a slim man with bushy black eyebrows. He was a few inches taller than Leopold, and probably twenty years younger. He carried an expensive brief-case, and when he came inside he removed his coat and produced a small tape recorder from the briefcase.

"I hope you don't mind if I tape this," he said, turning it on.

"Go ahead. Since my retirement, my wife Molly's been after me to write a book about my experiences, but I haven't gotten around to it."

Zach Brewster smiled. "This won't interfere with anything you might be writing, Captain. I'm only interested in the Clemmins case. Some papers say there could be new evidence implicating someone else."

"I know there's renewed interest now that the appeals process has been exhausted. But I don't know a thing about new evidence. That's tabloid talk."

"You think they'll go through with the execution?"

Leopold shrugged. "It's been decades since we've had one in this state, but the killing of children is a terrible crime."

Brewster nodded agreement. "The political climate is changing in the country, even in the more liberal Northeast."

"The Clemmins case never satisfied everyone, even after the jury brought in its verdict. People have been arguing about it ever since."

The writer leaned forward in his chair. "Suppose you tell me how it began, nine years ago."

That had been a snowy winter too, Leopold remembered, though by early March the snow on lawns and parking lots had retreated to little gray mounds which would soon be gone. It was a Monday morning and he'd gone into the squad room early to clear up some paperwork when the first report of the bombing came in.

Lieutenant Fletcher took the call. "Car explosion on Irving Circle, Captain. You want to come with me?"

Leopold shook his head. "Not unless I have to. Phone in if you need me."

Fletcher did just that some twenty minutes later. "Captain, you'd better get out here. It looks like a car bomb. Woman and two children dead at the scene."

Car bombs suggested one thing to most city police. "Any mob connections?"

Fletcher hesitated. "I don't know. There might be. The husband's in a state of shock. I haven't been able to question him yet."

"I'll be there."

Irving Circle was a nice street of middle-class homes looping around a grassy area at the center. A patrol car with its lights flashing was blocking the only access when Leopold arrived. He maneuvered around it and waved to the officer, pulling up to park across from an open-doored ambulance and two fire trucks. Virtually every home on the street must have been represented in the crowd of neighbors huddled together and talking among themselves in low voices.

Leopold nodded to the assistant medical examiner and others he knew among the team of investigators. "What have you got, Fletcher?" he asked, staring at the three body bags and the ruined car still leaking water from the fire hoses. The garage door, window-less and steel-clad, was undamaged, as was the minivan inside, but a side door into the garage had its window shattered by the blast. The windows of the house itself seemed intact.

"The woman is Frances Clemmins, the children are Kerry and Ben, ages seven and nine. All killed instantly. The boys from the bomb squad tell me it was under the driver's seat, attached to the ignition."

Leopold glanced at the minivan in the garage. Next to it was a small boat with an outboard motor attached. "Husband at home?"

"Alex Clemmins. He's in the kitchen, in pretty bad shape."

One of the detectives held the door open for him and Leopold stepped inside with Fletcher following. The house was brightly decorated, showing a woman's touch, and the sight of it immediately saddened him. He could see the man in the gray business suit seated at the kitchen table, his head buried in his hands as an older woman—a neighbor?—tried to comfort him.

"Mr. Clemmins?" This was the part of the job he'd always hated. "I'm Captain Leopold from the Violent Crimes Squad. I'm sorry to intrude on your grief at a time like this, but it's important to the investigation that we follow up any possible leads at once."

Clemmins lifted his head, revealing tear-streaked eyes and an expression of utter despair. He had a thin moustache and a receding hairline. "How can I go on after this? Who could have—?"

"Did your wife have any enemies?"

"No one! Everyone loved her."

The woman, around fifty with graying hair, introduced herself as Midge Proud, a neighbor from the next house. "Fran was wonderful," she confirmed. "And those dear children—"

"Did you notice any prowlers during the night, Mrs. Proud?"

She hesitated an instant. "No, but then my husband and I turned in early, before eleven. He has to be off to work by seven."

Because the undamaged car in the garage seemed to be the larger of the two, Leopold asked the obvious question. "Did Mrs. Clemmins usually drive the car she used this morning?"

Alex Clemmins gave a quick shake of his head, as if to clear it, then answered, "Not usually. It was mine, but I was blocking her and she had to take the children to school because they overslept and missed the bus. It often happens on Monday mornings. So I told her to take it. God, it's my fault they're dead!"

"It's no one's fault except the person who planted that bomb. Don't worry, we'll get him. What I need to know from you now is who might have done it. Are there personal or business associates who might want you dead?"

The shattered husband shook his head, still barely able to speak. "No one," he managed to say. "No one who'd do anything like this."

"Your wife's car is in the garage. Was it routine to leave yours in the driveway?"

"It depended. If she was out somewhere and I got home first, I took the garage. Usually mine was in the driveway."

"It's a two-car garage," Leopold pointed out.

"We keep a small boat there in the winter."

"Ever have trouble with prowlers damaging the car?"

"Never." Clemmins's voice was stronger and he seemed to have better control of his emotions. "This is a quiet, law-abiding neighborhood. Even the kids behave themselves."

"This wasn't the work of kids," Leopold pointed out. "What business are you in, Mr. Clemmins?"

"Real estate. I own a movie theater, a couple of bookstores, and some rental property."

"Any disgruntled employees you know about?"

He shook his head. "No."

"Write down the addresses of your businesses for Lieutenant Fletcher here. And let us know if you think of anyone at all who might have a grudge against you."

"Is there anything else?" he asked softly.

"Not right now, Mr. Clemmins. This is a terrible thing. You have our sympathy."

Later that afternoon Fletcher came into Leopold's office and sat down. "I've been checking on those addresses Alex Clemmins gave us, Captain."

Leopold caught the tightness in his voice. "What about it?"

"The movie theater is TorridTown, that porno house on Adams Avenue the city's been trying to shut down. The bookstores are pretty much the same thing. Sex books and videos."

"Why didn't we recognize the name? TorridTown's been in the news enough. I thought there was a man named Rockson involved."

"Rockson's been making the court appearances, but he only leases the property. Clemmins owns it."

"With a car bomb and ties to pornography, there could be a mob connection. See what you can find out. Meantime, I'll take a ride out to TorridTown."

The theater had once been a neighborhood picture palace, in the long-ago era when such things existed. Over the decades every other movie house within the city limits had been torn down but somehow this one survived, its name changed from the Odeum to TorridTown. Leopold remembered visiting it once around 1965 to see *The Sound of Music,* but he hadn't been back since they switched to fare like *Deep Throat* and *The Green Door* in the 1970s. Now the titles weren't even listed on the marquee outside.

A slim, brown-bearded man in a turtleneck was selling tickets to occasional customers when Leopold walked up. "Is Mr. Rockson in?"

"He's busy," the man responded without looking up.

Leopold flashed his badge and ID. "Police matter. Is Mr. Rockson in?"

The head came up, the eyes sleepy and sad. "What is this, more harassment?"

"Are you Mr. Rockson?"

"Yeah."

"Could I have a few words with you?"

"About the theater?"

"About three homicides."

That got his attention. "I'll close the ticket window. The show's started anyway. We can talk in my office."

Leopold followed him inside, with only a quick glance at the screen. Rockson's office was a tiny room behind the refreshment stand, cluttered with posters going back twenty years. He sat down in a worn swivel chair and asked, "Who's dead?"

"Frances Clemmins and her two children."

"Christ!" He pawed at the desktop for a cigarette. "Who did it?"

"It was a car bomb rigged to her husband's vehicle. We believe he was the intended victim."

"And you came here because he owns the place?"

"That's right. Car bombs require a certain amount of skill. It seems more the work of a professional killer—a mob hit. Are there any mob ties to this theater or the other places Clemmins owns?"

Rockson shook his head. "Nothing that I know about."

"It was all Clemmins's own money in these businesses? He never had visits from partners in New York?"

"Lately I've been busy with court appearances. I don't know what he's been doing."

The bearded man seemed to be avoiding a direct reply. "If you want to stay clear of trouble, you'd better tell me what you know," Leopold warned.

"Well, sure, he might have had a partner. I just lease the place."

"Do you book the films or does he?"

Rockson laughed. "This isn't exactly the Loew's circuit, you know. Someone phones me and says he has a block of films available, maybe a dozen or more. If they sound good and I'm familiar with the actors or the director I say sure, send them along. It doesn't take much to please the sort of audiences I get."

"Does Alex Clemmins ever suggest films or book them for you?"

"No."

His answer was so short that Leopold pursued it. "You're sure of that? Never?"

"He never books films. Once in a while someone calls me and says they got my name from him."

"So he does have some contact with the pornography business, and it's possible someone in that business might have had a motive for trying to kill him."

"Hey, anything's possible." He glanced at his watch. "I gotta go now, if you're finished."

"For the moment."

"Stay for the show if you want to. On the house."

"Thanks anyway."

Fletcher came back to the office around five. "Clemmins has mob connections, Captain. There's no doubt of it."

"Then he probably knows who tried to kill him. What did you find?"

"The Manhattan office of the FBI notified us last year that he made regular calls to a mob boss who controls porno houses and sex clubs in the Northeast. They had a tap on the guy's phone. From the conversations it seems likely this boss, Billy Cosetti, also known as Billy Goat Cosetti, was some sort of silent partner of Clemmins's."

Leopold sighed. "It looks as if we'll have to get back to Mr. Clemmins."

"Mrs. Proud is here too, if you want to speak to her. She came down to make a statement."

Leopold drew a blank. "Refresh my memory, Fletcher."

"Clemmins's neighbor, the woman we met at his house this morning."

"Of course! Where is she, in the interview room?"

Fletcher nodded. "Connie's with her."

Sergeant Connie Trent rose as Leopold entered the room. "I was just going to buzz you, Captain. I think you should hear what Mrs. Proud has to say."

Midge Proud appeared more attractive than she had at the Clemmins house that morning. The explosion had brought her running from her house during breakfast, but now she'd had time for makeup and grooming. She was still a gray-haired woman around fifty, but now she would be worth a second look.

"Nice to see you again, Mrs. Proud." He shook hands and sat down opposite her.

"Tell the captain what you just told me," Connie urged.

Midge Proud bit nervously at her lip. "I don't want to get anyone in trouble, but I keep thinking about Fran and those poor children."

"It was a terrible crime," Leopold agreed.

"I was telling the sergeant here that I couldn't sleep last night. I got up around one to take a pill and out of my bathroom window I noticed Alex just closing the door of the sedan on the driver's side."

Leopold came alert. "Are you sure it was Alex Clemmins you saw?"

"Oh yes. They keep an outside light on at night. I didn't think much of it. I figured he'd left something in the car and come out to get it."

"In the middle of the night?"

"They're usually up late. One o'clock wasn't the middle of the night for him."

Leopold had visions of Clemmins checking out the sex films on late-night cable. "Did he have anything in his hand when he left the car?"

"I didn't notice anything."

"Mrs. Proud, do you think Alex Clemmins could have been responsible for the death of his wife and children?"

"No, I can't believe that."

"And yet—"

"I just felt I should tell you what I saw."

"And thank you for doing so. Connie will take down your statement and have you sign it."

Leopold and Fletcher waited until late the following morning to pay another call on Alex Clemmins. By that time Fletcher had come up with information from Clemmins's bank and insurance company. The bereaved man answered the door himself, looking pale and drawn.

"Does this have to be today, Captain?" he pleaded. "I'm due at the funeral parlor in an hour."

"I'm afraid it can't wait, sir. We're at a crucial stage in the homicide investigation." They followed him inside.

"Your men were poking around the place all day yesterday—"

"Mr. Clemmins, I have to ask you about your dealings with a man named Billy Cosetti, sometimes called Billy Goat."

"I—" He shook his head, suddenly at a loss for words.

"He controls most of the pornography outlets in the Northeast, including your little operation in this city."

"I barely know the man," Clemmins insisted, recovering somewhat.

"Two weeks ago you tried to borrow three hundred thousand dollars from your bank here in town. They turned you down. Would you mind telling me what that money was for?"

"It was a business venture. I wanted to expand my theater holdings. Fran was urging me to get out of the sex business and buy into a first-run movie house in the suburbs, one of those with two or three screens. I agreed to try but the bank wouldn't go along."

Fletcher interrupted at this point. "You told your banker you needed the money to pay off some loans."

"Well, that too."

"Were these loans from Billy Goat Cosetti?" Leopold asked.

"Some of them," he admitted reluctantly.

"Mr. Clemmins, how much insurance did you carry on the lives of your wife and children?"

"Insurance? I don't remember exactly. The usual amount."

"One hundred thousand dollars on each of them. That's the exact amount you tried to borrow from the bank."

Clemmins's face twisted with sudden rage. "What are you trying to say—that I killed them for the insurance?"

"We're just investigating all the possibilities," Leopold said quietly.

"You're out of your minds, both of you!"

"Mr. Clemmins, we have a witness who saw you out at your car around one o'clock yesterday morning. You told us it was your idea that your wife and children take your car."

Alex Clemmins moistened his lips. "I want a lawyer."

Fletcher produced a folded document from his pocket. "We have a search warrant here for your house and garage."

"I want a lawyer," he repeated.

The bomb that killed Frances Clemmins and her two children had contained several sticks of dynamite and a detonator attached to the ignition. In the garage, wrapped in a dirty rag and inside an old tire, Fletcher found two additional sticks of dynamite and some electrical wire of the type used in the bombing. Alex Clemmins denied any knowledge of them.

Two days later, following the funerals of his wife and children, Clemmins was formally charged with their murder and the district attorney began building a case for presentation to the grand jury the following week. That was what took Leopold to New York City, to question Billy Goat Cosetti.

The Northeast's King of Porn wasn't in a topless bar or a bordello. Leopold found him in a Brooklyn warehouse, frowning over a clipboard of invoices while a forklift hoisted a pallet loaded with shrink-wrapped videotapes. He was a squat man with almost no hair, probably well past fifty. "You're the one who called me," he said, keeping the frown as he studied Leopold. "What can I do for you, Captain?"

"We're investigating the murder of Frances Clemmins and her two children. As I told you on the phone, we've arrested her husband."

"Alex Clemmins. Yeah, I've had some dealings with him. Come into the office and we'll talk."

The office was larger than Rockson's tiny room at the Torrid-Town theater but no neater. Leopold had to move a pile of paper-bound books off a chair so he could sit down. "Mr. Cosetti, I'll come right to the point. We have a report that Alex Clemmins owed you a considerable amount of money. Is that accurate?"

The squat man lit a cigar and shrugged. "Depends what you mean by a considerable amount. His operations there haven't been doing well. You got a very conservative town, Captain."

"Let's cut the games. How much is he into you for?"

"I don't even know. That's the truth."

"Take a guess."

Billy Goat shrugged. "A hundred grand, maybe. It's a lot of money."

"Could it be three hundred grand?"

"I doubt if it's that high." He shifted uneasily, not enjoying the conversation. "But, see, I put up the money for theater renovations, and then I did the same thing for the bookstores. Nothing's cheap these days."

"You supplied him with the films?"

"There's a fellow named Rockson who leases the place. My guy contacts him. Maybe he's been ripping Clemmins off. I'm not involved in that. I just know I got money coming."

"Would you kill him if you didn't get it?"

"You got the wrong idea about me, pal." He stood up, brushing some cigar ash from his pants. "You'll have to excuse me now."

Leopold took the train back home, wondering if the trip had been worth it.

Alex Clemmins was indicted and brought to trial amidst a media frenzy that ran on for months. The case against him was based upon three factors: He had the motive of needing money to pay off a loan from Billy Cosetti; he had the means, as shown by the two extra sticks of dynamite and wire hidden in his locked garage; and he had the opportunity, as sworn to by Midge Proud, who'd seen him by the car at one in the morning. Furthermore, he knew the children were often late on Monday mornings and he could urge his wife to take them to school in his car.

The murder of children, especially by a parent, always brought forth a public outcry. When the D.A. announced he would seek the death penalty only a few voices were raised against him. Presenting the state's case in court, he showed that the wire and the sticks of dynamite were the same type used in the bomb. The overhead door and the side door to the garage had both been locked, making it unlikely an outsider could have planted them there. And Clemmins's neighbor had no reason to lie about seeing him. They'd always been on good terms.

Defense attorneys argued that Clemmins was being prosecuted because of links to the pornography industry, and that could well have been a factor against him in the public's mind. The defense put him on the stand, where he vehemently denied all charges. The dynamite was not his and he had never hidden it in the garage. Midge Proud had seen him at one in the morning because he'd gone out to the car to have a smoke before bedtime. Fran hadn't liked him smoking in the house. The fact that he'd been denied a bank loan in the exact amount of his wife and children's insurance was nothing but a coincidence. He hadn't owed Cosetti that much but had tried to borrow a little extra so he could open another store. He told the jury he was convinced the mob boss had ordered him killed because of the unpaid debt.

The jury debated for three days before returning a verdict of Guilty against Alex Clemmins. That had been almost nine years ago.

Leopold was surprised to realize he'd been talking for nearly two hours when he finally reached the end of his story. Through it all Zach Brewster had sat spellbound on the sofa without moving except to ask the spelling of names and enter them on the yellow notepad on his lap. Now he said, "That's quite a story, Captain."

"I can hardly credit it to good police work," Leopold told him. "If the neighbor hadn't come forward we might never have gotten the break we needed."

"There was the dynamite in the garage."

"We had no reason to search for it. I still find it hard to believe he killed them just for the insurance."

Brewster put his pad and tape recorder into the briefcase. He took out a handful of newspaper reports, clipped together, and passed them over. Leopold saw again the press photos of the scene, the shell of the blackened car, the garage with its broken window in the side door. "Are these accounts fairly accurate, Captain?"

He glanced through a couple. "As accurate as the press usually is. The first reports usually need correcting as more facts come in." He handed back the clippings.

Brewster showed Leopold a folded cellular phone he carried in his jacket pocket. "I expect to be in town until tomorrow. If you think of anything else, you might give me a call on my cell phone."

Leopold nodded. "They're handy gadgets. My wife gave me one for Christmas."

He jotted down the number and handed it to Leopold. "Thanks for your time, Captain," he said, closing his briefcase.

"These days I've got nothing but time, Mr. Brewster."

The rest of the afternoon was free so Leopold took a ride down to headquarters. He rarely visited it these days, though he and Molly continued to see Fletcher and his wife socially every month or so. The place seemed to be running just as well without him and he was happy for Fletcher's success.

It was Connie Trent who greeted him as he walked in. "I thought you'd forgotten how to get here, Captain! How've you been?"

"Can't complain, at my age."

She grinned at him. "Thinking about coming back again?"

"I think I already came back once too often. Where's the captain?"

"You'll always be the captain around here, but if you mean Fletcher he's back in his office."

"Thanks, Connie."

Fletcher had recognized his voice and was already coming out to meet him. "Don't tell me! You're here about the Clemmins case."

It was Leopold's turn to smile. "You've been talking to Zach Brewster."

"Hell, sometimes I feel like I spend my whole day talking to writers and journalists. How've you been? How's Molly?"

"She's great. I'm just trying to keep busy."

"I told Brewster there was nothing new in the case but he wanted to interview the detective in charge of the investigation. I said you were retired and he asked for your phone number. I figured you could say no if you didn't want to see him, but I gave you a great buildup. Said you were like a bulldog in pursuing old cases, even though you're retired."

"I talked for about two hours," Leopold admitted. He frowned at a sudden thought.

"What's the matter, Captain?"

"Nothing. It was just that—Are the files on the Clemmins case still in the back room or have they gone off to the warehouse?"

"I've been keeping them here through all the appeals, just in case they were needed again. What are you looking for?"

"Didn't we have a diagram of the Clemmins house and its neighbors, showing the sight line from Midge Proud's window to the Clemmins car?"

"We sure did. As it turned out, they didn't need it in court because he admitted being out there around one o'clock for a smoke."

"Let's see if we can find it."

Leopold had always avoided trips to the warehouse at any cost, and the records room at headquarters wasn't much better. After they brushed off the dust, they were left with a thick cardboard file folder secured with a broken rubber band and a discolored ribbon. "We must get organized," Fletcher muttered.

"Ask the city fathers for more money so you can hire a couple of clerks."

"Sure! What do you think our chances are?" He carried the bulging folder to a work table and let the files and reports slide out of it.

Leopold recognized his handwriting on a number of documents and felt the years fall away. He was remembering the scene again, and Alex Clemmins's protestations of innocence. "Here it is!" He unfolded a diagram of the houses.

Fletcher squinted at it. "I remember now. This dotted line indicates the line of sight from Mrs. Proud's window. Is that what you wanted to check?"

"Not exactly. Look, Fletcher—this door on the side of the garage, where the window was broken. It's not visible to someone coming out the front door of the house and walking straight to a car in the driveway."

"What difference does that make?"

"None of the windows in the house were broken by the explosion. Why should that one at the side of the garage have broken?"

Fletcher shrugged. "I never thought about it. Shock waves can do funny things sometimes. What other explanation could there be?'

"Suppose the killer was a professional hit man hired by Billy Goat Cosetti. Suppose once he was on the scene he realized he had too much dynamite for the job. His target was one man, Alex Clemmins, and he didn't want to harm the family. He might have removed two sticks of dynamite to better limit the area of the blast, then hidden them and the extra electrical wire at the scene to avoid being caught with these items in his possession. He broke the window after planting the bomb, muffling the sound with a cloth, reached in and turned the bolt from inside the door. Then he hid the dynamite in that old tire and left the same way, locking the door behind him."

Fletcher's eyes narrowed. "It wouldn't have to be a hit man. Maybe that neighbor Mrs. Proud planted the bomb herself and didn't want her house to be damaged."

"Somehow I don't see Midge Proud or most women as bombers, Fletcher. It's a man's weapon. Besides, she was only a few steps from her own house. She could have hidden the dynamite there, or even buried it in the garden temporarily. And she'd be aware that Alex and Fran Clemmins sometimes switched cars, something the killer apparently didn't know."

"What's the bottom line on this, Captain?"

"It didn't have to be Alex Clemmins who hid that dynamite, and probably wasn't. Fran and the kids would have needed their coats in March, and hers at least was probably kept in a closet by the front door. If they came out that way they wouldn't have seen the broken garage window. If the dynamite was planted, one of the three cornerstones of the case is flawed. And how about the other two? He had an explanation for being in the car at one in the morning, and the amount of the insurance could have been a coincidence, as he claimed."

"After nine years you're telling me you don't think Clemmins is guilty?'

"I'm saying the evidence that convicted him might be flawed."

"The execution is only six days away, Captain."

"I know that. Is Rockson still running TorridTown?"

"You haven't been following the papers. After all these years the city finally got a restraining order against him. The theater has been closed for a month, though I guess he still has an office there."

Leopold glanced at his watch. "I guess I might take a drive over there."

"Don't get involved," Fletcher cautioned. "It's not your job anymore. I'll go see him in the morning."

Leopold drove home for dinner but the house was empty and he remembered that Molly had a meeting of her women lawyers' group that night. He was already planning to ignore Fletcher's advice and that decided him. He went upstairs to the bedroom and dug out the .38-caliber revolver he was licensed to carry as a private citizen. If he was going to seek out Rockson he had to be prepared for anything. As he was leaving the house he remembered the cell phone Molly had given him and that went into his pocket too, just in case he needed help in a hurry.

The area around the TorridTown theater and bookstore had deteriorated badly since his visit nine years earlier. Though Rockson still kept the marquee lit in promise of some future reopening, the place seemed deserted. Leopold was a bit surprised to find the lobby door unlocked. He entered and walked past the deserted box office, across the small lobby to the empty refreshment stand and the office beyond it. The office was empty, but one of Rockson's cigarettes still burned in the ashtray.

Leopold stepped out of the office and glanced around. If he was still in the building he could only have gone into the theater auditorium itself. Passing through the swinging doors, Leopold suddenly found himself in total darkness. "Rockson!" he shouted.

The place seemed deserted and he shouted the name again. "Rockson! I want to talk to you. It's Captain Leopold." Just for the moment, he thought, back from retirement.

Still silence.

He called the name once more and there was the flash and crack of a gunshot from the direction of the side aisle. He heard the thump of a bullet hitting one of the seat arms, and dropped to the floor in a sudden reflex action. He rolled over on his side and pulled his own weapon free.

Crawling along in the dark behind the seats he called out, "I know the truth. Throw down your gun!"

Another shot cracked out, from somewhere up near the screen. The gunman was circling, trying to get around the other side. Leopold wished the exit lights were on, but right now violations of the fire code were the least of his worries. He thought he heard a sound and stood up in a crouch. There was nothing but darkness around him.

He felt the cell phone in his pocket and found the key pad in the dark, keeping it in there to muffle the beeps as he pressed the numbers. Now if he could just remember it correctly—

First the power button, then the numbers. "Police! Throw down your gun," Leopold shouted again to further cover the muffled beeps. This time there was no answering shot. His assailant was moving closer in the dark, saving his bullets till there was a clear target.

Leopold raised his own gun and pressed the final button on his cell phone. Suddenly there was a muffled ring not twenty feet behind him. He whirled and fired a single shot at the sound.

Ten minutes later the lights in the theater were up, and the place was far from empty. Two patrol cars and an ambulance had responded to Leopold's 911 call, and now Captain Fletcher was hurrying down the center aisle. "What in hell happened here?" he wanted to know.

"I got him in the hip," Leopold explained, motioning toward the man being gently slid onto the ambulance gurney. "It was a shot in the dark, in more ways than one."

"It's Zach Brewster, that writer!"

Leopold nodded. "I believe he's the man who planted the bomb in Clemmins's car nine years ago."

They were interrupted by an officer calling from the back of the theater. "We've got a body here, Captain!"

It was Rockson, the TorridTown manager, and he'd been shot in the head at close range. Leopold stared down at the body. "So that's what he was doing here. If I'd arrived five minutes earlier I might have prevented this."

"You'd better explain," Fletcher said.

"All this recent publicity about next week's execution and possible new evidence must have worried Brewster—and maybe his boss, Billy Goat Cosetti. Brewster posed as an author working on a book and called on you for information. You gave me a big buildup and almost got me killed."

"Sorry about that," Fletcher said.

"He gave me his cellular phone number so I could call him if I remembered anything else. When someone shot at me here in the dark I took a chance that it was him and punched in his number on my own cell phone. His phone rang and I fired at the sound."

"You took a chance it was him?" Fletcher repeated. "Why would you even suspect him?"

"He was supposedly recording the interview with me on a small tape recorder, as writers often do. Those tapes only record about forty-five minutes per side. I talked for two hours and he hardly moved at all during that time, never changed tapes and didn't even turn it over. If he wasn't a writer, I got to wondering what he really was. They must have thought Rockson was getting ready to tell what he knew, so Brewster came here to ask some questions and then silence Rockson, just in case."

Fletcher watched them wheeling the wounded man out to the ambulance. "Do you think he's ready to implicate Cosetti?"

"I'd bet on it. And I'd bet the governor is ready to delay Clemmins's execution too!"

THE PHANTOM LOVER

Captain Fletcher first heard about Lynn Falkner's missing husband on Labor Day. He and wife, Carol, usually went over to the Leopolds' house for their traditional holiday cook-out, but this year Fletcher had invited Leopold up to his newly purchased cottage on Lake Conn, about forty-five minutes north of the city.

"It's someplace to get away to," Fletcher explained as he showed Leopold and Molly around. "I only wish we could have afforded it while the kids were still young."

"The years go by too fast," Molly said with a sigh, glancing over at her husband.

Leopold had grown older. There was no denying it. Fletcher still tried to keep him occupied with old unsolved cases from the department files, and Leopold's reasoning powers were as good as they'd been when he was Fletcher's superior on the Violent Crimes Squad. But his body was slowing down, and Fletcher and Molly both knew it.

"Beautiful place you've got here," Leopold said, leaning on the deck railing as he gazed out at the shimmering lake, its waters broken now and again by holiday boaters anxious to get in one last cruise before summer's end.

Molly was helping Carol with the food preparation and Leopold asked, "Got any more open cases for me to work on?"

"I'll take a look at the files. You did a good job on that last one."

"The Christmas trees? That was just luck." From the cottage came the ringing of the telephone.

"I'd call it more than luck—"

Molly had answered the phone, and it was she who called out to them. "Sorry, Fletcher. It's Connie, at the office."

He shook his head sadly. "There's not supposed to be any crime on Labor Day."

Leopold gave him a smile. "That's what I used to say."

Connie Trent was on duty that day so Fletcher knew it had to be business. "Captain, I'm sorry to bother you on a holiday, but we

have a missing-person situation here. It could develop into something more than that."

"What's so special about a missing person?"

"The woman who filed the report is Lynn Falkner. Remember
her?"

Indeed he did. About six months earlier she and her husband had
been involved in a very public tussle at one of the city's fancier res-
taurants. She'd jabbed him in the neck with a salad fork and drawn
a few drops of blood. The police had taken her into custody, but her
husband refused to press charges and she was released after a few
hours. Because of the very public nature of the brawl, it had been the
lead item on the eleven o'clock news that night and had made page
one of the following morning's paper. Falkner was a local Realtor
who dabbled in politics, and his name was fairly well known in the
city.

"I remember," Fletcher said. "So her husband's gone missing?
Maybe he just decided he was tired of getting jabbed with salad
forks."

"It might be more than that. She called in this morning to tell us
he'd been gone for twenty-four hours. He went off to church yesterday morning and never came home. Within the last hour we've had
a report of a car found in that gravel pit near the old rail yard. It's
Stanley Falkner's car and there's a body inside."

Fletcher sighed and glanced at his watch. It was just after one.
They wouldn't be eating till two. "Call me back when you have a
positive ID on the body, Connie. If it's Falkner I'll come right in."

As it turned out, Fletcher only arrived at the morgue later that
night, just before Lynn Falkner was brought in to identify her husband's body. Fletcher remembered her from the trouble six months
earlier, a tall, attractive woman with brown hair and tinted eyeglasses. She was thirty-one years old, about the age of Fletcher's own
daughter, and had been married to Stanley Falkner for eight years.
It had been the first marriage for both of them. She did not seem the
sort to murder her husband, but then she hadn't seemed the sort to
jab him in the neck with a salad fork, either. Seated across his office
desk from her after the identification, Fletcher couldn't have said
exactly what sort she was.

"Now then, Mrs. Falkner, can you tell me everything that happened yesterday morning, the last time you saw your husband alive."

She was clutching a handkerchief in one hand but her eyes seemed dry. "Stan was brought up Catholic, but he's never gone to church regularly. I don't know what impelled him to go yesterday, unless it was the fact that my sister and her husband were visiting for the holiday weekend. I assumed he just wanted a break."

"What are their names?"

"My sister is Joan Reagen. Her husband is Doug. We were having a brunch for them and we'd invited our friends Max and Marci McGuire over at eleven. He should have been home from church by that time, but I didn't think too much of it at first."

Fletcher had a memory for names and he immediately flipped through the rile file on the table in front of him. "The McGuires, aren't they the couple who were with you at Leonardo's restaurant the night you and your husband had that altercation?"

She nodded. "They're our closest friends. They've stuck with us through everything."

"Your husband never returned home after church?"

"No. I thought he was picking up some last-minute things from the store, and then I thought he'd gone into one of his unpleasant moods because of my sister and brother-in-law being there."

"How long were they staying?"

Lynn Falkner brushed a strand of hair from her eyes. "They were supposed to go back tonight, to get the kids ready for school, but when the police found Stan's body they said they'd stay on with me."

"You and your husband have no children?"

"No. Early in our marriage we wanted them, but lately things have been so ..." She left the sentence dangling.

Fletcher cleared his throat. "Mrs. Falkner, that altercation at Leonardo's restaurant involved a violent assault on your husband."

"No charges were filed against me," she answered calmly, not waiting for his question. "It was a family quarrel that got out of hand."

"Was there any time when you were alone after your husband left the house to attend church?"

"Are you asking me if I have an alibi, Captain?"

"I'm just trying to narrow the possibilities, ma'am."

"Max and Marci remained at the house with us until late afternoon. I think we were all surprised that Stan didn't come home after church. And of course Joan and her husband were there overnight. I was never out of their sight. Max phoned first thing this morning to see if Stan was back, and then he and Marci came over. They're the ones who convinced me I should call the police. My sister thought he'd just gone off and gotten drunk somewhere because she was in town."

"I gather there was no love lost between them."

"Hardly. When we had that trouble last March she hopped the next plane here and really lit into him, told him if he filed charges against me she'd finish the job I'd started with that salad fork."

Fletcher made a few notes and then said, "You're showing remarkable control, Mrs. Falkner, in view of the fact that your husband has just been murdered."

"There was no love lost between us."

"Then why didn't you divorce him?"

"He said his religion prevented it. I know a lot of Catholics get divorces or annulments these days, but Stan's mother would have disowned him. She's very strict on the subject."

"Did your husband have any enemies?" he asked.

"No one except me."

Fletcher asked some further questions, mainly routine, then said, "That's all for now, Mrs. Falkner. I'll probably need to talk with you again in a day or two."

After she'd gone, he sat alone at his desk for a few minutes. She'll certainly shed no tears at her husband's death, but did that mean she'd killed him?

Lieutenant Connie Trent had been busy checking the movements of Lynn Falkner and her guests on that Sunday and Monday. A young neighborhood college student named Gabe Smith had been there on Sunday afternoon to cut the grass, and he verified that Lynn Falkner and her four guests had spent much of the time on the deck at the rear of the house. He hadn't noticed any of them leave, and even after he'd moved onto the yards down the street he could see that all the cars except Stanley's remained in the Falkner driveway. A neighbor across the way confirmed his account.

Fletcher read Connie's report on Tuesday afternoon and summoned her to his office. "If it's any help, they've completed the autopsy on Stanley Falkner. He died sometime Sunday but they can't pinpoint it any better than that."

"Cause of death?" Connie asked.

"His skull had been fractured by a blow from behind. He was already dead when the car was pushed over the edge of the quarry."

"Do we have any evidence that he died in the car?"

Fletcher shrugged. "There's not much blood. Looks like he was killed outside the car, possibly at the quarry since some blood stains were found near the edge. Then he was put back in and the car went over the edge."

"On Sunday morning?"

"It's a pretty good assumption." He showed her a time line he'd worked out. "According to the witnesses, Falkner left the house around nine forty-five, saying he was going to church. We haven't found anyone who saw him there, but then he wasn't a frequent churchgoer and a lot of people were away for the holiday weekend. He may have gone and not been recognized, or he may have had another destination in mind."

"Such as?"

"Meeting his killer."

Connie considered the possibilities. "His wife seems to have the strongest motive."

"And the strongest alibi." He stood up. "Mrs. Falkner's sister Joan is still in town till after the funeral. I think I'll run out to the house in the morning and talk to her."

Wednesday had turned gloomy with the threat of rain, and the morning streets were crowded with school buses on this first day back to class. When Fletcher reached the Falkner house it seemed deserted and for a moment he thought no one was at home. Then a middle-aged man with a neatly trimmed red beard appeared at the door.

"I'm Captain Fletcher, sir, in charge of the investigation into Stanley Falkner's death."

The bearded man held out his hand. "Doug Reagen, Lynn's brother-in-law. Come on in."

Fletcher entered the comfortable living room, noting a few current magazines on the coffee table with a cellular phone resting on them. "I was hoping to speak with your wife."

"She and Lynn are making the funeral arrangements. The medical examiner just released the body. They should be back soon. Can I get you a beer?"

"I'm on duty," Fletcher said. "But maybe you can answer a couple of questions. Just how bad were things between Lynn Falkner and her husband?"

"Oh, you'd have to ask her. I don't know anything about that."

"This is a murder investigation, Mr. Reagen," Fletcher reminded him.

He measured his reply carefully. "Husbands and wives always have their little skirmishes. It's part of being married."

"Were you and your wife here in the house for the entire day on Sunday?"

"I certainly was. Joan might have gone out at some point to get a dozen eggs. We weren't sure the McGuires were joining us until that morning."

"Was this before or after Lynn's husband left for church?"

Doug Reagen snickered slightly. "Church? Yeah, I guess it was after."

"What's so funny, Mr. Reagen? He didn't go to church, did he?"

"Maybe he did, I don't know."

"The truth might help us find his killer."

Reagen was silent for a moment and then replied, "I suppose so. I don't know where he was going, but he told me he'd bring back a little pot for us to smoke later in the day."

"Had he done this before?"

"Not when I was around, but he and Lynn talked about it sometimes."

"What did your wife think about it?"

"Joan never criticizes her sister, no matter what."

As if on cue, the side door opened and Lynn Falkner came up the steps from the driveway, followed by a dark-haired woman who might have been a few years older. "We were at the funeral parlor," she told Fletcher by way of explanation. "This is my sister, Joan. I see you've met her husband."

"Captain Fletcher," he said, extending a hand to Joan Reagen. "I wanted to speak with you as part of our investigation. If you'd feel more comfortable at my office downtown—"

"This is fine," Joan Reagen replied. "I won't be saying anything Lynn shouldn't hear."

Fletcher ran over his timetable again, then asked, "Is it true that you went out Sunday morning to buy an extra carton of eggs?"

"I asked her to," Lynn interrupted. "When the McGuires phoned to say they were coming I discovered I was short."

"And your husband couldn't pick them up after church because—?"

"Because he was already gone."

"You could have called him on that cell phone," Fletcher observed.

Lynn Falkner shook her head. "That's mine. He didn't have one in his car."

Fletcher wanted to question Joan Reagen about the pot smoking but he knew she would say nothing that might harm her sister. Instead he asked, "How long did it take you to get the eggs?"

Joan shrugged. "Twenty, thirty minutes, I suppose. The nearest stores were closed for the Labor Day weekend, and Max and Marci were already here by the time I got back."

"How long did they stay?"

"Most of the afternoon. They were waiting for Stan to get back. They got really concerned about it, wanted to call the police right away until I convinced them to wait until Monday morning."

Later Fletcher tried to compartmentalize the five people who'd been at the Falkner house on the day Lynn's husband was killed. It was a technique he'd learned from Leopold and it certainly had worked well for him. If everyone was telling the truth, Lynn Falkner had been at the house all day, as had her brother-in-law, Doug. Her sister Joan had gone off for eggs and been away about a half-hour. Could she have connected with Falkner, killed him, and driven the body to the quarry in that length of time? It was doubtful, but possible.

And what about Max and Marci McGuire? Might they have killed their close friend Stan before arriving at his house for Sunday brunch? That seemed unlikely, but he knew he had to question them next.

The McGuires lived in a modern town house down by the Sound, one that had been built a few years back on the grounds of a country club. Connie had told him that Max McGuire was a teacher while his wife did book keeping part time on her home computer. Fletcher wasn't surprised to see two sets of golf clubs in the open garage next to a sporty new car.

It was Marci McGuire who answered his ring, wearing shorts and a country club T-shirt. After studying his identification, she said, "I'd rather you came back when my husband is home. He's out golfing right now. He only had a half-day at the high school."

Fletcher gave her an innocent smile. "Oh? I thought I saw his clubs in the garage."

That unhinged her nicely. "I—perhaps he returned when I was in the basement. Let me look upstairs." She left the door ajar and Fletcher edged his way through.

She came back in a moment with her husband close behind her. Both had the look of blond, tanned athletes, and his shorts and shirt matched hers. "We've already given our stories to your Lieutenant Trent," the man told Fletcher. "I don't know what more we can add." They all sat down around a coffee table that had a layout of the club's golf course on its surface.

"Excuse me if I run over the same material again. I need to verify the time you both arrived at the Falkner home on Sunday."

"A bit after eleven, wasn't it, Marci?"

She agreed, "Maybe quarter past, at the latest."

"They were all there when you arrived?"

"Well, no," Marci replied. "Lynn said Stan had gone to church, though that seemed unlikely. As you know, he never did come back."

"And Joan was out buying eggs or something," her husband added. "She came in just after we got there."

"Were there any other visitors during the day?"

"Not unless you count the college kid who cuts their grass. He came by in the afternoon."

"Did Falkner have any enemies you knew about? Did he ever mention threats to his life?"

"Sure, his wife told him she wished he was dead," Max McGuire said. "We were there when she tried to kill him with a fork, just because he made fun of the dress she was wearing. They passed that off as a family spat. He declined to bring charges against her."

"He'd have brought charges if it had happened now," Marci told him.

"How come? What changed?"

They exchanged glances and Fletcher knew they had more to tell. Finally Marci said, "Lynn has a lover. She's been having an affair for four months and Stan found out about it. He was looking for some keys in her purse and discovered a letter she was apparently going to mail. I think that was the last straw. He came here one night last week and showed us the letter."

"What did it say?"

Another exchange of glances. Finally Max McGuire stood up. "We have it. He gave it to us for safekeeping." He left the room to get it.

"In case anything happened to him," Marci added.

"He thought she was going to kill him?"

"She attacked him at least twice that we know about, once at the restaurant and once with her car."

"When was that?" Fletcher asked, making notes as fast as he could.

"Back in June. He was on foot, behind the car, and she backed right into him, claimed she didn't see him."

"Was he hurt?"

Marci shook her head. "I guess just a few bruises. He didn't report it."

Her husband returned with a folded sheet of notepaper inside a blank envelope. "He said he took this out of her purse."

Fletcher handled it carefully, at the edges, in case there was a possibility of fingerprints. The note was dated August 29 and read: *Angel, These past four months have been heaven. My nights without you are a sham. I must get rid of him before he drives me crazy. This time I'll make certain we succeed. Loving you in every dream. Your Lynn.*

"Do you have any idea who this Angel might be?" Fletcher asked, slipping the note back in its envelope.

"None," Max McGuire replied. "And neither did Stan. But she must have realized he'd found the note and taken it."

His wife shook her head, seeming close to tears. "They were our best friends once. We couldn't believe such a thing would happen."

"I'll have to keep this," Fletcher said, carefully storing the envelope between the pages of his notebook. He'd transfer it to a plastic evidence bag in the car. "Just one more question for now, Did Lynn Falkner and her husband ever smoke pot or use other drugs?"

"Once, I think. Maybe twice. It wasn't a regular thing, at least not when we were around," Marci said. Her husband nodded in agreement.

"When Stan Falkner said he was going to church Sunday, might he actually have been going to buy some drugs?"

Neither of them knew the answer to that question. Perhaps only Lynn Falkner had all the answers.

"Where do we stand?" Connie Trent asked him on Thursday morning. Calling hours were planned at the funeral parlor that evening, and Stan Falkner's funeral mass would be celebrated on Friday at the church he may or may not have attended the previous Sunday.

"We checked the fingerprints on that note," Fletcher told her. "I requested sample prints from Lynn Falkner, the McGuires, and the Reagens. As we expected, Lynn, her husband, and the McGuires all left prints on it. How about you?"

"I've got the lab report on the victim's clothing, but there's nothing unusual—bits of gravel in the bottom of his sneakers, some blades of grass on his pants, a dab of blue paint on his shirt which may or may not have been there earlier."

"That gravel interests me," Fletcher said. "It confirms he was out of the car at the gravel pit, as we already suspected from that blood on the ground."

Connie nodded. "It matches the gravel around the pit."

"He went there to meet someone…"

"Are you back to a drug deal again?"

"I don't know. There may be another explanation that gets back to Lynn Falkner or her lover. I want to question her again. Today, before the wake. I want to confront her with this letter."

"Can't it wait till after the funeral?"

"I think it has to be today," Fletcher said.

Lynn Falkner arrived at his office just before noon, looking distraught. "What's so important that it can't wait?" she demanded. "You said something about new evidence turning up."

"Please have a seat, Mrs. Falkner. I hope this won't take long." He pushed a pad and pencil across the desk to her. "We're going to need a sample of your handwriting."

"What for?"

He ignored her question. "Please write these words: *Angel. These past four months have been heaven—*"

She put down the pencil and said, very quietly, "I want a lawyer."

"I was about to advise you of your rights." He took out a photocopy of the letter and showed it to her. "Do you deny writing this?"

"Where did you get it?"

"Who is Angel?" he countered. "Were you having a love affair with him?"

Silence.

"Did he lure Stan out to the gravel pit and kill him for you?"

"I think it's time for a lawyer," she said.

"Very well. I'll give you a few minutes to think it over and then you can call someone."

He went over to Connie's desk in the squad room, watching Lynn Falkner through the glass partition to his office. "I showed her the note and she wants a lawyer."

"Are you going to arrest her?"

"I need a lot more than that note. But I think I've unnerved her."

He gave it five more minutes, pouring himself a cup of coffee, and then returned to his office. Lynn Falkner glanced up as he entered. "Would you like some coffee?" he asked.

"No, thank you." She moistened her lips. "I've decided to make a statement."

"Without a lawyer? Are you sure you want to do this?"

"I am. What's the use of dragging it out?"

"All right." He took the familiar printed card from his desk drawer. "I'll get Lieutenant Trent in here to record us while I read you your rights. Then we'll run through some questions and put it all in statement form for your signature."

"Fine." She smiled faintly. "You'll have to guide me. I've never confessed to a murder before."

Connie came in to join them and turned on a tape recorder. Fletcher read the statement of Lynn Falkner's rights from the card and then asked, "Mrs. Falkner, do you have any knowledge of the manner in which your husband died last Sunday?"

"Yes, he was killed by my lover, Gavin Stark, at my urging."

"How long has this Gavin Stark been your lover?"

"About four months. We met one day while shopping at the supermarket."

"What's his address?"

"He's divorced and has a furnished apartment on Maple Street. I'll give you the number."

"Suppose you tell us exactly what happened on Sunday."

She took a deep breath and began. "Stan and I had been bitter enemies for a year or longer. Sometimes he tried to beat or humiliate me and I struck back with whatever weapon was at hand. It wasn't always as public as that night at the restaurant. He wouldn't give me a divorce because of his religion, and I was thinking about killing him even before I met Gavin. During the summer I tried hitting him with the car but I botched it. When I told Gavin about that, he said that he would kill him."

"How did he go about it?"

"Stan occasionally bought small quantities of marijuana for us to smoke. He thought we fought less if we were a little high. Gavin struck up a conversation with him in a bar one night and mentioned that he could supply high-grade pot at a good price. He gave him a little just to try. Then he was going to lure him out to the gravel pit and kill him there. It was supposed to be later in September, but I moved it up to last Sunday when I discovered that Stan had found the note in my purse."

"What did Gavin Stark kill him with?"

"A jack handle, I think. I didn't ask the details. After Stan was dead he lifted him back into the car and rolled it into the gravel pit. He figured it might be a few days before it was found, but somebody spotted it on Monday."

"Have you talked to him since then?"

"He called Sunday noon to say it was done. I pretended it was a wrong number."

"You called him Angel. Why was that?"

She smiled sadly at the memory. "Because he looks like one. And he said his name, Gavin, is an Old Welsh word for hawk. I thought of calling him Hawk, but Angel seemed more appropriate."

Fletcher passed the address over to Connie. "Go pick him up, Lieutenant. Take a couple of men with you."

But Gavin Stark wasn't there. By the time Fletcher had a statement typed up for Lynn Falkner to sign, Connie had radioed in that the apartment seemed empty. "Get a search warrant," he told her.

"The landlord's never seen him, Captain," she said. "He just gets a rent check in the mail every month."

"Get a search warrant," he repeated.

Connie did so and returned to the squad room a few hours later. "There were a few clothes and toilet articles, a bottle of Scotch with two glasses, some condoms, and a few joints of pot. It looks more like a love nest than someone's living quarters."

He could tell she was holding something back. "What else, Connie?"

"Beneath a pile of his monogrammed handkerchiefs I found two more letters from Lynn to Angel."

"Is his name and address on the envelopes?"

"The envelopes are blank. She must have hand-delivered them."

"Let's see them."

The letters were much like the one he had, perhaps a bit more passionate but both addressed to "Angel" or "Dearest Angel." He read them over a couple of times, then returned the plastic evidence bags to Connie. "His fingerprints should be all over these. Have them tested right away."

"The landlord has the name of the bank the rent checks were drawn on. We can go after the account, too."

"Good idea," he agreed. "Keep me informed."

He went back into his office. Lynn Falkner had been formally arrested and charged with murder and conspiracy to commit murder. He said she could attend her husband's funeral service with Connie Trent escorting her, but she declined. Her arrest was a page-one story the following morning and the story stated that an unnamed accomplice was being sought. Two weeks later, Lynn was indicted by a grand jury and she hired the city's top criminal lawyer to defend her. The trial was set to begin the first week in January.

Autumn dragged on, and still there was no sign of Gavin Stark. In fact, except for the bank account used to pay rent on the apartment, there was no firm evidence that he'd ever existed. The love letters from Lynn Falkner in his drawer had been wiped clean of finger-prints, as had everything else in the small apartment.

Connie had questioned everyone at the bank branch where the checking account had been opened, but no one remembered ever seeing Stark. The customer service representative whose name was on the account record thought it might have been a woman who opened it. She told Connie she vaguely remembered the woman depositing five thousand dollars in cash. Connie showed her the mug shot of Lynn Falkner. The bank representative thought it looked a bit like her, but she couldn't be certain.

Two days before Thanksgiving, with the whereabouts of Gavin Stark still a mystery, Lynn Falkner's attorney, Clark Whitehead, announced that she had recanted her confession, claiming it was obtained under duress on the very day of her husband's wake.

Thanksgiving dinner with Leopold and Molly was always a plea-sure. Some years, when Fletcher and Carol's children came home, the Leopolds prepared dinner for everyone. This year there were only the four of them, and Molly insisted on roasting the turkey. While Carol helped her in the kitchen, Fletcher joined Leopold on the enclosed back porch for a glass of white wine. It had been a good autumn, with sunny days and crisp nights, and a few browning oak leaves still clung to the tree in Leopold's backyard.

The first thing he asked Fletcher was, "Any luck finding the Falkner woman's accomplice yet?"

"Lots of luck, all of it bad. I'll swear the man is a phantom."

Leopold smiled. "A phantom lover. I suppose there've been stranger things."

"I know she's conning us somehow, but I don't know how or why."

"The *why* part, is simple enough. If the jury finds her not guilty she can't be tried again, and without the lover I don't believe the D.A.'s office has enough evidence for a guilty verdict."

"What do you mean?"

"Lynn Falkner has been indicted on two counts, second-degree murder and conspiracy to commit murder. She has a solid alibi for the time her husband was killed."

"We just have her brother-in-law's word for that. Maybe they're in it together. Maybe he's the phantom lover."

Leopold shook his head. "I've been following this case closely in the papers. Even if they were in it together, there wasn't enough time. They'd hardly try something like that with her sister Joan due to return with the eggs, and the McGuires on their way over."

"Do you believe those letters from Lynn Falkner to Angel are genuine?"

"Probably. But you should keep in mind that Angel might not be a male. It's a much more common term of endearment for a woman."

Fletcher grunted, considering the possibilities. "All right, admitting for the moment that she has an alibi, what about the second count of the indictment?"

"Conspiracy to commit murder? Who did she conspire with?"

"Gavin Stark."

Leopold shook his head sadly. "A phantom lover. If you cannot produce this Gavin Stark, there is no way the D.A. can prove a conspiracy. For all we know, the man never existed."

"But—"

"As things stand today, with her confession recanted, the alibi firmly in place, and no sign of the supposed accomplice, I doubt if there's a jury in the country that would convict her. Come January she'll be acquitted and she'll be home free."

Fletcher got up to pour himself another glass of wine. "Tell me one thing. Captain."

"You're the captain now," Leopold corrected.

"Tell me one thing. Do you think she did it?"

"Of course she did it! Now you just have to find her accomplice."

Because he'd been at the cottage on Labor Day and Connie Trent had handled the preliminary investigation, Fletcher had never actually visited the scene of the crime. By the time he'd arrived downtown on that holiday evening the body was at the morgue and the wrecked car had been towed into the police garage. He'd studied maybe a hundred color photographs of the body and the crime scene, but that wasn't the same as going there yourself. On the Saturday after Thanksgiving he drove out to the quarry to get a feel of the place.

It was a barren, desolate location, without even a blade of grass growing anywhere near. A dusty dirt road ran all along the rim of the place, dipping at one point to start its perilous journey to the quarry's bottom. On this holiday weekend some machinery remained in place, unused, against the far wall of stone, ready to start running again on Monday morning. The leaden sky and chill air made it even more unattractive than it would have been on Labor Day. Certainly on a deserted holiday weekend it would be the perfect setting for a drug purchase. Or a murder.

From the crime-scene photos, Fletcher could identify the spot where the car had gone over the edge with Falkner's body inside. There was gravel here, no doubt spilled from the endless caravan of trucks that used this service road. Connie had told him it matched the gravel embedded in the bottom of the victim's sneakers.

He thought about it on the drive back to headquarters. There was something he was missing, some vital point he'd overlooked. He was sure Leopold would have had the case solved by now.

On Monday morning he met with District Attorney Webber at the Hall of Justice. He never liked these occasional sessions with Webber, who was quick to pass out blame but rather slow when it came to congratulations for a job well done. He was gray-haired and overweight, and had a reputation for trying cases only when they were cut-and-dried high-profile ones likely to help his re-election chances.

"Captain Fletcher," he began, "the trial of Lynn Falkner is scheduled to begin five weeks from today. What's the story on this recanted confession?"

Fletcher told him everything he knew, describing the interview during which the confession was obtained. "I stand behind it one hundred percent. There was no intimidation of any sort. I believe that confession to be true."

"Then why haven't you been able to locate this man, Gavin Stark? We're nowhere without him."

"He seems to have dropped off the face of the earth. The rent was paid by checks drawn on a bank account used only for that purpose. We found no fingerprints in the apartment even though it seems to have been used as a love nest."

Webber sighed. "We need him, Captain Fletcher. Without him, I may have to ask for a postponement, which might not be granted."

"We'll find him for you," Fletcher said with more confidence than he felt.

Later that same week, as the season's first snowfall dusted the December streets, Fletcher spoke again with Lynn Falkner, this time in the interview room at the county jail. Her lawyer, Clark Whitehead, sat beside her, and it was clear that she had no intention of changing her story another time. "You forced that confession out of me!" she insisted angrily. "It was the day of Stan's wake and I didn't know what I was saying."

"You assaulted him six months earlier," Fletcher reminded her.

"With a salad fork," her lawyer said with a dismissive wave of his hand. Fletcher could see him using the same gesture in front of a jury.

"Gavin Stark exists," he insisted. "He had some clothing in the apartment you told us about, along with more of your letters."

"Then where is he?" Whitehead demanded. "The contents of that apartment prove nothing, apart from the letters, which could have been planted."

And of course he was right.

Fletcher's frustration grew with each passing day. He found himself taking it out on Carol at home, and hated what the case was doing to him. "Why don't you call Leopold?" she said finally.

"You don't think I can handle this on my own? Leopold's retired twice from the department already. I can't keep dragging him back."

"Call him," she begged.

Molly answered the phone and put Leopold on at once. "I hate to bother you again with this Falkner case, but Webber's breathing down my neck."

"I saw the headline in the morning paper," Leopold said. "*Webber and Whitehead to Face Off in Falkner Trial.*"

"The D.A. is afraid of losing this one. He wants us to find Gavin Stark."

"Are you any closer to that?"

"Not an inch," Fletcher admitted. "No car registration in the state, no other bank accounts, nothing."

"It's obviously an alias."

"Connie has checked the alias file for known criminals and come up with nothing."

"Any other thoughts?"

"Just a wild one. Do you think all five of those people—Lynn, the Reagens, and the McGuires—could be in it together?"

He could hear Leopold sigh into the receiver. "Fletcher, you're making this too complicated. It's not. It's a simple case of a woman and her lover killing her husband."

"What should I do?" Fletcher asked quietly.

"Think about it."

Fletcher did just that, through most of December. Christmas shopping reached its peak, kids came home from college, and even in the squad room holiday decorations began to appear. He thought about all this, and considered some dates. By late August, according to Lynn Falkner's love note to Angel, the affair had been going on for four months.

Late April, maybe early May.

What happened at that time of year, every year?

"Connie!" he called out to the squad room.

"What is it, Captain?"

"What was the name of that college kid you questioned, the one who cut the Falkners' grass?"

She flipped open her file and replied after a moment. "Gabe Smith. Why?"

"Give me his address and get your coat."

"He's probably gone back to school."

"It's Christmas recess for most colleges."

The Smiths lived in a brick and stone house about two blocks from the Falkners. It was Mrs. Smith, a pale, slender woman, who answered the door. She studied Fletcher's identification and said, "Gabe is out with his friends. He should be home soon for dinner."

Fletcher went out to his unmarked car to wait. Connie was in her car, two blocks farther down the street. It was just under an hour, as the day was getting darker, when a car driven by a sandy-haired young man pulled up in front of the Smith house. Fletcher reached out the window and clamped his spinning red light to the roof of the car as he pulled up behind him.

That was when Smith caught him off guard. Instead of getting out, he threw the car into reverse and slammed backwards into Fletcher's car, setting off the airbag. It hit Fletcher in the face and chest with the force of a boxing glove. He was out of the car the instant it deflated, but Smith was already accelerating forward down the street.

He reached for the radio and barked, "He's headed your way in a red Saturn. Take him, Connie. He's our killer."

It was Leopold himself who answered the door the following evening, after dinner. He smiled at Fletcher but couldn't resist a little dig. "The old airbag trick, and you fell for it!"

"I never heard of it before," Fletcher grumbled.

"You haven't been reading the national crime reports."

But Molly came to his rescue with a couple of beers. "Don't let him bug you, Fletcher. He thinks you did a fine job, even if he won't admit it."

Fletcher accepted one of the beers and sat down. "Connie's the one who did the fine job. She had him out of the car and handcuffed before he knew what hit him."

"So tell me how it went down," Leopold asked, with a boyish eagerness for the details. "How did you know this Gabe Smith was the so-called phantom lover?"

"Her note spoke of four months of heaven. I thought back to early May and tried to remember what might have happened then. Two things came to mind. Some colleges end their classes around that time, and the grass begins to grow. I remembered Connie and someone else—Max McGuire, I think—mentioning a college kid who cut the Falkners' lawn on Sunday afternoon. He cut several lawns in the neighborhood, some probably on Sunday morning. I remembered there were traces of grass on Falkner's clothes, yet no grass grew near the quarry where he'd been killed. The grass had come from the killer's clothes when he lifted the body back into the car. Grass, and a young man who cut it."

"Keep going," Leopold said.

"The note Falkner found in his wife's purse, and those we found in the apartment, were in blank envelopes without address or postage. They hadn't been sent through the mail but delivered personally from Lynn Falkner to her lover. I wondered why that was necessary. If they met, she could simply tell him her feelings. But with her husband often at home it was necessary to slip these notes to Gabe Smith, probably when she paid him each time for cutting the grass. She rented an apartment where they could meet, setting up a bank account for the purpose in the fictitious name of Gavin Stark. Notice that the initials were the same—Gavin Stark and Gabe Smith. They could leave those monogrammed handkerchiefs in the room without any danger. They were a little gift from her, I suppose."

"She must be ten years older than he is," Molly commented from the doorway.

Fletcher shrugged. "That's nothing new."

"How did Smith lure Falkner to the scene?" Leopold asked.

"It was as we suspected. He struck up a conversation with him in the yard one day and offered to supply Falkner with small amounts of pot. That's what Falkner was after when he said he was going to church. Then, after killing Falkner, Smith phoned Lynn on her cell phone as a signal that it was done. He used a pay phone or we would have been onto him earlier."

"What about the notes addressed to Angel?" Molly asked. "Was that just a term of endearment?"

"Not entirely," Fletcher answered. "Gabe is short for Gabriel, of course, and we all remember that Biblical archangel, don't we?"

Leopold smiled and asked for another beer.

THE EMERALD EXPERT

In his retirement, Leopold paid little attention to criminal cases unless they involved a particularly baffling murder. The routine drug killings, robberies, and domestic violence held scant interest for him except as human tragedies that might have been avoided. On the occasional evenings when he and Molly dined with Captain Fletcher and his wife, little was said about the daily operations of the Violent Crimes Division. That was all in Fletcher's hands now, and he was doing a capable job of it.

Perhaps this accounted for the fact that Leopold had read little about the Jaspar case until a week before the trial was scheduled to begin, and then the news reached him in an unusual manner. "It's for you," Molly called out to him one Tuesday evening in April, holding the phone for him.

He took it and heard a voice from the past. "Captain Leopold, this is Henri Scarlotti. Do you remember me?"

"I certainly do, Henri! How's the jewelry business?" It must have been close to twenty years since they'd seen each other, but Leopold still remembered the jovial little Frenchman with the Italian name. He'd conducted a seminar for law-enforcement officers on jewel thefts, and later testified as an expert witness at a local trial.

"I am a full-time gemologist now, working with a team of French geochemists. It's a pleasure to be back in America for a few days."

"Where are you?"

"I flew into Boston today, but I'll be in your city tomorrow, to testify."

Leopold could hardly believe it. "You're coming here? For a trial?"

"The Jaspar case. Hasn't it been in the papers?"

"I may have read something about it," Leopold admitted. "Look, you must stay here with us."

"I believe they have a hotel room booked."

"Nonsense! You must stay with us. You've never met my wife Molly." Leopold was well aware of European visitors' inclination to stay in private homes rather than hotels.

"If you're sure it would be all right."

"Of course. What time will you arrive?"

"I'm taking the train tomorrow morning. I believe it arrives there at two-fifteen."

"I'll meet you at the station."

If Molly was unhappy about their sudden houseguest, she didn't show it.

"Can you pick him up?" she asked. "I have a meeting with a client tomorrow afternoon."

"Certainly. Shall we take him out for dinner?"

She thought about it. "Maybe we'd better tomorrow. I can make dinner on Thursday, and Friday if he's still here."

"They're probably figuring to go over his testimony on Thursday and have him in court on Friday. Know anything about this Jaspar case?"

"A jewel theft. A salesman was assaulted and robbed of some emeralds, and he later died. My friend Emily Benedict is one of the defense attorneys."

Leopold was at the station by two o'clock, and he recognized Henri Scarlotti the moment he stepped off the train. The trim Frenchman with the tiny black moustache hadn't changed much over two decades, certainly not as much as Leopold himself had. In his late fifties, Scarlotti could have passed for a much younger man.

"Retirement seems to agree with you," Scarlotti said as they walked to the car. "How long has it been now?"

"A few years. I retired and then they called me back. This time it's for keeps, though. Fletcher is doing a fine job. Do you still live in France?"

He nodded. "In Nancy, about a hundred and seventy-five miles east of Paris. I'm a professor at the Center for Petrographical and Geochemical Research."

"Are you married now?"

The Frenchman snorted. "No, no! Once is enough for any man."

"I'd disagree with that. I've never been happier than I am with Molly."

"I wish you well, my old friend. I'm anxious to meet her."

Molly had managed to get home early and start preparing dinner. Leopold saw that she and her guest liked one another immediately and he wasn't surprised. Henri Scarlotti was full of Gallic charm and Molly was a handsome woman. Over dinner she asked, "Is this case important enough for the prosecution to fly you over from France to testify?"

"Ah, dear lady, I am testifying for the defense in this case. As you may know, Alex Jaspar was a jewelry salesman who came here from New York to show a collection of unset stones to a wealthy client interested in having an emerald necklace designed for his wife's fiftieth birthday. She was born in May, and the emerald is her birthstone. Although such salespersons generally travel in the utmost secrecy, he was assaulted and robbed in his hotel room the evening he arrived. The jewelry company says the emeralds were worth upwards of a quarter-million dollars."

"I remember reading a little about it," Leopold said. "He died of his injuries a few days later."

"Which made the charge felony murder when the young couple were finally arrested," Molly said, starting to clear away their dishes.

"Your memory is better than mine," Leopold admitted. "Fill me in."

Molly returned with dessert. "The young man's name is Shields, Jeff Shields. He dropped out of college to make fast money on the Internet, only it didn't work out that way and he went broke. His girlfriend, Beryl Constantine, heard about Jaspar's visit and apparently persuaded Shields that they could make some easy money by stealing the emeralds. Both were arrested in New York City when they tried to sell the stones to a dealer on Forty-seventh Street."

"Where do you fit into this, Henri?"

The Frenchman dipped his spoon into the soufflé. "The young woman, who is nineteen, comes from a wealthy family that is convinced of her innocence. They have enlisted me to prove that the emeralds recovered from the pair could not have been the ones stolen from the victim, Mr. Jaspar."

"How can you do that?"

"At the research center in Nancy we have developed a method of emerald analysis in which a small sample from the gem's surface is measured for oxygen isotopes. There are only a few known mines that have produced emeralds, and each has had water with different isotope ratios. Therefore, we can identify the source of each emerald."

"You will testify to that?" Leopold asked.

"Certainly. Since the source of the stolen emeralds is known to have been a different mine, the accused must be innocent."

"Amazing!"

"I will meet with the defense lawyers in the morning to go over my testimony. They expect to call me on Friday."

"Who's the girl's attorney?" Molly asked. "I know a lawyer working on the case."

"I'm dealing with a Miss Emily Benedict, a very efficient young woman hired by the girl's family."

She nodded. "Emily's my friend. She's a good criminal lawyer and she's had some high-profile cases. You're in good hands."

"The young man has a different lawyer, someone named Richard Pfiezer."

"Don't know him." Molly started pouring coffee.

Leopold and Scarlotti sat up talking until after midnight. Leopold was fascinated with the Frenchman's work and wanted to learn more about it. "Did they have to send the emeralds to you in France?" he asked.

"No, no. A member of my team ran the tests in New York and faxed the results to me for analysis. A member of your police force was present at all times to make certain a substitution was not made with the stones."

"Where are these emerald mines you mentioned?"

Henri Scarlotti moistened his lips, as if warming to his favorite topic.

Leopold could imagine him giving a similar lecture to a room full of gemologists.

"One of the earliest and most fabled, of course, was Cleopatra's mine in Egypt, dating from about three thousand B.C. For a time it was believed to be the only source of emeralds other than a small mine discovered by the Romans in the Austrian Alps. Today we know there were also early mines in Afghanistan and Pakistan, and in the fifteen-hundreds an emerald mine was discovered by the Spaniards in Colombia. They tortured the Indians to learn its location."

"Just those five?"

"Basically, yes. Sometimes more than one mine exists in the same general area. The vaporization method we have developed can identify the country and even the individual mine from which an emerald came. In this case the stolen gems were known to have come from the Colombian mines. Our tests showed that the emeralds recovered from the accused couple came from the Panjshir Valley in present-day Afghanistan."

"Did they explain how they came to have them?"

"A vague story of winning them in a high-stakes poker game in New York. I cannot blame the authorities for pressing charges against the pair. The young woman is from your city and the robbery-murder took place here. If she didn't have a family who could afford a good defense, they would both be on their way to life sentences."

Leopold wasn't satisfied. "Surely the jewelry firm or its insurance carrier would have had accurate descriptions of the stolen gems."

"The stones were unset. Seven were stolen and only six recovered, but they appeared to fit the descriptions. They were the same carat weight and cut. Without my testimony that might convince a jury."

"Then Beryl Constantine's family made a wise investment."

The morning was damp and drizzly, typical of April. Leopold and his houseguest lingered over breakfast while Molly hurried off to an early court appearance. "I should be home afternoon," she told them. "I'll see you then, Henri. Here's an extra key in case you get back before I do."

Henri had an eleven o'clock meeting with Emily Benedict and the other defense lawyer to go over his testimony. Leopold drove him down to Emily's law office and then decided to swing by police headquarters, only a couple of blocks away. He rarely intruded on Fletcher at work, but once in a while he liked to drop in. The office hadn't changed much physically since his departure, though walking into the squad room now the only face he recognized was Connie Trent's.

"How've you been, Connie?"

"Fine. It's good to see you again, Captain." She brushed back the hair from her eyes, showing a few lines of age that he hadn't noticed before. None of us is getting any younger, he thought.

"You have to stop calling me that, you know. I'm retired."

"You'll always be 'Captain' to me. Are you looking for Fletcher?"

"I just dropped by to say hello. Nothing important. We've got a defense witness in a murder trial staying with us."

She nodded. "The Jaspar case. Fletcher heard that Frenchman was a friend of yours."

"Did you work on it?"

"A little. I took the emeralds down to New York for testing."

"Oh?" Leopold's interest was piqued. "What was that like?"

"I took all six stones down. It's a fascinating process, developed by the French. A small sample is actually vaporized from the surface of each emerald. It leaves a tiny pit on the stone, but one invisible to the naked eye. The French team and their collaborators have been allowed to test precious relics and even salvaged Spanish treasure. The New York people faxed their findings to France, and the defense had the results the next day."

"But the district attorney still went to trial."

"Of course. This particular test has never been used in a court of law. The prosecution plans to argue that it's unproved."

The squad-room door opened and he saw that Captain Fletcher had returned. "Good to see you again," Fletcher said with a wave of a hand as he entered his office. "I'll be right out."

He took off his jacket and came to join them at Connie's desk. "What brings you downtown?"

"I dropped off our house-guest, Henri Scarlotti, at the lawyer's office. We could have lunch if you're free."

Fletcher grinned, "Sounds good if we can make it brief."

Leopold gestured toward Connie Trent. "Join us?"

She shook her head, "Thanks, but somebody's got to work around here. Have fun."

Chatting with Fletcher over lunch seemed just like the old days to Leopold, though lunch had been rare when they'd both been working. "What do you think about that Jaspar trial?" he asked Fletcher at one point. "My French friend says they're innocent."

"We've got a pretty strong case. Shields and the young woman, Beryl Constantine, admit they were here in the city the night of the robbery and killing, and they have no alibis. More than that, Jaspar was in town to show the emeralds to Franklin Taft, the software guy, who wanted them made into a necklace for his wife. The Tafts are close friends of Beryl Constantine's parents, and she admits to being present when Taft told her parents about Jaspar bringing the emeralds up from New York. He even mentioned the hotel where Jaspar was staying."

"But there's no physical evidence?"

"Just the emeralds, but that's pretty strong. Or it was until the defense came up with this Frenchman's testimony."

"Did the salesman make any statement before he died?"

"He was in and out of consciousness. He answered his door, thinking it was room service, and a young man hit him across the head with something. He tried to struggle and the man kept hitting him. We found the weapon in the room. It was a sock with three heavy padlocks inside."

"What about the girl?"

"He didn't see her, but it was a woman's voice that got him to open the door. We figure she stayed in the hall as a lookout." Fletcher finished his coffee. "I have to be getting back."

"This is on me," Leopold told him, reaching for the check. That was when Fletcher's cell phone beeped.

"Fletcher here. What is it, Connie?" He listened grimly and then said, "We'll meet you there."

"What's happened?" Leopold asked.

Fletcher was already on his feet. "Molly phoned nine-one-one. There's been a shooting at your house. Somebody killed Henri Scarlotti."

The sight of police cars and detectives in front of his house, the shock of the yellow crime-scene tape already in place, had Leopold's heart pumping before he reached the front door. Connie met him there, blocking his path. "Molly's all right, she's fine. But go around to the side door. The body's right inside here."

Molly was seated at the kitchen table with one of the officers, still in the gray business suit she'd worn to court. "I came home and found him like that," she said. "He was on his face, right inside the door, with the back of his head all bloody."

Leopold took her hand in both of his, feeling the lingering chill on her flesh, "Don't worry Molly. We're here now."

"He's dead, isn't he? Murdered in our own home."

"Yes," he confirmed. "Molly, listen. Did you see anyone leaving as you drove in? Anything unusual on the street?"

"No, nothing."

Fletcher came into the kitchen. "Did you recognize him?" he asked Molly.

"I didn't see his face. It looked like Henri."

"I'd better have a look," Leopold decided, and went into the front hall.

Connie Trent lifted the head from the floor. "Is this him?"

Leopold sighed for his old friend, coming across an ocean to die like this. "Yes, that's Henri." He pointed. "There are powder burns around that wound."

She nodded. "Shot at close range."

"I'd driven him downtown to meet with the defense attorneys."

"How was he getting home?" Fletcher asked.

"He said he'd take a cab. I couldn't pick him up because I didn't know how long he'd be."

"Could someone have given him a ride back here?"

"I suppose so. You're thinking of the powder burns."

Fletcher nodded. "The killer walked in right behind him. Either he came with Scarlotti or he was hiding in the bushes. The ground's still soft from the rain and we haven't found any tracks there. That seems to rule out hiding in the bushes."

A cab pulled up to the house, behind one of the police cars, and a dark-haired young woman jumped out, shoving some bills at the driver and not waiting for change. Leopold didn't know Emily Benedict personally but he recognized her from television coverage of some of her high-profile cases. She saw them grouped in the doorway and sprinted under the crime-scene tape, heading for Captain Fletcher. "God, I just heard the news! Is it true?"

"I'm afraid so," Fletcher told her. "Someone killed your star witness. Now you'll have to get back behind the tape."

She ignored the request, staring down at the body as Connie Trent quickly covered it with a sheet. "Who would do such a thing? It'll only delay the trial."

"Please get back, Miss Benedict," Fletcher said again, and when she continued to ignore him Connie put a comforting arm around her shoulders and led her away. Leopold followed.

"Is that poor kid going to have to stay in jail?" she asked them.

"Did the judge deny bail?" he asked.

She nodded. "They went to New York after the crime and he was afraid they might flee again. I tried to point out that was false reasoning if they were innocent, but he still denied bail." She shook her head, as if trying to awaken from a bad dream. "I was with Henri just two hours ago, going over his testimony with Rich."

"That would be Richard Pfiezer, the young man's attorney?"

"He's court-appointed. Shields didn't have the money to hire an attorney. Beryl's parents hired me to defend her. I wanted a separate trial but the judge denied the request."

They were standing off in Leopold's side yard, just outside the crime-scene tape. Molly had come out of the kitchen to join her friend, and after a comforting embrace they stood with their hands joined. "A separate trial is usually requested when one defendant claims to be innocent of a crime committed by the other. Was that the case here?" Leopold wondered.

"Not at all. Scarlotti's testimony about the emeralds would have cleared them both."

"Then why press for a separate trial?"

"That was before I read about this new method of testing emeralds to determine their origin. Naturally I contacted Professor Scarlotti. The tests went well, and Beryl's family paid to have him fly over here as an expert witness. Because his testimony was crucial to both our eases, Rich Pfiezer sat in on this morning's meeting too."

"How long did the meeting last?"

"About an hour. We started promptly at eleven and finished up just after twelve. Professor Scarlotti was scheduled to testify for the defense tomorrow morning. I don't know what we'll do now. Ask for a postponement, I guess."

"How did Henri get back here?"

The question seemed to puzzle her. "What do you mean?"

"Did one of you give him a ride?"

She shook her head. "I asked if he needed one and he said he was meeting someone who'd give him a ride back. He'd mentioned earlier that he was staying here and I assumed you were whom he meant."

Molly had arrived home shortly after twelve-thirty to find the front door slightly ajar. She'd pushed it open and found Scarlotti lying there dead. Leopold learned that much seated at the kitchen table with her later. Fletcher and Connie had stayed on too, after the body was removed, as much to comfort them as to continue the investigation.

"I suppose there has to be a first for everything," Molly commented philosophically. "But a body inside my front door is something I wasn't prepared for."

"No one ever is," Connie agreed. "You're lucky, in a way that you didn't get home a few minutes earlier. If you'd stumbled onto the killer he might have shot you too."

That frightening thought had already occurred to Leopold. "If the killer was with Henri, it was most likely the person who drove him home. Perhaps Henri wanted to give him something from his luggage, a gift he'd brought from France."

Molly stood up. "Much as I hate the idea, we have to go through his things."

They went upstairs to the guest room with Fletcher and Connie following along. Connie checked the bureau drawers while Leopold placed the dead man's suitcase on the bed and unzipped it. "There might be fingerprints," Fletcher cautioned.

Connie thought that was doubtful. "The house key was still in Scarlotti's hand. He was killed as soon as he entered. If the killer wanted to find something he'd have kept him alive awhile longer."

Leopold opened Henri's toilet kit and glanced at the items. He was always surprised when people carried their own soap with them and he opened the plastic container to examine it. There was a French name embossed on the top, but what attracted his attention was a thin line around the circumference of the bar, as if it had been cut apart and stuck back together again.

"What did you find?" Molly asked, peering over his shoulder.

"Probably nothing. Get me a knife, will you?"

"Will a nail file do?"

"Maybe." He carefully pried apart the top and bottom of the soap bar while the others gathered around. Inside was a scooped-out area just large enough for the single unset emerald it held.

"What we have here is a puzzlement," Leopold said, holding out the bisected soap bar for all to see. "What does it mean?"

"Does it have to mean anything?" Fletcher asked. "The man was an expert on emeralds. Maybe he just liked to carry one with him."

"Hidden in a bar of soap?"

"It's a pretty good hiding place from thieves."

Leopold turned to Connie. "You took the six recovered stones to New York to be tested. What did they look like?"

"Well..." She thought about it. "Like these, I suppose, only smaller."

Fletcher picked the emerald from its container and held it to the light. "Any ideas?"

"There's one possibility," Leopold said. "But I hate to consider it in connection with Henri. Seven emeralds were stolen and only six were recovered from this Shields fellow and the girl. Could this be the missing one?"

No one answered. No answer was possible yet.

Fletcher decided that both the prosecution and the defense in the Jaspar murder case had to be apprised of this latest discovery, and while he contacted the district attorney's office he asked Leopold to track down the two defense attorneys. It wasn't a difficult task. A call to Emily Benedict's office revealed that she was in consultation with Shields's court-appointed attorney Rich Pfiezer. Leopold drove to her office to meet them.

Pfiezer was a short, intense man with dark eyes that seemed to bore into his audience when he spoke. Leopold could imagine him in front of a jury, arguing passionately for his client. Both he and Emily listened intently to Leopold's story of the emerald hidden in Henri Scarlotti's soap bar. "I don't know what it means," Leopold concluded. "But I think you may want it tested as the others were."

"And I'll have to find myself another expert," Emily Benedict said. "That won't be easy."

"What about the New York lab that performed the tests?"

"Their man is one of our witnesses. I planned to put him on the stand just before Professor Scarlotti tomorrow. But he's no expert at analyzing the data he collects."

"No sessions today?"

"The judge had another matter," Pfiezer commented with a trace of sarcasm, "as if the rest of us didn't. The prosecution has one more witness, the jeweler where they tried to sell the emeralds, and then it's our turn."

"The jeweler!" Emily Benedict flipped through her notes. "You know, there may be a way out of this without Professor Scarlotti's testimony. Do you have the jeweler's preliminary statement?"

"What's his name?" Pfiezer asked, shuffling through his papers. "Newman?"

"Jacob Newman."

"I've got it."

They'd become almost oblivious to Leopold's presence. "If you'd like me to leave—" he offered.

Emily smiled at him across the table. "You're retired, aren't you? And you're Molly's husband besides. I guess we can trust you not to run to the D.A."

She took the statement from Pfiezer and read quickly through it, looking for something. "Here it is! This Jacob Newman has a place in one of those big jewelry arcades on Forty-seventh Street in New York. Shields and Beryl came to him one afternoon last December with some emeralds to sell. He examined them at length and decided there was nothing special about the stones. He consulted some unseen partner and made an offer of five thousand dollars for the lot. Shields and Beryl insisted the gems must be worth many times that price. That was when he became suspicious and phoned the police. He kept them there on a pretext of reconsidering his offer until the police arrived."

"What does that prove, Emily?" the other lawyer asked.

"Look, we know from the professor's tests that the emeralds they tried to sell weren't the stolen ones. With him dead I can't use the tests unless I get another expert, probably all the way from France. But Jaspar's jewelry company swears the stolen emeralds were worth a quarter-million dollars or more. If this Newman places the value at five thousand, and that value can be verified, then it proves they're not the same stones."

"So what are you going to do?" Pfiezer asked.

"We'll let the prosecution finish their case by calling Newman. Then on cross-examination we'll bring out the value of the emeralds he saw. I'll ask for an adjournment until Monday so we can verify the value of the stones over the weekend."

The accused man's lawyer nodded. "Sounds like a good plan to me, Emily."

"What about the emerald we found in Henri's soap?" Leopold asked.

"Since we haven't called him as a witness, and can't call him now, the matter is irrelevant. The state can't introduce it unless they can link it directly to the Jaspar case, and that's not likely. Jeff Shields and Beryl Constantine are two people who couldn't have killed Henri Scarlotti. They're both in jail. And he was their star witness."

There was no arguing with her logic. "I'll try to be in court tomorrow," Leopold told them. He owed that much to Henri.

It was another cool and rainy morning. Leopold and Molly left home together shortly before nine, and as they entered their separate cars Leopold asked, "Are you sure you're all right?"

She smiled. "Of course. Though I would like to get the bloodstain out of our carpet."

"I'll be in court until they adjourn."

The trial day started with a sidebar conference of lawyers, and while they discussed their tactics with the judge Leopold had his first opportunity to study the accused couple. Jeff Shields was in his early twenties, and even a suit and tie couldn't hide the punk wise-guy attitude he assumed while seated at the defense table. He was handsome in a crude sort of way. Leopold could see how he would have attracted a nineteen-year-old woman like Beryl Constantine. She sat pale and emotionless, separated from her lover by the empty chairs the defense lawyers usually occupied. He thought they might exchange glances but they didn't, at least not that Leopold could detect. From his seat across the courtroom and slightly behind them he could only see the right side of Beryl's face. It was an ordinary face, not unattractive without makeup, and her body seemed understandably tense. Her brown hair was pulled back in a pony-tail perhaps deliberately designed to make her look younger. It seemed obvious that a middle-aged couple seated directly behind her were her parents.

Finally the sidebar discussion ended and the prosecution summoned its last witness. Jacob Newman was a bearded man with glasses who spoke with a strong New York accent. He told of his jewelry counter in one of New York's 47th Street arcades, of his advertisements stating that he specialized in fine emeralds, and of the two defendants who appeared on a damp December afternoon and offered to sell him six unset stones. He felt the two were acting suspiciously and remembered a police flier to jewelry stores reporting a recent theft of seven emeralds from a jewelry salesman. He said he'd have to show the stones to his partner in the rear of the store and went back to phone the police. He kept the couple at his counter, haggling over the value of the stones, until two officers arrived and arrested them.

Emily Benedict rose slowly at the conclusion of his testimony, gave a brief glance at her notes, and walked forward to confront him. Leopold admired her courtroom manner and the brisk directness of her questions. "Mr. Newman, what value would you place on the six emeralds the defendants attempted to sell to you?"

"I didn't have an opportunity to fully examine them."

"But what was your first reaction? Did you think of these stones as having high value, medium value, or low value?"

He thought about it for a moment. "Toward the low end of the scale. I made an offer of five thousand. That may have been a little low, but the stones were far from top quality."

"You're aware that the stolen emeralds were valued at a quarter-million dollars?"

"Yes. Of course that value may have been inflated. And I saw only six stones. The missing one may have been the largest, though a jeweler would be unlikely to create a necklace with one perfect stone flanked by six inferior ones."

Emily Benedict took a deep breath. "Mr. Newman, is there any possibility in your mind that the six stones you examined, even in a cursory manner, could have been part of a consignment of seven valued at a quarter-million dollars?"

He took his time answering, glancing over at the prosecutor, then said, "It's extremely doubtful."

Emily smiled and stepped back. "No further questions."

The prosecutor rose for redirect, stating, "Mr. Newman, the recovered stones correspond in carat size and appearance to the insurance-company descriptions of the stolen ones. Given that fact, and your very brief examination of the emeralds, isn't it possible that you were mistaken in your judgment of their value?"

Leopold could see the question made the witness uneasy. But he must have remembered his role as a prosecution witness and he answered, "I could have been mistaken, yes."

"No further questions. Your Honor, the state rests its case."

Emily Benedict was on her feet with an obviously prearranged motion. "Your Honor, due to the unavailability of a witness, the defense requests an adjournment until Monday morning."

"Granted." The judge banged his gavel. "This court stands adjourned until ten A.M. on Monday."

Leopold sought out Emily as the jury filed out and the prisoners were taken away. "That seemed to go well. The prosecutor must have agreed to your request."

She nodded. "But only until Monday. He won't allow me time to find somebody else in France. We'll have to go with the testimony on the value of the emeralds. I'm contending they were different stones entirely, won in a poker game as Jeff Shields alleges."

The couple whom Leopold had picked out as Beryl's parents joined them then, and Emily introduced Leopold. Mrs. Constantine was a dark-haired woman in her late forties, more attractive than her daughter but just as tense. "What do you think?" she asked. "Does Beryl have any chance without that Frenchman's testimony?"

"We hope so," Emily told them, outlining the argument she'd be using. "I think I can plant a reasonable doubt in the jury's mind."

"I'd give anything to have her out of this," Mr. Constantine said.

"If we're lucky," Emily told them, "a week from now it'll be all over."

When the Constantines left the courtroom, some of her confidence seemed to leave with them. "Yeah," she told Leopold, "it'll be over a week from now, but I wouldn't want to bet on my client's chances."

"Would it be possible for me to speak with her?"

"What?" His question had taken her by surprise.

"I want to speak with Beryl Constantine at the jail. Naturally I'd expect you to be present too."

"Why do you want to see her?"

"I think she can tell me who killed Henri Scarlotti."

Emily arranged the jailhouse meeting for three o'clock that afternoon. Leopold phoned Molly to tell her where he was and then phoned Fletcher at the squad room. For a moment it seemed like the old days as he told Fletcher what had to be done.

"You've got no evidence for this," Fletcher grumbled.

"I hope I will have, later this afternoon. I'll phone you as soon as I know for sure."

Leopold and Emily met with her client in the stark conference room at the jail. "Do you have any news yet?" Beryl asked, her green eyes full of hope.

"Nothing yet," Emily said. "This is Captain Leopold, retired from the police. He thinks he may be able to help."

She turned toward him. "Really?"

He spoke her name softly. "Beryl, that's a lovely name. Beryl, I have to ask you just one question."

"Yes?"

"Where did you hide the seventh emerald?"

Her face froze, the expectation draining from it. She panicked, turning to Emily for help. "Didn't you tell him I'm innocent?"

Leopold sighed and continued talking softly. "Beryl, you overheard your parents' friend talking about having an emerald necklace made for his wife's fiftieth birthday. You knew when the jewelry salesman would be at the hotel. That much came out at the trial. You told your boyfriend Jeff and he decided to steal the gems. According to the dying man's statement, he never saw you in the room, although you must have been in the hall because he heard a woman's voice before he opened the door. Jeff gave you the largest emerald and you both went to New York some days later to sell the other six stones. That's when you were arrested. Isn't that how it happened?"

"No!"

"The trial's not over, Beryl. There's still time for you to change your plea to guilty. Miss Benedict might even be able to work out a plea to a lesser offense, since you weren't in the room when Jaspar was fatally injured."

"It's a strong possibility, Beryl," she told her client. "I didn't raise it before because you wouldn't agree to a request for a separate trial."

The young girl stared at Leopold as if afraid of what he might say next. "Why don't you believe me?"

"Because you have lovely green eyes, child, and because emeralds are a transparent form of the mineral beryl. That's why Jeff stole the gems, and why he kept the biggest one as a gift to you."

She started crying then, but Leopold needed one thing more. "Jeff stole the emeralds from Jaspar, didn't he?"

"Yes," she said finally. And then, to her attorney, "Help me, I'm so afraid!"

As soon as they left the jail Leopold phoned Fletcher at his office. "She's admitted the theft and Emily Benedict is arranging for a plea bargain right now. The missing emerald is hidden in her parents' basement. That's all we need. Go get him."

Thirty minutes later, Fletcher and Connie arrested Jacob Newman on suspicion of murder as he was boarding a train back to New York.

"It was a simple case," Leopold told Fletcher later that evening, after Newman had signed a confession. "It only seemed complicated because Henri's murder became entwined with the Jaspar trial. Two kids, probably acting nervous and suspicious, went down to New York with six stolen emeralds and chose Newman's counter in the jewelry district because he advertised himself as specializing in emeralds. He realized at once that the jewels were valuable and probably stolen. Pretending to consult his partner in the back room, he substituted six very similar but inferior emeralds."

"It's quite a coincidence that he had inferior emeralds of the right carat, weight, and shape just waiting there," Fletcher said.

"The coincidence isn't so great when you realize the man specialized in emeralds. Naturally he'd have a great many sizes and shapes in stock for customers. And these seemed like safe kids to pull a switch on. When they complained about the price he offered, he simply reported them to the police."

"Go on. Before I read Newman's confession I couldn't figure out where the Frenchman fit into any of this."

"Newman figured he had nothing to worry about. It was his word against a couple of kids. But then he heard about Henri Scarlotti and the newly developed test tracing the origin of emeralds."

Fletcher shook his head. "How did you ever come up with Newman as a suspect? He and Scarlotti didn't even know each other."

"Scarlotti told the lawyers he was meeting someone who'd give him a ride home. It seemed clear that this person entered our house with Scarlotti and then shot him in the head. Why had Scarlotti met the person and invited him into the house? The answer came when I found that emerald hidden in Henri's bar of soap, probably to keep it safe and also to avoid customs duty. It wasn't the missing emerald from the Jaspar theft, not when it was hidden inside a bar of French soap. Henri had brought it with him, no doubt planning to sell it in New York. When he heard a jeweler specializing in emeralds was one of the trial witnesses he contacted him. Newman met him and drove him to my house, but he wasn't interested in more emeralds. He just wanted to keep Henri from testifying that the recovered emeralds couldn't have been the stolen ones. He carried a gun for protection, and as soon as they were off the street he shot Henri with it. I suppose he figured by the time the defense found another expert witness in France and flew him over here he could sell the stolen emeralds and maybe even leave the country. He was buying time for himself."

"He'll get plenty of time now," Fletcher said. "About twenty to life, I figure."

SOURCES

"The Woman Without a Past," *Ellery Queen Mystery Magazine*, April 1981.

"Captain Leopold Beats the Machine," *Ellery Queen Mystery Magazine* June 1983.

"Finding Joe Finch," *Ellery Queen Mystery Magazine*, February 1984.

"The Murder in Room 1010," *Ellery Queen Mystery Magazine*, November 1987.

"The Crime in Heaven," *Ellery Queen Mystery Magazine*, October 1988.

"The Killer Everyone Knew," *Ellery Queen Mystery Magazine*, March 1989.

"Captain Leopold's Birthday," *Ellery Queen Mystery Magazine*, February 1990.

"The Retired Magician," *Ellery Queen Mystery Magazine*, July 1991.

"Puzzle in a Smoke-Filled Room," *Ellery Queen Mystery Magazine*, November 1991.

"The Summer of Our Discontent," *Ellery Queen Mystery Magazine*, November 1992.

"Leopold at Rest," *Ellery Queen Mystery Magazine*, April 1993.

"Leopold Lends a Hand," *Ellery Queen Mystery Magazine*, October 1995.

"The Mystery That Wouldn't Stay Solved," *Ellery Queen Mystery Magazine* September-October 1997.

"The Phantom Lover," *Ellery Queen Mystery Magazine*, April 1999.

"The Emerald Expert," *Ellery Queen Mystery Magazine*, November 2000.

Books by Edward D. Hoch
Published by Crippen & Landru

The Ripper of Storyville and Other Ben Snow Tales. Available as a print book and as a Kindle ebook

The Velvet Touch. Available as a print book and as a Kindle ebook

The Old Spies Club and Other Intrigues of Rand. Available as a Kindle ebook

The Iron Angel and Other Tales of the Gypsy Sleuth. Available as a Kindle ebook

Hoch's Ladies. Available as a print book and as a Kindle ebook

Funeral in the Fog and Other Investigations of Simon Ark. Available as a print book and as a Kindle ebook

Constant Hearses and Other Revolutionary Stories. Available as a print book and as a Kindle ebook

The Killer Everyone Knew and Other Captain Leopold Stories. Available as a print book (and forthcoming as a Kindle ebook)

THE PROBLEMS OF DR. SAM HAWTHORNE

Diagnosis Impossible, The Problems of Dr. Sam Hawthorne. Available as a print book and as Kindle ebook

More Things Impossible, The Second Casebook of Dr. Sam Hawthorne. Available as a print book and as a Kindle ebook

Nothing Is Impossible, Further Problems of Dr. Sam Hawthorne. Available as a print book and as a Kindle ebook

All But Impossible, The Impossible Files of Dr. Sam Hawthorne. Available as a print book and as a Kindle ebook

Challenge the Impossible, The Final Problems of Dr. Sam Hawthorne. Available as a print book and as a Kindle ebook

The Killer Everyone Knew and Other Captain Leopold Stories is printed on 60-pound paper and is designed by G.E. Satheesh, Pondicherry, India. The type is Palatino Linotype. The cover is by Gail Cross. The first edition was published in two forms: trade softcover, perfect bound; and one hundred fifty copies sewn in cloth, numbered and signed by the editor, Roland Lacourbe. Each of the clothbound copies includes a separate pamphlet, "Captain Leopold Views a Crime Scene," a short story by Edward D. Hoch. *The Killer Everyone Knew* was printed by Southern Ohio Printers and bound by Cincinnati Bindery. The book was published in June 2023 by Crippen & Landru Publishers, Inc., Cincinnati, OH.

Crippen & Landru, Publishers
P. O. Box 532057
Cincinnati, OH 45253
Web: www.crippenlandru.com
E-mail: info@crippenlandru.com

Praise for Crippen & Landru Publishers

This is the best edited, most attractively packaged line of mystery books intro-duced in this decade. The books are equally valuable to collectors and readers. [Mystery Scene Magazine]

The specialty publisher with the most star-studded list is Crippen & Landru, which has produced short story collections by some of the biggest names in contemporary crime fiction. [Ellery Queen's Mystery Magazine]

God bless Crippen & Landru. [The Strand Magazine]

A monument in the making is appearing year by year from Crippen & Landru, a small press devoted exclusively to publishing the criminous short story. [Alfred Hitchcock's Mystery Magazine]

Subscriptions

Subscribers agree to purchase each forthcoming publication, either the Regular Series or the Lost Classics or (preferably) both. Collectors can thereby guarantee receiving limited editions, and readers won't miss any favorite stories.

Subscribers receive a discount of 20% off the list price (and the same discount on our backlist) and a specially commissioned short story by a major writer in a deluxe edition as a gift at the end of the year.

The point for us is that, since customers don't pick and choose which books they want, we have a guaranteed sale even before the book is published, and that allows us to be more imaginative in choosing short story collections to issue.

That's worth the 20% discount for us. Sign up now and start saving. Email us at orders@crippenlandru.com or visit our website at www.crippenlandru.com on our subscription page.

Title: Des Nouvelles d'Edward D. Hoch, Grand Maitre de l'Enigme (tome 1)

Authors: Roland Lacourbe (with Daniele Grivel)

Publisher: Semper Ænigma

Price: $ 55.00

Only available at lulu.com.

Title: Des Nouvelles d'Edgar D. Hoch, Grand Maitre de l'Enigme (tome 2)

Authors: Roland Lacourbe (with Vincent Bourgeois, Philippe Fooz, Michel Soupart)

Publisher: Semper Ænigma

Price: $ 55.00

Only available at lulu.com.

CPSIA information can be obtained
at www.ICGtesting.com
Printed in the USA
JSHW082122250623
43749JS00002B/3